PANTHEON

SAM BOURNE

ISIS
LARGE PRINT
Oxford

First published in Great Britain 2012
by
HarperCollinsPublishers

Published in Large Print 2012 by ISIS Publishing Ltd.,
7 Centremead, Osney Mead, Oxford OX2 0ES
by arrangement with
HarperCollinsPublishers

British Library Cataloguing in Publication Data
Bourne, Sam, 1967–
    Pantheon.
    1. Suspense fiction.
    2. Large type books.
    I. Title
    823.9'2–dc23

ISBN 978–0–7531–9066–1 (hb)
ISBN 978–0–7531–9067–8 (pb)

Printed and bound in Great Britain by
T. J. International Ltd., Padstow, Cornwall

For my mother, both the gentlest and strongest person I know

CHAPTER
ONE

Oxford, July 8 1940

It hurt him, this journey, it pained him, yet day after day he came back for more punishment. Every morning, whether the skies were dark with rain or, like today, lit by searing sunshine, James Zennor would be here on the water shortly after dawn, sculling alone on the Isis stretch of the Thames.

James loved these early mornings. The air smelled fresh, the sky was empty, everything was quiet. A family of moorhens puttered by the water's edge, but even they made no sound as if, like him, they preferred to keep their counsel.

The boat was gliding now, James's wrists flat and straight, the feathering motion — twisting the oars so that they entered the water vertically before slicing horizontally through the air — all but automatic. He gazed at the river ahead, sparkling as if jewelled by the sunlight. At moments like this, when the true exertion had only just begun, when the sky was blue and the breeze was as cool as a caress, he could almost forget what had happened to his ruined body. He could almost feel like the man he used to be.

Barring that one, fateful, year abroad, he had come to this same spot for a decade, ever since he had been an undergraduate, grateful for a place in his college team. He had even become the stroke for Oxford against Cambridge in a famously close boat race. But that was a long time ago. These days he was fighting only against himself.

He checked left and right but there was still no one else around. In term-time he might see some of the more ambitious crews on the water at this hour, readying for Torpids or Eights — younger men who reminded him of his younger self. James Zennor was not yet thirty. But he had been through enough that he felt twice that age.

He squinted upwards, enjoying the sensation of being dazzled, then returned his gaze to the job in hand. As his eyes adjusted, he could see the trees on the right-hand bank, shielding the path where he and Florence had so often walked, both before Harry was born and since. James liked bringing his son down here, fondly imagining he would fall in love with the river the way he had as a boy, just by being near to it. But in recent months Harry had become nervous, anxiously clinging to his mother's hand if they inched too close to the water's edge. But that would pass. James was sure of it. On a day like this, he felt that anything was possible.

He imagined how his son would look at this very moment. Still two months short of his third birthday, Harry would be fast asleep, one hand clutching Snowy, the little white polar bear who accompanied him to bed

2

every night. Just the way James had seen him this morning before creeping out for his rowing practice. Whatever else he and Florence had been through, they had made a beautiful child together.

Now, as James reached Iffley Lock again and turned around, the inevitable happened. His left shoulder began to scream for attention. The pain was no less sharp for being familiar, both burning and piercing, as if he were being stabbed by several thick, white-hot needles. Each day would begin with the hope that this time it would be different, that the pain would come later, that it might not come at all. Today, with the weather so perfect, that hope had shone brighter than usual. But as he rowed towards Folly Bridge he knew nothing had changed.

James tried to focus on those brief, blissful half-seconds of relief, when the blades were up and out of the heavy water: the recovery before the drive. He tried to imagine the river's coolness, the balmy, soothing effect it would have on his burning skin.

Each pull squeezed his lungs, his breaths coming as if they were the gasps of someone faraway; but his heart was as loud as the engine of a motor car revving too fast.

The boat scythed through the water, parting it silently, its bow lean and narrow. He knew that, viewed from the bank, the motion would look effortless. Team rowing, done well, always looked like that; human beings turned into a single, mighty machine, all their energies harnessed towards a single objective. If you had selected the right men, the strongest and best, the water seemed powerless to resist.

Single-sculls rarely looked so pleasing; a man on his own could not generate the same momentum or sense of order. James was certain his own rowing looked especially inelegant. His ruined left shoulder made sure of that. Fated now to be forever weaker than his right, his left arm could not keep up; perfect symmetry was out of reach. He pictured his boat zigzagging its way down the river, even though he had been told a dozen times that it did no such thing.

He gulped for oxygen, looking up as he did so. Folly Bridge was just visible in the distance. Once there, he would have rowed himself along the Isis stretch, to Iffley Lock and back, three times, a distance of four and a half miles. His body was demanding to stop; he had already done his usual morning circuit. But he could not help thinking about the men — his own age or younger — in combat on the continent, or the pilots preparing to defend the skies over England, giving their all for what the new prime minister had warned would be a "Battle of Britain". With each stroke, he contemplated how feeble were his exertions compared to theirs, how if they could carry on doing their part, the least he could do . . .

But now the perennial shoulder pain suddenly sharpened as if something had splintered. He wondered if perhaps a shard of bone had cracked out of place. The agony was unspeakable.

James firmed his jaw against the pain. In a bid to distract himself, he forced his mind to recall what he had heard on the wireless last night. The main news remained Britain's sinking of the French fleet in Algeria. Typical Churchill, that. Bold and brazen with it. Unlike that damned fool Chamberlain, Churchill understood there was no room for messing around, no time for niceties. Now that Paris had been conquered, France's ships would fall into German hands. Better they were destroyed altogether. Not that the French saw it that way: they were furious, the recriminations still rumbling on.

His shoulder was sending shockwaves of hurt through him now. He refused to listen. What had come next? The BBC generally tried to begin the broadcast with something positive to offset the bad news that was to follow. What pill was the discussion of the sinking of the French fleet meant to sweeten last night? The agony tugged at his nerves, but he refused to succumb. That was it. The Channel Islands. Sark had surrendered to the Nazis, two days after Alderney: the Channel Islands were now entirely under German rule. The idea was shocking. He had never been there, but he had grown up on the English south coast knowing that Jersey was just a ferry ride away. The people there spoke English. In just the last few weeks the swastika had been raised over Norway, France, Belgium, Holland; and now a little corner of Britain. Hitler was getting closer.

James shipped the oars to let the boat drift on the unruffled water and let out what he thought was a gasp of relief. It was only when a flock of coots scattered wildly that he realized the sound he had made was a scream. A man on the towpath opposite turned suddenly and then, alarmed, walked briskly away.

James took himself to the bank, as close to the boathouse as he could manage, then hauled himself out onto dry land and braced for the most demanding moment in his morning routine. Bending low, he tugged at the loop of cord on the bow of the boat, to bring the scull out of the water and onto his good shoulder. One, two, three and, with a strain that made him want to howl, it was out and up. He staggered the few yards to the boathouse and dropped the scull into its rack.

Then he stood for a few seconds, catching his breath, gazing up at the sky. The glorious cornflower blue of it struck him as a kind of lie. The skies over Britain were becoming a battlefield, the air-raid sirens sounding in cities night after night. German planes had bombed Cardiff just a few nights ago. What right did they have now to look so peaceful?

James walked quickly past the college boathouses, one each for St John's, Balliol, New and the others, all now locked up and empty. And though that owed more to the Long Vacation than to the war, he silently cursed his fate once again.

Reaching the post where he had left his bicycle, he threw one long leg over the saddle and began to pedal hard, savouring the kinetic change for his body after the relentless back-and-forth of the river. He pushed himself over the little bridge, as steeply arched as a rainbow, then across Christ Church meadow, noting both the grazing cows — who, since the onset of rationing, looked useful rather than merely decorative — and the patches that had been ploughed up for growing potatoes. That was happening all over Oxford now, even the smallest private garden or square of lawn turned into a vegetable patch to boost the nation's food supply.

He pedalled between Merton and Corpus, up past Oriel and onto the High Street. The colleges were deserted at this hour, though many of them would soon fill up for another day of requisitioned wartime service. Turning right towards St Giles, he did his best to avoid a glimpse of the Martyrs' Memorial, and headed north for home.

It was not yet seven, so there were not many cars on the road. But even when rush hour came there would be fewer today than there had been a year ago: petrol rationing had seen to that. James knew of one adventurous fellow who had found a solution, filling up his tank with a brew of whisky and paraffin — he complained his car now smelled like a "lamplighter on the piss" — but by the looks of things most of Oxford's motorists preferred not to take the risk. Those that did would now encounter checkpoints guarding the exits north, south, east and west of the city — roadblocks designed to ensure the authorities knew exactly who was coming in and out, as if Oxford were a military base rather than an ancient university town. There was even a roadblock between Pembroke and Christ Church. But they tended to be rather less bothered by a chap on a bike.

Not that you could ever forget it was wartime, no matter how you got around. There were the traffic lights cloaked in their monk-like hoods, one of the countless little transformations demanded by the blackout. But stranger still was the complete absence of street signs and signposts, removed in order to give a headache to any future occupying army. Let Jerry find his own damned way around Oxford.

The pain in his shoulder had returned. He glanced at his watch and began to make the calculations that might distract him from the agony. If he cycled at full strength, he should be back at the house in four and a half minutes.

As he powered along Banbury Road, the wind rushing past his ears, he became conscious of a roaring appetite. A meagre four ounces: that was his entire bacon ration for the week. He could wolf all of that down this instant, in a single breakfast! And what good to anybody was one egg every three and a half days?

At last the turning for Parks Road was just ahead of him, a large black car parked on the corner, its engine humming.

Florence looked over at her son, sitting at the kitchen table, his chair piled high with cushions so that he could reach his plate, though his toast and margarine were barely touched. Harry was instead hunched over his drawing pad, a stubby red crayon in his hand.

"Not long now, Harry, I promise." Yet again she opened, rummaged through and closed every drawer in the kitchen. Where the hell had it gone?

Everything else was ready: the suitcase, methodically packed, coats for the journey, sturdy shoes. She had been careful with the passport, deliberately placing it at the back of the second drawer in her dresser, tucked in among her underwear, a private realm James was unlikely to probe. And yet when she had checked for it nearly an hour ago it had not been there. It had been the first thing she had done, after a long time spent in bed, her eyes closed feigning sleep, as she heard James wash, dress and head out to the river. Unmoving, she had lain there listening to his routine, waiting for the sound of the front door closing behind him. She had waited another two minutes after that, timing it by the bedside clock, just in case he had forgotten something and turned back. Then, when the coast was clear, she had got out of bed, her mental checklist clear and straight. But when she opened the second drawer, there had been no sign of her passport. Had James somehow twigged, and hidden it from her? Had somebody revealed her secret? If her husband did know, why had he said nothing? What trap was he setting for her?

She glanced over at Harry again. His head was down, intent on his drawing. She moved to stand behind him, peering over his head, and abruptly felt a hardness in her throat. "What's that, darling?"

Harry looked up, his eyes two round blue pools. Florence saw in them a terrible melancholy, before realizing it was a reflection of herself she had glimpsed in her son's eyes.

"It's our house," Harry said, his voice low and husky, so different from other children his age and yet so like

James. "Inside, there's me," he said, pointing at a shape that vaguely resembled a window. His chubby finger pointed at another shape: "And there's you and Daddy."

Florence felt her eyes smarting. "It's lovely, Harry," she said, trying to sound jolly. "It's lovely." It was the third house he had drawn in the last twenty minutes.

She resumed her search, trying not to think about Harry or his picture. She didn't want to dwell on anything that might corrode her resolve. Where in heaven's name had she put the passport?

Perhaps in her panic she had missed it. Determined to be more methodical, she returned to the kitchen drawers for the third time, now removing the cutlery tray from the top one and then proceeding to the next. Tea cosies, napkins, a wooden spoon, a spare torch and a fresh set of batteries. Finally the bottom drawer, full of James's man things: screwdrivers, pliers, a spanner, a can of bicycle oil and more batteries for the torch. Since the war began, there seemed to be torches and batteries in every corner of the house. But it wasn't there.

Florence glanced at her watch. Six forty-five am. They had to be out of here by seven at the very latest. James was never back before seven fifteen. She just needed to keep her head.

She ran into his study. Such an awful mess, tottering piles of papers, books and what appeared to be a complete set of the *Journal of Experimental Psychology*. Lifting the biggest tower, she moved it gingerly onto the chair. Then she removed the February issue of the *New Statesman*, its cover marked by the ringed stains of multiple cups of coffee, a copy of *Tribune* underneath. More letters, a heavily dog-eared copy of *Homage to Catalonia* by George Orwell — though her husband always referred to him as Eric, after meeting him in Spain — a thick copy of *Wisden*, but no sign of the passport. A weeks-old clipping from the *Daily Sketch*: "Conscription extended to age 36", read the headline. It was five minutes to seven.

"Mummy!" A shout from the kitchen.

"Not now, Harry."

"Mummy." More insistent.

"Mummy's busy." She worked her way through a desk drawer full of typewriter ribbons, paperclips and a spare blotter. "Why don't you make sure Snowy is comfortable in your satchel?"

"There's a man at the door."

She froze. Could James be back already, so much earlier than usual? It made no sense; if he were here, he would let himself in. Why would he be standing outside? Unless he had left his keys behind. And he was refusing to ring the bell, lest he wake up Harry. Good God, what should she do?

She crept into the hall. Instantly, through the coloured glass at the top of the door, she could see that it was Leonard, the outline of him tall and taut. Her shoulders dropped with relief. She opened the door.

His brilliantined hair was still in place but his face was flushed with exertion. "He finished early. I saw him just now."

"What?"

"I came as fast as I could. James has stopped rowing: I think he must have been quicker than usual today. Or I timed it wrong. But he's finished. He'll be back here in ten minutes, fifteen at the most."

She grimaced and, as if he had misinterpreted her expression, he added sharply, "Remember, there are too many people depending on this, Florence. There's too much at stake."

"Just wait there a minute."

Desperate, she tore at the rest of the desk drawers, foraging through the cigarette papers, used up matchboxes and foreign coins, most of them Spanish. She turned to the bookshelves, pulling out volume after volume, then whole blocks at a time, including the entire Left Book Club stretch in orange, throwing them to the floor. Still no passport.

Harry had begun to cry, maybe at the sight of Leonard, a stranger, at the front door. Or perhaps because of her barely-contained frustration. But she would have to ignore him. She ran back into the bedroom. Breaking one of the tacit taboos of their marriage, she had already peered inside James's wardrobe, but now she would do a thorough search. She swept past the two or three suits and dark cloth jackets hanging on the rail then sank to her knees, padding the hard wood at the base of the cupboard. She felt something and snatched at it.

A shoebox. She tore at it hopefully. But inside were just two black leather brogues, still wrapped in tissue paper, the ones, she realized with a stab of guilt, he had worn for their wedding or, rather, the wedding party they had had nearly six months later in England.

A shadow fell over her and she turned to find Harry, escaped from his chair, standing in the doorway trembling. "Mummy?" Tears streaked his cheeks.

She felt her own eyes pricking. Despite all her preparation, weeks of it, she was about to fail. "Don't cry, darling. Everything will be all right."

One last chance. She grabbed the stool by the bathroom door, stood on it to look into the top shelf of her husband's clothes cupboard. Two thick sweaters sat, unworn, on the shelf. She pushed them apart. Nothing there. She was about to give up when a faint outline caught her eye. It was barely visible, brown against brown. She reached out and felt the touch of leather. Her heart sank: another damned book, with musty-smelling pages and no words on the cover. When she opened it a picture slipped out. Harry snatched it up, gazing at the handsome young man in uniform surrounded by pals, a rifle in every hand, before crying out with happy recognition: "Daddy!"

Florence felt defeat settle in her bones. James must have found the passport and taken it to the river with him. What a cruel trick.

Only desperation sent her back to the place where she had started her search: her underwear drawer. She emptied it of the remaining items one by one, as if in a final show of thoroughness. As she lifted up a pair of black stockings, her heart jumped. She pulled at the material and there, somehow caught inside, was the small, stiff, dark blue booklet. How on earth had she missed it? Her passport was there, exactly where she had left it, all along.

"What did Mummy tell you, Harry? You see, everything's going to be all right." She could hear the crack in her own voice as she lifted her son in a single move, settling him onto her right hip. With her left hand she picked up the suitcase she had placed in the hallway, in readiness for this moment, nearly an hour ago. She walked out of the front door to join Leonard. There was no time to look back. In his small hand, Harry was still clutching the picture of his father.

CHAPTER
TWO

Barcelona, four years earlier

James saw more of Florence's bare flesh the first time he laid eyes on her than he did until the day they were married. Which was not strictly true, but became a line he liked to use — though rarely in mixed company.

They met in Barcelona, in the heat of July 1936. He had never been to Spain before. In truth, he had never been anywhere before. He walked around the city, along its gorgeous wide avenues, round-eyed, his chest tight with excitement and pride. Hanging from the buildings with their strangely-shaped, weeping-eye windows were banners and bunting welcoming him and some six thousand other foreigners to the Olimpiada Popular: the People's Olympiad. The event's official flag depicted three heroic, muscular figures in red, yellow and black clutching a single standard. It took a while for James to realize that at least one of the notional athletes on the emblem was a woman; the second was a red-skinned man and a third figure was quite clearly negro.

He should not have been surprised: this was the alternative Olympics, designed to steal the thunder of the official games taking place a week later and more

15

than nine hundred miles eastward in Berlin. While those games would be a showcase of Aryan supremacy, the People's Olympiad would be a festival of socialists, idealists and radicals who had refused as a matter of conscience to take part in Herr Hitler's Nazi carnival.

"Well, we're not going to win, I can tell you that much," James had said the very moment he and his friend Harry had arrived, off the train after a journey that had begun nearly eighteen hours earlier at Victoria Station. "Not in this heat. We're used to freezing dawns and Cherwell fog. This is the bloody tropics."

"Now, Zennor, you listen to me. If I'd wanted a gloom merchant, I'd have brought Simkins or that other twit, Lightfoot. I brought you for your *rhetorical* powers. You're supposed to be here to lift our spirits, to exhort the team to victory!"

"I thought I was here because I'm a bloody good oarsman."

"And so you are. So no more of that defeatist talk. We won't lead the masses to revolution with soggy English pessimism now, will we?"

Harry Knox, Winchester and Balliol, hereditary baronet and one-time lead organizer of . . . now what was it? James thought it was the ILP, but it might have been another socialist group with another set of initials: it was hard to keep up. Coming to Barcelona had been Knox's idea, a way to make up for missing the real Olympics — as he insisted they *not* refer to them — and a chance to take a stand against Fascism. James had been tipped to row stroke in the Great Britain boat in Berlin; this was to be his consolation prize.

Along with all the other foreign athletes they were put up at the Hotel Olímpico in the Plaza de España, where the lobby was already teeming with fresh arrivals from the United States, Holland, Belgium and French Algeria. Most were just like Harry and James, there with the backing of a workers' association, a socialist party or a trade union, rather than their government. James rather doubted the selection process had been as athletically rigorous as it was for the official Games. But, as Harry had said, "That's hardly the point, is it?"

The atmosphere was raucous and did not let up for a week. The door of their room remained open, as Marxist Danish hurdlers or anarchist French sprinters came in and out as they pleased. The entire building seemed to host a single, unending party. James had barely put down his suitcase when a huge Italian shot putter, who later turned out to be a communist exile, thrust a bottle in his hand, urging him to knock it straight back, no sipping. James read the label — Sangre de Toro, "bull's blood" — and did as he was told. It tasted musky and heavy with fruit. He hadn't much liked it at the time but thereafter he would forever associate the taste of that Catalan wine with freedom.

At last they had spilled out onto the street, wandering from one tapas bar to another. James had no memory of paying for either his food or his drink, as if all the Barcelona bar-owners were grateful to the visiting Olympians for supporting their infant republic, for doing exactly what the International Olympic

Committee had refused to do five years earlier —
choosing Barcelona over Berlin.

He was munching on a plate of *calcots*, charcoal-
grilled spring onions that, had you offered them to him
in England, he would have rejected as terrifyingly
exotic, when Harry, already sunburnt, the sweat
patches spreading under his arms, turned to him with a
lascivious grin. "Rumour is the ladies' swimming team
are having a late night practice session."

"Harry, even you can't be that desperate," James
replied, doing his best to sound like a man of the
world. He had some experience with women, more
certainly than Harry. He had spent most of his
second year at Oxford stepping out with Daisy, a
blonde, long-necked Classicist from St Hugh's,
fumbling his way towards a familiarity with her body,
albeit through her clothing, but he had lost his
innocence with Eileen, studying at a secretarial
college on the Woodstock Road. She lacked Daisy's
fine features, but her edges were softer and she was
more like him: provincial, from Nottingham. He
would see her every Wednesday evening with the
occasional Saturday night trip to the pictures. He
kept her entirely separate from his college friends, so
that she was more like a mistress than a girlfriend. It
slightly shamed him now to think of the secrecy he
had maintained about their affair, but she had never
questioned it. Instead, on Wednesdays at around
6.30pm, when her room-mate was at choir-practice,
she would usher him into her digs — and into her
bed.

"Well, don't come then, James," Harry said, feeling his friend's scorn. "I'm sure there's an exciting new academic monograph you could be reading."

"Since it's clearly so important to you, old chum, I'll come and keep you company."

For once, Knox's gossip turned out to be accurate. By the time they arrived at the outdoor baths a crowd had already gathered. Mostly men, but also families out for an after-dinner stroll on this steaming night, young children, ice-creams in their hands, some on their fathers' shoulders — all watching the moonlit swimmers.

Knox elbowed his way through the three-deep throng in order to get closer. But James, at six foot four, had a clear line of sight to the start podiums at the right-hand end of the pool — and he saw her straight away.

Her hair was hidden by a swim cap, but he could see that she was dark, or at least darker than the rest of the girls. There were two fine black lines above her eyes — eyes which even at this distance seemed to sparkle: later he would discover that they were a jewel-like green, as if illuminated from within. Her nose was perfect, not tiny, not a button like some of the other girls', but somehow strong. She was the tallest among them, her legs long, lean and, thanks to the Catalan sun, bronzed. But it was the animation of her face, her laughter, the way the other women looked to her that marked her out as singular, the natural leader of the group. He was transfixed.

He watched as she organized the team, assigning each of the six a lane. They were giggling, aware of their

19

audience. The white of their swimsuits was almost florescent in the searchlight-bright moon, their figures defined in silhouette. As she turned side on, stepping onto the starting block readying for her dive, he marvelled at the shape of her, and when she bent her knees, her arms forming into an arrowhead, it struck him that this was probably how the ancients imagined Diana the huntress, a goddess of perfect strength and beauty. With the moonlight on her and her hair swept up into the white swim-cap, she could have been made entirely of marble.

The races went on for a while, the crowd eventually dwindling. But Harry didn't want to leave and James was only too happy to let him think that staying on was his idea. Once the women were out of the pool and had pulled on their robes, the two of them headed over, trying terribly hard to saunter.

"I say, you all did terribly well," Knox offered as his opening gambit, his voice plummier than usual — a nervous tic which, James recognized, surfaced whenever Harry came face to face with what he called "the fairer sex". James could feel his own heart rate had increased: rather than risk a joke that fell flat or some other gaucheness, he said nothing.

Two of the ladies laughed behind their hands, a third stared intermittently at her feet, stealing shy glances upward. James noticed that five of the six girls were looking at him rather than Harry, a pattern that, he had to admit, he had seen before. All that spoiled the moment was that the goddess was paying him no attention, instead rounding up the equipment and collecting a stopwatch left hanging on the back of an observation chair. Finally she walked over and, assessing the scene, extended her hand immediately towards Harry, bestowing on him a thousand-watt smile.

"Miss Florence Walsingham," she said. Her voice was confident and melodic but with a gentleness that surprised. As Harry stammered a reply, she nodded intently, her eyes only for him. James might as well have not existed. But, curiously, he did not mind. It meant he could stare at her, savour her smile, listen to that voice which instantly suggested the West End at night, dinner on the Strand, cocktails in Pall Mall and a thousand other delights he could only guess at.

As she turned to him, she reached up and removed her swimming cap, allowing long, glossy curls of dark brown hair to fall to her shoulders. Not all of it was dry: the damp ends clung to her cheekbones. Involuntarily, he found himself imagining how this woman would look when she was sweating, while she was making love. His outstretched hand had to remain suspended in mid-air for a second or two before she took it. But when she did, fixing him with that high-wattage gaze, he was over-run. By desire, of course, but also by an urge he had never known before: he wanted to lose himself in her, to dive inside and let the waters close over him.

James and Florence spent every moment of the next four days together. She watched him row, he watched her swim. Both tall, dark and striking, they became one of the more recognizable couples around the Plaza de España. They accompanied one another to the permanent parties in the hotel, on his floor and on hers, but mainly they just wanted to be with each other.

After Florence's morning swimming practice, they would walk and walk. The swimming baths were in Montjüic, a raised area that had once been a fort and a jail but which had been revamped in time for the International Exhibition seven years earlier. They would start at the newly-landscaped gardens, soaking up the view, then stroll down the hill past the pavilions built for the 1929 exhibition, stopping at the Poble Espanyol, the model Spanish village, and eventually gazing in awe at the fabulously elaborate Magic Fountain. In the warm sunshine, he in a white shirt, sleeves rolled up to the elbows, she in cotton dresses that seemed to float around her, they told each other how they had come to be fraternal team-mates at the People's Olympiad.

"Blame Harry and his pals in the ILP," he had said, during their first proper conversation.

"The Independent Labour Party?"

"Yes, that's it. Independent Labour Party."

"Are you a member?" she asked.

"No. I'm what Harry calls a fellow traveller. You?"

"Well, I'm certainly a socialist if that's what you mean." Hers was an accent he had never heard before he went up to Oxford, certainly not in his home town. It wasn't the received pronunciation you'd hear on the National Programme. It was the voice Harry lapsed into towards the bottom of a bottle of wine or when he spoke to his mother or, of course, when he was around young ladies: James supposed it was the accent of the upper class, or something close to it. "Inevitable, really, given my field."

"Your *field*." He marvelled at the arrogance of a twenty-one-year-old girl, four years younger than him, speaking of herself as if she were some kind of expert. "And what is your 'field', Miss Walsingham?"

She turned her face up to catch the sun. "I'm a scientist, Mr Zennor."

"A scientist indeed."

She ignored his condescension. "I've just completed my degree in natural sciences at Somerville. I'll be returning there next year."

"Whatever for?"

"To get my doctorate, of course. I am specializing in biology."

He considered making a joke — something about undertaking practical research — but wisely changed his mind. "What's that got to do with being a socialist?"

"You're a scientist, aren't you?"

"Well, some would dispute that, as it happens. Some call psychology 'mental philosophy'. Others say it's the newest branch of medicine."

"I don't care what 'some' say." She clutched his arm. "I want to know what *you* say."

He wanted to kiss her there and then, in front of all these people. She only had to look at him like that, with that electric-light smile, and he fell several hundred leagues deeper. "All right then," he conceded. "I say that it's science too. The science of the mind."

"Good. So we're both scientists." She squeezed his hand and he felt her energy flow into him.

He forced himself to concentrate. "You still haven't explained what any of this has to do with socialism."

"It's obvious, isn't it? Science is reason. It's about seeing what's *rational* and eliminating everything else. Socialism aims to do the same thing: to organize society rationally."

"But human beings are not rational, are they?"

"I don't know what you mean."

"Just look at us. Here." He glanced down at his forearm, on which lightly rested Florence's slender fingers. "What's rational about this?"

A worried look fleetingly crossed her face, like a wisp of cloud passing the sun. It was gone almost as soon as it had appeared. He could not tell whether she had been concerned at the blow to her argument or at the thought of what she was doing, walking arm in arm in a foreign land with a man she barely knew.

"Oh, I would say this is *perfectly* rational," she chirped, her enthusiasm recovered. "But to persuade you I would have to blind you with science."

Their love affair continued for the rest of that hot July week, preparing for the start of the Games on the nineteenth. They stayed up late at the street corner bar, listening to Harry play his ukulele along with his impromptu band — two Americans on trumpet and bass, one of whom turned out to be Edward Harrison, eminent foreign correspondent, with a gymnast from Antwerp as the singer — but they remained inside their

24

own cocoon. James wanted to know everything about Florence, and was prepared to tell her more about himself than he had ever told anyone before.

"So what's Zennor then? Is that foreign?"

He laughed. "Cornwall originally."

"Not now?" she asked, as if disappointed.

"My ancestors headed east," he said. "To Bournemouth."

"Bournemouth. I see. I thought from 'Zennor' you'd have at least, oh, I don't know, some pirate blood. From Zanzibar —"

"Or Xanadu."

"Cheat," she said, giving him a mock slap on the back of his hand, which was in truth another excuse to touch.

He said, "Bournemouth is not very exotic, is it?"

"Not really, I'm afraid, my darling. No foreign blood at all?"

"My parents are Quakers, if that counts. Both schoolteachers and both Quakers. Maths for him, piano for her. Two more solid, provincial people you could not hope to meet. They're not quite sure what to make of me."

"Aren't Quakers pacifists?"

"That's right." He watched as Florence did some rapid mental arithmetic.

"Does that mean, your father was, you know —"

"A conshie? Right again."

"Heavens. Did he go to jail?"

"Nearly, but not quite. Sent to do 'work of national importance'. In his case, farming."

"I see," she said, biting her lower lip in a gesture he was already coming to love. "So that's why they moved away from Cornwall. They couldn't return home after the war: too shaming."

He stared at her, wondering if he had been the victim of some kind of confidence trick. He had never told anyone that story, not even Harry. But she had intuited the truth.

This is how it was for that short, heady week, the two of them peeling off layers from each other. Sometimes it took the presence of another person, like the night they stayed at the tapas bar long after the rest of the rolling Olympics party had moved on elsewhere.

"I do hope we're not keeping you," Florence had asked the manager, a rotund man probably twice their age, as he began wiping the tables around them, sometime around two am. He insisted they were not and thanked them for being in Barcelona. In a fractured, bartered conversation — a bit of pidgin English in exchange for a phrase of broken Spanish — they began talking, he explaining that Spain would soon be a model for the world, a communist utopia.

"Well, if that's what the people vote for, then that's what it should be," Florence said.

"Quite right," James added. "That's what the army and the church need to get into their heads: the government was elected by the people of Spain. If you don't like it, vote it out at the next election."

"No, no, no," the man said, rag still in hand. "No voting out. Once we have communism here, it stay that way. Forever."

"Even if the people vote against it?" Florence had asked, her brow furrowed.

"They won't vote against it."

"Yes, but if they do."

"They won't. They shouldn't be allowed. Once the revolution is secure, then they can vote."

"And how long will that take?" James asked, picking up where Florence had left off. "How long till the revolution is 'secure'? That could take decades. Just look at Russia."

"The Soviet Union is the greatest democracy in the world!"

Florence and James looked at each other, before Florence said, "I don't think Mr Stalin has to face the voters too often, do you?"

The man looked puzzled.

"Communism is all very well but only if it's democratic. Otherwise it's just as bad as all the other rotten systems, if you ask me," James said.

The man resumed his clearing up, then rebuffed James's repeated attempts to pay the bill: "You are guests in my country and you support the republic!" When James produced a bank note, he shooed them out.

"It's like boycotting Berlin," James said as they walked slowly back towards her digs. "You don't have to be a communist to detest Hitler and the Nazis. You just have to be a half-decent human being. The man's a vile brute."

They were speaking of politics and the world, but really they were exploring each other, discovering with every conversation, every new encounter, how well the curves and contours of their minds fitted together. Then, at stolen moments in the mid-afternoon or late at night, they would do the same with their bodies — cautiously at first, with Florence teasing more than he could bear, then surprising him with sudden passion. His strongest memory was of her face close to his in the dark, their mouths sometimes speaking to each other in a lovers' hush, sometimes kissing.

The result was a fever for the taste, touch and smell of the other that shocked them both. Merely walking beside Florence, close enough for her scent to reach him, was enough to make him ravenous for her. What was more, and this he had never experienced before — even with sweet, giving Eileen — Florence seemed to feel the same: her desire was equal to his.

And so, while the political skies over Barcelona began to darken, and as the welcoming faces of their Barcelona hosts turned to distracted anxiety, James and Florence focused on the deadly serious business of falling in love.

Only when they heard about the broadcast of a coded message — "Over all of Spain, the sky is clear," was the plotters' signal to each other over the radio — did they understand that a coup d'etat was underway, fascists and nationalists bent on overthrowing the republican government that had invited the flower of international radical youth to Barcelona, to thumb its nose at the Nazis on parade in Berlin.

Suddenly the notion of sprints, heats and semi-finals seemed horribly irrelevant. Even those who thought the coup would be rapidly put down, who did not imagine the country was about to plunge into a vicious civil war, could see that this was no time for a pretend Olympics. When the rumour spread through the Hotel Olímpico that the games had been cancelled, few waited for confirmation.

James was packing his bag when Harry, his skin fire-engine red, found him. He had, James saw instantly, sobered up fast.

"Where are you going, Zennor?"

"Don't tell me you haven't heard. The Games have been —"

"Cancelled, I know. But where are you off to?"

"Well, I thought . . . if there are no Games. That is, I was going to ask Fl —"

"You're not proposing to leave, are you? In the republic's hour of need?"

James scanned Harry's face. He seemed entirely in earnest. "What are you suggesting?"

"A few of us are staying on. To defend the republic."

"But . . . but, you're not a soldier."

"I can train. The point is, Zennor, we've been enlisted, whether we like it or not."

"Enlisted?"

"History is enlisting us."

James stopped stock-still, holding the lid of his suitcase. It was quite true that, since the day he had arrived, he had understood that something much larger than a sports tournament was at stake. He knew it was easy to romanticize a gathering of fit and handsome young people coming together in the sunshine in a noble cause — but it was not just romance. Barcelona with its People's Olympiad had become the focus of international opposition to Adolf Hitler and his nasty so-called Third Reich. It was here that the world had said no, taking a stand not only against the Berlin games but against the entire Nazi project. And so an attack on the republic led by ultra-nationalist army officers and backed by fascist thugs was not solely a domestic matter for Spain. It was an attack by fascism itself. There would be a new fault-line now, running through Spain, yes, but dividing all of Europe. Hitler and Mussolini would doubtless be on one side of that line and those who believed in democracy and free speech and all the promise that the twentieth century held in store would be on the other. James Zennor found that he was asking himself a question: whose side are you on?

He snapped his suitcase shut and went to find Florence.

James had to fight a throng of athletes flooding out of the Hotel Olímpico lobby, stampeding for the railway station, to reach her. He was bewildered to find her standing outside, bags already in hand.

"I was just coming to see you," she said. She bit her lip in a way that instantly resolved him not to say what he had planned to say.

"Where are you going?"

"I'm going to Berlin."

"Berlin?"

"If I leave now, I can make it."

"*Berlin?* Why the hell would you be going there?"

"It's not how it looks, James. You have to trust me."

"But, what about —" he gestured at the crowd shoving and pushing around them, at the banners and the bunting.

"I know, but I have —"

"All that talk about the 'wicked Nazis' and how the Olympics will be just a 'glorified Nuremberg rally'. That was all rubbish, wasn't it? You meant none of it!"

"That's not fair."

That cloud that he had once seen pass across her face so briefly was lodged directly above her now, darkening her eyes. The light within seemed to be faltering. But he could not stop. "'I refuse to play any part in it'. That's what you said. Just talk, wasn't it? Cheap talk."

"How dare you talk to me like that?" She was glaring. "This is beneath you, James. And it's certainly beneath me."

"Listen —"

"No, you listen. I don't know what kind of women you've been with before me but this one" — her index finger tapped her breastbone — "makes up her own mind, OK? I will not be told what to do by any man. Not by my father and certainly not by you. You can decide to do whatever you like. But this is my decision. I've realized I need to make my point in my own way." She paused. "Besides, I haven't done all this training for nothing."

"Oh, so that's it, is it? You don't want your precious training to be in vain? You want the glory of a bloody medal!"

"No, that's not it," she said in a low voice, her eyes not meeting his. She was briefly knocked off balance by a group of women hurrying to cross the road and board a bus. "I have to leave. I'm sorry."

He reached out and grabbed her shoulder, forcing her to turn back to face him. "And what about this? Us." The word tasted awkward in his mouth; he instantly regretted it. "You and me. Has this meant nothing to you?"

She tilted her head to one side in an expression he didn't quite know how to read. Was it pity? Regret? He wondered if he could see tears in her eyes.

"You don't understand at all, do you? All that 'experimental psychology' and you don't understand a thing."

And with that, she broke free of him and disappeared into the swell of people clamouring to get out.

James stood for a while, letting the crowd shift around him, like a stream around a pebble. He could not quite believe what had happened, how quickly he had let her go. How quickly he had pushed her away, more like. What a fool, sounding off like that to a woman he had known for, what, a week? And this was not any woman. You might be able to tell an Eileen, or even a Daisy, what to do — some women positively seemed to like being bossed around. But not Florence. That much should have been obvious. She was independent, strong-willed, with a mind of her own: it partly explained why he was falling in love with her. To have attempted to control such a woman — a brilliant, beautiful woman, who could have any man she wanted — was the mark of a prize idiot.

He had embarrassed himself, there was no other word for it. He had sounded desperate, like some lovesick drip. All that talk of "you and me", of "us" — why, he had got it all wrong. To her, this was a holiday romance, nothing more — a casual fling. How naïve of him to have presumed it was anything more. He was like a girl in a port, stupid enough to believe the sailor who says he loves her. She was young and gorgeous and for her this probably meant no more than a furtive kiss in the chapel during an Oxford ball.

He had a strong urge to turn around that very instant and make the long journey back to Victoria Station. But the thought filled him with cold. The very idea of England without Florence felt barren. Returning to his routine of seminars, papers and long, silent sessions entombed in the dust of the Bodleian . . . No, he couldn't do it, not after a week like this.

Perhaps he should chase after her. He could apologize, tell her he had got it all wrong. He could tell her that whatever she had decided, he was sure it was right. Maybe he should follow her to Berlin. It would be worth it, even for just one more night with her, touching her skin, smelling her hair, hearing her laugh.

But that would sound more desperate still. He would be clinging to her, like a limpet. She would soon want to shake him off. And what respect would she have for a man so ready to abandon his principles, decrying

Hitler and the "fascist circus" of the Berlin Olympics one minute, only to come scurrying to the Games the next? It was one thing for her to do it; she had her own, mysterious reasons. She had her point to make, "in her own way". He would have no such excuse.

Anyway, she had not asked him. If she had wanted him at her side, she would have asked, and she had done no such thing. It would be humiliating to follow her to Berlin, trotting after her like a devoted little spaniel.

He looked upward, watching the red and yellow of the People's Olympiad banner come down, replaced by a flag of deepest red, and let himself fill up with the sensations he had felt earlier: the call of liberty, the demand of justice, the imperative that all those who were fit and able fight the good fight, saving the republic from those who would destroy it and much of civilization along with it. The void love had left in his heart would be filled by history.

CHAPTER
THREE

Oxford, July 8 1940

James slid his key into the lock noiselessly. He always tried to be quiet on these early mornings, so as not to wake the baby. But there was the smell of human warmth in the hallway, suggesting Florence and Harry were already up. He called out, "Good morning!" There was silence.

He wandered into the kitchen, noting that two of the three drawers were still open. Had they had to rush out for something? Had his son been ill while he was on the river? He called out again. "Harry? Daddy's home."

Once in the bedroom, his concern rose. Clothes were strewn over the floor, a chair from the bathroom dragged in front of his cupboard, whose door was flung wide open. His scrapbook was on the bed, several pictures shaken loose. Now James ran into his study, only to have his worst fears confirmed. The drawers were pulled from the desk, the floor covered with their contents along with dozens of books. There had been a robbery, just now, while he was out.

And yet the most valuable objects in the house, a pair of solid silver candlesticks, worth several years of his fellow's salary — a wedding gift from her parents —

were still sitting, untouched, on the mantelpiece. If they had been robbed, and if Florence had rushed from here to the police station to report it, a screaming Harry in tow, then the culprits must be the stupidest men in Oxford.

As he went back to the bedroom, a new thought began to form. He opened his wife's cupboard and, while he could not have said exactly which items were missing, he could see that the shelves were unusually bare. A look under the bed confirmed that the suitcase was gone.

Now his head began to throb. He ran into Harry's bedroom, looking for one thing. He went straight to the bed, pulled away the pillow and then tore off the blankets. No sign of Snowy, the boy's toy polar bear. His place was always here, in Harry's bed. If they went anywhere overnight, whether staying at the Walsinghams' London home in Chelsea, as they had done a couple of times, or at the country house in Norfolk, Snowy always came with them. Harry couldn't sleep without him. The fact that the bear was missing, even more than the absent suitcase, could mean only one thing.

Instantly and without conscious thought, James ran back into the hall and out of the front door, down the garden path and onto the wide, tree-lined road that was Norham Gardens. He looked left and then right, then left again: nothing, save for a large, heavy black car pulling away at the Banbury Road end of the street. All else was tranquil at this hour, the larger buildings opposite — once among the grandest houses in Oxford, but which were now often satellite buildings for assorted academic departments — were still locked up and empty, their gravel driveways undisturbed.

With no more reflection than before, he ran in the opposite direction, stopping just before Norham Gardens came to a dead-end at Lady Margaret Hall. The college porter, sweeping outside the front gate, lifted an arm in acknowledgement but James ignored him, instead turning hard right down a narrow pathway. This would lead to the University Parks. Would Florence have taken Harry here so early? Perhaps the boy had had a tantrum, perhaps he had developed that child's version of cabin fever for which the only remedy was fresh air. But then why had the house been turned upside down and why was the suitcase missing?

James vaulted over the gate — officially this entrance was for members of Lady Margaret Hall only — into the wide, flat stretches normally green but now a dry, sun-scorched brown: ahead and to his right was a strip of turf the colour of a digestive biscuit. This was the Oxford University Cricket Club, still and dormant.

A flicker of movement to his left: a matronly woman with a headscarf, walking her dog. He scoped the horizon one more time, left to right and back again. There seemed to be no one else around. And certainly no sign of Florence and Harry.

He walked the short distance back but now it felt like a long trudge. It was becoming impossible to avoid the conclusion that Florence had not left the house for some early-morning exercise, nor because there had been a break-in, but because she had left him.

Back at the house he felt instantly mocked by the outward serenity of the scene: the creeping white roses around the front door, the low wall containing a small, pretty garden with its trim lawn and single chair. He could picture Florence and Harry sitting there, the boy on his mother's knee, turning the pages of his illustrated edition of Grimms' Fairy Tales. With one shove of his right arm, James sent the chair crashing to the ground.

Once inside, he went straight back to his wife's wardrobe, standing closer this time, so that the scent of her rose from the few remaining clothes. He pulled out a drawer, now empty but for a few forlorn items: an old comb, a broken brooch. Her jewellery box was there. He opened it and saw that all the pieces he had given her — including the bracelet that was a gift to celebrate their reunion — were gone. He picked up the Japanese lacquerware box and, without thinking, hurled it against the far wall. The shattering sound provided a momentary shock of relief.

She had left him. She had left him, just as he had always feared she would. Who was it, he wondered? It could only be a much older man. All those his age or younger were at war. McGregor at the lab, working with her on "research"? Or that Fabian smoothie, what was his name? Leonard something.

He started running through all the possibilities, each time inflicting on himself the image of his wife in the arms of another, her mouth on his, her hair touching his shoulders . . .

Now he began pacing the house. How long had it been going on? How long had she been planning for this moment, never letting on a thing? Smiling at him, chatting away as if there was nothing out of the ordinary, when all the time she was scheming, preparing . . .

And to take little Harry with her, treating their son as if he were her personal property . . .

He could feel it returning, the sensation which these past three years had become as familiar to him as an old friend. He could almost hear it, like the first intimation of distant thunder or the tremor of an approaching underground train. It was building inside him, getting stronger with each beat, until it was rushing through his veins, a rage that could not be stopped. He could picture it too, hot and viscous as lava, a physical substance that, once stirred, would swell inside his body, surging forward, searching for escape. The rage controlled him now; it would brook no restraint until it had erupted. He was merely its vessel.

The terrible truth, that he had admitted only once and never to Florence, was that he did not loathe or despise this feeling. Instead, he greeted this molten fury when it came with something close to relief. For weeks on end he had to hold it all in, to speak calmly, to smile at acquaintances, to feign interest in students, to discuss cricket or Herodotus with some fossilized nonagenarian at high table. But when the fury came, it came with elemental force, a force that cared for nothing but his appetites, his fears and his rage. When James was in the grip of this anger, he did not care about the consequences of his actions or what the neighbours would think. He did not think at all. It made him free.

He reached for one of those damnable candlesticks and, satisfied by the weight of it in his hand, threw it squarely at the window looking out on the back garden: it sailed through, smashing the glass but clipping the window-frame on its exit, splitting the white wood. He heard it land hard on the flagstones beyond. To hell with the bloody Walsinghams and their bloody adulterous daughter!

Next he turned to the dresser, containing their best china. He opened the glass-fronted door and removed the largest plate, and hurled it, discus-style, in the same direction as the candlestick. It went askew, smashing on the wall to the right of the window. The noise was too feeble to sate him, so he took another plate and threw that one to the floor. Softened by the rug, it broke in two with a single crack. Reaching for a third, he smashed it on the table before him; it cut his wrist on impact, producing a jagged wound. The sight of the welling blood brought the eruption to a halt and suddenly he felt tired, spent.

And now came the reckoning, the feeling of disgust that followed release. He surveyed his surroundings, strewn with rubble of his own making. So much destruction. Again.

He stumbled towards Harry's room and slumped onto his son's infant bed, imagining he could still feel the boy's warmth. At this moment, Harry was probably walking between Florence and the man who had stolen her from him. They were each holding one of the boy's hands, calling out "one-two-three" then lifting and swinging him through the air. The man was smiling at Florence who was looking more beautiful than ever. How long before Harry called him Daddy?

As if trying to escape the thought, James headed to his study, now as cavernously empty as the rest of the house, suddenly desperate for a cigarette. The first hit of nicotine flooded through him, swamping his neural circuitry, just as he wanted it to. As he exhaled, a fresh thought occurred to him, one sparked by the ache in his shoulder, now pulsing with increased voltage. Florence had tired of him, and who could blame her?

She had tired of living with an invalid. Not yet thirty, James was already a veteran with a war wound. A cripple. Yes, he could row, though at nothing like his former strength and at such enormous effort. He was still a cripple, rejected three times for military service, despite his repeated appeals and best endeavours at string-pulling in Whitehall. So what did that make him? A cripple who tried hard. A Victorian oddity, on display in a travelling show. Good old James: shoulder smashed to pieces, but still he does make a jolly good effort, I'll say that for him.

Florence, on the other hand, was twenty-four and in her impeccable prime. Why would such a perfect creature want to be paired with a physically damaged specimen, why would she tolerate it? She needed more than he could give her.

He thought of the first time, not long after it happened, when he had realized this. They were back in

England, married for less than a year. He had woken with a terrible thirst and croaked out, "Florence! Florence?"

And then he had seen that her side of the bed was empty. He had hauled himself up and staggered to the kitchen. He had been about to go inside when he had stopped short, halted by the sound of sobbing. He had watched her for what seemed like an hour, though it was probably no more than seconds. Her back had been to him, her shoulders rising and falling in rapid, short jerks. She was pregnant and he had decided that she must be in pain, that there must be some kind of complication and that she needed his help. He had stepped forward, drawing level with the doorway, before realizing that she was, in fact, crying for him — for what he had once been and for what he would never be again. He had opened his mouth, his lips forming his wife's name, but they emitted no sound, just a dry, papery rasp. She did not turn around.

He had returned to their bed without her ever noticing that he had left it. And that was hardly the last time he had seen her cry.

The memory left a bitter taste: he decided he needed a drink. He poured himself a full glass of Scotch, downed it, then poured another. Florence had left him before, he now thought. After their very first week together, she had left him. Or that was how he had understood it at the time.

She had told him she was going to Berlin, to take up the place she had never formally surrendered in the British Olympic team. He had accused her of vanity, of betraying the principles that surely they both shared. He had embarrassed himself, speaking of "us", as if they had sworn solemn vows, when they had known each other for little more than a week. He had sensed in Florence Walsingham a kindred spirit. She was not like Harry, with his ideological tracts and his alphabet soup of political parties. She seemed to see things the way he did: that what was happening around them was not really about politics, but about right and wrong. You didn't have to carry a party card to know the difference, to know on which side of the line a decent person had to stand. By heading to Berlin, she had announced she was crossing over to the other side.

He was the older of the two of them, and yet he had been so bloody juvenile. So naïve. She had told him to trust her, that she was going to make her point in her own way, but he had not listened.

Instead he and Harry Knox had stayed in Spain, to do what they could to defend the now-endangered republic. They had watched as a flood of French communists who had made the same decision poured into both the Basque country and Catalonia. As those volunteers and others from all over Europe and beyond gradually formed into the International Brigades, he and Harry gladly signed up.

There had been quite a few people in their position, two hundred by one estimate: athletes who had been expecting to take part in the People's Olympiad but who would soon find themselves learning how to dig a trench or use a rifle. (It was a Czech, tipped for gold in the twenty-five metre rapid-fire pistol event, who had first taught James his safety catch from his trigger.)

Most there were like Harry, serious men driven by political conviction — and that conviction was usually Marxism. Some saw the Spanish republic as a laboratory experiment, a test bed for socialism that had to be protected. But plenty saw it the way James did. He had been adamant that he would not be used as an extra in Hitler's pageant of the master-race in Berlin, and he was equally clear that Francisco Franco and his fascist allies in the Falange could not be allowed to overturn the will of the Spanish people by toppling a government the people had chosen. It was a clash of democracy versus brute force: pretty straightforward really.

And what James could not deny, though he would not have admitted it out loud or even quietly to himself, was that this epic struggle between good and evil had come along at the right time — just when he needed a cause in which he could lose himself.

So he was happy to join the internationals as they journeyed first to Valencia, where they paraded through the streets, greeted by flags, placards and ragged banners, their slogans chalked in white, and by endlessly-repeated chants. James heard lots of *vivas*, quickly echoed by the French communists leading the column, who began to shout *Vive le Front Populaire!* or *Vive la Republique!* But the most constant refrain was *No Pasaran!*, the slogan James would see daubed on walls and hear at rallies for most of the next year. As he and Harry walked with others from the International

44

Brigades, diffident and surprised to be feted in such fashion, the townspeople would sometimes join in, walking among them for a block or two, before joining the crowds stretched along the pavements. They were being hailed as heroes, like the warriors of ancient myth. And they had not yet fired a shot. When they came to leave Valencia, and their train was delayed for a long while before moving off, the local women compensated them by offering free kisses to anyone who stuck his head out of the window.

James remembered the mood of almost reckless idealism that had gripped him and his new comrades in that late summer of 1936: young men, from all over the world, united in a cause that was just and noble. And in his mind it was intertwined inseparably with the love that he carried for Florence, the spark lit during that brief, exhilarating week in Barcelona and which burned in the months afterwards. It burned even as that train took him to Albacete, the nowhere city in La Mancha where the International Brigades would have their headquarters and training camp. Though that term flattered it: there was no formal training, just a period set aside early each morning for exercise. Perhaps in a nod to the anarchists then so influential in the republic, each unit was to devise its own exercise programme with no order from any commanding officer telling them what to do. James and his group had prepared for war by playing leapfrog.

Now slumped in his chair in Norham Gardens, the whisky doing its work, he gazed up at the mantelpiece, at the picture frame that contained no photograph but

45

only a small, singed newspaper clipping. He had preserved it because that little piece of paper had brought Florence back to him.

He had been on guard duty at the Albacete camp, his group having been saddled with the two am shift. The war was in its eighth week, it was late September and the nights were getting cold. A Yugoslavian comrade had passed him a shred of newspaper, urging James to use it to relight a dwindling fire. He had just put a match to it when he noticed it was in English; indeed it was a page from *The Times*. Hungry for news, he had blown out the flame so that he could scan the items: a ship lost in the Atlantic, troubles for Mr Baldwin's government. Then a name leapt out at him.

"Miss Walsingham's withdrawal from the Games disappointed British organizers, who had believed she was a racing certainty for a gold medal, having secured her place in the final with the fastest qualifying time. But the champion swimmer said that she had never intended to compete in the last stage of the Olympic swimming competition. "I wanted to show Herr Hitler that his nasty little Nazis are not the best in the world, whatever they might say. Whoever comes first on Sunday will be second best — and they will know it."

James reached for it now, reading it again, nearly four years later, as he let a third glass of whisky warm his throat. For months that clipping had stayed in his wallet, second best to having a photograph of her. He had kept it with him until they had made contact again, kept it with him, in fact, until they had set up this house as their marital home (thanks to some help from Papa Walsingham).

Once in its frame, it became quite a conversation piece: Florence used to like telling the story. But for James it was more than just a memento of their romance. It was also a reminder to him of his own naïveté. He kept it lest he forget that sometimes — often — she was right and he was wrong.

He had written to Florence immediately, addressing his letters to her Oxford college. He had little confidence in the wartime postal service of a country divided against itself, but whenever he passed a mailbox, even in the remotest Spanish village, he would send another letter. When he ran into Ed Harrison, covering the war for *Time* magazine, the American journalist had let slip that he was returning to the States via London: James promptly pushed a letter into his hand.

In each version he wrote the same thing, apologizing for his pig-headedness, applauding her bravery for what she had done in Berlin — and then congratulating both of them for taking a stand for what was right. He described the action he was seeing, at first doctoring the actuality just a touch to ensure he gave a good impression of himself. But eventually he simply recorded the unvarnished truth, flattering or otherwise. He faithfully recorded, for example, the midday attempt he and a contingent of mainly British volunteers had made to storm a hilltop monastery deep in the Castilian countryside, now converted into a Nationalist fort. He had been inching forward on his stomach, the earth scratching his face as he advanced. Within moments, he had heard bullets swish through the grass above his ears. Only the sound of gunfire coming from his comrades behind made him realize that he was meant to fire back. He pointed his rifle in the direction of the enemy and squeezed the trigger — only to hear a single, dull click. He suddenly felt utterly exposed, vulnerable to instant death (though, he wrote to Florence, "I soon learned that the ability to shoot back is no guarantee of safety"). Still lying prone, the air around him whizzing with gunfire, he had emptied out the failed ammunition and loaded a fresh clip of cartridges. Still nothing. So it wasn't his fault; his weapon was a dud. Only the presence of Harry Knox, scrabbling up the hillside just behind him with a functioning gun had saved him.

In his letters, he would offer his half of the conversation he imagined they would be having — about the course of the war, the intervention on the Nationalists' side of the Germans and the Italians, the republic's desperate need for Britain to get involved. He wrote often, once a week at least, and kept writing even when he had reached Madrid for what he and his fellow volunteers believed would be the decisive battle of the war.

Madrid. By rights his memories of Madrid should have been sources of horror — and plenty of them were. He had spent twelve long days with the XII International Brigade in an event that would be named,

48

in the heroic language of such things, the defence of Madrid. On the ground and in the moment, it felt much less epic. For a man raised on English schoolboy notions of battles — at Agincourt or Hastings — it was a shock to realize quite how messy, confused and appalling was the reality.

The battle was fought in the northwest of the city, where Franco's forces were attempting to break into the capital, with the action focused on the university district. The result was a crazed, shifting series of skirmishes in and around the academic buildings. It might have been funny if there had not been so much death around — the notion of an armed advance to capture the geography block, followed by a retreat back to the literature department. James was involved in a series of particularly furious counter-attacks to recapture the Hall of Philosophy.

In one operation, James and a dozen others had had to run across an open space of some forty yards. They did it in threes, a frantic dash in which the men at James's side had simply fallen away as they ran, shot noiselessly it seemed to him. By the time he reached the other side, he came across perhaps a hundred dead bodies, Moroccans mostly, men of the Army of Africa, veterans of Spain's colonial wars enlisted into Franco's forces. James had been transfixed by the sight of the corpses. Most had not been killed cleanly, by gunfire. Instead shells had shredded their bodies; Mills bombs had blown off their arms and legs. He could smell burning and turned to see a small fire, no larger than the ones he remembered from the scouting weekends of his boyhood. Except this time, in place of logs, were two dead men burning steadily. He had not vomited, nor wept, as he might have expected of himself. Instead he had simply stared, feeling as if he had failed these men by arriving too late. But perhaps by looking at them, really looking at them, as if they were men rather than corpses, he could give them a small measure of dignity.

He had, to his surprise, become an effective soldier, his willingness to take risks winning the admiration of his superiors. A few called him El Corajudo, the brave one. Eventually, he had been given intelligence duties, including surveillance of those the Republican brass suspected as infiltrators or spies. Until the day whose details he could not remember, the day whose consequences he was never allowed to forget.

And yet, despite everything, the word "Madrid" did not fill him with dread. For he associated Madrid with Florence.

Eventually, after perhaps his dozenth letter, he had got a reply. She explained that, not long after the fuss about her performance in Berlin had faded, she had decided that she too ought to be in Spain, to give what she could to the cause of freedom. Like him, she was reluctant to write down the complete truth: that she wanted to be with him. And he, no less ardently, wanted to be with her.

Florence became a nurse, treating the wounded at the Red Cross Hospital in Avenida Reina Victoria, in northwest Madrid. She had no training to speak of, but that was hardly unusual. She relied instead on the instruction of Marjorie, a stout and seasoned volunteer from Baltimore, who had abandoned her job as a sister on the wards of the city hospital there to treat the besieged people of the republic; she taught Florence and the other women under her the basics. And, Florence being Florence, she had read several books on medicine and anatomy en route to embattled Spain, mugging up on the ship from Marseille to Valencia, leaving James in no doubt that she had rapidly become as expert as any of the doctors.

His service at the front and hers at the hospital meant they could not see each other much, but that only made their encounters through the autumn of 1936 the more exquisite. Instead of sleeping in a shallow trench — little more than a ditch, bolstered by a few sandbags — surrounded by unwashed men, James would find himself in a room in the Hotel Gran Via where, before anything, he and Florence would soak in a hot bath together, then make love and then make love again. They would eat a long dinner, trading tales of what they had seen, before climbing the staircase and returning to bed. No matter how exhausted they were, they would stay awake much of the night — believing that to sleep was to squander the strictly-rationed supply of time they had together.

During the day, they might walk out, surveying the latticework of tramlines and improvised barricades Madrid had become. "It looks like London during street-mending," Florence said, pointing to braziers just like those English labourers might use to warm their hands.

Once they were out walking together during an air raid. The city was all but defenceless in the face of attack from the air: there were no anti-aircraft weapons and the Republicans were reduced to mounting cinema projectors on the rooftops to do the work of searchlights. But this raid came in the middle of the day. Florence and James were at a street market when suddenly they heard the overhead whine of German planes and, seconds later, the thudding crash, the cloud of dust and the screams caused by a falling bomb.

They ran together to a scene of appalling destruction, lumps of blood and flesh barely recognizable as bodies. James was quickly drafted into helping move a slab of concrete under which a man, conscious and still wearing his hat, had his legs trapped. Only later did he notice Florence kneeling by a little girl, who lay as still as a doll.

Perhaps it was because the people of Madrid themselves returned to normal so quickly — the shops lifting their shutters within a few hours, the elderly couples strolling once more in the late afternoon — that somehow these events did not obliterate all other memories of their time together. Despite everything, James thought of those final months of 1936 as among the happiest times of his life. "It's not despite the war, it's because of it," Florence had said once as she gazed out of the window of their hotel room, watching the blue beams thrown into the sky by machines that a few months earlier had lit up the local cinema screen with Fred and Ginger, dancing together cheek-to-cheek.

"Because of it?" he had asked from the bed.

"Yes, because. Fear of death makes love more intense: isn't that what it says in your psychology books?"

"'Make love'? Did someone say 'make love'?" And he dragged her back under the covers so that he could touch her skin and taste her mouth all over again.

On Christmas Eve, after less than two months together, they went to the *ayuntamiento*, the town hall on the Plaza de la Villa, to be married by a grandly-moustached socialist councillor, who hailed theirs as a "revolutionary wedding", a civil ceremony conducted in defiance of the Catholic church, now fatally identified with Franco. The ceremony was brief and chaotic, punctuated by rowdy cheers from the crowd of well-wishers that had gathered all but spontaneously. Harry was best man and held the ring, bought from a jeweller whose shop window had been blown out in that afternoon bombing raid but who had reopened for business the very next day. Sister Marjorie was there as Florence's witness. They had had to utter their vows in Spanish, so that James would forever cherish the words, *Sí, quiero*, the Spanish equivalent of "I do", seeing them as somehow belonging to him and Florence alone — their private language.

Now, he considered pouring himself another glass of Scotch, but thought better of it: he drank straight from the bottle instead. That had all been less than four years ago, but it might as well have happened in another age. To another man. Florence had left him because she had grown to despise him. He had been a good, loving husband and father, but it had not been enough. She

53

would now shower that exceptional vigour, energy and beauty on another man. He felt the anger rise in him once more, his old sparring partner back for another round.

He got up, not wanting to be in the same room as that framed newspaper clipping, and walked into the kitchen, stumbling in the hallway on a chair he couldn't remember knocking over, and saw it straight away, wondering instantly how he could have missed it.

On the table, resting against the conical flask Florence had brought home from the lab and converted into a vase, was a small envelope — quarter-sized, the kind that would usually contain a florist's card accompanying a bouquet. No name on it.

He tore it open and recognized her handwriting instantly.

She had written just three words: *I love you.*

James felt a pricking sensation behind his eyes. He blinked and then read it again. Was this some kind of trick?

She had left him, taking Harry with her, and yet she still loved him? What sense did that make? It was insincere, a fake greeting card, "I love you", scribbled to offset the cruelty of her actions. That must be it.

And yet he did not believe that either. Florence was only ever sincere about love. She did not use the word lightly; they had been together a long time before she told him that she loved him. He knew, too, that he was the first man ever to hear those words from her lips. If she had written it, she meant it. That there was no other message made it truer still. That she loved him was her entire meaning.

He held the card and read it a dozen more times, turning it over, then reading it again. The words were balm to the bruise she had left on his heart, but after the relief came another sensation: a bafflement that grew deeper by the moment.

CHAPTER
FOUR

It sounded like a fusillade of gunfire, distant rather than deadly. The sun was high and James's shirt was sticking to his back. He squinted against the brightness of a Spanish noon but he could not see where the noise was coming from. He was in the bombed-out ruin of what, he guessed, had once been a farmworker's cottage. The walls still stood, though they were pocked by bullet-holes. Whole chunks of plaster were missing, exposing the brick underneath, like snatched glimpses of flesh. The windows had no glass, the doorways were empty arches. And when he looked down at his feet, he saw that the ground itself seemed to be sinking slowly. He was in a house that was crumbling before his eyes. And now the gunfire started again . . .

He woke with a start, his heart thumping. He looked around, confused. When he realized he was slumped in an armchair, he sat bolt upright, knocking over the bottle of whisky lodged at his side. *Damn*. It had soaked the top of his trousers, drenching his left thigh. And then came that rat-tat-tat again; not gunfire, but someone at the door.

James remembered after a moment of delay what had happened, the recollection landing like a deadweight on his chest. Harry and Florence were gone.

The knocking again. He stood up, aware of a chill draught in the house. Of course: the hole in the kitchen window, shattered by the candlestick.

"Dr Zennor?"

Oh no. The voice, unmistakable, belonged to Virginia Grey. James encountered her most often as one half of the couple that together ran his college: her husband was Master. But that accounted for only a small part of their influence. Bernard and Virginia Grey were luminaries of the British intellectual Left. You couldn't open a copy of the *New Statesman* without coming across an article by or about them, the latter usually reviewing a pamphlet or book they had produced either singly or together. They were a dominant force in the Fabian Society and, through that, the Labour party, their ideas and proposals constantly debated in the national press or taken up as policy. They hosted a high table that was regularly graced by Westminster politicians and the country's most eminent theorists.

The Greys had taken Florence and James under their wing almost as soon as they had returned from Madrid, insisting that Florence transfer her doctoral work to the college, demanding they have their Spanish marriage blessed in the college chapel — where they had acted as if they were the parents of the bride. His own parents had sat polite, quiet and thoroughly overwhelmed through the whole event.

Now in their late sixties, the Greys had their doubts about James's field, regarding psychology as new-fangled and experimental. They urged him to switch to political science instead — though, to his irritation, they always appeared riveted by Florence's work on evolutionary biology. James suspected they rather fancied the Zennors might become the future Greys of the 1970s, seeing themselves in this "handsome young couple"; seeing too, perhaps, an opportunity to extend their influence beyond the grave. They had no children of their own.

Brushing crumbs of a half-eaten sandwich off himself and onto the wooden floor, he opened the door. "Good mor —" He stopped, suddenly aware that he had no idea what time it was.

"Thank heavens. I was beginning to wonder if you were *dead*! I've been knocking on your door for seven minutes."

"I'm sorry, Mrs Grey. I wonder if I could call on you later. Now is not —"

"Are you unwell, James dear? You do sound a little off-colour." Her tone was bossily familiar, a mother talking to a recalcitrant child.

"I am feeling a little under the weather, as it —"

"I think I ought to come in."

"I really would rather —"

"Chop, chop, James."

That was how the Greys were: they would not take no for an answer, so no one ever gave it to them. He opened the door.

"Oh Lord. You look absolutely dreadful!" Her eyes darted past him, no doubt taking in the devastation; then she wrinkled her nose in distaste: she had smelled the whisky.

"What *has* been going on here?" She marched into the room uninvited.

"Would you like a drink, Mrs Grey?" He took an almost malign pleasure in the appalled expression on her face.

"I rather think you've had enough of that already, don't you?"

"I was actually offering one to you, Mrs Grey. But if you won't, I will."

She ignored this remark, instead finding a chair and making herself comfortable. Then in a voice that was kindly, and nearly free of the usual imperiousness, she said, "Can I suggest you tell me what happened?"

James sat down too, realizing that he was grateful for the chance to speak to another person. "It would appear that Florence has left me."

Grey stifled a gasp. "Good God, no. When?"

"This morning. I came back from sculling and the house was empty."

"And Harry?"

"She's taken him with her."

James watched a thought flicker across Grey's face, stern beneath its bun of silver hair. Her initial shock seemed now to give way to urgency, the practical desire to act and to act immediately. "Have you spoken to her? Has she telephoned?"

"She left a note."

"A note? What did it say?"

"Nothing." He paused, weighing up the temptation to tell her everything. But something held him back. Was it loyalty to Florence? Was it embarrassment? "Nothing that explains anything anyway."

"Had she ever talked about leaving before?"

"No. Never."

"So why do you presume she left?"

"She must have met someone else. She is the most beautiful woman in Oxford, after all. Your husband called her that, as I recall, at our wedding celebration."

A picture instantly sprang into his head. That Indian summer's day, late September 1937, in the college garden: Florence, heavily pregnant and glowing with good health. Next to her, on crutches, James himself, his smile for the photographer more of a wince. Though the Greys had insisted on the location, the idea of the celebration had come from Florence's parents: "Darling, you've denied us the delight of seeing our daughter married; you will *not* deprive us of our right to throw an enormous party." So nine months after they had exchanged their Spanish vows, they had listened as Sir George Walsingham made a toast extolling the qualities of his wonderful daughter while Bernard Grey made jokes at James's expense and, like a man who could not help himself, offered repeated paeans to the beauty of the bride.

"Her attractiveness has no bearing on her willingness or otherwise to pair with other men, nor to leave you. Unless you have any evidence to the contrary, James?" Virginia Grey asked tartly.

60

James closed his eyes. "No, I don't suppose I do."

"You have made a telephone call to Florence's parents of course."

He sighed. "No, as a matter of fact, I haven't."

"Well, why ever not? She's probably on her way there now. It's the first place any young girl goes when there's trouble at home."

"She's not gone there. Believe me."

"Well, it's the obvious place to start and I insist that you check. Now where's the number? I'll —"

"Please! Mrs Grey. Florence hasn't spoken to her mother in . . . for a while."

Virginia Grey frowned.

James looked away, guilty to be breaking one of his wife's secrets. "They're not speaking to each other at present."

Silence hung in the air until eventually Mrs Grey spoke again. "I imagine it will be awkward, but I fear you will have to do it all the same. She has almost certainly gone there and no proper search can begin until you have at least eliminated that possibility."

James could hardly fault her logic; but the thought of making such a call filled him with dread. What would he say? If he announced that Florence had gone missing, he would be admitting that she had left him. If Mrs Grey was right, that would make no odds: the Walsinghams would know already. But if she was wrong, well, then he would be making an entirely needless confession. And before he knew it, Sir George Bloody Walsingham would be taking charge, alerting his contacts in the Oxford constabulary until they had tracked down his daughter and grandson, while Lady Walsingham would be giving him that withering look of hers, a woman's look that said "No wonder she's left you: you're not a proper man any more."

They already blamed him anyway. He was the reason why Florence had stormed out of that dinner in London with her parents, back in April (or was it February?). He could scarcely remember what the row had been about, probably something trivial about the menu or the taxi home. But the underlying cause was obvious. The Walsinghams believed their daughter had married beneath herself: she, whose pedigree breeding would have secured the richest, most desirable man in the kingdom, married to this son of provincial schoolteachers who was crippled to boot. To announce that he could not find Florence or Harry, that he had been discarded, would be to confirm their verdict on him: he was not good enough.

A voice called out from the hallway. "They live in Norfolk, don't they?" As good as her word, Virginia Grey was standing by the telephone table, about to make the call.

James ran out and grabbed the phone from her. "I'll do it," he said quietly. This was how the Greys operated, bending everyone to their will.

Virginia hovered as he heard his own breathing through the heavy, Bakelite receiver and then a click as the operator came on the line. "The name is Walsingham, please," he said. "In Langham in Norfolk. Thank you." He waited, listening to the clicks and switching sounds, picturing the exchanges as they plugged in the series of cables that would send his voice eastward across England.

Eventually there was the ringing sound, followed after four rings by a female voice: middle-aged and aristocratic. "Wells 452."

"Lady Walsingham? It's James. Florence's husband."

"Good afternoon, James. I'm afraid Sir George is out." *Ite.* "Is there something wrong?"

"No, there's nothing wrong." The echo on the line was confusing him, making him trip over his words as they bounced back to him two seconds later. "I just wondered if I might speak to Florence."

"Florence? I don't understand."

"Florence and Harry. They're not with you?"

"No. Why ever would they be with us? You always come in August."

He listened closely to the voice, trying to detect a lie. They were polished, people of her class, he had learned that much after more than a decade in Oxford, whether as undergraduate or fellow. She and Sir George — a powerful figure in the City and a decorated officer in the Great War — were as elegant in their manner as in their looks. They were a handsome couple: Florence's mother, once a society beauty, had her daughter's piercing eyes and perfect bone structure. Was Florence standing nearby, mouthing answers to her? If she were, he would never know it. And yet, he had to confess it did not sound like that at all.

"James? Are you still there? Has something happened?"

"No, no. Not at all." Hearing his own voice played back to him, even he did not believe it. "Just some confusion on my part."

"Is Florence unwell? Is Harry all right?" The concern was genuine, he was certain of it.

"Yes, yes. Everyone's well. I just thought they might have . . . perhaps . . ." He mumbled a farewell and hung up.

Virginia Grey did not say anything. She bit her lip and headed towards the kitchen. "Time for a pot of tea, I think."

While she was fussing over cups and spoons, she asked, her tone as casual as if she were inquiring where she might find the sugar, "How have things been between you? Recently I mean."

He hesitated, reluctant to confide in her. But it was clear she was keen to help and it was somehow comforting not to be conducting this search entirely alone. "We're not newlyweds any more, Mrs Grey. But I believe our marriage is strong."

She stopped her tea preparations and gazed at him.

"You're not convinced," he said.

"It does not matter a jot whether I am convinced, my dear. That is not at issue here."

"Did she say something to you?"

Grey stared out into the garden and her hair caught the sunlight, turning the silver to bright white.

"I don't think it was anything specif —"

"So she did say something! What the hell was it?" Now he stood up, looming over her. He could feel his veins engorging, the rage stirred and beginning to surge.

Grey's expression looked more pitying than alarmed, which only fuelled James's ire. "Come on," he said loudly, "answer me!"

In a voice that was studiedly calmer and quieter than before, she said, "This." She gestured towards him. "She told me about this. Your aggression. She told me about your fights, James."

"We have had disagreements. Every couple has dis —"

"She was not referring to *disagreements*, James. She was referring to violent displays of temper. I can see for myself the broken crockery here today."

"Today is hardly typical."

"She told me that there was a constant *tension* in the house."

"Nonsense."

"Her exact words were, 'I feel as if the ground is covered with eggshells. And I'm tiptoeing my way through them.'"

"Eggshells? I know what that's about. That's my punishment for demanding quiet when I work. Any scholar would be the same. It's impossible to do serious reading with an infernal racket going on."

"What infernal racket?"

"Harry shouting and shrieking when he's playing. I lost my temper a few times." He could picture the tears trickling down his son's cheeks, the little boy standing in the garden crying after James had exploded again, Florence holding Harry tight, explaining that it was not his fault, not his fault at all, James standing apart from them, too ashamed to step forward and hug Harry himself — a shame whose sting he felt again now. But what he said stiffly was, "I'm sure the Master would have been the same in my position."

The silver-haired author of half a dozen books and a couple of hundred learned articles eyed him coolly. "Yes. Even I might struggle to do my needlepoint with that distraction."

James realized his mistake. "I'm sorry, Mrs Grey. I didn't mean —"

"Don't worry, Dr Zennor. I've been condescended to by far greater men than yourself." She now placed the teapot at the centre of the table and took a seat. "Florence was worried about you. She said you were drinking heavily."

"For heaven's sake, can a man not drink a glass of Scotch in his own home?"

"At high table the other night, you had Perkins return to the cellar at least twice."

"So you think my wife left me because I'm some kind of dipsomaniac?"

"No one is saying your wife has left you."

"She's not here, is she?"

"No, she is not. But there is no evidence that she has left you, in the rather melodramatic sense of that word. You don't know where she is. And you don't know why she's gone."

"Precisely."

"Well, I think you need to begin by putting yourself in her shoes."

James straightened his back, as if to signal that the discussion was over. "Well, thank you, Mrs Grey. I appreciate your efforts. But nothing you have told me will help me get my wife back."

"Is that what you want? To get her back?"

"Of course, that's what I bloody want!" His voice cracked at that and, ashamed by the show of weakness, he dipped his head.

"Well, perhaps I can help you."

He looked up, the rims of his eyes a bloodshot red.

"Florence came to see me yesterday."

James gave a small nod, determined to do nothing that might stop Grey from going on.

"She seemed agitated. She told me something of the . . . *strains* at home."

"Yes." His mind was whirring, processing what he was hearing at top speed, already working through the possible implications.

"She said nothing concrete, she made no mention of any plans."

"But . . ."

"She was clearly in a hurry. She broke off our conversation, saying there was something she had to look up urgently at the Bodleian." Grey focused on her fingers, as if she needed to concentrate and choose her words carefully. "I thought nothing of it at the time. After all, your wife is a dedicated scholar. But given her departure first thing this morning, I wonder if the two are connected. If there was something she had to check, something she had to find out, before she could leave. It might perhaps give you a —"

But Virginia Grey did not get the chance to complete her sentence. She looked up to see James had simply turned around, grabbed a jacket from the hall and marched out of the front door.

CHAPTER
FIVE

It was only when he passed the clock outside the Post Office that he discovered the time. It was quarter to six: he had, he realized, spent most of the day in a stupor fuelled by anger and alcohol. But now, at last, he had some action to take. It was not much — after all, his wife was in the Bodleian fairly regularly — but Grey was a shrewd judge of character: if she believed Florence's visit yesterday might be significant, that his wife had somehow seemed agitated, then that had to be taken seriously.

He had peddled furiously past Keble when a blur from his left suddenly slammed into view. He swerved to avoid it, but it was too late: a fellow cyclist had sprung from South Parks Road without looking, clipping the back of James's rear wheel.

He landed hard, thankfully on his backside rather than his shoulder. His right hand, which had taken some of the impact, was scratched, the graze revealing itself as a grid of blood spots.

"So sorry, Zennor. I am so frightfully sorry."

James looked upward, shading his eyes to see Magnus Hook, research fellow at New College and wearer of the roundest, thickest glasses in Oxford, standing over him. Poor eyesight had kept Hook out of the army, but he was doing his bit for the war effort: he had been seconded by the Ministry of Food, which had taken over large chunks of St John's to control the national supply of fish and potatoes. "I now work at the largest fish and chip shop in the world," was his pet conversational gambit; James had heard it at least three times.

Just the glimpse of Hook sapped his energy. For one thing, he embodied the category in which he, Zennor, now belonged. Thanks to his damned shoulder, he too was a D-band reject, just like Hook and the rest of the other half-blind cripples. But combined with this contempt was envy: for Hook had taken his place alongside the hundreds of dons of non-military age who had been drafted as civil servants. That was why Oxford in July, usually empty thanks to the Long Vacation, was teeming: the city had become a displaced Whitehall. Merton housed parts of the Department of Transport, Queen's had the Ministry of Home Security and Balliol, characteristically for a college which regarded itself as *primus inter pares*, was host to a good part of the most prestigious of all departments, namely the Foreign Office. Word was that the section in question was intelligence. A further rumour insisted that one unnamed college was being kept empty, ready to house the royal family should the King flee London.

James had watched as this gradual transformation of the university had happened — Brasenose College becoming a hospital, the Ashmolean Museum opening its doors to the Slade School of Art — and wondered when the call would come for him. He had a first-class mind, at least that was what it said on his degree certificate, and he had military experience — experience that had not come cheap. He had even picked up a grounding in intelligence, before . . . well, before. When James heard that Oriel was taking in the War Office Intelligence Corps, he had stood by, waiting for the call. But it never came.

Instead he was supposed to spend the war in the Department of Experimental Psychology, reading Viennese scholars and drafting learned monographs. A mere five-year-old department in a university that measured its life in centuries, it lacked all status. Located far up the Banbury Road in a converted house, it would have had to be sited in Slough to be any more peripheral. All that had been true before the outbreak of war. Afterwards, its irrelevance increased tenfold.

It was obvious to James that his work there was pointless. Once the requisitioning of college buildings and senior faculty was underway, he had put himself forward, either by means of a discreet chat with colleagues or twice writing formal letters of application. He had heard nothing back. He told himself it was the chaos of war. So he had gone to see Bernard Grey, who knew everyone in Whitehall, and asked him to put in a word. He assumed it would be a formality. But Grey had eventually had to apologize over sherry in the Master's Lodgings. "I'm afraid, Dr Zennor, it seems this is one war you're going to have to sit out."

And now here was Hook in his grey flannels, smiling smugly even under his cringing apologies and clumsy, myopic attempts to help James to his feet.

"Are you sure you're all right? I feel awful. I thought you could see me, but you were haring along at such a speed, I —"

"You should have been looking, you damn fool."

"That's just it you see, Zennor. I have the most appalling eyes. Hence these binoculars." He gestured at his spectacles which, Zennor guessed, would have enabled a normal man to gaze at the surface of the moon.

James pulled himself up to full height, so that he was now looking down at Hook with the advantage of at least a foot. Maybe it was the imploring, not to say intimidated, look on the poor man's face; or the recollection that Hook was a staunch anti-fascist — as intolerant as James himself of the appeasers who had had quite a presence in Oxford not so long ago — but James felt a dose of sympathy for Hook, standing there in his bottle glasses. And with the sympathy came shame for his rudeness, and the attendant need to make amends.

"Apology accepted." He extended his hand, which Hook took gratefully. "So what you working on then, Hook?"

"Well, strictly speaking, I shouldn't say."

"Good man. 'Careless talk' and all that. I'd better be —"

"Put it this way, though. All this focus on fish and potatoes complements my research very well." He looked expectantly at James but, getting no response, went on. "Nutrition."

"Glad to hear it," James said, lifting up his bike.

"You see, consumption patterns map very precisely onto income and education levels. I'd intuited that before, but now — thanks to the ministry — I have very precise data. They show that in those social categories we would define as weak, potato consumption outstrips fish by a ratio of up to three to one. Among those we might classify as defective, the ratio rises to five to one. In superior groups, the data —"

"You're saying the poor eat more chips?"

"Well, that's obviously a great simplification. I'd prefer to put —"

"Yes, of course. Well, I really do have to —"

"Oh. But I hadn't explained the link between oily fish in the diet and mental performance. And the benefits of school milk on national strength indices for teeth and bones!"

"Another time, Magnus." James got back on his bicycle, relieved to see that the rear wheel was bent but still functional. He had pedalled a couple of yards when he stopped and looked back over his shoulder. "I don't suppose you've seen Florence recently, have you?"

Hook looked down at his feet, his face flushing. James had seen this reaction before: Florence only had to walk into a room to reduce men to stammering wrecks. He had not appreciated that the mere mention of her name could have the same effect. The realization of it brought that deadweight of melancholy back onto his chest.

"The last time I saw her was on Tuesday. I was on my way into college and she was coming out with her friend, what's her name?"

"Rosemary?" James had only met her a couple of times, but he had found her irritating. And she clung to Florence like a growth.

"That's right. Rosemary." Hook squinted at James once more. "I say, Zennor: is that a rowing shirt under your jacket?"

The last leg of the ride down Parks Road took no time at all, but as he leaned his bike against the low wall outside Wadham College, James had a dread thought. Opening hours at the libraries were shorter now, the New Bodleian included. And it was nearly six o'clock.

He dashed across, heading into a building that still stood out for its novelty. Where almost every other structure in the town was covered in grime, stained with the soot generated by coal fires in every room, the brick of the New Bod was still a pristine beige. Not only was it clean but it was made of straight lines, free of the gargoyles, gnarled brickwork and battlements that made university Oxford resemble a walled city from the Middle Ages. That gloom had only deepened thanks to the strictures of the blackout, demanding that every college cover its windows in blinds or curtains or, when supplies of those had run out, brown paper or even black paint. At first, pride ensured that the curtains were drawn back or the paper removed each morning. But staff were short and so was patience, and so, with the war now in its eleventh month, many of Oxford's medieval or Tudor windows remained cloaked in darkness all day long.

And to think it had only opened a year ago: James and Florence had gone together, invited as the Greys' guests. The speeches had looked forward to a bright future, full of dreams for the scholars of the next generation. Even at the time, James remembered, those seemed to owe more to hope than expectation. Only the hopelessly deluded, or those fanatical for appeasement, believed war could be avoided. For some, like James, the war had begun long ago.

Sure enough, the New Bodleian was closing its doors. "Have to wait till tomorrow now, sir," said the commissionaire, producing a key from his belt in the manner of a gaoler.

"Of course," James replied. "I just need to retrieve some notes I'd left in one of the reading rooms."

"Opening hours are nine am till —"

"Yes, yes, I know the opening hours. But —" He leaned in, his voice dropping to a whisper. "This is for the, er, war effort. If you get my meaning."

The doorman pulled back as if to assess James's honesty from a distance. All he had to do was feign confidence. That, his instructor back in Spain had told him, was the key. So he held the commissionaire's gaze, convinced in his own mind that he was engaged in intelligence duties at Balliol or Oriel, until the man eventually stepped out of his way, gesturing him towards the stairs.

He noticed that the landings were full of what he guessed were paintings wrapped in brown paper and string, stacked together against the wall: those must be the artworks he had heard about, brought here for safekeeping. All the colleges were doing it, emptying out their collections, even removing stained glass windows and statuary, using the newly-built Bodleian building as their refuge. And not just the colleges. The House of Lords library had sent some of the nation's most precious documents here, packed into four tins — among them the death warrant of Charles I. Quite why they thought such treasures would be safer here than anywhere else in Oxford, James was not sure: perhaps they simply put their faith in the modern.

On the first floor, he could see a last remaining librarian, a woman around his age. She had a wireless set on her desk and it was switched on, a sign not only that she was off-duty and packing up for the day but also of how different life had become: you would never have seen a wireless in a library before, but everyone was glued to the device these days, awaiting word of the war. As he approached the desk, he heard the BBC announcer conclude that afternoon's play, *Adolf in Blunderland*. Some satirical effort aimed at lifting the nation's spirits, James guessed.

The woman turned around. She looked nothing like Florence but something in the brightness of her eyes reminded James of his wife and, for a split-second, it seemed to suck the wind out of him. In that instant he was somewhere else entirely, in a pokey little café not far from here — The Racket — where, thanks to

76

rationing, he and his wife had had to make do with a supper of baked beans on toast. They had been arguing, he had gone too far and she had calmly got up and walked out, leaving him to face the embarrassed stares of the staff and the other diners. He had run out after her, searching street after street, eventually finding her just a few hundred yards away from their home. They had patched it up, he couldn't remember how. But for nearly an hour he had feared that he had lost her. And something in this woman's face brought back that fear now, made him realize he had been fending it off all day.

"I'm sorry, sir, the library is now closed for the day. We will be open again tomorrow morning."

James stared back at her, suddenly unsure what to say, where even to begin.

"Sir?"

She had dipped the volume on the wireless, but he could hear the start of the six o'clock bulletin: something about Vichy France formally breaking off diplomatic relations with Britain. Unplanned, he began to speak. "I'm afraid something serious has happened. My wife has gone missing. One of the last places she was seen was here. I'd like to know what she was here for. It may enable us to find her."

The woman blinked a few times, then glanced over James's shoulder, as if checking to see if anyone else was around. "The rules are quite strict on —"

James looked directly into her eyes. "I quite understand that. And that's how it should be. But this is quite an exceptional situation." She said nothing, which he took as a good sign. "I'm desperately worried for her, you see."

"I'd like to help, but the request forms are not kept here. I'd have to —" She looked away again, towards a door just behind her. He couldn't tell if she was worried that someone might come — or hoping that they would. She was a woman alone in a large, empty building with a man who had just described himself as desperate.

"Would you? I really would be extremely grateful."

Speaking hurriedly, conscious that she was breaking the rules, she handed him a yellow slip and asked him to write on it the name of the lender concerned. "And the date please, Mr . . ."

"Zennor. Dr James Zennor."

She took the piece of paper, turned and went through the door behind her. James looked upward then around, taking in the vast room. He had barely visited here since the opening: he preferred to do his reading in the Radcliffe Camera, where he came across fewer of his colleagues. But Florence had embraced it right away. "Just think: I will be one of the very first scholars to have worked in a building that will probably stand for a thousand years." She paused, then gave him that smile he could not resist. "I like being first."

He began to pace, looking at the rows of desks, new and barely scratched — lacking the dents, cracks, blemishes and the gluey, human resin accreted through centuries that coated the wood at the "Radder". He looked at the clock. The librarian had been gone more than five minutes, closer to ten. He wondered what could possibly be keeping her.

Where on earth would Florence have gone? Mrs Grey was right: the obvious answer was her parents' house, but he had ruled that out. He could feel a swell of anger rising inside him. He needed to see what the hell Florence had been looking at here. It could be her regular studies, Darwin and the like, but it could be something else, something more urgent. What was it Grey had said? *Something she had to check, something she had to find out, before she could leave*.

So what the hell was it? What had Florence had to find out? And where was that damned librarian?

He marched at full speed past the administrative desk, breaking through the invisible barrier that separated clerks from readers, and through the door the librarian had taken nearly quarter of an hour earlier.

Behind it, he found himself on a landing for a service stairwell. Dimly lit by a single sickly bulb, it was painted a functional grey, the floors covered in a thin linoleum. Instinctively he headed downstairs.

Two flights down he came to a pair of double doors. He pushed them open to see what struck him at first as a long corridor. He called out. "Hello?"

The echo on his voice surprised him. This was no corridor. He stepped into the almost-dark, calling out again. No answer.

He walked further, slowly becoming conscious that the path he was taking was narrow. He put out his hand, expecting the touch of cold concrete. Instead he felt rough metal, the texture of a bicycle chain. Slowly he began to make out the shape of a conveyor belt.

He had read about this innovation. He was inside the tunnel, the one that connected the New Bodleian to the Old, stretching under Broad Street. It had been lauded as a feat of engineering and great British ingenuity. Instead of librarians scurrying back and forth between the two buildings, a mechanical conveyor would do the work for them, dumbly transporting whatever had been requested, whether it were *Principia Mathematica* or *Das Kapital*.

James squinted upward to see a stretch of pipework attached to the ceiling. That must be the pneumatic tube system introduced with equal fanfare last year: put the request slip in the capsule and off it whizzed, powered by nothing more than compressed air. Aeroplanes, the wireless, the cinema — the world was changing so fast. It was already unrecognizable from the Victorian age his parents still inhabited.

"Miss? Are you there?" Where had the librarian gone and why was she not answering?

There was a sharp turn right; he wondered how far he had gone. Could he already be under Radcliffe Square? He didn't think he had walked that far, but perhaps the absence of light had confused his senses. He suddenly became aware that he was cold; he shivered, feeling the film of sweat that still coated him.

What was that? Was that a flicker of light far ahead? There had been some kind of change, perhaps a torch coming on and off. He quickened his pace.

He broke into a jog. "Miss, is that you?"

There was a delay and then an answer, one that made his blood freeze.

The answer was "No." And it was spoken by a man.

CHAPTER
SIX

"Who's there?" He could hear the alarm in his own voice.

"Is that Dr Zennor?"

An accent. What was it? Dutch? German? He couldn't even see where the voice was coming from. What exactly had he walked into here? "Where has the librarian gone?"

"I am the librarian."

As that moment, James was dazzled by a bright-yellow beam aimed directly in his face. He turned away, lifting his hand to his eyes.

"My apologies, sir. For the light, also I am sorry."

The torch was now angled away from his face, but still James remained blinded. He blinked and blinked again to regain his vision. "Who the hell are you?"

"Please." *Pliz.* "Do not swear at me."

James could feel his rage building again. In a low voice, the calmness of a man repressing fury, he repeated, "Who are you?"

"I am Epstein. I am now the night librarian here."

So that would explain the accent: an émigré German. "And what happened to the woman?"

"I saw her down here after six of clock and told her to go home already. Such long days they work, these girls. Working for seven days she has been, without a break. On a trot."

"On the trot."

"Yes. On *the* trot. That is what I mean."

"But she was helping me. I had a request."

"Yes, yes. I know this. I am helping you myself. I was trying to find the books."

"The books Mrs Zennor was borrowing?"

"That's right. But why you come down in the tunnel? This is prohibited, yes?"

James exhaled. His heart was pounding, at a pace that refused to slow. The light shining in his face had rattled him. He was still dazed, but it was not just the light. Something else.

The man spoke again. "Please. I have them now. You are to follow me."

They walked in silence, James embarrassed by his pursuit of this man underground. And also fearful — that he would, by saying the wrong thing, induce a change of heart in the émigré librarian, that he would come across as too sweatily anxious. So he curbed his impatience to see the books in the man's hands and waited till they emerged into the relative light of the stairwell, moving from there back inside the reading room.

"We have to save the power, you see. At night. That is why there is no lights down there. Only this." Epstein waved his torch. "And no conveyor of course. So this I do by hand. It takes a long time, for which I apologies."

"No need to apologize," James replied.

"Apolog*ize*, yes, of course. Sorry for my English. I can read it perfectly, but I never had to speak it before so much."

"No. It's excellent." James momentarily considered speaking to him in German, then imagined the delay that would entail — explaining how he knew the language, his reading of the great Viennese analysts and all the rest of it.

"In Heidelberg, I did not need so much English. But now I am here."

"I see." James was trying to identify the three books the German had placed on the desk, their spines facing — maddeningly — away from him.

"I did not choose to leave, Dr Zennor. You see, I am of a type considered, how to say, *undesirable* by the new governors of my country. I came here two years ago."

"You are a Jew?"

"Yes, sir."

"Well, welcome to England. And thanks for finding these books so quickly." James nodded towards them, hoping he would get the hint. "You're obviously a good librarian."

"Thank you. I am learning. In Heidelberg, I was not librarian."

"No?" James glanced again at the books, but the man was still laboriously engaged in signing them out, taking what seemed an age over each word.

"No." Epstein smiled a wistful smile. "My last job at the university was as a cleaner. I had to mop the floors."

"Oh."

"Before that, I was Professor of Greek and Chairman of the Department of Classical Studies."

"I see." James looked into the old eyes, seeing a terrible sadness and longing. He had read about the ghastly things the Nazis were doing to the Jews; he knew of the laws banning them from the professions, burning down their synagogues and God knows what else. But it was different to meet one in person, to see the human consequences of such barbarism standing in front of you.

The librarian must have grown used to this reaction. "Oh, do not feel sorry for me, Dr Zennor. I am very grateful. For my job and for this country. The only country in the world fighting this evil."

James glanced once more at the pile on the desk between them.

The professor pulled himself upright. "I am forgetting myself. Please."

James picked up the books and shifted over to one of the desks. He turned the first one over. To his surprise, it was a bound volume of journals: *The Proceedings of the British Psychological Society for 1920–1*. He flicked through it, trying to work out what might possibly have drawn the interest of his wife. This was not her subject after all.

As he turned the pages, he caught a slip of white paper, the tiniest bookmark that had been left inside.

Instinctively, he held it close to his face, hoping that he might catch a scent of her. But it carried no trace. Instead it marked an article entitled: "A survey of British veterans of the Great War".

Odd. Florence had no particular interest in the last war. If she was not a psychologist, she was certainly not a historian.

He turned to the next book, written by an American scholar affiliated with Harvard Medical School: *Studies in Pediatric Trauma*. He flicked through the pages again, looking for one of those tiny white slips. He found it and began reading:

" . . . *sustained exposure of a non-traumatized child to a traumatized adult can result in* secondary or passive trauma. *Symptoms range from selective dumbness, melancholia, extreme shyness, impaired development, bedwetting . . .*"

Instantly, he thought of Harry: how he had been slower than the other children to control himself at night, how he had still not mastered it. Florence had been anxious, refusing to be placated by James's insistence that their son would "soon get the hang of it". Until now James had thought nothing more of it.

He picked up the third book. *A Compendium of Advice for Mothers*. So very unlike Florence, who usually cursed such things. He didn't need to thumb through the pages. The book opened automatically, the spine already cracked. The chapter heading: *Preparing a child for a long journey or separation*.

He read the title again and then once more, the dread rising in him. Any hope he had harboured that this might be a stunt, an attempt by Florence to make a point, was fading fast. There it was in black and white. What his wife had planned for was a long journey. Or, worse, a separation.

He went back to the first volume, to the article on former combatants in the last war, reading a paragraph at random:

" . . . *subjects in the trial revealed a set of behaviors which recurred. Among them were acute insomnia, including difficulty both falling and staying asleep; excess anger and temper; poor concentration. Others reported a heightened state of awareness, as if in constant expectation of danger."*

He skimmed a few paragraphs ahead:

" . . . *several of those interviewed displayed an extreme reluctance to speak of their wartime experiences, flinching from even indirect reminders. Perhaps paradoxically, many of these same people complained of unwanted memories of the event, 'flashbacks', as it were. The most common complaint, experienced by some sixty-eight per cent of those surveyed, was of distressing dreams, often violent . . ."*

James slammed the book shut, his heart hammering. He was beginning to feel light-headed. He was hungry. He had barely eaten since last night and he had exerted himself strenuously on the river early this morning. The alcohol would not have helped either. The room was beginning to spin.

He stood up and saw Epstein at the desk, the old man's bespectacled face appearing to shrink and swell, waxing and waning like the moon. He had to get out, into the fresh air. He mumbled an apology, left the books where they were and stumbled towards the exit.

Outside, he gulped down large draughts of oxygen, clutching the handrail by the entrance. Across the street, the Kings Arms was filling up now with the after-work crowd: not students but academics-turned-civil servants.

He needed to think but his head was throbbing. What had he been expecting? He had assumed something more direct: an atlas, perhaps a road map, maybe a train timetable. But this, what he had just seen . . . he felt nauseous.

Where the hell was his wife? Where had she gone? It unnerved him to imagine that she was living and breathing somewhere — perhaps arriving at a distant railway station or walking down a street or sipping a cup of tea — that she existed somewhere now, at this very moment, and he had no idea where. He told himself he could survive being apart from her, so long as he knew where she was. But he knew that was not true. Ever since those nights and days in Madrid, holding each other as the bombs fell, he felt that nature itself demanded they be together. As a scientist, he was not meant to believe in fate or destiny, so he could not say what he truly felt. Nor did his education have much tolerance for a word like "souls", but that too was what he felt: that their souls had been joined.

Harry's arrival had only confirmed it. He loved his son with an intensity that had surprised him. He pictured him now, rarely saying a word to anyone, clinging to his little polar bear. The thought of life apart from his son struck sudden terror into his heart.

The words appeared before him, floating in front of his eyes: *a long journey or separation*. A black thought raced through his mind, like a virus carried on his bloodstream. Could it be, was it possible . . .

Suddenly and without any warning even to himself, as if his mouth, chest and lungs had a will of their own, he heard himself screaming at the top of his voice. "WHERE ARE YOU?"

The sound of it shocked him. A group of young men drinking on the pavement outside the Kings Arms looked towards him, their faces flushed, their necks taut with aggression. James wondered if these were the veterans of the Dunkirk retreat — or *evacuation*, as the BBC delicately phrased it — brought here for treatment at the Radcliffe Infirmary. Florence had mentioned them only yesterday, reporting the scandalized reaction of some superannuated don or other who had been outraged by the soldiers' constant state of drunkenness. James had shrugged, refusing to condemn servicemen for seeking comfort wherever they could find it.

Ignoring them, he crossed the road, retrieved his bike from outside Wadham and cycled away.

He pedalled maniacally, trying to keep his thoughts at bay. And yet they refused to be halted. He could almost feel them in his head, speeding around his cerebral cortex; as soon as he had blocked off one neural pathway, they re-routed and hurtled down another, shouting at him inside his head, forming into words.

He smothered them with another idea. It was Thursday, nearly seven o'clock in the evening and it was summer. Ordinarily, this was when Florence would be out with her friend Rosemary for the weekly walk of their rambling club. As far as James could tell, most were communists, all but ideological in their zeal for strenuous exercise in the British countryside.

The group would probably be walking back by now and, if they were sticking with their usual routine, he knew just where to find them.

And so, for the second time that day — though it felt like another era — he was back by the river, cycling along the towpath towards Iffley Lock. And, sure enough, there they were: Rosemary at the front, in sensible shoes, her sensible brown hair in a sensible bob, carrying one handle of a picnic hamper, the other taken by a strapping young female undergraduate. James let his bike slow, then swung one leg off it, so that he was perching on just one pedal, before hopping off, trying to look calm and composed. No red mists now, he told himself.

"Hello there," he called out, giving a wave.

"Is that you, James?" she asked, peering through spectacles which, while no match for Magnus Hook's, consisted of two substantial slabs of glass.

"Yes, yes it is. I was just —"

"Don't worry, I can guess." She nodded at the young woman on the other side of the picnic basket who immediately and deferentially yielded her handle to James, falling back to join the chattering group of women a few paces behind. How Florence fitted into this group, James could not imagine, except that it was a pretty safe bet that several would have had a strong "pash" for her. Perhaps Rosemary too. He took the basket in one hand, wheeling his bike in the other, and waited for her to speak first.

"So, you're looking for Florence?"

"I am, as it happens. I don't suppose you know where she —"

She cut him off, her gaze fixed straight ahead: "How long has she been gone?"

"Since," he made a gesture of looking at his watch, "this morning, as a matter of fact." He was carrying the hamper in his left arm, which was already buckling under the strain. But he was reluctant to say anything, lest he distract Rosemary whose brow was fixed in concentration. But it was she who stopped.

"Audrey!" she shouted, turning to address one of the walkers behind. "Could you and Violet take the hamper? There's a love."

Two of the girls rushed forward to do as they had been told. Rosemary supervised the handover, then waited while the rest of the group overtook them, ensuring that she and James were well out of earshot. "Gone since this morning, you say," she said at last.

"Yes."

"And you thought she might be with us."

"Well, it's Thursday evening. She never misses her weekly walk, rain or shine."

"Ramble, Dr Zennor. We call it a *ramble*. And, you're right, Florence is a stalwart. She hated missing the last couple of weeks."

"Missing them? She didn't miss them."

"Well, she wasn't here."

"I think you must have that confused. I remember it distinctly, Florence left at five o'clock, walking boots on. Same as always. I can picture her coming home, telling me about it."

"Well, I run this rambling club, Dr Zennor, and I've never missed a week. Not one. And I can tell you that Florence was absent last Thursday, as she was the week before. She's not the kind of woman whose presence goes unnoticed."

James was baffled. "Did she give any explanation?"

"Only that something had come up. Something important. She was very apologetic."

James was working through the different logical possibilities, trying to rank them in order of probability: that Rosemary was lying; that Florence had joined some other group and lied to her friend in order to spare her feelings; that on both Thursdays Florence had indeed been somewhere else, somewhere important, and had lied to him about it.

Rosemary spoke again. "This is very awkward, Dr Zennor. When speaking about the affairs of others, one never knows how much one is meant to know. Or how much the other parties themselves know."

"Affairs? What do you mean, 'affairs'?"

"Sorry. That was a very poor choice of word. Sorry about that. When one is speaking about the lives of others, let's put it that way, one is never quite sure where the boundaries lie."

"Look, Miss —" he ran dry, immediately regretting the attempt at a name.

"Hyde, it's Rosemary Hyde. And that rather makes my point, Dr Zennor. I have been your wife's friend for at least ten years, since we were at school together. I suspect I am her closest confidante. And yet you are not entirely sure of my name."

"That's not true," he said, without much conviction. "It's just that I always thought your friendship was . . . well, I just left you two to get on with it." He was still preoccupied by the notion of his wife pretending to have gone out walking the last two Thursdays, putting her boots on, arranging for Mrs Brunson to look after Harry. Why would she have done that? Where would she have gone?

"It's not a criticism," Rosemary was saying. "Rather it might illustrate your problem."

He could feel the red mist descending. "Yes? And what exactly is my 'problem', Miss Hyde? Because as far as I can see my only 'problem' is that my wife and child are missing. I have been sent on a wild goose chase to the Bodleian library that proved no use at all and now you want to play games with me — suggesting that my wife has been lying about her recent movements — rather than just spitting out where the hell she is. That's all I want to know, Miss Hyde. Where *is* she?"

It came out as more of a plea than he had intended, his voice desperate and imploring. That much was apparent from the change in Rosemary's expression.

Her features had softened into a look unnervingly close to pity.

"I don't know where Florence is," she said quietly. "That is the truth." She resumed walking. "But I am not surprised she's gone. I expected it."

"You expected it?"

"Didn't you? If you're honest. Given everything that's been going on?"

"I don't follow."

"You know what I mean."

"I really don't, Miss Hyde. And I'm getting pretty damned irritated with people speaking to me about events I know nothing about."

"These are not 'events', Dr Zennor. This is about day-to-day life. At home. You and Florence and Harry."

"Our day-to-day life is fine, thank you very much. We're a very good family. I love my wife and I love my son." His eyes widened in sudden understanding. "Oh, so that's why you spoke about 'affairs'. Well, let me tell you, I have always been faithful to Florence, from the very first moment —"

"Nothing like that," she said, looking at her feet. She lifted her eyes and met his gaze directly. "Tell me, how well do you sleep?"

"I don't see this is any business of —"

"It's no business of mine at all. But your wife needed someone to talk to and that turned out to be me. So: how well do you sleep?"

"And if I answer you, is that going to help me find my wife?"

"It might."

"I go to bed late and I get up early, and I sometimes wake in the night. There, I've told you. Now, what can you tell me?"

"Florence told me that you often wake up in the dead of night, shouting and screaming."

"I know the incident you're referring to. It was —"

"Incident? Florence said it happens all the time. You're in a sweat, sitting bolt upright, bellowing out —"

"I really don't see . . ."

Rosemary ignored the interruption. "Night after night. And that would set Harry off. He'd be crying so hard, he couldn't be settled. And if he did fall asleep, he'd only wet the bed an hour later. Then there was the time she found you sleepwalking."

"I don't remember any —"

"She found you in the kitchen, holding a knife. She said you just stood there, your eyes staring, frozen still with a knife in your hand. She was scared half to death."

"You're making this up!" he roared suddenly.

Rosemary turned and faced him, her teeth clenched tight. "And this is what she said was making life utterly impossible. Your constant pretence that nothing had happened. And your aggression. 'Is he lying, Rosemary — or does he just not remember?' That's what she would say to me. And she didn't know what was worse: the thought that you would deny what she had seen with her own eyes or that you were so ill you couldn't remember your own actions."

"*Ill?* I'm not ill."

"I know about this too. Your refusal to see a doctor. She's been begging you to see —"

"Oh, for heaven's —" He struggled to get to the end of the sentence; the bright light in his head was becoming unbearable . . . but he couldn't stop her. Not if she knew something he needed to know. He tried to speak calmly. "I did see someone. About the insomnia."

"Yes, but you didn't tell him the truth, did you? You just said you had 'the odd bad night'. You said —"

"How the hell do you know all this?"

"Because your wife had no one else to turn to. She didn't dare speak to her parents. She knew how much you resented them for —"

"Resented them?"

"— for the help they had given you." His puzzled expression prompted her to be more explicit. "Resented the *money* they had given you."

"Look," he said, his voice firm and steady. "All I want is to know what information you have. You need to tell me that. Now."

She paused, looking out over the river unwinding ahead, gazing at the top of Christ Church Cathedral in the middle distance. "All right," she began. "The important thing is Harry. Florence wanted to protect him."

"From what?"

"From you, of course. *Initially.*"

He was about to object, but the throbbing in his head was getting too insistent. It was easier to be quiet, to walk and to listen.

"She said she had almost got used to you being angry all the time. After the —" she glanced at his shoulder. "After the, um, accident. But once Harry was born, it began to worry her. The truth is, she was frightened."

"Of me," he said quietly.

"Yes, James. Of you. Of what you might do. She was worried that you might hurt Harry."

At this, his heart seemed to cave in, a physical sensation, felt in the muscle and blood. He could say nothing.

"You once left him by a boiling kettle. Do you remember that, James?"

He shook his head, unsure.

"Well, you did. You'd left the boy on his own, in the kitchen. You'd put the kettle —"

"That's enough," he said softly.

"That's what I said," Rosemary said, sardonically. "I told her it was enough. That she should leave you. Several times. Especially after you hit her."

"After I did what?"

"Oh, don't pretend you don't remember that. You'd had an almighty row. And you slapped her, clean across the face. Her cheek was stinging. I had to soothe it with cool flannels all evening."

"That's a damned lie!"

"Don't shout at *me*. All I am —"

"It's a damned lie and you know it." He felt giddy, as if he were about to topple over. It could not be true. It could not. Could it?

Everything else she had said had sounded some distant bell in his head, a distant but undeniable ring of truth. But not this. Yes, he had a temper, that was a fact. But the target of his rages was always himself. It was his own wrist that had been slashed when he punched his fist clean through the French windows onto the garden, his own head that had been bruised when he had rammed it into a bookcase in an eruption of fury. But he had never harmed his wife. No real man would ever do such a thing. His voice quieter now, he said once again, "It's a lie."

"So you keep saying. But how can you be sure? Your memory seems a touch unreliable in my book."

"And you say she came to you?"

"Straight away." The pride with which this was declared sent the rage surging through him once more, rising like mercury in a thermometer.

"But she'd never do it. Leave you, I mean. Absurdly loyal, Florence. I hope you appreciate that."

"But she's left me now."

"For Harry's sake. She feared for his safety with you in the house. That was at first. Florence no longer sees you as the biggest threat to her son. Not directly anyway."

James spoke quietly, more to himself than to her: "It's the war."

"Yes. She's been getting gradually more terrified since the day the war started. The sirens, the air-raid shelters, the gasmasks, that thing you've just built in the garden —"

"The Anderson shelter."

"All of it scares her. She feels like it's getting closer."

"They bombed Cardiff last week."

"Exactly. She was convinced Oxford would be next."

A dozen times Florence had expounded her belief that Oxford was a natural target, not only because of the car plant at Cowley now converted into a munitions factory but also because of the university. "London is the nerve centre, but Oxford is the brain," she had said.

Rosemary was still talking. "I explained to her the statistical probabilities. As you know, mathematics is my subject: my specialism is statistics. Actually, you almost certainly don't know: typical man, you probably think I'm a secretary. Anyway, I explained the probabilities, but it was no use. She kept torturing herself with the thought. 'What if, Rosemary? What if?' "

The haze was beginning to clear in James's mind. It was so obvious he couldn't fathom how he had been unable to see it, why he had not thought of it till now. Still, if even half of what this woman was telling him were true, there was so much he was not seeing, so much he was forgetting, so much he had — what was the phrase in that book Florence had requested at the library? — *blacked out*.

Rosemary had not stopped: "It made no sense, of course. If I told her once I told her a hundred times, Oxford is not an evacuation area. Children are being sent *to* Oxford, aren't they? We were entertaining some of them just yesterday, lively little things from London. A few of the girls from Somerville went out to cheer them up . . ."

But James was not listening. He was remembering the conversation — the row — he and Florence had had . . . when was it? A month ago? They had just come home from an evening at the Playhouse, watching a top-drawer play: the West End theatre, like so much else of London, had sought sanctuary in Oxford.

"I won't hear of it," he had said.

"What do you mean, *you* won't hear of it. You do not have sole authority over our child. We are *both* Harry's parents."

He had tried to get out of the kitchen, walking past her as if to signal the discussion was over. But Florence had stuck her arm out across the doorway, barring his way. "You need to listen to me," she had said in a low voice, her teeth gritted. "I will do whatever it takes to protect him."

"It's a surrender, Florence. You're asking me to surrender to the fascists."

"'Surrender'? We're not talking about a bridge or a railway line, James. This is not some strategically important piece of land. This is a *child*."

"If people like us run away, Hitler will have won, won't he?"

"Don't ask a two-year-old boy to do your fighting for you, James."

"What did you say?"

"You heard what I said. You want us to be heroes because you can't be. And it's not fair."

He had stepped back from her, not wanting to look her in the face. She had extended her hand, but he had

100

brushed her away. "Don't touch me," he had said, spitting out the words.

She tried again, her voice gentler. "When are you going to understand that you already did your bit? You made your sacrifice, James. And you were one of the first to do it. You took your stand against fascism when everyone else here was fast asleep. You don't need to do any more."

He had looked up at her, his face red with anger. "That's easy for you to say. You're a woman: no one expects you to fight. But I should be there, killing as many of those bastards as I can. I'm not though, am I?" She had said nothing, prompting him to repeat his question, this time bellowing it: "Am I?" Once she had sighed and nodded, he went on. "This is my frontline — here, this house. And I'll be damned if anyone will make me retreat from my own bloody home."

He stared ahead now, all but forgetting that Rosemary was there, and still talking. He now knew why his wife had left — and, much more important, he had an inkling of where she had gone.

CHAPTER
SEVEN

James cycled home, the energy coursing through his veins and into his legs. He was full of determination, a plan forming in his mind. Back at the house, he rushed into his study to find his atlas of the British Isles.

Rosemary had forced him to remember what he had forgotten, that Florence had indeed been in a state of high anxiety about the war and what she felt was its creeping proximity to their own lives. It was natural that Florence would want to get out into the countryside, with her parents' estate in Norfolk the obvious destination. But she was not there.

Now that it had proved a dead end, he could see it was always going to be an incomplete explanation. For one thing, it could not account for the mystery of the last two Thursday evenings — the elaborate lengths his wife had taken to deceive him, apparently withholding the truth even from her best friend. No, she must have made an alternative arrangement, joining the rest of the hundreds of thousands of British people who had left their homes in cities for rural safety. It made no sense to him: Oxford was hardly an urban metropolis; a quick cycle ride and you were in the countryside. But Florence, unlike almost every other mother in England, had seen the aftermath of a bombing with her own eyes. He remembered his wife crouching by that little girl in Madrid, still and lifeless. Florence had been so calm; she had not sobbed or become hysterical. But clearly it had left its mark.

He found the page for Oxfordshire. This was what he would do. He would get on his bicycle and keep going until he had found them, cycling to every village if he had to. Start at Botley, then Wytham, then Wolvercote, Old Marston, Marston — ringing the city in concentric circles until he had covered the whole county. And after that the next county and the next and the next.

He looked out of the window. The summer light had at last faded. There was no chance of going now, whatever fantasy he had spun as he had raced back here from the river. It would mean cycling in the dark, no lights allowed in the blackout. He was confident he could navigate sufficiently well, even without road signs, but what he would do once he arrived in, say, Botley? He could hardly start walking the country lanes, calling out their names — though he imagined himself now doing exactly that, hearing the echo of it in his head: "Florence! Harry!" He would have to wait till morning.

He reached for the whisky bottle beside the chair. Despite the spillage caused by Virginia Grey's arrival, there was still some left. He raised it to his lips and, without opening his eyes, knocked it back.

As the liquid ran down his throat and he felt the alcohol travel through his veins, he thought of what the insufferable Rosemary had told him. That he had been sleepwalking, shouting in the night, waking Florence and Harry with his screaming. He wanted to deny it, but it sounded true. And the boiling kettle? If he forced himself, he could picture it: Harry on his high-chair, the steam rising inches from his face. How he, in a fit of absent-mindedness, had put the kettle down on the child's table . . . But slapping Florence? Hitting his own wife? He had no memory of that whatsoever.

He saw her as she had been in Madrid, during their first weeks together as husband and wife: her floodlit smile, her body bursting with energy, vitality, sex. And then he imagined her in the Bodleian, her brow furrowed, poring over dry journal articles, detailing the symptoms of a kind of delayed shellshock in veterans of the Great War. Was that what she believed was wrong with him? Was she right?

He saw again the page as he had read it. Whatever else had gone wrong with him, his memory for printed words had retained its near-photographic ability. He could read the lines as if they were still there, recalling their precise position on the page: acute insomnia, including difficulty both falling and staying asleep; excess anger and temper; poor concentration. Others reported a heightened state of awareness, as if in constant expectation of danger.

With his mind clarified by the whisky and the serial shocks of this day, he could recognize himself in that list.

And then he thought of the second book in that pile the old Jewish librarian had handed him: *Studies in Pediatric Trauma*. That was what she feared most, he

104

could see. She worried that he was passing on some of his own troubles to his son. Symptoms range from selective dumbness, melancholia, extreme shyness, impaired development, bedwetting . . .

It was true that Harry had not yet mastered staying dry at night, but James had put that down to his age: he did not know when boys were meant to learn that particular trick. But impaired development? Everyone had always joked that, with his parents' combined IQ, Harry would be on course for a double first before his tenth birthday. He had started speaking early and could deliver neatly composed, relatively complex sentences. But in recent months he had become shy. Did that amount to selective dumbness? Surely not. Though, try as he might, James could not recall the last time he had heard his son speak at length.

His headache was returning. He could see the bright lights again, miniature explosions inside his brain. Now he could hear Florence's voice, pleading with him: "James, you're supposed to be the expert in how the mind works. You're so clever about 'the human brain'. But why can't you understand yourself?"

Eyes closed, he attempted to formulate an answer. But the words would not come. Instead, he heard a voice repeating the sentence in the book Florence had been studying. The voice, he realized as it became more distant, belonged to Epstein, the refugee professor. He was lecturing, in that calm, patient German accent, as if he were Sigmund Freud himself: ". . . several of those interviewed displayed an extreme reluctance to speak of their wartime experiences, flinching from even indirect reminders.

Perhaps paradoxically, many of these same people complained of unwanted memories of the event, 'flashbacks', as it were. The most common complaint, experienced by some sixty-eight per cent of those surveyed, was of distressing dreams, often violent . . ."

It is dusk, not yet six o'clock. A cloudless day has ensured a severe drop in temperature, so that now he longs for his overcoat. Or perhaps that tremble he feels is a last rush of nerves. Or, as he likes to think of it, stage fright.

He has done a few of these missions and he is becoming rather adroit, if he says so himself. He is quick on his feet, but quick of eye too: if there is something to see, he will see it. That's what matters most, Jorge is very clear on that. "This is not a job you do with your hands or your legs." He would point. "Your eyes do all the work."

It is the starting rung in the intelligence corps of the republican army, that's how he explains it. James's job is to be a courier of messages, those too secret, sensitive or elaborate to be trusted to radio signals. The enemy is outside Madrid, but also inside: it is known that there is a "fifth column" of Franco sympathizers lurking in the city. That he is a foreigner has its drawbacks: he is more visible, no matter how hard he attempts to dress, walk, smoke like a Spaniard. On the other hand, he has an excuse if a fascist gang pounce. He will say he is a journalist, writing for . . . it doesn't matter who.

This journey has been more elaborate than most, but that has not dimmed his confidence. Besides, he has his pal with him, his "comrade" as Harry Knox would put it. They will be one hundred yards apart at all times, with Harry in front — but the important thing is that James will not be alone. James

106

is the message-bearer, Harry the scout who will spot trouble, then either walk around it or walk away, thereby protecting them both.

But on this evening, it is James who has been unsettled by something he has seen. An older man in a creased grey suit walked past him twenty minutes earlier and walked past him again just now, heading in the opposite direction. There is nothing unusual about his manner or his appearance. But Jorge's words, repeated a dozen times, are too firmly etched on James's mind: "Nothing is a coincidence. If you see the same thing twice, run!"

He thinks of doing that but hesitates, anxious that, if they are being followed, the sight of him sprinting up the street will immediately confirm their pursuers' suspicions. And what if only he, James, has been spotted? A dash to warn Harry will simply serve to expose his friend as an accomplice.

So he chooses to walk instead, to increase his pace only subtly, to make the gear change from steady to brisk. He has closed the gap to just a few yards when it happens. He feels it before he hears it, the rush of air behind his ear as the bullet races over his shoulder and into Harry's back. His partner jerks upward, arcing his back, an oddly balletic movement, slow and graceful. As Harry begins to fall, there is a second shot directly into his head, exploding his face into a thousand pieces of flesh and gristle; the glass of his spectacles, lit red with blood, sprays into the air like sparks from a bonfire. A third shot and a fourth and James darts into a side alley, propelled there by instinct alone.

He stands there, panting heavily, his brain juddering over the image he has just seen: the head blown off, the head blown off, the head blown off. Harry there one moment, gone the next. The rainshower of skin and bone.

He is digesting this when he realizes that his shirt is wet. Some of Harry's blood must have landed on him. But under his jacket is a red patch, covering the left side of his chest. It takes him a while to realize that the stain is spreading. Oh, he thinks. That's my blood. I've been shot.

Harry's looking at him, tut-tutting over James's wound and shaking his head, as if to say, "Who's a silly boy, then?" Until once again, his brain explodes. And again. And again . . .

James woke to his own scream. Immediately his hand reached for his left shoulder and, as always, it was wet. Not with blood, but with sweat. That dream, again.

It was light, which only added to his confusion. He was home, in the armchair, the whisky bottle close by. Was it still the afternoon? Had Florence left that morning? The clock on the mantelpiece said seven. But was it morning or evening? Had he dreamed his visit to the Bodleian, his underground encounter with a strange old German Jew and Rosemary Something by the river, shouting at him?

There was a rattling sound outside, muffled and indistinct. He leapt up, to see a shadow of movement shift across the doorway, visible through the stained glass. His heart leapt. Was that Florence, putting her key in the door? Had she come back to him? But there was no smaller, second shadow, no Harry . . .

He rushed to the door and snatched it open. No one there. He called out. "Hello?" He heard a rustle, but whether that was a person slipping past the trees on this wide, quiet avenue or merely a breeze, he could not tell. He called out once more, stepping forward this time. But no one replied.

The smell of the air, the height of the sun, told him it was a new day. He had slept all night in that chair and they were still gone. It had been twenty-four hours now, twenty-four hours without them. Their absence was not some temporary aberration, a lost afternoon. It was, he felt now, solid and real. The thought of facing another day alone and then another and then another filled him with gloom.

But as he came back inside he caught a glimpse of one of Harry's favourite toys, left abandoned on the living room floor: a wooden Noah's Ark, complete with its own pairs of animals. Perhaps it had been too big to take, perhaps Harry had cried as Florence had prised it from his hands, explaining that there was no room for Noah on their long journey. Whatever had happened, the mere sight of it restored James's determination. He would not be engulfed by despair; he would not give up. No matter what it cost, he would find his wife and child.

He decided to wash, eat and ready himself for the full-scale search. Sleep had given him the clarity to realize that his effort needed to be organized, that it should not begin with the random searching of nearby villages. He girded himself for the task ahead, taking care as he towelled himself dry not to shake his morale by looking too closely at the wreck of his shoulder in the bathroom mirror: collapsed and thinner than the rest of him, as if his chest simply petered out on that

109

side, it was repulsive for him to contemplate. The wound had been treated in a hurry, in the crowded, overworked military hospital in Carabanchel, in the south-west of Madrid, near to where he had fallen. In time the city's doctors would get used to such operations, as sniper fire became a favoured tactic of Franco's Fifth Columnists. But on that night they had stitched him up fast, stretching the skin too tight and with little regard to appearances. The result was that the top half of his chest looked like a wall covered with paper from two separate and clashing rolls.

And all the while, as he foamed up the shaving brush and splashed on the hot water, he could not shake the odd feeling he had had since the moment he awoke, one akin to the sensation of being watched. The only reason for it was that faraway rattling sound the instant he had been pulled from sleep, that fleeting glimpse through the glass of the front door — and yet the feeling lingered, like a shiver.

His plan was to see Bernard Grey in college. He would ask him to deploy all his contacts in the Health Ministry running the national evacuation effort, so that they could rifle through their voluminous card index and discover which generous soul had taken in Florence and Harry Zennor. It could not be that difficult, not for a man like Grey, for whom Whitehall might as well have been just another Oxford college.

James parked his bike and guiltily received the greeting of the aged porter in the lodge, a nod he always translated as, "What the hell are you doing here, a man your age? Why aren't you in the war like everyone else?"

To his surprise, the quad was covered with people, around a hundred and fifty men at least, standing in neat lines. The shock was that Oxford had no more strictly imposed rule than the prohibition on walking on the grass. You could steal another man's essay and pass it off as your own; you could, in the immortal phrase, bugger the Bursar. But you could not, under any circumstances, tread on the trim green of the college lawn. Yet here that hallowed turf had been transformed into a parade ground and there, standing at the head of it, was none other than Grey himself.

He had heard about this but scarcely believed it could be true: that the Oxford South Company of the newly-created Local Defence Volunteers, made up chiefly of Royal Mail employees, had been put under Grey's command. But here they were, row after row of middle-aged postmen taking orders issued not by a bullying sergeant major but by a white-haired philosopher, one whose voice was known to millions through his regular talks on the BBC Home Service. Heaven preserve them all if, come the invasion, these men represented the first line of defence.

Invasion. The word triggered a memory of yesterday's ill-tempered exchange with Rosemary. She had been talking about invasion just before he climbed back on his bicycle and returned home, once he had switched off and stopped listening properly to what she was saying. Something about the countries that had fallen in just the last few weeks — France, Holland and

Belgium in just a single day last month. Saying that Florence was convinced Britain would be next. Mr Churchill was doing a manful job of stiffening the nation's resolve, but that was how most people felt: that there was a very good chance that, before long, there would be German boats landing on England's beaches and German troops walking on England's streets. Was that why she had not gone to her parents' house, because she feared Hitler's men might come across the North Sea and march right into Norfolk? He began to wish he had listened to what the damned Rosemary woman had been saying.

James turned on his heel, avoiding the embarrassment of explaining why he was not among those on parade, and walked back to the porter's lodge, this time going inside.

Another raised eyebrow semi-smile to the man on duty and straight to the pigeon-holes. Much less for him these days, now that term had finished. There was a letter inviting him to a lecture on birth control by Marie Stopes: *Population Science and the Path to Radiant Motherhood*. No, thank you. He wouldn't go within a hundred yards of that woman, not since hearing that she had attended some conference in Berlin a couple of years after Hitler had become Chancellor. Completely unacceptable to lend aid and succour to the Nazis like that. The only exception: if you were going in order to poke a finger in the Germans' eye, as Florence had done. But there were not many like Florence, not many at all.

A circular urging donations of books for prisoners of war via the Red Cross; a notice about new rules aimed at reducing coal consumption in college; a letter asking for revisions on an article he had written on group behaviour for the *Journal of Experimental Psychology* and, finally, at the bottom of the pile, a postcard from Florence.

There was no doubt it was from her. The handwriting was unmistakable; just glimpsing it was enough to make his heart squeeze. The same three words again: *I love you.*

He flipped it over to see the image, a photograph showing the construction of the Sagrada Familia, Gaudi's magnificent, unfinished church: they had visited it together during one of their long, meandering walks through Barcelona, the week they had met.

He turned it over to check the postmark. It had been posted last night. Thank God for the Royal Mail, carrying on as if there were no war on: with a first class stamp, it seemed they could get a letter to anywhere by the next morning. And this had not come from some village in the Oxfordshire countryside. This has been posted from Liverpool.

Liverpool? It made no sense. If she was worried about bombs, the last place to go was Liverpool — an industrial port so strategically indispensable it was surely close to the top of Berlin's target list. She might as well have fled Oxford for London. It made no sense at all.

Then he spotted a detail that he had initially assumed was a mistake. Registering it now revived the

113

shiver he had felt first thing this morning. The address Florence had written on the card was their home in Norham Gardens, not the college. Yet here it was in his pigeon-hole. It had been sent from Liverpool only last night; there would have been no time for the Post Office to have redirected it.

There could only be one explanation. Someone had moved it.

But who? And why?

CHAPTER
EIGHT

He was halfway to the station before he realized he would have to make a detour back home to pick up some essentials, starting with money. Adrenalin pumped through his system. He passed the old stone buildings, with their gothic arches and medieval chapels, in a blur, his brain moving faster even than his body. There could be only one possible reason why Florence had gone to Liverpool: in order to leave it. It was no place to hide from the bombs; on the contrary, she had placed herself more directly in harm's way by going there. Which meant she would be there for the shortest time possible before heading somewhere else. The obvious, closest destination was Dublin. Was Florence thinking it would be safer in neutral Ireland than in occupied Britain? Was this, then, her great fear — not bombs, but life under Nazi occupation?

The postcard had been sent last night. It was conceivable that she and Harry were still there, that with a bit of luck on the trains, he might just make it in time, catching them before they left. He would have a chance to persuade her to stay. The fact that he had chased her all the way to Liverpool would surely demonstrate how much he cared: what, after all, was

115

the purpose of that postcard, except as a summons, urging him to follow her if he truly loved her? Of course she could have simply telephoned and told him where they could meet. But James preferred to see the card like a challenge set for a medieval knight, imagining that Florence had chosen to test him, to make him prove his devotion. He pictured their reunion: they would meet at the docks, Harry would hug him tight and she would instantly realize the folly of separating a boy from his father. Everything would be all right. Just so long as he could catch a train.

At the station, all was chaos and noise. Ever since they had removed the signs from the railways, the staff had to march up and down the platform barking, "Oxford, this is Oxford! Oxford, this is Oxford!" (Was it really likely that German pilots would be able to read station signs from the air, especially in the dark?) The platform was crowded, with piles of baggage everywhere, doubtless belonging to soldiers on the move. Everyone seemed confused, especially by the special troop trains, which looked like the others and ran on the same lines but which were barred to the civilian population.

Eventually James found a clerk who told him that he needed to cross the bridge and wait for the next LMS train to Bletchley, due in twenty-five minutes. From there, the man — elderly, probably brought out of retirement so that the permanent holder of the position could do his bit for the war, a thought which triggered in James the usual spasm of shame — explained that he could catch the main line to Crewe, which should take two-and-a-half hours, and then change for Liverpool

Lime Street. It would be a long, circuitous journey but James could see no alternative. He had considered asking to borrow the Greys' car, but petrol was so scarce and the trek northward might not be any faster. To say nothing of all the explanations and gushing thanks he would have to produce.

Once on board, standing wedged between two young conscripts and their kitbags, the man apparently heading back to war after a spell of leave, he turned over the riddle of the postcard — addressed to one place, his home, and delivered to another, his college. Did that explain the sudden movement he had glimpsed this morning? Had someone intercepted his post, collaring the postman just as he was about to put the card through the door? But he was sure he had not seen two people, and there had been no sign of a postman when he had looked outside, let alone any lurking stranger.

But now he wondered. Perhaps there had been a stack of mail lodged in the letterbox and someone had taken it. Maybe that was the faint rattling noise he had heard, not the sound of letters being posted through the slot, but being *pulled out*. But who would do such a thing? It had achieved nothing except a delay, given that he had seen the postcard from his wife little more than an hour or two later. If someone had wanted to steal his post, then why not simply steal it: why go to the trouble of delivering it to an alternative address that very morning? Whoever had done it had clearly known plenty about him, including his college affiliation.

Or was this exactly what Rosemary Hyde — that was it, Hyde — had in mind when she accused him of going off the rails yesterday? Was he imagining things, constructing a menace that wasn't there out of a simple mix-up with the morning post? He remembered the book: *Others reported a heightened state of awareness, as if in constant expectation of danger*. Was this an example of the very hyper-vigilance he had read about, little more than mindless paranoia?

The train had stopped, halted in a screech of metal and a cloud of steam for no reason he could discern. An argument was getting louder in the next carriage, an inspector telling a gang of servicemen to get out of the first class compartment. James felt himself tense. He couldn't afford even the slightest delay. A minute lost here could be the difference between winning Florence back and seeing her go. He craned to look out of the window, where he could see the train's fireman had jumped off the plate and was inspecting one of the engine's wheels. James's hands were beginning to tremble: come on, *come on*. And then, mercifully, there was a blast of the whistle and they were back on their way.

Partly to keep his mind occupied, he constructed a list, refined and refined again, of people who might benefit from the switch of the postcard. As the train chugged through the Oxfordshire countryside, he went through them all, starting with the obvious category: those who were infatuated with, or covetous of, his wife, a category that would include most of the red-blooded men in Oxford and probably a fair smattering of Rosemary's glorified Brownie pack, including the Brown Owl herself. He worked through each of them, paying particular attention to the myopic Magnus Hook, promoted up the suspects' rankings for having seen James dishevelled and out of sorts the previous day: that would only have had to prompt a few questions in the right places for Hook to have discovered Florence's absence. And then there was Virginia Grey, in the picture from the very start. Round and round he went, working through the carousel of friends, acquaintances and colleagues. Albert Wills, Professor of Natural Sciences and Florence's head of department, had taken an instant shine to her: who knew what he, what they, might have been plotting in the labs? There was the slick-haired Leonard Musgrove, Chairman of the local Fabian Society and undeniably handsome. *Damn*. James had meant to check when the Fabians met, wondering if, by any chance, it was early on Thursday evenings. And what about Edgar Connolly, eminent biologist and vegetarian fanatic who had come to see Florence as something of a protégée? He was her father's age, but that meant nothing; Oxford morality was not the same as the provincial variety he had grown up with. It could be any one of them.

He tried to be disciplined, even — when he got off at Bletchley and found a seat on a platform bench — pulling out a notebook and pen, writing out his thoughts methodically. But constantly his mind would wander back to the more important enigma. If his wife had left him because he had become impossible, why tell him she loved him, not once but twice? And if she did love him, why run away from him? The Crewe train arrived on time and he got on board. As it headed north past Rugby, he tortured himself that Florence and Harry had been kidnapped, taken hostage by some maniac. Had she smuggled out these postcards or perhaps written them under duress, the abnormal brevity of the message a kind of code for her situation? If so, how obtuse he had been not to have seen it earlier. Perhaps he was meant to realize that his wife would never sign off with a mere three-word farewell and that he had been a fool not to have read the signal.

But then he remembered the suitcase taken from under the bed, the clothes removed from the cupboard, even Snowy missing from under Harry's covers. Also, when he had gone to look for cash, he had seen that some had been taken already. If all the money had been gone, that might have been further evidence of a kidnap, one compounded by theft. Taking just some, leaving the rest for him, suggested a degree of deliberation, surely impossible with a kidnapper's knife at her throat. He shuddered at the thought, as if the movement might physically shake the image loose from his head. Instead he saw something worse: a blade pressing against little Harry's skin. He coughed and opened his eyes wide, hoping the view of the busy platform opposite would expel the thought he had just conjured.

Harry. He had meant the name as a tribute to his dead friend, one of the most vital men he had ever known. It was not supposed to be a morbid gesture, quite the opposite. It was a way of keeping Harry Knox alive and in the present, rather than sentencing him to an eternity in some non-existent next world. He would be in the here and now, not the hereafter. James was not a religious man — he had emphatically rejected his parents' creed by taking up arms in Spain — and if anyone had put the idea to him out loud he would have laughed it off as superstitious nonsense; but privately he had also hoped that his old comrade's strength and energy might somehow be passed onto his son, via their shared name.

Yet now James was gripped by the fear that he might have placed on his son's infant shoulders a curse, that it had been arrogant to name a little boy after a man who had died such a violent death — that he had offered the fates too great a temptation.

He trod over this same ground, forward and back, as he travelled north through Staffordshire and as he waited for a desperately frustrating two hours under leaden skies at Crewe, midday turning to afternoon and then evening. And throughout, even when he was trying to sift through the possibilities with all the logical power a first class degree in philosophy had given him, a larger subject lurked, like a vast, grey whale shifting through the water. It had been there all this time, only occasionally breaking the surface. When it showed itself, it was as a question: had Rosemary Hyde, describing a violent, dangerous man possessed by demons, spoken the truth?

His brain had been scrambled just as surely as those poor boys back from Ypres and the Somme mentioned in the journal article Florence had been reading in the Bodleian. He had spent only a short time in the trenches on Madrid's north-western outskirts, but he had seen his best friend's head explode like a watermelon smashed by cricket bat.

He had always believed he had coped admirably. He had never blubbed for Harry; he had followed the doctors' instructions for the rehabilitation of his shattered shoulder. He had been a faithful husband and, barely two months after he was shot, a devoted father. Yes, he had usually been furious when he woke up and furious when he went to bed, raging against an injury that had prevented him avenging Harry's murder. It had thwarted him first by forcing him out of the Spanish Civil War, sending him back to England the instant he was discharged from hospital. And it had thwarted him a second time when he was branded unfit to join the battle against Hitler and the Axis powers. What man would not be boiling with rage? But he had kept it to himself and got on with his work, hadn't he? Why had that not been good enough?

And finally, in the fading summer light, the train crept into Liverpool, wheezing its last gasps as it stuttered to a halt. James edged his way through the soldiers on board, some looking weary from war, others nervous at returning to it. He ignored the tut-tutting at a civilian failing to defer to men in uniform. But there was not a moment to waste. The instant his feet touched the platform, every step he took thereafter would take him closer to Florence and Harry. And he had so little time.

CHAPTER
NINE

Perhaps it was because of the dark, with the station lights dimmed in deference to the blackout, but this city looked grimier than almost any he had seen, the sides of every building stained with soot. The trams were dusky with dirt and so, it seemed to him, were the faces of the people, or at least those hanging around the railway station at this late hour.

He hurried past them all, determined to reach the docks. He knew it was unlikely that any ferries would be sailing so late, but it was wartime: none of the usual rules seemed to apply. Perhaps Harry and Florence had been booked on an afternoon crossing and it had been delayed. He did not care so long as he got there in time.

He turned down Hanover Street and onto Liver Street, fairly marching down the pavement. With his head down, and in the dark, he saw the policeman standing by a doorway only after he had barged into him. It was James's left shoulder that had caught the man and the impact sent a rocket of pain shooting down his arm.

"Watch yourself, lad," the special said, brushing the sleeve of his uniform to signal that he had been struck, his torch throwing jagged shadows with each movement.

"Sorry about that," James replied, resuming his near-run. He had gone no more than two paces when the policeman took hold of him. "Where are you off to in such a hurry? Don't answer. I want to deal with this so-and-so first."

James sighed and waited, a picture of impatience, as the constable aimed his torch at the door to the shop. A blind was covering it, save for a gap cut into the middle to reveal the single word "open". The word was picked out by a blued lamp just behind, which revealed that this was not a shop but a café. Standing to one side was a man who had remained hidden until now; James guessed he was the proprietor. Suddenly all three of them were in pitch darkness, as the policeman switched off his flashlight.

"See," he said in an accent thick with the Mersey. "It's too bright, in't it? You're showing too much light."

"Yes, yes. I'm a-sorry. I thought it not so bright."

"Are you Italian or what?"

"I live here thirty-five years, constable."

"Yeah, but it's different now, in't it? Let's have a look at your documents and that."

James closed his eyes in despair. "Officer, I really do have to be going. My —"

The policeman turned round, shining the beam directly into his face. "I told you. I'll get to you when I'm good and ready."

"It's just that my wife and child may be leaving on a ferry to Ireland any moment now. I need to —"

"Ireland, eh? We got all sorts here, in't we?"

"Please, officer. I need to get there as soon as I can. I'm sorry I bumped into you."

The special looked him up and down, taking in the flannels and satchel, then shining the torch back at the proprietor. "All right," he said to James eventually. "Scarper."

James all but ran now, trying to shake off the after-image of the torch beam that still lingered. Soon he was enveloped in complete darkness. He could see no movement ahead of him or behind. The only sound came from his own feet, and he could barely even see them. Then, passing a row of steel-shuttered shops, there was a glint of light — the beam of a human eye — accompanied a second later by a voice. "How are you, darling? Don't you think I look like Betty Grable?"

To his left in a shop doorway was the painted face of a woman in a low-cut dress. "Just two bob and I'll make you happy, you'll see." As she smiled, James saw the missing teeth and deep lines that suggested she was old enough to be his mother.

That was one of the unforeseen consequences of the blackout, an epidemic of prostitution. The dark offered anonymity to women who would never have considered such a thing before. Wives whose husbands were at war, who needed to make a few extra shillings, could offer themselves from the shadows, knowing their secret would remain hidden. Shame, it seemed, could not flourish in the pitch black. Oxford had not been immune from this new outbreak. The proctors had warned the undergraduates that they would be expected to maintain the highest moral standards, no matter what offers came their way from the darkness of Holywell Street.

Eventually he reached the port, the thin crescent moon leaking speckles of light onto the water. The harbour was packed, with both troop ships and container vessels bringing supplies from across the Atlantic. But the dockside was silent: no one was around. What he took to be the harbourmaster's office was bolted and padlocked. He was too late.

He had played out the scene in his mind so fully that the realization that it was a delusion came as a shock. There would be no last-minute boarding of a ferry about to set sail for Ireland, no sprint up the gangplank, no cry of joyous surprise from Harry.

He checked his watch: it was past eleven. Life on the sea probably began at dawn; this place would be awake in just a few hours. In the meantime, he would get some sleep. No point finding a room. He would bed down here, in the port, so that he would hear the first stirrings of activity in the morning.

In the gloom he saw what looked to be an unloading area, under a wooden roof. He was walking towards it when he saw the briefest glimpse of light, in front of him and at waist level. A reflex, learned not instinctive, told him it was a knife and he looked up to see the hooded, sad eyes of the man holding it. The man said nothing but his eyes angled pointedly towards the satchel over James's shoulder, the whites illuminated in the darkness.

In Spain he had been trained to know that if you needed to disable a man's arm, you stepped forward and isolated it from the shoulder. *Apply pressure in the armpit and the blade will eventually drop*, Jorge had said and, James discovered now, Jorge was right. But it was not the training that told him to twist the man's arm behind his back until he was screaming in pain. Nor was it the training that forced the man to his knees and began to kick him hard in his guts repeatedly, with a final precise blow to the chin, leaving him moaning and writhing on the ground.

As he walked away, James felt his system flood with a mixture of relief, adrenalin and swaggering pride. What do you say about that, eh, men of the Medical Examination Board? Not bad for a D1. Too unfit to fight? If I can do that with my bare hands, imagine what I could do with a gun.

But soon the bounce went out of his step. He had none of the soldier's discipline. He was out of control, in the grip of furies he barely understood. What he had done just now was the behaviour of a brute. He appalled himself.

He had been walking in circles, ending up almost where he had started, close to the harbourmaster's office. He would not bother with — he thought he barely deserved — a shelter. Instead he found a spot between two crates, retrieved a pullover from his bag, put it on and used the satchel as a pillow as he curled into the narrow space. But sleep would not come. He was picturing the man he had beaten so hard, he had left him lying semi-conscious on the ground.

Finally, James dug into his pocket to look again at the postcard. He wanted to think about something else, but also to reassure himself that the card was real, that he had not imagined it, that his wife had been here, in Liverpool, the previous day. The sight of those three words, inked in that curved, gorgeous script of hers — amused, amusing, confident, flirtatious, just like her — warmed him: *I love you.* And somehow, in the cold of the night, alone in an empty dockyard, surrounded by the stench of oil, grease and working ships, and lying on hard, rough ground, he fell into deep, exhausted sleep.

"Oi. Up. Let's be having you."

He opened his eyes, trying to make sense of the confusion of sudden consciousness.

"I said *up*. Now."

"Where am I?"

"*Now.*"

In a rush of memory, it came back to him: where he was, why he was here and how he needed to behave. He leapt to his feet, the action of a man embarrassed to have been caught asleep, straightened his jacket, swept a long forelock of hair out of his eyes and attempted a charming smile. But the clerk in front of him — peaked cap, officious expression and in late middle age — was not in a mood to be charmed. "Harbour-master's office, now."

James was about to protest but, after a second's delay, realized there was no need. With luck, he would be taken exactly where he needed to go.

Within a few minutes he was standing before a desk, the walls around him covered in nautical charts, lists and time-tables. It reminded him of nothing so much as his multiple childhood appearances in the headmaster's study. The clerk at his side was explaining to the bespectacled man in a three-piece suit, whom he took to be the harbourmaster, where "this gentleman" had been found and asking whether the police should be summoned. James decided it was time to play the class card.

"My name is Dr James Zennor of the University of Oxford. You can verify that by contacting the Vice Chancellor, Professor George Stuart Gordon, or the master of my college, Professor Bernard Grey." He hesitated, reluctant to mention his subject: he had learned that the less educated sometimes baulked at the mere mention of "psychology", suspecting that only those a bit funny in the head would dabble in such matters. "My wife is Florence Walsingham, daughter of Sir George and Lady Walsingham, and I believe she may have set sail from this port in the last day or two. A ferry for Ireland seems most likely. I would like to check the manifests for all the passenger vessels that have left Liverpool in the last two days." He paused. "Please."

The harbourmaster produced a pipe and set about the business of stuffing it, tamping it and lighting it — happy for the task to take as much time as it needed if not a little longer. He then used the end of the process to gesture the clerk towards the door, leaving him to size up the newcomer on his own.

Finally, he spoke. "Zennor, you say." He sucked the pipe, turning the compacted weed bright orange. The sudden smoke, fragrant, wooded and warm, transported James in an instant back to his childhood, to the parlour of that small house in Bournemouth, his father puffing on his pipe as he worked his way through a pile of small, neatly-lined children's exercise books. That triggered another memory: his father's face the first time they saw each other after James's return from Spain. His expression had been pained, though whether by the anguish of seeing his son so badly wounded or the hurt that James had rejected his parents' most sacred creed by fighting at all, James never knew.

Another suck on the pipe. "*Zennor.*" The accent was Scottish. "Is that foreign?"

"Cornish, actually."

"Not German, then?"

"No."

"Because we're on the look-out for enemy aliens, you know. There's a camp not far from here. Huyton. You sure you didn't escape from there?"

"Of course I'm sure."

"Not planning to stow away? It's just I don't really see an Oxford man — a professor, if you please — kipping like a dosser out here on the docks. Doesn't quite add up."

"I didn't say I was a professor. I'm Dr James Zennor, in the Department of Experimental Psychology of Oxford University." *Damn.*

"Psychology, you say. Isn't that a bit German?"

"Look, I'm not bloody German. Here's my passport."

Another suck on the pipe, then an adjustment of the spectacles as the harbourmaster turned the pages, studying each one carefully. "I see you spent a lot of time in Spain, Dr Zennor."

"I fought with the International Brigades. Against the Fascists. I was wounded." James nodded toward his shoulder: "That's the only reason I'm not in the army now."

The harbourmaster sat back in his chair and relit his pipe. The passport remained on his desk. "What do you know of the *Arandora Star*, Dr —" he looked again at the document before giving an exaggerated pronunciation of the last name, as if determined to make it sound like that of a Viennese shrink, "*Zennor*."

James's mind whirred. *Arandora Star*. Almost certainly a ship. Could that be the ship Florence and Harry were on? Did this man know something? Would it be better for James to appear ignorant or informed? With no better plan, he opted to tell the truth: "It sounds like a ship, but I've never heard of it."

"You sure of that, Doctor?"

"I'm sure. Do you have reason to believe my wife and son might be on that ship, Mr —"

"It's Harbourmaster Hunter and no, I don't. That ship sailed from here just over a week ago. Mostly krauts and wops on board. Internees. You sure you don't know about it?"

"For heaven's sake, I've told —"

131

"Because that ship was hit by a German torpedo and sunk, Dr Zennor. Loss of more than eight hundred lives."

"Good God."

"It's not been in the papers, not yet anyway. But I should expect word has reached Huyton. The camp, I mean. Relatives and what have you. There'll be a lot of angry people, I expect. Well, I don't need to tell you, you're the psychology expert." His tone was softening, but his eye remained sceptical.

"Oh, I see," said James, with a bitter smile. "You think the 'krauts and wops' might be planning some kind of revenge. You think I'm a saboteur who came here to plant a bomb!"

"There's nothing funny about it, Dr Zennor. It does happen, you know. And after *Arandora Star*, the police have told us to be especially vigilant. And there you are, sleeping rough on the dockside. Now why would a gentleman like you do that? Doesn't make sense. Put yourself in my shoes."

James decided that the man was extending a hand, that he wanted to be persuaded that James posed no threat. "Harbourmaster Hunter, I appreciate what this looks like. Downright odd for a man like me to behave this way. I spent all day travelling here from Oxford and I was, frankly, exhausted. I wanted to be first in the queue to —"

It wasn't working. He could see that the man remained unmoved.

"Forgive an intrusive question, but tell me, Harbourmaster, are you married?"

132

"I am."

"Would I be right in assuming that, if one day, your wife and child were missing, but your wife sent you a note leading you to — I don't know — let's say, for the sake of argument, my office in Oxford; would I be right in assuming, in that situation, that you would camp outside my door until you found out where they were?"

A long suck on the pipe, then a cloud of smoke bearing the scent of childhood. Then: "Yes, you would be right, Dr Zennor." He paused, as if waiting for something more. On an instinct, James reached into his breast pocket and pulled out the postcard and handed it to Hunter.

The harbourmaster examined the picture on the front, then the postmark and finally the message, his eyes closing briefly — the modest gesture of a man acknowledging that he has just intruded into the private space of another. He put his pipe in the ashtray, bowl first, letting the ash tumble out, before standing up and announcing, "The ships' manifests are kept in the log room next door."

And so, a moment later, James was staring over Hunter's shoulder as he pulled down the thick volumes containing records of recent traffic in and out of Liverpool. He went first, and deliberately it seemed to James, for a liner called *Antonia*.

"The *Antonia*," James said out loud. "Was that bound for Dublin?"

Hunter ignored the question, instead running his finger down the list of names, heading straight for the end of the list. Nothing under Z. He searched again, his finger moving more slowly. Still nothing. Now he checked other traffic, working his way through the passenger vessel manifests before turning to cargo ships, examining the crew lists. They found a Zander, but no Zennor.

It was, James thought, with genuine disappointment that Hunter finally shook his hand and ushered him from the office. "I wish you the best of luck, Dr Zennor," he said, adding with an extra squeeze of the hand, "and well done on fighting in Spain, sir. That was a good cause if ever there was one."

As James walked away, struggling to repress a sense of defeat, he took another look at the postcard. The picture of the Sagrada Familia: was that purely sentimental, a reminder of happier times, a reminder of why they were together? Or had Florence been trying to tell him something more specific? Was there some clue contained there that he was missing? He looked again at the postmark — Liverpool — and the message: *I love you*.

He remembered the first letter he had ever had from her. It was after he had seen that press clipping, the one that revealed the ingenious truth about her participation in the Berlin Games. He had written to her, to apologize, of course, but also to express his fierce admiration for the stance she had taken. He was taking his own stand, he explained, fighting the barbarism that spoke in a Castilian, rather than a Bavarian, accent. (He was showing off.) He was fighting for the people who had hosted them so warmly in Barcelona. But the war would not last forever. And when he came back to

England, he would very much like to see her again. He had not been sure how to sign off. He had not wanted to seem too infatuated, as if misreading the importance of their week together. Perhaps, for her, it was no more than a holiday romance. In the business of love, for all her freshness, young Florence Walsingham had been no ingénue. So he had opted for "Yours". Capable of two readings, it could simply be the formal, conventional "yours" but surely it could also carry a sense of "I am yours," as in —

Walsingham.

James turned around and sprinted back to the office. He burst through the doors, ignoring the shocked expressions of the clerks, and demanded to see Mr Hunter right away. When one official asked him to take a seat and wait his turn, James just spoke right over him until, hearing the commotion, the harbourmaster reappeared.

"What is it?"

"Her maiden name. I didn't try her maiden name," James panted, attempting a smile to cover the embarrassment at his own stupidity. "Will you check the manifests again? For Florence Walsingham."

Once again Hunter opened first the record for *Antonia*, running his finger along the names until he stopped and turned to James. "I thought as much. There, you can see for yourself."

James stepped forward, finding the spot where in a clerk's Victorian hand it stated simply, "Walsingham, Florence. F. Age, 25." Next to it was an entry for "Walsingham, Harry. M (minor). Age, 2 yrs 10 mths."

His blood cannoning through his veins, James looked at the harbourmaster. "Where is this ship going?"

"Canada."

"What? What did you say?"

"The ship is sailing to Canada, sir."

"Canada? But that —" His voice gave way, unable to push through his own incredulity. Canada? That was half a world away. Why on earth would Florence go there, why would she take Harry so far from his own father? Ireland would have been bad enough, but at least it was just a ferry ride away. Canada: she might as well have decided to live on another planet.

He forced his voice to speak, emitting a croak that implored the harbourmaster. "When do they leave?"

"I'm afraid you're too late, Dr Zennor. The *Antonia* set sail yesterday morning."

CHAPTER
TEN

London, later that same day

He checked himself in the mirror and was pleased with what he saw. He had never worn "white tie" before and feared he would look like a two-bit Fred Astaire, but he found the whole get-up flattered him immensely. Back home no one outside Hollywood ever dressed like this, but these Brits knew what they were doing. Any man who wasn't a cripple could look suave and dashing wearing tails.

He looked again at his invitation, printed on a card so stiff you could use it as a drinks tray. *Dinner at the Russian Tea Room in South Kensington, 7.30p.m. for 8p.m..* And there was his own name, rendered in fancy, curly script, as if he were a regular earl or viscount.

Of course the invitation omitted the crucial information, about the host. Sure, there was a name of an individual, but that didn't reveal the full picture. Keeping it vague was smart, given the nature of the gathering. And also exciting.

He checked his shoes: clean without being mirror-clean. One thing he was beginning to understand about these Brits: no time for those who tried too hard. "Amateur" was an insult back home in the States, but here it was a compliment. An English gentleman gave the appearance that he regarded everything as a game. Anyone who was in earnest was automatically a bore.

Why, he asked himself again, had they invited him? The obvious answer was Anna. She had made him her ... what was he exactly? An escort, a protégé, a plaything? If that last was it, then he did not object. It was a privilege to be toyed with by such a woman. She was at least ten years older than him, far from beautiful, her features uneven, her nose positively crooked. But she was sexy. Her manner oozed sin and smoke. She made even the most mundane task a seduction; the way her fingers caressed the length of her cigarette-holder when lighting up, why, he had to look away. She would glance up, notice his embarrassment and rock her head back with lascivious laughter, showing her throat, her lips parted. The dresses she wore, the way the satin moved around her hips and ass, the cloud of perfume that hovered over her, carrying the whiff of afternoon sex ...

So Anna was the obvious explanation. She would only have had to mention his name to her husband and that would have been enough. It wouldn't be like that back home in the States of course. No husband could tolerate such behaviour in a wife, it would be too humiliating: most would give her a good beating. And the way she conducted herself in public, they would be quite within their rights. But this, Taylor Hastings was coming to realize, nine months to the day after he had

138

arrived in London, was not the States. This was Europe. Different, more decadent standards applied.

Here it was quite possible to believe an adulterous wife would introduce her cuckolded husband to her lover and that, far from punishing the affair, the husband would regard the association as a recommendation. "Come on in, Taylor, old boy. I hear you're engaged in bit of hanky-panky with my better half. Well, good for you, old chap. Only a thoroughly *good egg* would do that." Nine months in and he hoped he was getting the hang of how these guys spoke. The old *lingo*.

He stepped beyond the porch and into Cadogan Square. Still light, there was the smell of summer rain. Only a July shower, it had left the city smelling fresh rather than damp, as if it had been cleansed. He hailed a cab and asked for Fifty Harrington Road, Kensington, his voice further betraying his good mood.

"What you got to be so cheerful about?" the driver asked. "Don't you know there's a war on?"

Hastings mumbled something, the sound rather than the words doing the work of apology. The last thing he wanted was to get drawn into a mindless conversation with some British prole. He wanted to stay with this train of thought. He was enjoying the ride.

His dalliance with Anna — or, rather, her dalliance with him — only went so far as an explanation for tonight's invitation. He knew the summons had not come solely on account of his sparkling dinner table wit and the quality of his conversation over brandy. (Less comfortably, he knew that Anna's interest in him did

139

not solely draw on the appeal of a former college football player in his twenties whose physique represented hard granite to her husband's wrinkled prune.) He was young, no denying that. But he was not naïve. He knew that he was expected at the Russian Tea Room because of his job.

Or rather his place of work. He had not yet confided the details of his duties to this circle, though he half-feared he had given Anna enough clues over the course of four months of pillow talk for her to have worked it out. Half-feared and half-hoped. The desire to impress her, especially when he knew that his reward might be some new and previously unimaginable delight in bed, was too hard to resist. Anyway she had sworn she would say nothing to her husband. "My lips are sealed," she had said, licking them as she said it, then rolling over as if to offer herself up to him.

Could he believe her? Did it matter? He stepped out of the taxi, the door held open for him by a doorman, successfully avoiding the small puddle that had collected just in front of the sidewalk, and swept inside, his head up and his shoulders back, handing his hat and coat to the second man inside. He announced the name of his host with pleasure, gratified by the nod of recognition the name prompted. He let himself be led up the staircase, noting the portraits of assorted Russian aristocrats, most of whom he guessed had lost their heads to the Bolsheviks, then followed as the butler turned and headed down one thickly-carpeted corridor and through a heavy door.

140

On the other side stood what he estimated were two dozen gentlemen dressed, as he was, in white tie, around a table laden with silver, china and crystal, apparently set for a feast. He wondered what his censorious cab driver would make of this little scene, where there was not a ration book in sight. *Don't you know there's a war on?*

He checked his watch, worried that he had arrived too late. But his host, standing at the head of the table moved fast to dispel any anxiety. "Ah, Hastings, perfect timing. We're just about to drink a toast. Come on someone, give the man a glass! That's it. All right then." He raised his flute of champagne, so that it caught the light from the candles and even the glow of his white hair. "To the Right Club!"

The other twenty-odd men, each standing behind his chair at the table, echoed the words back, full and hearty. None heartier or more enthusiastic than the young American in their midst who felt the uniquely delicious joy of the man who had *arrived*. He could hear his own voice in among the chorus as he too chanted, "To the Right Club!"

CHAPTER
ELEVEN

James must have visibly weakened, perhaps he had even stumbled backwards, because the next thing he could remember was watching the steam rise from a thick mug of sweet tea, placed on the near side of the harbourmaster's desk before him. He could not remember when it had appeared or who had asked for it.

Canada. What sense did that make? Leaving him was one thing, but to head to the other side of the world? Why would Florence do such a thing? Had living with him really become that unbearable?

Meanwhile, he could hear Hunter speaking. The man seemed to be answering a question James could not remember asking. There were knots and nautical miles in the sentences that were coming from the official's mouth; put together, he seemed to be explaining why it was impossible for James to catch up with Florence's ship and join her on board. Had he really asked such a question? He needed to pull himself together.

He looked at the tea in front of him. That was the way they always ended their long walks, his parents and their fellow Quaker friends. Through the New Forest or perhaps taking the chain ferry over to the Isle of

Purbeck, wherever they had gone, the day would always conclude the same way. Hot cup of tea in his parents' front room, heavily sweetened by his mother: a reward for their exertions. Somehow he guessed Rosemary Hyde allowed no such indulgences to her walking women; they needed to be lean, fit and strong if they were to lead the proletariat to the Marxist utopia or some such rubbish. No sweet tea for them.

The harbourmaster was watching him, a look that combined concern and fear, a look that said this man in my office could be capable of anything. James decided it was time to get out. He spoke with a clarity that surprised even himself. "Mr Hunter, I need to make an urgent telephone call in the light of the information you have so kindly given me. To Oxford. I wonder if I could use your —"

"That's a trunk call."

"It is, I'm afraid. But I will be brief, I assure you."

The harbourmaster took a hard look at James, as if he were worried that he had taken in some kind of lunatic. In a bid to reassure him, James added that the man he needed to telephone was the master of his Oxford college. And so, after a convoluted conversation with a telephone operator and multiple clunks and clicks, he heard his own voice meet down a crackling line with that of Bernard Grey, scholar, broadcaster and guiding sage of the British intellectual left. James pictured him as he had glimpsed him just before he sped away from Oxford, in the muddy green uniform of a commanding officer of the Local Defence Volunteers, the cloth as thick as carpet. The image still struck him as ludicrous.

"Professor Grey, it's Dr Zennor."

"James, you sound terrible. Where in God's name are you?"

"I'm in Liverpool."

There was a hesitation, followed by, "Ah. I see."

"I'm here because Florence has taken our son Harry on a ship bound —" He stopped himself. "What do you mean, 'I see'?"

"You followed Florence to Liverpool. Did you see the ship off?"

"No, I missed it by twenty-four hours. I don't understand. How do you know about the ship?"

"Are you all right, James? You sound distressed."

The calm, consoling voice had precisely the reverse of its intended effect; James felt his initial politeness congealing into cold anger. "Yes, I am distressed rather. My wife has fled thousands of miles away from me and taken my child with her. And while this has come as an enormous shock to me you seem already to be in the picture. So in fact 'distressed' barely begins to cover it, Professor Grey."

"James, I think you had better return to Oxford where we can discuss all this in person. In my lodgings. You could dine afterwards at high table. We are to be joined tonight by William Beveridge. Do you know his work? Excellent ideas on the appropriate allocation of citizen rights to those with what he calls 'general defects'. Unsentimental fellow and the detail is a bit wobbly but —"

144

"I have no intention of returning to Oxford, Master. I want to find my wife and my child and I now know they are nowhere near Oxford." He seized on the mental recording he had made and which was now playing back in his mind. "And what do you mean, 'all this'?"

"I'm sorry James, I'm afraid you're not making much sense."

"You said 'all this'. We can discuss *all this*. What did you mean by that?"

"Oh I see. You don't know."

"Know what?" On hearing a moment's silence, James repeated the question, shouting it this time. "I don't bloody know what?" Through the glass of the harbourmaster's office door he could see secretaries' heads turning and staring. For all his efforts, he was once again the crazy man who had been found sleeping rough.

Eventually Bernard Grey began speaking, his voice low and regretful, as if he had been forced into saying something he had hoped to avoid. "I sincerely thought someone would have informed you of this by now. At least Virginia if no one else."

"Master."

"Your wife and child are on a ship together with twenty-five Oxford mothers and approximately one hundred and twenty-five children. They are on their way to Yale College, which has graciously offered them a place of refuge during the war."

"Yale? In America? But she's going to Canada."

"Canada is a stopping-off point. I believe they are to be accommodated at the Royal Victoria College in Montreal for a few days, before travelling by rail to New Haven in the United States."

"Yale," James repeated, uselessly. "In America." Whatever the precise geography, this seemed so much more remote. Canada at least was a dominion of the British Empire, under the same King and fighting the same war. But the United States? For the first time, he wondered if he would ever see his wife and child again.

He closed his eyes, forcing himself to focus on this moment and on the words he had just heard, "How long have you known about this?"

"It's been in the offing for several weeks."

"Several weeks!" He had tortured himself with the idea that Florence had been plotting behind his back for weeks, and now here was Grey telling him that his worst fears had, in fact, been utterly realistic. "Several weeks," he said, letting the weight of that amount of time hang in the air for a while. "No one told me."

"It would appear not."

"Why? Why in God's name —"

"I'm afraid —"

"Florence is my wife, Master Grey. Harry is my *son*."

"No one told you, James, because we knew what you would say."

"'We'? Who's 'we'?"

"All I —"

"You mean *you* were involved in this?"

"I played a very minor role. Many others were far —"

146

"I don't believe this. *Lots* of you were involved, were you? *Many others*, you say. What, in a secret plot to take my wife and child away from me?"

"Now, James. Calm down."

"Don't you tell me to calm down," James said, spitting out the words. "You've just told me you conspired in the break-up of my family, sending them half way across the world. So, no, I will not be calm. I want to know why you did this. Why you and all these 'many others' plotted against me like this."

"You see this is exactly what we were afraid of."

"There you go again: *we*."

"This ranting and raving. This paranoia. This is what scared your wife out of her wits. This is what scared her away. You've been like this a long time now, James. It explains why . . . you're in this situation."

That stopped him, the way Rosemary's words had stopped him yesterday. What she had said then and what Grey said now sounded too much like the truth. Whatever help these others had given Florence, no one had forced her onto that ship: the decision to leave him, and to travel an ocean away, had been hers. More quietly than before, he spoke again. "And I suppose there were meetings, to iron out all the details?"

"Yes, of course. The families involved, mothers mainly, met several times to make preparations. Helped by various university officials of course. Discussing visas, legal guardianship, that sort of thing."

"I don't suppose these meetings were on Thursday evenings by any chance, were they?"

"They were as a matter of fact, yes: 5p.m. at Rhodes House."

So that's why she had missed the last two walks with Rosemary and her Marxist Girl Guides. She was with other mothers, planning her escape — not to Norfolk or Bedfordshire, like other evacuees, but to America.

"And who else knew about this? About Florence I mean?"

"James."

"No. Go on, who's this 'we' you mentioned?"

"I'm not sure this is healthy."

"Don't worry about that. I'd like to know." He was trying hard to sound reasonable, as if they were no more than two Oxford dons trading college gossip.

"Virginia, of course. Myself. Other concerned friends."

"Rosemary Hyde?"

"I don't think it's necessary to mention any names, James."

"And why did this group of 'concerned' friends believe that the one person who could not be trusted with this secret was the husband and father of the woman and child concerned? Why was that then?"

"To repeat myself: we knew what you would say."

"And what was that?"

"We knew you would say no."

He couldn't argue. Of course he would have said no. The very idea of his family becoming evacuees across the Atlantic, he could not have discussed it, let alone approved of it. He believed a move to Herefordshire or the Cotswolds amounted to a surrender to the Third

148

Reich; but the United States? It was abominable. It represented an abandonment of the country, as if they were pulling down the shutters and shutting up shop, leaving Britain for the Nazis to inherit. They might as well run up the white flag now. How had these other men — the fathers of those one hundred and twenty-five Oxford children — ever agreed to such a capitulation?

And yet, these convictions dragged behind them a nag of doubt. He could not quite articulate it even to himself but he could feel it. It was the guilty sense he had that these other men, these other fathers, were allowed to take such extreme action to protect their young but that he was granted no such privilege. They would perform their act of sacrifice on the battle-field or, failing that, in some war ministry or other, now relocated in Oxford. But staying put, keeping his family in England even under Nazi occupation, even in the shadow of Hitler's bombs, was the only act of resistance available to James Zennor. If he buckled on that, then he was doing precisely nothing to defy the fascist barbarians who had killed his friend and nearly destroyed him. There was nothing else he could do. And the realization of it — that he was using a woman and a not-yet three-year-old boy vicariously, to make up for his own failure to play any part in this essential and wholly just war — filled him with shame.

And then the mental recording of the words just spoken caught up with him. "What was that you said?"

"James, I really cannot stay on the telephone much longer. I —"

"You said, 'This explains why you're in this situation.' Now, what did you mean by that?"

"I, I, I was referring of course to your wife being on that ship. That is to say . . . she knew you refused all talk of evacuation, which is —"

"No. You meant something else. You said I've been like this a 'long time'. You meant something else, didn't you?"

"James, please."

"DIDN'T YOU?" He bellowed it, prompting more turned heads in the outer office. When Grey spoke again, James was sure he could hear a tremble in the older man's voice.

"Yes, I did. It was a slip, I'm sorry."

"I know all about slips. They never are entirely accidental, are they? What were you trying not to say?"

"I regret you pushing me in this manner, James. But since you seem determined to twist my arm, I was referring to your recent . . ." He paused again. "Rejections."

"You mean from the civil service? From the ministries? What about them?"

"I have already said far too much."

And then James saw it. "Oh, I don't believe it. You bastard."

"How dare you speak to me that way! It was not down to me. I had next to nothing to do with it. They run their own checks, their own independent assessments."

"But they would have consulted you. Whitehall doesn't order a box of bloody paperclips without asking what Professor Bernard bloody Grey thinks about it."

150

"It was not like that, James. You must accept my word on that. They had already concluded that you were . . . not suitable for sensitive work, long before they spoke to me about you."

"'Not suitable for sensitive work' is that how we put it now? And I thought my lot were fond of euphemism. Crackers, is that the word you're looking for? Poor Zennor, he's round the twist: is that what you told them? Saw a bit too much action in Spain and now he's out of his mind. Eh? Would that be the gist of it, Professor? The 'burden of the argument' as you philosophers like to put it?"

Grey sighed and then replied quietly. "Something like that, yes. And this little exhibition has only confirmed the accuracy of the analysis, Dr Zennor. Now I suggest you put down the receiver and head back to Oxford where Virginia and I will see what we can do for you."

"You've ruined my life."

"I am going to say goodbye now, James, before you say anything you will come to regret."

And it was at that moment that James added another decision to the one he had already made. He had vowed the second he had learned where Florence had gone that he would somehow get to America and find his wife. But now he saw how he was going to do it — and just who would pay the price.

CHAPTER
TWELVE

He lost track of the number of hours he spent pacing in
and around Liverpool docks that day and yet, if you
asked him to sketch the place or draw a map, he would
have been blank. He had paid no attention to it, looking
no further than the ground beneath his feet. He was a
brain grappling with a problem: when he was like this,
everything else, everything physical, was a distraction.

The problem in this case was multi-layered. The
harbour-master had shaken his head and sucked in his
breath, leaving James in no doubt as to the
near-impossibility of him sailing across the Atlantic any
time soon or at least this side of a German surrender —
and "Adolf doesn't seem the surrendering type". There
were few ships daring to make the crossing now,
running the gauntlet of German U-boats and their
deadly torpedoes, like the missile that had taken out the
Arandora Star. Those that did had to travel in convoys
for their own protection, escorted by at least one or two
warships, which meant ships could not sail as and when
they pleased: they had to wait till there were enough
vessels to constitute a group. Even if James was lucky,
and there was another crossing, there were next to no
regular passengers these days, travelling for simple

business or pleasure. If they weren't troops on the move, enemy aliens or POWs deported to Canada or young evacuees transported by the Children's Overseas Reception Board, there had to be a damn good reason for an ordinary member of the British public to make the journey, which meant official permission. And the difficulties did not end there. At the other end, while a British subject could simply walk into Canada, to enter the United States required a visa.

There was only one person who could get James through all those hoops — and he had just called him a bastard down a long-distance telephone line. He was pretty sure that at the moment Bernard Grey would rather drop him to the bottom of the Atlantic than help him cross it.

The harbourmaster had begged him to find a boarding house — he had even recommended one on Kitchen Street — and told him to get a good night's sleep. But James could not rest, he could not even eat, until he had cracked this problem. And so he had paced.

Only once was his concentration broken. To his alarm he saw two police officers, apparently interviewing people on the dock-side. Had they found the man James had beaten last night? Was he dead? Were they conducting a murder inquiry? He could feel his heart thumping. It wouldn't take long for them to point the finger at him; anyone in the harbourmaster's office could tell them about the strange man they had found sleeping rough, a man who had already admitted that he had been here, down at the docks, late last night. A man who they had just overheard shouting down the phone, in a state of high distress.

James turned around, attempting to walk away discreetly, when he caught a snatch of the conversation the police were having with the man they had stopped.

"Now, don't get lippy with me. I told you before, all I need to see is your licence. You know the rules on selling."

A woman standing close by, with huge forearms, was chipping in. "Them batteries only worth tuppence ha'penny and he's selling them for fourpence. You should bang him up for that n'all."

"No one asked you, madam," the second policeman said firmly, as a small crowd began to form. The man at the centre, James could now see, was wearing a shiny suit, the cheap and nasty uniform of the black marketeer. He was protesting that he "wasn't forcing no one to buy my torch batteries", that that was their choice and it was still a free country — "till Jerry gets here at any rate". James turned away with relief.

He called in at the harbourmaster's office at frequent intervals, making a nuisance of himself but picking up new and, on his last visit, useful information. It was not long after that, as he was pacing along a pier sloppy with bilge water and stinking of fish, that it struck him. He had been thinking of Harry Knox. He remembered him holding forth on all manner of topics at the most improbable times and in the unlikeliest locations. This little lecture came during the defence of the university district in Madrid, as they stood together, shivering with cold in an abandoned block, its walls pocked with bullet holes, between rounds of shooting. Conversation was the only distraction.

Not that conversation was the right word. Tutorial, more like. Harry would lecture him on political theory, on the difference between Menshevik and Bolshevik, on the treachery of Ramsay MacDonald, on the true evil of Hitler and his lunatic worship of the Aryan superman. "There's a man who's swallowed his Nietzsche neat," Harry had said of Hitler, "while I always recommend the taking of German philosophers with gentle sips and plenty of water."

On that particular night, Harry had been expounding on human motivation. Officially, this should have fallen into James's area of expertise but there was no field in which Harry was not the most well-read man in the room. So James tried to clean his rifle — oddly they had discovered that Nivea handcream worked wonders on the weapon — and listened.

"I prattle on about all these great ideologies and you, James, are good enough to hear me out," Harry had said, "but do you know what really motivates men to act?" James stopped poking inside the gun chamber and was contemplating offering an answer when he realized that Harry was not waiting for one. His question had been rhetorical. "God, money and sex."

James had laughed but Harry had continued in earnest. "And power of course. Not power to do x or y, but the thrill of wielding power itself. That's why people risk their lives or do things they would, in normal circumstances, run a mile to avoid: power, religion, moolah or getting their oats."

"And which one of those is it with us?"

"Beg pardon, James?"

"Why are we sitting here waiting to get our nuts blown off in the middle of nowhere in a country neither of us come from? It's certainly not for the money. And I don't see any ladies around."

"Ah," said Harry, paying his friend the respect of appearing to think about the question. "This would be faith. What we have created here is a new religion. Still the battle of good and evil that your parents and their Quaker Friends would recognize — but this time the devil is played by Francisco Franco."

They had laughed and the conversation had moved on but Harry's rule had proved surprisingly durable. And as he paced around the docks, feeling the wind off the Mersey, chill even in July, it struck James with new force. *Of course.* How could he not have thought of it before?

Thank you, Harry and thank you, Florence, James said to himself now, breaking into a sprint in search of the nearest telephone box. He checked his watch; every chance Grey would be out.

He wondered what he would do if Virginia answered. He would have to hang up; it would not work unless he spoke to the Master directly. Two rings, three. Damn. He could be anywhere, trading Whitehall chit-chat at Balliol or out drilling the pot-bellied warriors of the Local Defence Volunteers. Four rings — and then the voice of the college butler. He pressed Button A and heard the coins tumble through the machine.

"Ah, Forsyth," James began. "It's Zennor. I need to speak with Master Grey. Urgently."

"I'm afraid, he's not available at —"

"Tell him he will regret not speaking to me. Immensely."

A pause, in which was contained several years of college gossip about the mental state of poor Dr Zennor, as well as the calculation by Forsyth the butler that he was not paid to act as nursemaid to the fellows and that this was a matter best dealt with by the Master himself. "Please hold on, sir."

James waited, looking up at the Liverpool sky through the red-bordered glass squares of the telephone box.

A rustle, the muffled voice of the butler and finally, "This is Grey."

"Bernard, it's James, again." Bernard. A different tone.

"Yes, James? Forsyth tells me you are telephoning on a matter of great urgency."

"That's right. I need your help in getting across the Atlantic. I need a United States visa and I need you to contact the Ministry of Shipping to get me a berth on the next ship out of here. There's due to be another crossing in —"

"That's completely impossible, James. How would I possibly justify you travelling to North America? You're not a woman, you're not a child — even if you are, to my great sorrow, behaving like one. You're not an evacuee. It's completely out of the question. Besides, and I say this kindly, the reason why many of us sought

to help Florence was in order to deliver her to safety —
and that, in part, meant getting her and her child away
from you."

Once again, James could feel the fury bubbling
through his veins. *Her child*. He was being steadily
removed from his own family. Any compunction he had
felt about using the weapon Florence had unwittingly
handed him a few months ago now dissolved. He
thought back to the moment Florence had come home
with the news of Grey's affair with the college secretary,
some thirty-five years his junior. At the time, James had
affected heard-it-all-before nonchalance, easy to do
because he had indeed heard it all before. But there was
no room for nonchalance now.

He closed his eyes and began, bracing himself as if he
were about to jump into a pool of bottomless water. "I
know about you and Miss Hodges."

Grey cleared his throat before replying. "You'll have
to do better than that, James. As you must surely
appreciate, Virginia and I do not believe in the
suburban conventions of marriage. She is a much more
enlightened woman than you give her credit for."

"Is she enlightened enough to approve of her
husband having got his mistress pregnant?"

A long pause. "Virginia is a very understanding
woman."

"I wonder if she would also understand that you
demanded Miss Hodges get an abortion."

A longer pause, then a reply from Grey delivered
with an ice James had not heard before. "No one would
believe a word you say. These claims would be

dismissed as the ravings of a madman. I would make sure of it."

James had anticipated this move too. "That might work with your wife, though I would not bet on it: Virginia knows me too well for that. But I certainly doubt it would work with your mistress's father."

"Good God," the Master said into the telephone.

"That's right. I suspect Sir Herbert would be rather less persuadable. These Whitehall mandarins tend towards the sceptical, don't they, Master? Professional requirement, you could say."

"You wouldn't dare."

"Wouldn't I? I thought you just said I was crazy. No telling what a crazy man might do. Besides, it would be very easy. Sir Herbert's ministry is just down the road these days, isn't it? I'm surprised you haven't run into him at high table."

"He wouldn't credit a word that came out of your mouth."

"Maybe not. But the suspicion would linger, wouldn't it? Sir Herbert might eventually ask his daughter if there was any truth in what that lunatic Zennor had suggested. And, as we know, the girl is talking."

"This is blackmail of the crudest kind, James."

"You can call it what you like. Now, why not get Forsyth to fetch you a pencil and paper?" James spelled out his demands slowly, as if Bernard Grey were a junior secretary, pad perched on her knee. He wanted a berth on the SS *Santa Clara*, which Hunter had just told him was due to leave Liverpool in the coming week, a US visa and a visiting research fellowship, with suitable accommodation, at Yale University. "None of that should give you too much trouble," James had added breezily. "And if it does, you can always give the Chancellor of Oxford University a call: he used to be the Foreign Secretary, after all."

Any delay on any of his demands and the letters James had already written and stamped would be on their way to Mrs Grey and Sir Herbert in the next post. "And don't try pulling strings with the Liverpool constabulary to get me arrested: I've left word with my new friends here at the port to post those letters for me if I don't come back and collect them." That last threat was a pure lie, but the white-haired social reformer and distinguished scholar had not risked proving it.

The calculus of interest, Harry used to call it. "Almost mathematical. You can work it out like an equation." That's what James had done, reasoning that Bernard Grey would soon see that acceding to James's demands was actually in his own best interests. Given what James knew, wasn't it obvious that the Master would want him out of the way?

CHAPTER
THIRTEEN

On board the SS Santa Clara,
somewhere in the North Atlantic. One week later
All around him, people were vomiting. Some were
puking directly over the rail and into the ocean; others,
apparently paralyzed by the horror of the experience,
simply emptied their guts where they stood, three, four
or five times.

James stood a distance away, wearing an expression
that, had anyone noticed it, would have appeared
unnervingly serene. He was so relieved to be on this
ship, he could not care less about a swell so big it was
sending waves over the ship, crashing onto this deck
and several below. This sea, no matter how rough, was
preferable to dry land because it could do for him what
static, stationary *terra firma* could not: take him closer
to America and to Florence.

During that brief sojourn in Liverpool he wrote to
Florence several times a day, writing and rewriting,
eventually settling on a bland few lines that scarcely
expressed a fraction of what he was feeling, before
addressing the air-mailed letters with a simple, hopeful
"care of Yale University". Now, on the *Santa Clara*, he
carried on the habit, thinking of his wife and child in

every minute of every hour. During the long, uneventful hours of smooth passage, during the meandering conversations with the enemy aliens on board, the Germans and Italians, some of whom had been resident in Britain for decades, set now for deportation to Canada — including one watery-eyed old man originally from Frankfurt who made a point of saluting when referring to "King George" — when the sun came up in the morning and when he finally pulled the covers over him in the darkness of his tiny bunk, from the start of the day to its end, he thought of his new, small family and how he had come to lose them.

The long, empty hours allowed him to go over and over the strange sequence of events that had begun with him sculling on the Thames one bright July morning and had him sailing across the Atlantic less than a week later. He examined in minute detail those last twenty-four hours in Oxford, concluding that little of it had been accidental. Grey had admitted that Florence's departure had been a team effort, that the Greys and their unnamed co-conspirators had worked together to ensure she would get away safely. It followed, then, that little or nothing about that day was as it had first seemed. He reconsidered it all in the light of Grey's confession. That morning visit from Virginia Grey and her kind-hearted suggestion that he visit the Bodleian Library? Surely a delaying tactic, designed to gobble up crucial hours when he might otherwise have been en route to Liverpool. Similar logic surely explained why someone — Rosemary Hyde perhaps? — had intercepted and moved the postcard from his letter box to his college pigeon-hole, thereby keeping James in the dark just long enough to deny him the chance to catch Florence and Harry before they set sail. (He wondered why Rosemary had not simply stolen the card altogether: perhaps some curious sense of honour prevented her, or whoever it was, depriving a man of a farewell message from his wife.) How elaborate had this strategy of delay become? He half-suspected the half-blind Magnus Hook had staged their little collision on Parks Road on purpose.

When he was not replaying the immediate past he was flagellating himself with the possible future. What if he had got out just in time, abandoning England days or weeks before a German invasion? It was a contemptible act, he told himself, an act of desertion if not outright treachery. He had taken up arms to defend Spain, for heaven's sake, and yet had not been prepared to stand and fight for his own country. He had deserted England in its direst hour. He was a rat jumping off a sinking ship and he hated himself for it. Who cares if he had not passed the army's bloody medical? There would have been something he could do. What if Nazi troops tried to march on London, the way Franco's men had sought to break into Madrid? James could have acted as a trainer, teaching the Local Defence Volunteers how to do what he, Harry Knox and the XII Internationals had done on the Madrid university campus. There might be battles to defend the coast, shootouts on Southwold Beach, trench warfare in Eastbourne — and he could have helped. So what if a piece of paper classified him as a D1? He would have

163

been able to hold a gun and shoot, more effectively than most of the codgers in the LDV anyway. Better than Bernard bloody Grey at any rate. The British resistance would need every man they could get, especially those with fighting experience. And he would be far away, safely across the Atlantic thinking only of himself.

And yet he had not hesitated to board the *Santa Clara*. His prime mission was to find Florence and Harry. It didn't feel like a selfish act, even though his own need to see them again was overwhelming. It also felt like a duty, a sacred obligation. He loved his country and was ready to make any sacrifice for it. But he felt exactly the same way about his family. Even though both had rejected him.

He turned such thoughts over in his mind for hours at a stretch. Some, especially among the crew, lamented the tedium but James had no such complaint. One gift of a Quaker childhood: a high boredom threshold. Besides, on at least one occasion during that ten-day voyage, there was a moment of high drama.

One came after the *Santa Clara* had been at sea for a little over four days. They had already bade farewell to their warship escort and were now officially unprotected and on their own. The powers that be had decided that, at this distance, they were beyond the reach of the long arm of the enemy. A crewman who had become something of a pal to James — a Pole called Andrzej, early twenties and a fanatical anti-communist — had already tipped him the wink that something was up, that there had been an outbreak of alarmed activity on the bridge. He spoke to James as a fellow soldier, once he had heard about his combat experience in Spain, granting him a respect which surprised James. He had assumed that Andrzej would regard him as a dirty communist for having taken up arms against Franco. But, as he slowly understood, there is a bond that unites men who have seen war and which separates them from those that have not. Far from providing James with any smug satisfaction, it reminded him that in the current, essential conflict he was a mere spectator.

Thanks to Andrzej's tip-off, James was not surprised when he heard the order ring out over the ship's address system, instructing everyone on board either to go down below or to remain stationary on deck. There was to be no visible movement.

Despite the order, James stayed close to Andrzej, watching as he removed the cover from the fixed gun on the starboard side of the ship. There was a great hush, as if the whole ship were watching and waiting, and then the grinding, wheezing sound of the boilers cranked up to maximum effort, so that the ship might forge ahead at speed. Still, Andrzej kept his hands on that gun. James was carrying his lifejacket but, unlike the handful of other passengers who remained frozen still on deck rather than risk movement by going down into the ship, bravado prevented him putting it on. All they could do was wait, hoping that somehow the bridge had been mistaken, that there were no enemy subs in this area, that the threat, if it had existed, had passed.

And then, at great speed, there was a foaming, hissing sound below. James leaned over the railing just in time to see a torpedo passing, just yards astern of the ship. Seconds later, there came another of these "tin fish", this one passing within six feet of the hull, certainly no more.

There was a massive jolt, the ship lurching to one side — but it had not been hit. Andrzej explained that they had been saved by the torpedo having turned upright, rather than horizontal, at the last moment. James imagined such a feat, like a circus seal standing on its hind paws, and gave thanks for such good luck. His gratitude, he realized once he felt it, was not that his own life had been saved — but that the life of Florence's husband and Harry's father had been spared. Did that make any sense? It did to him.

Suddenly, hands on the lower decks were hurling white canisters overboard, which exploded with a judder that made the spine shake, as if the liner had just hit a rock. "Depth charges," Andrzej explained.

The Pole waited a little longer, concluding that the U-boat was "too chicken" to surface, doubtless because the Germans wrongly believed the *Santa Clara* was still under armed escort. He replaced the gun cover and went to check down below. James looked at his hands and saw that his fist was still balled around the lifejacket he had been holding since the order had first come across the ship's address system. His knuckles were white. As he relaxed his fingers, he saw his palm was shiny with sweat, the strap of the jacket where he had clutched it drenched.

Two more days passed before they saw icebergs, the first glimpse of something solid after nearly a week at sea. James imagined how Harry — who had surely passed through this same stretch of water a few days earlier — had reacted on seeing these majestic, almost mythical structures: mountains of glistening white ice, the brilliance of the white rendered dazzling by the bright sunshine. Some had broken up, their fragments, mammoth in themselves, taking on all kinds of shapes in the imagination. He pictured Florence pointing at these very shards, comparing that one to a shark, the other to a submarine and that one there to a fairytale castle. In the hour after he first saw them, James opened up his notebook and wrote a poem for his son: "The Iceberg Dragon". He doubted it was much good as literature. But he liked imagining the moment he would read it to Harry, picturing the boy laughing at the story of the hapless seagull who had landed on what it thought was ice only to find himself lost in the fiery mouth of a dragon.

They had been at sea eight long days when they first saw land ahead, passing eventually through the straits of Belle Isle and then along the coasts of Labrador and Newfoundland. The St Lawrence estuary was gorgeous, as stunning as any of the Highland lochs: tall mountains, broken up by the occasional clearing on the wooded slopes, containing a small settlement of twenty or so wooden huts or white cottages, with a church spire towering above them.

It was beautiful but James Zennor had no time for beauty. As the ship finally came to dock in Quebec, ten days after it had grunted and groaned its way out of the mouth of the Mersey, he was impatient to set his foot on the North American continent and begin the final stage of his journey. Only the Canadian border with the United States and the train journey south to New Haven stood in his way now. Soon he would walk into Yale and be reunited with his wife and child.

CHAPTER
FOURTEEN

London

She had turned her back on him now, the clear signal that at last she was sated. He looked closely at her skin, paler than he was used to in the American girls he had had. Not that she was a girl; twenty years too late for that. Lady was not quite right either, though that would be the word most would use for the wife of an eminent Tory MP. But during the last hour and a half she had behaved like the most outlandish whore.

Taylor Hastings let his eye rest on a dark spot beneath her right shoulder blade. What was that? A birthmark? A mole? A beauty spot? It was far from the only one. In fact, now that he looked closely, there were little imperfections all over. The skin on her arms was not taut; the traces of past pregnancies were visible on her hips and thighs. Very different to the young flesh he was used to. And yet he didn't mind. The opposite: her age excited him, somehow confirming with every caress that he was sleeping with another man's wife.

She was breathing heavily now, falling into a deep, exhausted sleep. She had tired his body, as always, but she had not been able to still his mind. The dinner had ended more than three hours ago but the thrill of it remained fresh.

Back in the States they always liked to talk about big names and he had grown up among plenty of them at St Albans and Princeton. But no names as big as this. He smiled at the thought of who had steered the evening's conversation, acting as informal chairman: only the fifth Duke of Wellington! How do you like that, Pa? That beats the Deputy Undersecretary of State for Near-East Paperclips?

He had sat next to a Lord Redesdale, father of the famous Mitford girls. "You ought to meet my daughter," he had said to Taylor within minutes of shaking hands. "Not Decca, she's mad of course. Red as a bullfighter's cape. But Diana. She's sound."

He had counted several other lords — though, he had learned tonight, you were meant to call them "peers". There was a Galloway and an Agnew, though he suspected one of them was a "sir". Or rather a knight.

Who cared if it was confusing? It was magnificent. Such lustre gathered in one room: newspaper writers and publishers of pamphlets trading ideas with aristocrats and eminent industrialists. This, Taylor reflected, must be how a London salon in the eighteenth century would have been: men of stature seated around a fine polished table, the room heavy with wealth and pedigree.

But not, Taylor Hastings noticed, confidence. Anna's husband, Reginald Rawls Murray, member of parliament for some far-off part of Scotland and animating genius behind the Right Club, was energetic in his efforts to lift the spirits, but the faces gathered around him remained stubbornly sombre.

"Churchill has us on the run," was a remark offered more than once. The arrival of the new prime minister and the departure of Chamberlain, humiliated over the failure in Norway, represented a grievous, perhaps terminal blow to their cause: the campaign for what they called "an honourable, negotiated peace". Now the nation's leading warmonger was in Downing Street, seizing on Hitler's march through the Low Countries and recent conquest of France as proof positive of what he had said all along: that Germany was intent on global domination and could not be appeased, only defeated.

But Churchill's threat was much more direct than that. He had wasted no time in rounding up and jailing suspected Nazi sympathizers under the dreaded Defence Regulation 18B, a move which had badly depleted the ranks of the Right Club. Around the table tonight were those whose status and rank made them harder fish to catch or who had been careful to present themselves as "anti-war" rather than "pro-Hitler". But tonight, in private and among friends, there had been no such need to conceal their true views.

Murray had set the tone early enough when, in a bid to lighten the mood, he had asked the assembled to join him in a chorus of the country's much-loved, if unofficial, national anthem. He began humming the tune of "Land of Hope and Glory", but then, when it

171

came time to sing, he bade the table hush while he could present his new, alternative lyric:

> "*Land of dope and Jewry*
> *Land that once was free*
> *All the Jew boys praise thee*
> *Whilst they plunder thee.*"

There had been a roar of approval and a banging on the table, spreading a wide smile across Murray's face. Encouraged, he went on:

> "*Land of Jewish finance*
> *Fooled by Jewish lies*
> *In press and books and movies*
> *While our birthright dies.*"

That, though, was one of the few moments of good cheer. The consensus that night held that the Jews had won yet again, dragging the country into war — and that to suggest seeking peace while Churchill was hailing the country's "finest hour" and speaking of a "Battle of Britain" was doomed, if not suicidal. The phoney war was over; the real war was on in earnest. To stand against it now was to be branded a traitor.

All of which contributed to a gloomy mood in the Russian Tea Room. Murray was the only man present who remained both jolly and overt in the expression of his views, confident both that the room contained only those who could be trusted and that the privilege of his seat in parliament would protect him from the loathsome Regulation 18B.

The rest threw out various general observations of disgust and despair. "For years, all that we value has been in peril," said one man with a title, who might have been an earl or a viscount, a word which Taylor remembered came with a silent "s", but whose suit looked surprisingly shabby. He rattled off the list: the Empire, Christian beliefs, England as the land of freeborn Englishmen and of freeborn Englishmen alone. "All of that has long been under threat — from the Bolsheviks, from foreigners, from the masters of international finance." The last phrase delivered with a knowing look. "But this war will destroy it, once and for all."

Why, then, had none of this gloominess infected him, Taylor wondered now, as the bedside clock nudged towards three in the morning. Partly it was the childish thrill of a young man allowed to sit at the grown-ups' table: he had been decades younger than everyone else there. Partly it was the secret knowledge that, after the food and wine, he would be savouring the host's wife, thanks to Murray's midweek habit of staying overnight at his club.

But mainly it was a vague sense, one not fully formed until he articulated it now, that he was somehow immune from the pessimism around the table. He had great sympathy for these Brits; but he was an American and in America the game was all still to play for. In the US, unlike Britain, it was not yet — to use the two words that had come up again and again over dinner — too late.

Taylor shifted to a cooler patch of the bed, taking care to move stealthily so that Anna would not stir, wondering for a passing moment if Murray himself had ever done to his wife what Taylor had just done — wondering indeed if Murray had ever even slept in this bed. There certainly seemed to be a separate, gentleman's bedroom on the other side of the landing. Maybe it was simply a condition of being an American that made him more upbeat than his fellow diners this evening. Wasn't that what set most Americans, certainly those his age, apart from their British cousins: that sense that their best days were ahead, not behind them?

No, it was more personal than that. In the end, Taylor had been in a good mood when all around him were down in the mouth because he had the growing feeling — almost a premonition — that he was about to play a part in events of great import.

It had been budding even as he had slicked the brilliantine through his hair at Cadogan Square, this sense of imminence, but it had been confirmed by Murray several times through the evening. At intervals, the old man had winked in Taylor's direction, sometimes offering opaque asides: "Not the same for you though, eh, Hastings?" or "You're in a rather different boat, wouldn't you say?" By the time the waiters cleared away the main course — beef in a gravy more luxurious than the thin brown liquid served up at these so-called British Restaurants around town —

Murray had left no doubt in the mind of anyone in the room that he had seen something in young Taylor Hastings. This dinner was only their second meeting, the first being that introductory tea at the Savoy with Anna, and yet Murray was treating him like a trusted confidant. Once the room was clear of serving staff, the MP had tapped his glass with the side of a dessert spoon.

"I hope you've all had a splendid dinner," Murray began, to a murmur of approval around the table. "As you know, we've already welcomed our guest, Taylor Hastings from the colonies." A polite smile from the American. "But I know you will agree with me in saying that we strongly hope young Mr Hastings will be more than a guest in our country and more than a guest in our cause." A couple of "hear, hears", including, Taylor was glad to note, from the Duke of Wellington.

"So, for that reason, it is my great honour to present Mr Hastings with membership of our little society. In accepting it, he joins us in the first rank of those fighting for England. For the real England, that is. And against the real enemy. Not our fellow Aryan, the great nation of Germany, but the race which has been at war with Christendom from the very beginning. So let me present Mr Hastings with the crest that marks him as a valued member of the Right Club."

There was applause as Taylor rose from his chair and walked the three or four paces to where Murray stood waiting to greet him. The MP gave him a strong handshake and then passed him a metal badge.

Hastings looked at the dulled silver brooch. It showed an eagle killing a snake, beside two capital letters: "PJ".

"Who's PJ?" Taylor asked, without thinking.

"My good fellow, you surely know the motto of the Right Club, conveying our purpose in its pithiest form. PJ stands for 'Perish Judah'."

CHAPTER
FIFTEEN

My darling Florence,
I feel as if I am writing into a void. I know you are in
America, I know you are at Yale. And yet I have no idea
of your situation, of where or how you are living. The
last time I knew this sensation was four years ago when
I had been rash and stupid and knew only that you were
in Berlin. Your decision was right then, though it took
me some time to see it. I understand why you could not
be straight and truthful with me then: we had only just
met. But now we are man and wife and yet you still felt
able to deceive me. It may be like Berlin again: that, in
the end, I will see that you were right and I was wrong.
But that is not how it feels at present. Not least because
in Berlin it was only our romance — our fledgling
romance, you might say — that was at stake. Now there
is a child involved. Your child, yes. But mine too . . .

James screwed the piece of paper into a tight paper ball
and put it in his pocket, to join the other letters to
Florence he had drafted and aborted. Too angry, even if
the anger was controlled. He wanted her back, didn't
he? Well, letters like that would never do the trick. He
dashed off something shorter and simpler, telling

Florence that he was looking for her and that he would not rest until they were back together, once again addressing the envelope "care of Yale University", just as he had countless times before, whether from the dockside at Liverpool, the harbour at Quebec or Penn Station in New York City.

"New Haven, New Haven! Next stop, New Haven."

It was the third time the guard had marched through the carriage making that announcement in the last twenty minutes. James was ready, his bag packed and above his head. He took another look out of the window, taking in the American countryside. In the several days he had spent on trains, hopping from Quebec to Montreal to Boston and now, at last, New Haven, he had alternated between two conflicting impressions. Most often he was struck by the vastness, the sheer scale of North America, where everything was wider and taller than in little England. He was used to the odd grand old man of a tree — there was one in his college quad, after all — but here you could pass whole forests of thick-trunked trees, majestically scraping the sky. The clouds themselves seemed to loom larger in skies that stretched further to the north, east and west. In America, God seemed to paint on a bigger canvas.

And then, less often, would come an unexpected jolt of familiarity. Perhaps it was his expectations that were at fault. With some shame he realized that he had pictured a land of deserts, cactuses, saloon bars and fighting Indians, as you would see at the pictures. But in Boston there had been elegant buildings in solid grey

178

stone that would have sat comfortably in Edinburgh or Manchester. The train had stopped at Providence and Mystic, names that might have come from a fairytale, but had also passed through New London. It made the place confusing: at once both utterly like and unlike England.

And of course the biggest difference was not in the physical details that caught his eye, the motor cars as big as boats — including one blue, wooden-sided monster he had spotted when the train was chugging alongside a road outside Boston and which a fellow passenger had identified as a "station-wagon" — or the perennial chewing gum in the mouths of porters and ticket collectors. The biggest difference was the expressions on the faces of the people. They were not tight or drawn, as they were, constantly, in England but open and relaxed: mothers smiling at their children, businessmen doing the crossword puzzle in the morning paper, all of them going about their ordinary lives, worrying about paying the bills or cutting the back lawn, rather than fearing for their country's very survival. Here, war was so far away, it might as well have been happening on another planet.

There was a bright sound of a whistle and the exhalation of a fresh cloud of white smoke. The rhythm of the pistons was slowing down, the train heaving itself to a halt, like an aged rower on the river running out of puff. Through the billowing steam he could see the name on the station platform: New Haven.

He felt his jaw clench three or four times in quick session, an involuntary move that used to precede every race on the river. During the long voyage from Liverpool and the journey south from Canada, he had not had to prepare himself: he could think about the past and concentrate on reaching his destination. But now, as he stepped off the train, he had arrived. New Haven was home to Yale, which meant she was here. It was quite possible he would run into her any moment now; she might even be at the station. He spotted a balloon, the string held by a boy around Harry's age. Next to him was a woman buying something from a cart. (He squinted to read a sign that said "Pretzels", a word he had never seen and could not pronounce.) She was not the right height for Florence — few women were — but the sight of a mother and child, and the possibility that, logically speaking, it could have been Florence and Harry, hit him hard. He looked away.

Only now did he notice the station itself, the ceiling almost as high as St Pancras in London. But where such places in England were permanently drab and dirty — the shabbiness exacerbated by nearly a year of war — this was clean and stylish, the ceilings, from which fancy chandeliers were suspended, elaborately decorated in a complex pattern of gold. Even the rooves of the tunnels leading from the platforms were clad in gleaming stainless steel. Not for the first time, he felt as if he had left England, the ageing mother country, for America, the vigorous young son.

Once he had popped his letter in a blue post-box, he looked down at the note he had scribbled in his book. *459 College Street.* This was where Grey had arranged rooms for him, a late addition to the list of demands

James had put to the college Master in return for his silence. He asked a porter for directions, struggling first to be understood and then to understand: divided by a common language indeed.

With just a single knapsack, picked up in Liverpool, he had travelled lightly enough to walk. The short journey up George Street took him to College Street, a right turn and then he was inside the university district. What he saw astounded him. He had been expecting a place bursting with 1940s modernity, a *Flash Gordon* landscape of shiny towers, strange shapes and clean lines.

True, the cars were once again something to behold. Vast, bulky machines that moved like mighty beasts of the jungle, hippos or rhinos who would trample over any creature reckless enough to stray into their path. But the university itself seemed as rooted in the ancient past as Oxford.

The streets were lined with faux-medieval arches and stone walls, punctuated by churches with steeples and Gothic spires, as if by the wave of a magician's wand an entire thirteenth century English university town had been moved across the ocean and planted on this other continent. He peered inside one college building at random (it might have been called Calhoun though he was barely taking in the names). There was a quad, complete with a perfectly maintained lawn. Two tall, fair-haired men passed him, both carrying tennis rackets, just as their counterparts might do back home. He passed a grand entrance to a tower that clearly aspired to be a castle, bearing the motto *Lux et Veritas*, carved in a pale stone. Perhaps an expert would be able to see, on closer inspection, that the likes of Bingham Hall or the Battell Chapel belonged to the last or even the current century, rather than seven hundred years earlier. But to the layman's eye, the illusion was complete.

He glanced across the street, spotting with relief the number 459 — attached not to the grand structure with pillared portico next door, but to a relatively modest colonial-style house, clad in pale clapboard. He had half-expected Grey to put him up in a college dormitory, like some of the younger fellows back home. The last thing James needed now was small-talk with scholars, eagerly making awkward inquiries about his precise "field of research" at Yale. For the short time he hoped to be here, a room in an anonymous boarding house with regular meals would suit him fine.

But the comfort of that delusion was not allowed to persist for long. A knock on the door, answered by a butler — who, to James's startled surprise, was a negro in late middle age — soon revealed that this was no boarding house but the Elizabethan Club. With its chairs in well-worn leather, the same shade as the elbow-patches Florence's father had taken to wearing on his tweed jackets in a nod towards wartime thrift, and well-stocked fireplace, even now on a warm, humid day in high summer, it too might have been winched into the skies from Oxford, flown across the Atlantic then dropped, unaltered, on this street in New Haven, Connecticut.

182

The butler took his name and said that they had been anticipating his arrival. He apologized that Dr Zennor would have to make do with the steward's quarters, since there was no other accommodation in "the Clubhouse". It took James a moment to realize that the butler was referring not to some sporting pavilion, but this very building. As he huffed his way up the stairs, the servant delivered a potted lecture on "the Lizzie", founded nearly thirty years earlier by a wealthy undergraduate who yearned for a little oasis of calm where literary-inclined students might speak about the arts and suchlike. He stopped on the middle landing to point out the vault where the club kept its priceless collection of Shakespeare Folios, including one of the three surviving copies of the 1604 *Hamlet*. James imagined the select membership of the Lizzie as the American counterparts of the effete, privileged young men at Christ Church or Magdalen whom he had gone to such lengths to avoid when he was a new undergraduate, nervous, naïve and just off the train from Bournemouth. It had not been all that long ago, at the tail end of the 1920s; but it seemed like a different epoch.

The room, however, was monastic in its simplicity. There was a bed, a chair, a desk and a basin and not much else. The asceticism of it appealed to him, but he did fleetingly wonder about Grey's motives. Was he punishing James with this garret room, or had he deliberately wanted him away from the heart of Yale life, where he might meet fewest people — so keeping his secrets to himself?

James sat on the bed and wondered where he should begin. It was a Sunday, which made it impossible simply to present himself at an administrative office and ask where he might find the Oxford families. If this were Oxford, he would select a college at random, pop in and ask a porter, who were, after all, the best-informed people in the university.

He splashed some water on his face then headed down the stairs, two at a time. He was striding down College Street, deciding that he would stop at the first college he saw — the butler had told him there were ten to choose from — when he heard it: a drifting melody from across the road, the universally familiar sound of a church choir.

Among those Oxford mothers, there was bound to be at least one woman pious enough to attend, maybe even to give thanks for their safe passage across the Atlantic. Not Florence of course; she wouldn't be seen dead in church. But someone who, on hearing James identify himself, might smile warmly and say, "Oh yes, I saw young Harry just this morning. They're staying two minutes from here; I'll take you there myself if you would like."

He ran up the few steps leading to the doorway and went inside. To his surprise, the church was packed, every space on the wooden benches taken. No church in Oxford would get a turnout like this on a warm Sunday in July. Perhaps this was what the experts meant when they said America was a country founded by "the Protestants of the Protestants" — religious zealots whose zeal, it seemed, lived on.

He stood at the back, loitering by the door, suddenly self-conscious. Should he affect to be a churchgoer, late to arrive but here in earnest? Or pose as a tourist, come to admire the gold-inlaid walls and pillars and to gaze at the half-dome above the altar, an artful compromise between grandeur and modesty?

James did a quick scan of the faces before him and recognized none of them. Not that he could conclude from that that there was no one here from Oxford: there might well be several, he just didn't know them. Inwardly, he cursed the habits he had fallen into since his return from Spain. He had been fairly sociable as a student, avoiding the aristocratic crowd, but jolly enough with everyone else. He was popular in the rowing club; Daisy's friends had always liked him. But after his return, he had turned inward; could not be bothered remembering names, barely even noticed faces. And now, when he needed the help of someone familiar, he was paying the price.

The music had ended and a cleric had taken his place at the pulpit. White-haired and in his early sixties by James's reckoning, he looked more earnest than forbidding. The man cleared his throat, then said in an unexpectedly strong voice, "My fellow members of Yale. I'm glad to see so many of you here — proof, I guess, that you've all had a week so full of sin that you've rushed here to repent." A ripple of gentle laughter. "Well, you're all welcome. This is God's house, which means it's your house. Welcome, welcome."

The man's style of speech was a surprise too. He was much more informal than any vicar James had heard speak in England. Even the way he stood seemed to be looser, as if he were wearing more comfortable shoes.

"Now you heard the lesson we read earlier. From Isaiah," — *Eye-zay-ah* — "chapter two, verse four." There was a rustling of tissue-thin pages, as many in the congregation consulted their bibles.

The vicar's voice boomed out loud, the word of God delivered with an American accent: "'And he shall judge among the nations, and shall rebuke many people: and they shall beat their swords into ploughshares, and their spears into pruning-hooks: nation shall not lift up sword against nation, neither shall they learn war any more.' " He paused letting the words linger a while. Then he spoke again.

"I do not believe we can argue with those words. I believe their meaning is as clear as a freshwater stream: 'in the last days', when we are on the brink of redemption, we will put aside the tools of war. They play no part in the Second Coming of Jesus Christ our Lord. If we are to be worthy of His return, if we are to live life as it is meant to be lived, then we should start now, making ploughshares from swords and pruning hooks from spears. We would grow food, instead of death. We would water the ground with God's sweet rain, not with the blood of our fellow man."

There was an emphatic "amen" from some in the room and an unmistakable silence from the rest. James was slowly becoming aware that this was no ordinary Sunday service.

The preacher looked down at the lectern, a tiny gesture that suggested he was coming to a close. "I have

186

been chaplain here for most of the last decade. You all know me well and you know my views. They are best summarized not with words, but by our Lord's eloquent action. A small action, as it happens, but one that is still so radical, still so revolutionary. Struck on one side of his face, Jesus did not hit back. No, he did not. Instead he offered his other cheek. That's right, he turned the other cheek. And that — that action that is so small but so large — is how we will abolish war. Even when we are provoked — and yes, our consciences are provoked by the violence in Europe — we will resist the urge to shed more blood. We will not fight war with war. As Isaiah says, 'neither shall we learn war any more'."

The words were very familiar to James. How many Quaker meetings had he sat through where the speaker, often his father, had repeated those same points, citing the same sources? The only difference this time, besides the accent and the charisma of the delivery, emanated from the congregation. James was used to hearing the case for pacifism presented to a room full of pacifists. Yet here was a man preaching to a crowd which, it was obvious, was anything but converted. The pastor had his supporters, but there was a low, unvoiced hum of discontent throughout that was undeniable. Now the preacher moved to address it.

"As I say, you know my views. You don't need to hear them again. And I know the Yale fellowship is not of one mind on this topic, that our community of scholars has been debating this question fiercely. That's how it should be. And I want that debate to live here, in God's house. For as the holy texts tell us, 'These and these are the words of the living God.' These *and* these. There is always more than one view.

"Which is why I'm sharing this pulpit today. I have invited Dr Ernest West from the Philosophy Department to speak about the theory of the just war. Not that I think there can be such thing —" He stopped himself with a smile. "Forgive me, I'm used to having the floor all to myself. Dr West, please come and address the congregation."

James watched as the room seemed to shift, a wave of energy rippling through it. Some sat forward in their seats, others pulled back and folded their arms into a posture of sullen disapproval.

The new man at the pulpit was younger and more uncertain. He was clasping a text, which shook slightly in his hands.

"I'd like to thank Pastor Theodore Lowell for welcoming me here today," he began, as if addressing the wood of the lectern. "And I come before you humbled by the scale of the task. I want to persuade you that the right place for the United States of America is by the side of those Europeans fighting for their lives and against the tyranny of Herr Hitler and his Third Reich."

"America first!"

James swung around to his left in search of the heckler, but the acoustics had confused him. The voice could have come from any of the wooden benches on that side of the church. He looked up and saw that the speaker too was confused, thrown off balance by what he had heard. Dr West gathered himself and looked up to face his audience.

"'America first', you say and I understand that. I agree with it too. America should always put its interests first. But I tell you, this war *is* about our interests. Only Britain now stands between us and the Nazi menace. If Britain falls, then Germany will control the Atlantic. We could wake up any week now, any day now, with Nazi warships in Boston harbour and U-boat submarines off New York."

The heckler was silenced by that and the hush of the church seemed to catch the speaker by surprise.

"And let's remember that Germany will not be alone in this part of the world. It has friends — in Mexico and Argentina and throughout Latin America. Just imagine what Hitler would be capable of with a network of military bases throughout that continent. I say to you, we would face the very same threat now faced by our British cousins: bombs. A Blitzkrieg could come from the south, German bombs landing on San Diego or Houston or Miami, even, who knows, Chicago. So I do put America first. I put American safety first."

James noticed that the man's voice was less nervy now; he was beginning to hit his stride. "That's why we have a direct, vital interest in making sure Europe does not get swallowed up in Nazi tyranny. America cannot exist alone on this side of the Atlantic, hiding away from the world."

"Warmonger!"

The same heckler or a different one, James could not tell. Now there were a few cries in response: "Pipe down!" "We came here to hear him, not you!"

James noticed that the pastor did nothing to impose order on his church, but was watching the unfolding scene with an indulgent smile.

Dr West chose to ignore the last interruption and press on. "We cannot hide ourselves away. We need Europe. Not just to buy our goods. Though I have to say America will only be the leading power of this twentieth century if we sell and trade with the rest of the world. And there will be no trade with Herr Hitler's empire. No, we need a Europe that holds to the same ideals as we do."

"Our ideal should be peace!"

"Of course it is. But you cannot make a pact with the Devil. And we should be clear what kind of enemy we face. 'Know thine enemy', that's what the Bible tells us, doesn't it, Pastor Lowell? And there can be no denying that we face a new and terrible enemy in Adolf Hitler and his Nazi party. America will not be able to live in a world where such brutality holds supreme. As President Roosevelt —"

"Rosenfeld!"

"As President *Roosevelt* has argued so forcefully, it is a delusion, a fantasy, to think that we can let America become, I quote, 'a lone island in a world dominated by the philosophy of force'. Our ideals as Americans, the very ideals set out by our founding fathers —"

"'Beware of foreign entanglements', that's what Washington said!"

190

"I know what he said: you don't have to shout his words at me. But these are different times. There was no threat then equal to the threat we face today, a dictator bent on ruling the world."

There was more commotion now, as a small group to James's right attempted to start a chorus of "America first!" James fought the urge to stand up, march over to the pulpit and deliver a speech of his own. Did these people have no idea what was happening across the sea? He had left a country already at war, its men either at the front or preparing to defend the homeland; a place plunged into unbroken darkness at night, where people, including him, were digging holes in their gardens to shelter from bombs; where even a two-year-old boy like Harry was told to carry a gas mark lest Hitler attempt to fill the air with poison; where the enemy was a matter of miles away, just twenty-two of them in fact, Dover to Calais.

Yet here in New Haven war was a debating topic, with arguments to be made for and against. This was how Britain itself had been three or four years ago, back when Chamberlain reckoned he could make peace with Hitler. There had been debates like this, plenty of them, at the Oxford Union and elsewhere, with young gentlemen making speeches about whether they would fight for "King and country" and all that. But not any more. That argument was over.

In the United States, however, here in this chapel, the argument was just beginning. He was suddenly aware, more keenly than he had ever been before, that Britain truly did stand alone. Stalin and the Soviet

191

Union had become Hitler's allies; Italy had joined in, declaring war on Britain a matter of weeks ago; France, Belgium, Holland and Luxembourg had fallen to the Germans. And America was still debating with itself.

It struck James with sudden, painful force. Britain was on the brink of extinction. If it were to survive, if its people were not to live under the boot-heel of the Gestapo, they would have to defeat the German menace with their own bare hands.

He didn't wait for the speaker to finish, leaving him instead to take on the hecklers over whether Roosevelt was agitating for war as an excuse to build up the might of the federal government.

As he got up to leave, he caught sight of something that stopped him in his tracks. Someone he recognized. A face there, then gone. He scanned the congregation again only to see what he had seen before: the same sea of undifferentiated, unfamiliar faces. But the vague sense of recognition, someone spied in his peripheral vision, lingered. He craned slightly, to see around a pillar, but found nothing.

As quietly as he had entered, he retreated to the chapel door and left.

CHAPTER
SIXTEEN

The gentle tap on the door did not wake him, though the offer of a cup of "the Lizzie's own tea" was welcome. He had woken early, relieved that today was Monday: that offices would be open, that all he needed to do was find the right secretary, in front of the right card index, who would swiftly run through the list of Oxford children and their new, temporary homes. And soon after that, he told himself, he would have Florence and Harry back in his arms. Today would be the day they were reunited. What he told himself was the hardest part — the shock, the separation, the long journey across the Atlantic — would be over. Whether Florence would see it that way, whether she would immediately embrace him as if nothing had happened, whether the mere fact of his having come all this way would nullify the concerns that had driven her away in the first place — on those questions James preferred not to linger.

He washed and dressed quickly, taking directions for the old campus, a quadrangle of lawns and redbrick colonial buildings that were neither modern, nor ancient in the Oxford sense but rather of an eighteenth-century colonial style rarely glimpsed in

England. He found the administrative building and went inside, following the signs.

The Dean's office boasted an outer area roomy enough for two secretaries and which, James noted, was probably twice the size of Bernard Grey's entire study. Clearing his throat, he announced himself.

"Hello, my name is Dr James Zennor, here to take up a fellowship from Oxford," he began, attempting his most charming smile. "I've come about the Oxford children."

To his great relief, the woman — in early middle age and with a wave of brunette hair so unmoving it appeared to be sculpted from rock — smiled back. Encouraged, he explained his situation, that his wife and child were among the evacuees and that he had come to join them. Having learned his lesson in Liverpool, he asked if she might check her files and let him know where a Miss Florence Walsingham or Mrs Florence Zennor was now resident.

The secretary's relentlessly professional smile did not waver. "I'm afraid that won't be possible, Dr Zennor. These records are strictly private and confidential."

He had expected that. "Of course. I wouldn't ask you to divulge the details of anyone but my own immediate family. Here's my passport, just so there is no doubt as to my name. If my wife is here under her married name, it will be a simple matter of matching me with your records. I'm happy to wait." It was an effort to resist the urge he had to push past her and ransack the files himself, but he forced himself to take a couple of paces backward, deliberately relaxed.

"Sir, perhaps I was not clear," the secretary said, her face still frozen into a rictus of apparent delight. "The Dean has left very specific instructions that the Oxford children and their parents are here as guests of Yale and, as such, we cannot divulge any private information."

"But I am one of the parents! I am Harry's father. Harry Zennor. Just check your list." He gritted his teeth in an attempt to remain polite. "Please."

"Dr Zennor. If you would care to write to the Dean, I'm sure he will —"

"Ah, you need him to give authorization. I understand. Well, perhaps I could see him now, if he's available. The Dean, I mean."

"What I was going to say is that if you wrote to the Dean, he would explain to you what I have tried to explain."

"Could I speak to the Dean, please?" The temperature in his bloodstream was rising, he could feel it beginning to bubble.

"I'm sorry, sir, but the Dean is not available."

He advanced again, menacing. "He's behind that door, isn't he?"

"Sir, I'm going to have to ask you to step away from the desk."

"Now you listen to me," he said, leaning in. "I've just travelled across the Atlantic, and then from Canada all the way here. I want to see my wife and child. That's all."

"Please sir, step back. Otherwise, I will have to have you removed."

The woman stood up and moved rapidly to the empty desk behind her, where she reached for the telephone and, with her back to James, spoke hurriedly into it. She seemed genuinely frightened.

James retreated, aware that he had gone too far, that he had already made a hash of it. When the far door opened, he was not surprised to see a stocky man in a cheap uniform enter. Instinctively, James raised his hands, showing his palms in a gesture of surrender, and headed for the door.

Outside, in the sunshine, he wanted to howl with rage, to break a window with his fists, such was his frustration.

He walked briskly away, trying to formulate a plan. The silver lining was that he had clearly come to the right place; the secretary with the plastered-on smile had not looked at him blankly as she might have done: she knew about the Oxford children. The bad news was that her instructions had clearly been strict and unambiguous, as if he had asked her to breach a state secret. He wondered why.

He was pacing down College Street now, past the brick facades of the colleges and into a parade of modern-looking shops, as if he had stepped out of the eighteenth and into the twentieth century. He stopped by a "drugstore" that advertised a "soda fountain". He had seen one of those at the pictures, but could hardly believe it was real. He went inside.

The place was filled with students, sipping milkshakes or drinking coffee. James took a seat at a window table and looked at the options on the menu wedged between the salt and pepper pots: eggs fried, scrambled, boiled or poached; a three-egg omelette; buttermilk pancakes with blueberries optional; cheesecake, poundcake, pecan pie. On it went, promising a banquet, plates spilling over with food and glasses filled to the brim, enough to stuff the bellies of the greediest, most gluttonous diners. A three-egg omelette! Three! That was eleven days' rations blown in a single breakfast. And what would it be like to eat a cake that was made from real butter? He could hardly remember how such a delicacy tasted.

By the door was a stack of newspapers: the *Yale Daily News*. The main story on the front page told of the imminent retirement of the university football coach; only lower down and far less prominent was an item related to the war. There had been a conference in Havana of all the governments of the western hemisphere, apparently to discuss their common interest in "neutrality". Neutrality? The very word made him sick. The Nazis were on the rampage: to be neutral was simply to step out on their way. You saved your own skin and someone else got clobbered.

An unnerving thought came to him then: he was as alone in this country as Britain was alone in the world.

Though he was hungry, he ignored the waitress heading his way, got up and walked out, feeling disgusted. He kept walking until drawn by a sign promising "Imported Pipes, Tobaccos and Cigars". It was called the Owl Shop, but it also appeared to have a bar. Even though it was not yet nine thirty in the morning, and he strongly doubted they would serve a real drink, he suddenly craved one. But a cigarette would be a decent consolation prize. He went in and bought a packet of Pall Malls.

He lit up straight away, sucking the smoke deep into his lungs, then, at the very moment he should have exhaled, breathed in deeper — a trick he had learned from Harry Knox and not forgotten — and gazed ahead, unseeing, as the nicotine snaked its way through his system.

"Can I help you, sir?"

It was the man behind the counter. Without realizing it, James had been staring. Except only now did he see how young this bartender was. Slight and with bad skin, he looked like a schoolboy.

James forced himself out of his cigarette reverie and asked, "Do you work here?"

"Excuse me?"

"Sorry. You just seem rather —"

"Yes, sir. Gotta work my way through college. Three mornings, five evenings a week." James had not worked during term-time as an undergraduate at Oxford, but he had during the vacations: he had once sold ice-creams on Bournemouth beach. "Can I can get you something, sir?"

James shook his head. He picked up a copy of the *New Haven Evening Register* left discarded on the counter, scavenging hungrily for items of war news. There was a brief story about the Duke of Windsor, "formerly King Edward VIII of England", was how the paper put it, taking up his new post as governor of the

Bahamas. Good riddance to the appeasing bastard, James thought.

As the cigarette glowed its last, he admonished himself for falling at the very first hurdle, threatening the college secretary and keeper of the Oxford files that held the secret of his wife's location. What an idiot. Rosemary Hyde was right: his temper had become a liability. He was unable to control himself, even when he desperately needed to. What on earth could he do now?

He looked up, inadvertently making eye contact again with the bar-boy. The lad smiled, then glanced up at the old clock, clad in tobacco-stained wood on the wall. Counting the hours till his shift ends, James thought, I know that feeling . . .

Hold on. James stared at the clock. It was worth a try at least.

He took up a position on a low wall on the opposite side of the street. That way, he reasoned, he could keep an eye on the entrance of the administrative building without being too obvious. He had his newspaper, but not much else by way of distraction. Even a park bench would have been helpful; that way, he could have at least pretended to be having a rest or taking a nap. He had no visible reason to be sitting there, just hanging about.

So he paced, contemplating the entrances to the other buildings nearby, waiting for the hours to pass — and never letting his gaze slip for more than a second from the doorway he had come to watch. At one point, the porter who had ejected him earlier came out carrying a box, as if on delivery duty. James rapidly turned his back and lifted his newspaper higher.

Perhaps forty-five minutes had passed when, just before twelve-thirty, the secretary herself emerged. She had the prim, purposeful walk of a woman who had taken lessons in posture. He remembered Eileen demonstrating it for him in her small Oxford rooms, exaggerating the upright back and small, demure steps, the pair of them laughing at the absurd demands of a ladies' secretarial college.

She turned a sharp right down Elm Street but James waited till she was completely out of view. Never move too fast, that's what Jorge had said. *Allow for the possibility that a subject might turn around for one last look; that they might even double back, believing they have forgotten something. Unless the urgency is too great, give yourself room for error.* So James watched the second hand of his watch sweep a complete circuit before folding his paper and striding confidently towards the entrance, approaching the Dean's office as if for the first time. Once outside, to his great relief, he saw that his hunch had been right: now it was the second desk that was occupied, with a different secretary on duty. Just like the teenage bartender, they worked shifts.

He would try a different tack this time. "Good afternoon," he said quietly. "I'm a research fellow over at the Department of Psychology." He kept his eyes down, thinking of the likes of Magnus Hook, the socially inept, shuffling academics that were surely as common a species in Yale as they were in Oxford. He hoped even his accent would not be noticed, buried in the international scholars' language of mumbling.

"Yes? And how can I help?"

"My department is keen to undertake research into the effects of," he hesitated, recalling the book he had found at the Bodleian, the one Florence had been reading. "We're researching the effects on children of a long separation. This has been an area of interest for many years but we think we now have the ideal test subjects. Right here in Yale."

"I'm sorry, I didn't catch your name." Instead of a rictus smile, this woman's forehead was furrowed with a kind of puzzled concern.

"My name is Zennor," he said, the mumble dipping, he hoped, into the positively inaudible. "We would like to approach the Oxford mothers about their children taking part in a study. We would interview the children at the start, then at later intervals —"

"That sounds a very interesting idea."

James brightened, lifting his chin to face the woman directly. He was about to give her his charming smile before remembering Magnus Hook; he instead resumed staring at the floor and mumbled something about consulting the files so that he might contact the children.

"I'm afraid that won't be possible. The Dean has given strict undertakings to the families concerned, to the British authorities and to the State Department, regarding confidentiality."

"Yes, I appreciate that —"

"This is something you would have to discuss with the Dean directly."

He was about to explain why the nature of the research project did not allow for delay, that it was vital to record the children's sentiments at the very start of the period of separation, when instinct made him look up and meet her gaze. The second he did so, he knew it was a mistake. A thought passed across her face, as visible as a shadow. "Could you repeat your name for me, sir?"

"It's Zennor."

"Were you here earlier this morning, talking to my colleague?"

At that moment, a door from the inner office opened and a man — tall, long-faced, bespectacled and probably no older than James himself — stepped through. "What seems to be the trouble, Miss Rodgers?"

In desperation and knowing it was folly, James made a last attempt. "Are you the Dean?" He extended his hand but the man ignored it. "I'm Dr James Zennor from Oxford. I believe my wife and son are here at Yale and I need to find them."

"Are you the man who threatened one of the secretaries here today?"

"I'm begging you. Just tell me —"

"Either leave this office now or I will have you forcibly removed."

"Just let me see the bloody file!"

With surprising speed, the man advanced towards him, grabbing him by the elbow, then placed his other

202

hand on James's left shoulder. Unavoidably, James howled in pain, a sound that made Miss Rodgers scream.

That did it. The man tightened his grip, swivelling James's arm behind his back into an instant half-nelson, and frogmarched him back down the corridor.

The porter who had ejected James a few hours earlier appeared from the other end, looking aghast. "Assistant Dean, I'm right here."

"No need, Murphy. I have this under control." As if to prove his point, he raised James's arm a further two inches, making him cry out in even sharper pain.

Through the agony, James assessed his torturer. The Assistant Dean. A fellow athlete, he reckoned. Maybe an American football player, though he looked too thin for that. Maybe a rower. Whatever his training, he was a bastard and a sadist to boot.

They had reached the front entrance by now, the blue sky of a summer afternoon visible. James could see people rushing by, cars gliding along the road, the bustle of a busy American city. But he was about to be cast out into the desert — into a land where he knew no one and no one knew him, where every path led nowhere.

Now on the steps, with the porter watching them from just a few paces behind, James prepared himself for the moment of expulsion, picturing how it must look, like a drunk turfed out of a saloon bar in a western. His hand still on James's shoulder, the Assistant Dean leaned in closer. James could feel the man's breath in his ear, the plosive blasts as he spoke: "Meet me tonight. Seven o'clock at Frank Pepe's. I can help you." And with a last, hard shove to his back, the Assistant Dean despatched Dr James Zennor as if he were throwing out a sack of garbage.

CHAPTER
SEVENTEEN

London

The afternoon passed slowly, the work laborious. No matter how often Taylor Hastings looked up at the clock, it insisted on advancing with slow, heavy steps. He looked down at the pile of documents awaiting decoding. He could gallop through it, but a new pile would take its place: it wouldn't make the time pass any quicker.

He needed another excuse to go back into his briefcase. He had already retrieved a pencil sharpener from there; he couldn't pull that stunt again, not without his beetle-eyed colleague becoming curious. Yet he was desperate to look inside.

Help came in the form of a phone call, the distraction allowing him to bend low and retrieve what he wanted from his case. It was a card in an envelope, the card stiff, both in a rich shade of cream. He slipped it in among his papers, so that when, a few minutes later, the beetle-eyes were averted, he could steal another look at it.

Embossed at the top was the green, portcullis crest of the House of Commons. On the right, in the blue ink of an expensive fountain pen, today's date, the month rendered in roman numerals. Below that, the time of writing: ten am, an indication, along with the missing postmark on the envelope, that this message had been hand-delivered. Had Reginald Rawls Murray taken a risk by despatching it here, of all places? A calculated risk, Taylor concluded. Using the Royal Mail would have been far riskier, given the likelihood of surveillance and interception: thanks to Regulation 18B, Murray's mail was surely opened and checked routinely. Hand delivery by courier was much safer. If Murray had delivered it himself, so much the better.

On the other hand, if minimizing risk had been the MP's objective it would have been better to have dropped off the card at Taylor's home rather than here. But not if the message was urgent: Taylor wouldn't have seen it till late this evening. Very late, most likely, since he had "dinner" plans with Anna (though it was not food that was on the menu). It wouldn't have surprised him if Murray knew as much and so had opted to get this message to him at work. Looking at it again, it certainly seemed urgent.

Meet me tonight, House of Commons terrace. 7.30 pm. RRM.

The evening was close and sticky. Taylor Hastings had known a thousand such humid nights, the air choking with ragweed pollen, in Washington. But the Brits seemed to find it unbearable. Murray was constantly running his finger along his shirt collar, as if breaking a seal formed by the sweat on his neck.

206

But perhaps it wasn't just the weather that made him agitated. After ten minutes of chit-chat on the terrace — admiring the view over to the South Bank, eyeing up County Hall, watching the river in the still-bright evening — Murray finally got down to business. What was it with the English, always feeling obligated to pretend that a transaction between parties was really a conversation among friends?

"The situation's getting awfully tight for us, Hastings, I'm sure you appreciate that. Awfully tight. They've banged up Diana and Oswald under the bloody 18B and they've done the same with Norah. Pretty soon, there'll be more of us inside than out," he said, knocking back what was left of his gin and tonic. "Which is why we need you."

"Me?"

"Well, they can't damn well put you in choky, can they? Against the rules. Immunity and what have you. Which is why I have a little gift for you."

"That's very kind, Mr Murray."

"You haven't seen what it is yet," the MP said sharply, a hint, Taylor decided, of the boarding school bully in his voice. He was unzipping a slim, leather portfolio case that Taylor hadn't noticed. Perhaps it had been tucked under Murray's suit jacket. "On the count of three, take this from me and put it inside your briefcase, all right? Ready? One . . . two . . . three."

Taylor took the object Murray had removed from the portfolio and put it in his bag, without looking at it. Touch told him that it was leather and had a metal lock on the front. It had the weight of a book and was roughly the size of a large desk diary. He wouldn't have sworn to it, not in the fading twilight of a terrace with no lamps, but he was almost certain it was red.

He should have waited, but he couldn't help himself. In the back of a taxi, his briefcase on his lap, safely out of sight of the driver's rearview mirror, he removed Murray's gift and let it sit on his knees for a second or two while he gazed at it. Yes, red. Red leather worn through use, the binding grown soft. The sides were ragged, like a diary stuffed with scraps of paper and odd receipts. There were so many extra leaves inserted into this book that it appeared to have bloated to what Taylor guessed was twice its regular size.

He probed inside his breast pocket, feeling the outline of the tiny metal key that Murray had given him as they said goodbye. "I am not only trusting you with my life, Mr Hastings. I am trusting you with the lives of many others. Don't let us down."

Taylor took his time, examining the Bramah lock on the side of the book. Little more than a small brass tab, it would surely not be too hard to break — though Murray had assured him that appearances were deceptive, that the mechanism was tougher than it looked. Gingerly he inserted the key, no bigger than a coin, and turned it.

To any observer, including the cab driver, it would have looked like an ordinary address book. Pages and pages filled with names. Instantly his eye picked out the familiar ones: the Blackshirt propagandist AK Chesterton and the fascist agitator Arnold Leese were, he knew after just a few short months in London, permanent fixtures in the country's Jewhating scene. Lord Redesdale he had already met and there was Lord Lymington. Taylor had heard about him: an eccentric by all accounts, who yearned to turn back the clock and dreamt of an England populated solely by ruddy-cheeked farmers and blonde-haired milkmaids, tilling the land and eating only the purest food. "Organic", he called it. Anna had laughed, deliberately mishearing, and had declared that she quite liked the sound of "orgasmic food".

He flicked through the pages until one caught his eye. The name — Colonel GG Woodwark of Kings Lynn — was new to him, but there was an intriguing scribbled note in the margin: *judge of the Führer's Special Prize for Best of Breed at the Cologne Dog Show in November 1938.* Another annotation appeared by the name of Captain George Henry Drummond of Pitsford Hall: *Diana M.'s bank manager, bottom of swimming pool decorated with swastika.*

Diana M, he thought. Must be Diana Mitford, now Mrs Oswald Mosley. The pair of them were legendary: they'd got married four years ago in Goebbels's home and Hitler had been a guest.

Such elevated company. And to think that he, Taylor Hastings, had been entrusted as keeper of their secrets. He would take one more peek, then close and lock the book, leaving plenty of time before the cab reached his home.

He had come across what he presumed was a list of affiliated organizations. A few leapt out: Mosley's

British Union of Fascists was there, obviously, along with the Anglo-German Fellowship, the Imperial Fascist League and the Nordic League. He strained to read Murray's handwriting before deciphering something called the January Club, followed by the White Knights of Britain and an outfit that seemed to be called the English Mistery, whatever that might be. And now an individual's name, though it was included in the list of groups: Lady Alexandra Hardinge.

Then he spotted a name that surprised him. He read it twice to make sure he had it right, but there could be no doubt. How interesting.

He closed the book and locked it carefully, looking up to see the driver, his head turned, staring at him. Only then did he realize the cab was still. It was parked outside his building, on Cadogan Square.

"How long have we been here?"

The driver made a show of consulting his watch. "'bout five minutes. I tried to tell you, but you weren't listening. Immersed in your book, weren't you? Good one, is it? One of them murder mysteries?"

"Not quite," Taylor said, handing him a few coins, kicking himself for his mistake. How long had the driver been watching him like that? What if he could read upside down?

Asked to guard the membership list of the Right Club, he had failed his first test. To be worthy of these people's trust, he would have to do better. He would have to curb his curiosity, no matter how intense. He would have to be vigilant, watching out for anyone nosing around. Above all, and this would be hardest, he would have to be discreet. That meant no bragging to Anna when he saw her later tonight.

He walked up to his apartment, strode into his bedroom and pulled the empty suitcase from under his bed. He placed the red book at the bottom, then placed two blankets on top. He closed the lid and locked it, returning the key to his night table, then put the suitcase inside his wardrobe, behind two pairs of boots. Tomorrow he would buy a lock for the cupboard.

Three separate locks, three separate keys, standing between any would-be spy and the information he had sworn to protect. He looked around his apartment — his "flat" as Anna called it — and headed for the bathroom. He found his box of shaving cream, lifted the lid, and popped the red book's small key inside.

That done, he felt a sudden rush of pride. He had been in this country less than a year and already he was at the centre of things. He held the fates of some of the most important men in England in his hands. He would prove himself deserving of their faith; he wouldn't let them down. And yet, thrilling as this was, he longed to do more than merely safeguard their secrets. He wanted to help their cause.

The clock in the hallway chimed nine. Anna would be waiting for him. He wondered if he should stop off somewhere to get something to eat first. There would be no food on offer from Anna. Just martinis and . . .

The thought aroused him, sending a surge of blood to his groin. He made one last check of the apartment and headed out into the London night.

CHAPTER
EIGHTEEN

James Zennor spent the afternoon in the Sterling Library. He knew what he was looking for, but this time decided he would speak to no one and ask no questions. He would search on his own.

It did not take him long to get used to the place. Fifteen storeys high and as imposing as a Gothic cathedral, the library nevertheless felt familiar, solid and rooted, the stone as dull and pitted by age as if it had stood there for centuries, like one of its Oxford counterparts. But it turned out that the Sterling Library was a kind of confidence trick and he had fallen for it. An information booklet set him straight: work on the library had only finished in 1931, just nine years earlier. The aged appearance was an act of artifice. The booklet explained that, before construction began, the stones from which the library had been built had been deliberately buried in soil for two years, pulled out only once they looked suitably eroded and weather-beaten. As for the stained-glass windows, with their jagged strips of black leading, some of those panes had been deliberately cracked and then leaded to get that ancient monastery look. James could only marvel at the mentality that would go to such lengths: the university of a young country spending a fortune pretending to be old. Who would have thought youth, energy and vigour could be so unsure of itself? He had never before diagnosed a building, but he concluded that the Sterling Library had a distinct case of what his fellow psychologists referred to as an "inferiority complex".

He found what he was looking for: the newspaper reading room. It was full of deep leather armchairs and tables piled with papers clasped in long, wooden binders. He ignored the stacked copies of the *New York Times* and *Wall Street Journal* and pounced instead on the *New Haven Evening Register*. He had already worked out the edition he wanted: the *Antonia* had left Liverpool on the tenth of July, arriving into Quebec on the nineteenth. There would have been a few days in Canada with arrival at Yale on or around the twenty-second. There, he had it: the paper for July 22nd 1940.

He scanned the front, turned to the inside pages, then back again. Nothing. Maybe they had stayed in Canada longer than he had estimated. He went to the twenty-fourth, riffling through the paper. Still nothing.

Then on an inside page of the *Register* of July the twenty-fifth, he saw it: a photograph showing the window of a railway train, the frame filled with the faces of six children, one a baby on the lap of her mother. The caption read "Refugees Find New Haven in Land Holding Promise of Peace" — but the woman was not Florence.

His eye combed the story, searching for names. There was a Spokes, a Handfield-Jones and a Phelps-Brown, but no Zennor and no Walsingham. Still, this at least was written confirmation that he had not gone on a wild goose chase, that he had been right to cross the ocean and come to Yale. The Oxford children were here. Then he spotted another, smaller photo lower down. Was that Harry, a blurred little face in the corner? He desperately wanted it to be, but now that he looked closer, he doubted it.

Of course there were two dozen mothers and five times as many children; it meant nothing that his wife and child had not been mentioned in the article. And yet he had never met any man with a camera who had been able to resist taking photographs of Florence. Half of the press stories about the People's Olympiad seemed to be accompanied by a shot of the beautiful British swimmer Florence Walsingham. As a result, he had all but assumed that if the New Haven papers had made any mention at all of the Oxford arrivals, his wife would feature prominently.

But there could be other stories. He advanced to the editions for the subsequent days, eventually finding this: "Dress of British Refugees Here Sets Them Apart From US Youth". There was another picture, of older girls, and a story about the long outer coats and long "short pants" of the younger boys — but no photograph and no mention of Harry. There were references to the sandals and school blazers, with insignia "emblazoned on the pockets", and much excitement over the "natural color straw hats to protect them from the rays of the sun", especially the hat worn by one little girl on top of her pigtails. Back numbers of the *Yale Daily News* served up similar offerings, but of Florence and Harry there was not a trace.

He could see immediately why the Assistant Dean had wanted to meet here. A good twenty-minute walk from the university district, all the way down Chapel Street as if descending to some lower realm, this place was on the literal other side of the tracks — across the railway bridge and in the poor part of town. James was no longer among students in varsity football jerseys and professors in seersucker suits, but Italian immigrants, dark young men with slicked-back hair standing on street corners, their mothers swaddled in black, escaping the late summer heat in the house by sitting out on the stoop. If it was a secret meeting the Assistant Dean was after, this was just the place: surely no one would recognize him here, in New Haven's Little Italy.

There was no missing Frank Pepe's: a sign covered an entire wall of the building announcing it as a Pizzeria Napoletana, a phrase that meant next to nothing to James. Had he heard one of the Italians in Spain mentioning pizza? He might have done, but he still had little idea what it was.

Once inside he saw something that looked as if it belonged in a locomotive: on the far wall, surrounded by white tiles as wide as bricks, was a gaping hole filled by a roaring fire. Several chefs were standing before it, like the crew of a steam engine, apparently stoking the flames. Once he had watched, mesmerized, for a while, he realized they were in fact clutching long paddles which they used to deposit and retrieve discs of dough larger than gramophone records in what was a giant oven.

He was not sure of the etiquette of such a place. Would the Assistant Dean have made a reservation? It was no good if he had: he had never caught the man's name. James decided to take up a position under the green awning just outside, and wait.

He hoped that if he looked out of place now it would be as a Yale man in the wrong part of town rather than as an Englishman abroad. At the J Press store on York Street he had invested in a jacket like those he had seen worn by college men his age, as well as a couple of shirts. The article in the local paper had made him realize that clothes that might strike an Englishman as perfectly ordinary could look strange and exotic to an American. And he did not want to stand out.

He wondered yet again why the Assistant Dean, an official whom he had never met, had offered to help him. How did he even know what help James needed? Was the rough manhandling and forced ejection from the building all a show and, if so, for whose benefit? What help was the man able to give him and why did it have to be secret?

James had no good answers to any of these questions and over the last six hours he had damped down his expectations, suspecting the Assistant Dean would probably not even turn up. But now, at twenty-five past seven, he glimpsed the outline of the man who had earlier whispered so urgently and promisingly into his ear, and he could not help but feel excited. Did this man know where Florence and Harry were and was he about to pass on that information?

On the pavement by the open door, the Assistant Dean gave him no more than a nod of greeting, beckoning him to follow him inside. He asked the waitress for a booth and was taken straight away to an arrangement of dark green benches with high wooden backs, with a tall post marking one booth from the other. Clearly familiar with this layout, the Assistant Dean instantly removed his jacket and hung it on the coat hook at the top of the post. There were two wide rings visible under the arms of his white shirt, sweat patches which, James concluded, suggested nerves rather than merely the sticky heat of a summer night in Connecticut.

"George Lund," the man said, offering a brief, cramped handshake across the table. "Best if we look like we know each other." He gave James a wide and painfully artificial smile. If it was intended to convey long friendship with and affection for James, it would have instantly failed: the man simply looked strange.

"Well, it's good of you to see me," James began. "My situation is —"

"We should order. There's no one on that table over my left shoulder is there? No one who can hear what you're saying or see us talking?"

James frowned. "Just a family; the adults have their backs to us and the children aren't interested."

At Lund's insistence, they ordered right away, James opting for what was called a pizza margherita, which his

217

host said was the best introduction to the dish for a novice. Lund made a point of doing the ordering. "Best if no one hears your accent," he explained once the waitress had gone.

Quietly, James attempted to restart the conversation and keep it light, calm the chap down a bit. "So how long have you been at Yale?"

"Ten years. Straight out of college and into the faculty. The medical school."

"So you're a doctor."

"Qualified but not practising. Preston recruited me straight after my final exams, to help him run the department."

"Preston?"

Lund looked puzzled. He was about to say something when the food arrived. Two plates the size of wagon wheels, steam rising from vast patches of melted cheese and deep gory smears of red that revealed themselves to be cooked tomatoes. James thought back to The Racket in Oxford, where this very evening there might be a few couples hiding behind the blackout curtains, sharing a small plate of tinned baked beans on a single slice of toast. What a contrast. Everything about this country screamed plenty; a single one of these pizzas would probably account for a month's rations.

"Preston McAndrew," Lund continued when they were alone again. "The man you came to see today."

"Oh, the Dean."

"Yes, though he wasn't Dean then. Only head of the Medical School."

"And he's your boss."

Lund nodded, his eyes darting to a far corner of the room. "Listen, I should have said this before. You won't tell anyone about this meeting, right?"

"Not if you don't want me to."

"I mean it. This entire conversation, even the fact that I'm here, is confidential. Are we agreed?"

"We're agreed." James noticed that Lund was methodically cutting up his pizza into even-sized slices but had not yet eaten any of them. James was not sure if he was allowed to begin eating or should wait. Was this an American custom?

"I've taken a risk doing this," Lund said, still not eating.

"What kind of risk?"

"Never mind that. Now, why did you come into the Dean's office today?"

"I thought you knew. Isn't that why you said you could help —"

Lund glared. "Don't repeat that here."

"But I thought you heard what was going on outside your door. With me and the secretary. I thought you knew."

"I heard the secretaries discussing your earlier visit, when Miss Kelly had you thrown out. I wasn't there, but they were talking about it. And then I heard you when you came back."

"So you decided to throw me out?" James bit into the pizza, scalding his tongue on the hot cheese. It burned, but it was also delicious, like a thinner, tastier version of Welsh rarebit.

"I did that for your own sake," Lund said, picking up the first of his carefully segmented slices of pizza with his hands and letting it hover before his mouth.

"My sake? There had to be an easier way to do that than chucking me onto the street like a bag of rubbish."

"I'm sorry about that. But I didn't want to arouse any suspicion. Now to my question: what are you looking for in Yale?"

"I'm looking for my wife and son. They're here in the Oxford evacuation party. Here in Yale, I mean."

"Do you have proof of that?"

"Proof?"

"Any evidence that makes you sure they're here."

James leaned his back against the hard wooden panel, attempting to assess the man opposite him. Did he need to be careful? Was the promise of help some kind of trap? Who was this man? He decided to limit how much he revealed. "I saw the ship's manifest to Canada, with their names on it. And a colleague in Oxford assures me they are part of the evacuation group."

"Canada? Are you sure they made the journey to New Haven? Could they have stayed there?"

James was seized by a sudden squeeze of panic. He had never considered that possibility. He had taken Bernard Grey's word at face value, even though, he now thought, he had known that the Greys and the rest of their Oxford co-conspirators were capable of lying to him and had done so several times. If Virginia Grey had felt no compunction in pretending to be shocked by Florence's disappearance that morning, why would her

220

husband hesitate before serving up some cock-and-bull story? To think he had been in Canada and had done nothing to look for her there. He was suddenly furious with himself. The anger that rose in him spilled out towards this man. "Are you telling me that my wife is not in Yale after all? Because if that is the case, I would like to know right away so I can make arrangements to leave."

"Please," the Assistant Dean said in an urgent whisper, his eyes imploring. "You must speak quietly. No, that is not what I am saying. I just need to know what you know."

"And I need to know what *you* know," said James, pushing aside his plate. "It's a simple enough question. Florence and Henry Zennor, possibly travelling under the name of Walsingham: are they here or aren't they?"

Lund sighed and again looked left and right. His forehead was gleaming with sweat. "I believe they came here to Yale, yes. I am not exactly sure where they are now."

James exhaled and sought to steady himself. "Thank you," he said with genuine relief. "It would be terrible if I were barking up the wrong tree entirely." He paused. "Now, I presume the paperwork for the Oxford group is kept in your office. I don't understand why we can't simply look up my wife's file and find out where she's staying."

"It's not as simple as that."

"I understand. The foster families want their privacy respected and there's the confidentiality —"

"No," Lund snapped, catching James by surprise. "You don't understand at all. This is much bigger than the lives of just a few families."

"Of course, I see that. There's a hundred and twenty-five children, so that must involve, what, perhaps as many as fifty families, with an average of two children —"

George Lund seized James's wrist. "You have no idea what you've walked into here, do you?" The man's hand was clammy. "You've stumbled into something much bigger than you realize. Bigger and more dangerous."

He broke his grip, almost tossing James's hand back at him. His whole face was covered with sweat now and beginning to look pale, as if suffering from a fever. Lund rose to his feet, swaying unsteadily. Then he dashed in the direction of the lavatories, leaving James alone at the table, fielding the embarrassed stares of several diners, including the mother from the family table ahead, who had turned around to assess the commotion for herself.

What on earth had got into the man? James had simply asked for Florence and Harry's whereabouts. He had mentioned the ship's manifest and Canada. And that was it. Yet this man seemed as alarmed as if James had been threatening him. Or did he believe that simply meeting James exposed him to some grave danger? If it did, why had he been the one to suggest it?

James cut another slice of the pizza. Cooling now, it had lost its initial appeal, the cheese beginning to congeal. James thought it highly unlikely that such a

222

dish could catch on back home: Brits would always prefer the reliability of meat and potatoes.

Still no sign of Lund. Had the man upped and fled for home? He seemed perfectly capable of such histrionics. On the other hand, he had left his briefcase on the bench where he had been sitting. James could see from the clasp that it was not locked.

His eyes flicked across the room, from left to right. In one rapid movement, he leaned across and pulled Lund's bag to his side, shuffling up so that he could wedge the case between himself and the wall. Determined to look natural, he did not open it straightaway. He cut up and ate another slice of pizza instead, before taking a sip of the glass of iced water that he had never asked for but which had been placed in front of him all the same. Then, with his left hand, he found the clasp on the case, a button-release that needed only to be slid downward. The tag of leather that bridged the two halves of the case sprung free, so that now he could easily slip his hand inside. He could feel a hardback book, then another. He glanced down to see what looked like medical textbooks.

He looked up, briefly making eye contact with the boy of the family nearby, then let his hand carry on probing. Now he felt what he guessed was a large manila envelope. His fingers inched toward the top, where he could tell the envelope was unsealed. He pushed inside, his fingers finding the unmistakable texture of photographs. There seemed to be dozens of them, forming a thick wad. Peeling a few away from the set, he brought them close to the opening of the briefcase so that he might glance down for a quick look. It took him a while to absorb what he had seen. Once he had, the images both shocked him — and explained everything.

CHAPTER
NINETEEN

A moment or two later, a flushed George Lund returned. "I can't go through with this, I'm sorry," he said and, before James had a chance to reply, he reached down for the briefcase — now returned to its place — turned and quickly walked towards the exit.

James got to his feet: "Stop!"

Lund did not turn around.

"Don't just storm out like that. Stop, will you!" James called, much louder this time.

The mother at the next table was staring again. Digging into his pocket, James slapped down a couple of dollar bills and dashed out. He stumbled, knocking a glass over on his way to the door; he heard it smash to the ground. Once on the street, he looked left and right among the small knots of teenagers and geriatrics hanging around together in the warm evening, but he'd lost him.

It wasn't the first time James had encountered one of Lund's type, he thought as he headed back towards town. There were plenty like him in Oxford and, on two occasions, they had made their feelings known to James. Years later, he had told Florence about it and she had said it was his fault for being so damned handsome.

Even so, the photographs were pretty shocking. Shots of naked young men from the front, back and side on. At first glance each man looked as if he were standing before a medical examination board — facing the panel, then offering a profile, then showing them his back. James had wondered if that was how these pictures had been taken, by an official army photographer, or maybe by a hidden camera smuggled into the examination room.

But then he had spotted the strange spikes. At regular intervals along their spines, the men had sharp metal pins emerging from their backs. They were especially visible in the profile photograph, the spines silhouetted against the plain white background.

James liked to think he was a man of the world. In Spain a couple of the other volunteers had pornographic magazines which James had seen, featuring knickerless girls bent over chairs and tables, often prising apart their own buttocks in order to expose themselves more fully. He knew from his academic research that sexual desire was a complicated business and that some people were aroused by the unlikeliest of things — fetishes for women's hair or feet, for example. But he had never contemplated anything like this, that a man could want to look at images of other men whose bodies had been elaborately pierced.

As James knocked back his second Scotch at the bar of the Owl Shop, he contemplated his rotten luck. He had hoped that Lund would prove to be his lucky break, the man who would prove that every now and again you could rely on the kindness of strangers. Instead he had run into a homosexual and pervert, who had somehow deluded himself into thinking this visiting Englishman would be interested in a quick, queer embrace.

No wonder Lund had wanted to meet far out of town, where no one would discover his shameful secret. James should have been suspicious from the off, starting with Lund's suggestion that they meet in the evening and at a restaurant. And all that flustered placing of his moist hand on James's wrist: the man was clearly nervous, uncertain of how James would respond to him. What was it he had said? *You have no idea what you've walked into here, do you?*

James ordered another whisky. And yet, he could not be sure. If Lund really were a homosexual out to make a conquest, why would he suggest meeting in public and early in the evening? If he had summoned James to his home at 11 o'clock tonight, promising some information on Florence and Harry, James would have gone there without hesitation. Meeting at Frank Pepe's had only made it harder for the man.

Lund had said something else too. He'd been all but jabbering by then, so James had not taken it too seriously. But the message was clear enough: You've stumbled into something much bigger than you realize. *Bigger and more dangerous.*

That could be nothing, loose talk from a man determined to exaggerate his own importance, to increase the value of his information. Perhaps that was it: Lund was going to demand certain favours from him in return for the file on his wife and child. The very thought made James shudder.

In the morning he would make an appointment with the Dean himself. Reluctantly he would have to tell him what his subordinate had been up to, attempting to pressure a visiting fellow of Yale into . . . unseemly behaviour. James might then be able to propose a little exchange of his own: he would keep silent about the deviant interests of the Assistant Dean in return for the location of his wife and child.

He downed the last of his whisky, his fourth double. Or perhaps his fifth. He emerged from the Owl Shop, breathed the night air in deeply, then turned left and headed for his garret room in the Elizabethan Club, stumbling more than once on his way back.

He had woken so often to the fusillade of gunfire that he had almost learned to sleep through it. Somewhere in his unconscious, a voice told him that the pounding rat-tat-tat he could now hear close by was a creation of his own mind, part memory, part imagination. He could just stay here, under this thick, warm quilt of sleep — made thicker by the alcohol still in his bloodstream — and eventually the sound would disappear.

He started suddenly and was bolt upright: the noise had got louder. Now it was not a knocking sound, but a banging on the door and it was not coming from inside his head, but outside it — from the door of this small room. It was accompanied by voices too, which only now became distinct. It took another second for him to hear what they were saying: "Dr James Zennor, this is the Yale Police Department. Open up."

"What is this?"

"Open up this minute, sir. Do not think about fleeing through that window, we have a man on the street outside."

James's heart was thudding in his chest; his head was cloudy with dreams and drink. His shoulder was sending volts of agony through him; in his stupor, he had slept on it, the alcohol anaesthetizing the usual pain that prevented him making such a calamitous mistake. He staggered towards the bedroom door, which he did not remember locking, and opened it.

The frame was filled by two uniformed police officers, one of whom spoke immediately. "Are you Dr James Zennor of Oxford, England?"

"Yes."

Instantly his partner snapped a pair of handcuffs on James's wrists.

"What the hell is this? What are you doing?"

"You're under arrest."

"Arrest? What for?"

"For the murder of George Lund. He was found dead this morning. And you were the last person who saw him alive."

CHAPTER
TWENTY

London

Taylor was practised in this now. He could wake,
remove himself from the bed and tiptoe to the
bathroom without disturbing Anna. She slept deeply,
especially when she had been so . . . active during the
night.

Last night she had begged him to spend the morning
with her: they could have breakfast together and then
go out shopping. She wanted to buy him something,
she had said. When he had asked what, she had
dissolved into a girlish giggle — a trick he guessed she
had developed back when she was a debutante, coming
out at just eighteen years old. It probably worked
wonders then, which was why she had kept it up. But
the gesture seemed strange in a woman approaching —
how old was she? He had never been rude enough to
ask and had never tried to find out. Thirty-six?
Thirty-eight? Over forty? Jeez, even his mother was
barely forty-five.

Anna had been agitating to go shopping with him for
a while. She had mentioned Piccadilly or St James's.
She probably had in mind one of those country sports
shops, where they sold oilskin jackets, fly-fishing rods

and sturdy umbrellas. She had some crazy idea about getting him invited as a fellow guest to a weekend house party of friends of theirs, Lord and Lady Somebody. She would have a quiet word with the hostess, discreetly requesting that the room she would nominally share with her MP husband be close to Taylor's. "Darling, don't you think it would be so much fun? I could come creeping along the corridor just after lights out and then slip into your room and jump into bed. I haven't done that since boarding school!"

"I thought your boarding school was all-girls," Taylor had said.

"It was," she had replied, biting her lip naughtily, then breaking out into more of those giggles.

Or perhaps she would take him to Savile Row or Jermyn Street, to buy an expensive shirt or even a suit. She had already given him a pair of silver cufflinks, far too expensive to wear, especially at work. They were bound to raise suspicion.

He was not sure what to think of this urge of hers. He recognized it of course. Plenty of wealthy men liked to cover their mistresses in dollar bills, dressing them up in expensive couture they would never buy for their wives. It seemed a woman with a young lover could be just as stupid.

He kept a couple of pressed white shirts in readiness for such overnight stays on the shelf in the linen cupboard. He had asked Anna if it wasn't taking a terrible risk: surely, if Murray spotted them there, he would connect the dots. She had dismissed his concerns so blithely he wondered again if the

Conservative MP knew all about the affair already, whether indeed he sanctioned it. He put one of the shirts on, finished dressing and scribbled a note, which he left on the nightstand. *Another time, my love. T.*

Since it was not yet seven-thirty, he decided to walk to work. It wouldn't take too long and it was a beautiful morning. He walked by the river, along the Chelsea Embankment, before heading north and into Hyde Park. That was the joy of London, these gorgeous oases of countryside dotted all through the city. He caught a glimpse of the Serpentine, vowed once more to swim there before the summer was through, then carried on until finally he emerged at Park Lane. Everyone said Park Lane and Mayfair were the swankiest parts of town, but these days they were looking distinctly rough at the edges. You only had to look up at the windows of some of the grand hotels and see the black paint to know you were in a country at war.

At last he reached Grosvenor Square. He could see the flag of his country fluttering through the trees. He checked his watch. He was early, though wartime meant everyone was working odd hours: some staying late in order to be in touch with Washington, others getting in before eight, so that they could be in step with Whitehall. He looked up at the marine on duty at the door, giving him the sharp nod he deemed the civilian equivalent of a salute. And so began another day's work for Taylor Hastings at the London Embassy of the United States of America.

CHAPTER
TWENTY-ONE

"Everything points at you, Dr Zennor. The bust-up in the restaurant, you storming out after him, smashing the place up — all witnessed by at least a dozen people. Why don't you tell me what happened?"

"I've already told you this."

"Well, tell me again."

James sighed. He was sitting in a grey holding room in the Yale Police Department headquarters which was, to his dismay, a real police station. The name had misled him: he had assumed the Yale Police Department would be an outfit equivalent to the "Bulldogs" who policed Oxford, an arm of the academic authorities rather than a genuine force. But these men were dressed like the policemen he had seen in gangster films back home and they sounded and acted that way, too. Once out of the squad car, he had had to pose for a man with a camera — face on and sideways, like the men in Lund's photographs — then press each one of his fingertips into a small pad of black ink. This was, he realized, serious.

The bureaucratic processing was long and drawn-out: his mind wandered back to Oxford and the autumn of 1937.

He remembered being surrounded by the paraphernalia of new life, a cot in the nursery, a pram in the hall — signposts pointing to the future. Florence had tiny Harry at her breast, her body fuller and, to James, more beautiful than ever. They were newly married in a new house, a new family brimming with hope and possibility.

That was what the visitors saw, at any rate — the likes of Virginia Grey, pitching up with chicken livers wrapped in greaseproof paper from Harris's because, "My dear, as a nursing mother you will be suffering from depleted stocks of iron which you will need to replenish immediately."

But neither she nor anyone else saw Florence repeatedly pleading with her husband to pick up their baby and to hold him, urging James to overcome his fears that his shattered shoulder would let him down. No one else was there to witness his insistence that he held no such fears, that it was just that he had to be in college in fifteen minutes or that he had an urgent journal article to complete, or that the baby clearly wanted his mother. *Go on Florence, take him, he's obviously crying out for you.*

Just as no one had seen the late November afternoon when, while Florence napped, James had gingerly approached the crib after Harry had woken. He had stared at his child for a long minute, like a wrestler sizing up an opponent, before reaching down with his good arm and trying to scoop the baby up one-handed, curling his right hand under and then around Harry's back. It had worked at first, the child effortlessly light in his father's grip, James almost managing a smile as he carefully hoisted Harry upward. But then the baby, not yet two months old, had wriggled. James's left hand tried to come to the rescue, but it was too slow, its movements still too jagged and awkward. Little Harry escaped from his grasp, tumbling out of his hand and into the empty, dangerous air, while James watched uselessly, frozen in place.

Only luck ensured that the child bounced back into the soft blankets of the crib. A few inches to the left or right and Harry would have crashed onto the hard, wooden floor. At that realization, James had let out a sound he had never made before: part scream, part roar. And either that or the impact of the fall had set Harry off, crying silently at first, his baby jaw trembling, his tongue oscillating until James was terrified he was taking in no oxygen, before giving voice to loud, hoarse bawling. Florence had rushed in, her features stretched wide with anxiety, as if a jolt of electricity had just shocked her from sleep.

She had picked Harry up in a single smooth movement, placing him on her shoulder, letting him feel her warmth, his face nuzzling into her neck. He was still crying, but soon the register altered, the sobs becoming calmer and more regular. Keeping her eyes on her husband, who had retreated into the corner, on the other side of the cot, Florence had moved towards him, stretching out her free hand in a gesture that said she knew what had happened. James had recoiled, then pushed her arm away. He refused to be comforted. He refused to be pitied. She had soothed Harry, but she would not soothe him. He fled from the room.

Now, nearly three years later and thousands of miles away, he let out a deep sigh. Fear had prevented him from trying to pick his boy up again. Until this moment he had thought that the mistake he had made that day had been dropping the baby. Now he understood better — but he had left it too late.

"Do you speak English in England? Or are you deaf?"

Startled, James looked up to see a detective glaring at him. "I'm sorry?" Like a gramophone record spinning at half speed, it dawned on him only slowly that this man had replaced the officer who had arrested him. He took in the man's face: pale, fleshy with thinning hair. What was his name? Riley? It struck James that the name went along with his accent, an accent that he had heard several times this morning from other officers. All older, grey- or white-haired, with the air of men who had worn uniforms all their lives. He forced himself to listen to what the man was saying.

"I'm afraid it's not your lucky day. You're staring at an Irishman and we ain't too fond of the English. No offence, but that's how it is."

"You're from Ireland?"

"No. But my Pa was. Once you lot had starved him out, he went to Boston, didn't he?"

James looked through the door, which had been left open, spotting two more of Riley's colleagues. So that was it. They were retired officers from the big city, men used to dealing with thugs and thieves rather than plagiarist scholars and exam cheats, or whatever kept them busy at Yale. Which meant they were probably relishing the prospect of a proper crime, like a murder. Well, they could damn well find somebody else to liven up their day.

"Like I said, everything points at you, Dr Zennor. The only thing I can't for the life of me figure out is motive. Why d'you do it?"

"This is outrageous!" James said, slamming his fist onto the table. "I insist that you contact the Dean's office immediately. They'll explain who I am and what I'm doing here. Jesus Christ!"

"Don't you dare swear at me, you limey bastard, or I'll shove you in those cells so fast you won't know what's hit you."

Riley was staring at him, his pointed finger hovering in the air in front of James's face. James stayed exactly where he was, his gaze meeting the detective's without wavering. "I did not kill that man. I am here to find my wife and child. That's why I'm here, in America. She is one of the Oxford mothers who arrived here a week or so ago."

"So you say."

"And Lund confirmed it! For heaven's sake —"

"I warned you once, Zennor. Now calm down. One thing I've learned in this job is you university men are very good at talking fast and spinning a story. You Brits probably the best of the lot. I may not be as smart as you, but I know my job. So you take it nice and slow unless you want to be telling this story all over again to a jury."

So for the third time, James explained how he had gone to the Dean's office — twice — how he had adopted a different tack the second time, inventing a story about research simply because he was desperate to find out where his family had gone. Without planning to, he repeated to Riley the question he had asked the harbourmaster in Liverpool: if your family had gone missing, wouldn't you resort to any means to get them back?

"That's what worries me, Dr Zennor. That you were ready to resort to anything. Even murder."

James leaned forward again, baring his teeth. "This is insane. The man threw me out of his office, but whispered that I should see him later that evening. I went to meet him, I asked what he knew but he wouldn't tell me. He was speaking in riddles."

"This was at Frank Pepe's?"

"Yes. He was very agitated, and he became more so the longer we spoke. Then, when he went to the lavatory, I saw the —"

"I know. The photographs. You see how this looks, though, don't you? You're angry. You threaten a secretary. You somehow track down the man who —"

"I didn't track him down! He told me to meet him there."

"We only have your word for that. You track down the man who holds the information — which you've just admitted you will do anything to get — to the place where he's eating dinner. You argue. People in the restaurant hear that. Then he goes to the bathroom, you break into his briefcase and snoop through his personal property —"

"It wasn't like that! I thought he might have Florence's file in there. That's all I wanted. That's all I want: to know where the hell she is." James dipped his head, exhausted.

But the detective was not to be diverted. "You rush out of the restaurant, shouting and screaming. People hear that too. You chase after him, following him home. You watch the house and then later — while his wife is sleeping upstairs — you kill the guy, trying to make it look like he killed himself."

"His wife?"

"That's right. His wife and his new baby."

"But I thought —"

"I know what you thought. That he was a pervert with obscene pictures in his bag. You told me already."

"But I saw them!"

"Well, they weren't in his bag when his wife found him dangling this morning. A wife, incidentally, who swears her husband was making plans for the future and would never, ever contemplate suicide."

"He hanged himself? Bloody hell."

"Or you hanged him and made it look like a suicide. That's what I'm trying to figure out."

James rubbed his temples. None of this made sense. A wife and a baby? Now that he thought about it, such things were not unknown: there was a legendary Classics professor at Oxford who used to joke about buggering the more promising undergraduates. His wife was utterly devoted to him.

Riley closed the door, then returned to his seat. "You still want to stick to this crap about the homo pictures? Are you sure about that? Much better to change your story now than when you're in the dock at a murder trial, believe me. You plead guilty, tell the judge you were going crazy looking for your wife, maybe he'll be lenient with you. But you mess us around, he's going to be measuring you up for the electric chair. Oh, you didn't know that? Yep, that's how we do it these days in Connecticut. Three years now. Not a nice way to go, I can tell you. They strap you in, so you can't move. Then they pass electric currents through you — two thousand volts, I think it is. The first current's meant to knock you out and burn up your brain, and the second's meant to blast all your vital organs, your lungs and heart and what have you. But it doesn't always go right, see? Maybe the charge is not enough: the brain might stop, but the man's still breathing. These new machines, something always goes wrong, you know how it is. We had a man whose blood vessels, under the skin, they starting popping and bleeding; then his head was on fire. His head! Oh, that was awful. Took him eight minutes to die. Imagine that. You'd just cry out to be hanged, wouldn't you? I would. Get it over with."

James knew what the detective was doing, that he was trying to break his spirit, to force him into some spurious, panicked confession. He knew it, but he would not succumb to it. He knew the evidence the police had was circumstantial at best. But he also knew that juries were unpredictable. Who knew what might be his fate before a dozen Rileys, pumped up by some

240

fast-talking lawyer to fear this strange Englishman, abandoned by his wife and deemed too mentally unstable to wear his nation's uniform? They would hear that this foreigner was the last person to see Lund alive and that he had been seen chasing after him in anger only hours earlier.

Riley was sitting back now, staring at James silently. James recognized this trick too. He had deployed it himself during some of his clinical interviews: say nothing and let the subject squirm until they eventually revealed themselves, if only to break the silence.

James would not fall for that. Instead he would use the pause for his own purposes, to think. He tried to put aside the question of how things looked and to focus on reality. What had actually happened here? It was conceivable that Lund had taken his own life, perhaps in shame at his deviant urgings. His wife could have come down in the morning, seen his body, discovered the photographs and then destroyed them, for fear they would disgrace the reputation of her late husband and taint her family name.

But the same was true if Lund had been murdered, the killer merely disguising it as a suicide. In that situation, Lund's widow would still have destroyed the photographs to save her shame. Or perhaps the killer had taken them for some reason.

James pinched the bridge of his nose, as he did whenever he was struggling to untie a knotty problem. The best method, he had found, was discussion with his wife. She had a fine logical mind, ordered and rigorous, but she also had a creative intellect: she could generate new ideas, wholly new possibilities that he had not considered. So often a conversation with her would unlock a puzzle that had seemed insoluble. The irony of it did not elude him: to find Florence, he needed Florence.

"Are you sure you don't want to tell me something?" Riley said. "'Cause I'm watching you, closing your eyes, frowning, holding your nose and all that and I'm thinking you look like a man with a lot on his mind. Lot on your conscience."

"I'm thinking, Detective, that's all. Just thinking."

"Looks painful." Riley leaned back, assessing. His lips adjusted a fractional amount, a gesture that somehow, like a silent clearing of the throat, signalled the imminent introduction of a change in topic.

Riley let his fist open to reveal a glint of metal inside, like a magician producing a coin from an empty hand. "Is this yours, Dr Zennor?"

James leaned forward.

"Go ahead, pick it up."

At first James thought it was a tie-pin but it was too small and the pin at the back was the wrong shape, long and thin, like a needle. This was to be worn in the lapel. It took the form of an Egyptian cross, a crucifix with a loop rather than a vertical line at the top. In this case, the loop was filled with the image of an animal head. As he peered at it, he could make out the face of a wolf.

"Well," said Riley. "Is that yours?"

"I've never seen this before in my life. What is it?"

Riley was staring at him, trying to read his face for signs of mendacity. "Never seen it?"

"Yes, I've never bloody seen it. What is it?"

"You really are going to have to learn to control yourself, Dr Zennor," the detective said, though this time, James noticed, the edge in his voice had softened. "This was found in the deceased's mouth."

"In his mouth? I don't —"

"The coroner says that's where you'd hide something if you wanted it to be found after your death. Least, that's what a medical man would do. He'd know there's no point holding it in your hand. Muscles relax when you die and the thing drops out. Seems Lund was pretty determined: the pin was stuck right into the inside of his cheek."

"Did it belong to him?"

"Excuse me?"

"The pin. Was it his?"

Riley let a hint of a frown pass across his forehead, before chasing it away. "I asked the widow exactly that. Turns out Lund did have one just like it, but that's still upstairs in the bedroom. In its case, just like always. She showed it to me. So this belongs to someone else."

"His killer."

"Are you asking or telling?"

James bit down hard, a technique that always used to help him suppress his anger, though it had fallen into disuse in recent years: too feeble a weapon. "You think Lund might have ripped this off his killer's jacket during a struggle. Then put it in his mouth so that you would find it, to identify the man who murdered him."

"You're getting carried away, Dr Zennor. We leave the theories to you gentlemen in the university. Facts is all I want. Facts."

"Well, do you know what this is, this badge? Or why Lund had one?"

"Leave the questions to me, OK? Let's go back to Pepe's restaurant. You say —" He was interrupted by an urgent knock on the door. Riley called out and another police officer came in, bending down to whisper in the detective's ear. Riley nodded, whispered another question to his colleague, then nodded again. The officer left.

Riley leaned across the desk to retrieve the pin, placing it on top of a pile of papers he now squared up. "I guess this is your lucky day after all. The guy behind the bar recognized your mug shot. Says he remembers serving you six double whiskys and telling you to get lost, just after eleven. And the butler at the Elizabethan Club says he put you to bed last night: you were so drunk, he had to take your pants off. Which is embarrassing but also an alibi. The old boy says he slept downstairs on a camp bed and would have heard if you'd left during the night. Which means you're no longer an official suspect in the death of George Lund."

James let out a long sigh, a sensation of relief he had not felt since completing that last, agonising row on the Isis. He was free. But then a thought intruded. The butler? He had no memory of that at all. Had he really got that drunk? Or was this the amnesia Rosemary Hyde had taunted him about?

He stood up and faced the detective. "If I'm not a suspect, does that mean you won't be treating this case as murder?"

"You're not an official suspect, is what I said."

James looked down at the table that separated them. To his shame, he realized that it was only now he was not defending himself that he was fully taking in what had happened. A man was dead; a man who had taken what he clearly felt was a great risk to meet him; a man who had told him *I can help you*; a man who had become feverish with anxiety in the restaurant, in the last hours of his life.

"And, Detective, you're sure those photographs I saw were not in his briefcase when you found Lund this morning?"

"When his *wife* found Lund this morning," Riley corrected him. "No, there were no photos. Our men have searched the place thoroughly: no sign of any homo pictures, no magazines, nothing. You may be off the hook for murder, but that doesn't make your story about last night the truth. I'm going to be keeping a close eye on you, Dr Zennor."

James eyed him steadily. "I'd like you to keep an eye out for my wife. No one will tell me where she is."

"That's between you and the university. I've got work to do." With that, Riley offered a brief handshake and ushered him out of the room, leaving James Zennor relieved, puzzled — and absolutely clear where he had to go.

CHAPTER
TWENTY-TWO

He had once heard Bernard Grey joke that the best-informed people in England were the tea ladies at the Palace of Westminster: they overheard everything. It wasn't just hatred born of hindsight that made that quip grate on James. He had found it irritating even before he had discovered that Grey was centrally involved in the plot to spirit his wife and child to North America without his knowledge. Because the joke rested on what was meant to be a shared assumption, that it was surprising, and comical, to imagine tea ladies knowing anything about anything.

Still, grudgingly, James had to admit that there was a grain of truth in the old bastard's little apercu. If you wanted to know what was happening in college — which undergraduate had been caught cheating in his prelims, which fellow had been found masturbating in chapel — then there was no point idling about high table. The place to go was the porter's lodge, where the true authorities were to be found.

He couldn't do that in Yale, a place he had never visited until two days ago. He knew no one here. Except for one man, whom he needed to thank anyway.

James knocked on the door of 459 College Street. In the rush of his arrest this morning, he had barely been given time to get dressed, let alone pick up the key to the Elizabethan Club he had been given. But the butler was in and opened the door to him. As he did so, James realized that he did not know the man's name.

"Ah, good morning —" James met his eye.

"It's Walters, sir." The dark skin of the butler's face was creased with age; he was much older than James had first appreciated. "Good morning to you too, Dr Zennor."

"I'm very grateful to you for what you did for me, umm, last —"

"There's no need to say anything, sir. We look after our guests here."

"But what you told the police; it's largely because of you that they released me."

"I just told the truth, Dr Zennor. They asked me and I told them."

"Well, I'm grateful all the same." James paused. "Could we . . .?" He gestured at the main drawing room, as if to introduce a topic that was best not discussed standing in the doorway.

Once safely out of idle earshot, James said, "I wondered whether you might be able to help me track something down. A pin."

"A pin, sir?"

"For a lapel. One was shown to me this morning, and my guess is that it's something a Yale man would recognize immediately, but it meant nothing to me." The butler nodded, as if awaiting guidance. "It was an

Egyptian cross, you know with the loop at the top?" James sketched the pattern in the air. "Inside the loop was an animal head. A dog or something. Perhaps a wolf."

Walters looked away, weighing what he had just heard. At last he looked up. "I think I know what you were looking at, Dr Zennor. And you're right. It would be recognizable to most Yale men."

"What is it?"

"What you had there was a wolf's head pin. And Wolf's Head is one of the most powerful secret societies in the university."

CHAPTER
TWENTY-THREE

James wanted to get started right away, but the butler steered him to a mirror. "With all due respect, sir . . ."

The reflection that came back was of a man dishevelled, unshaven and rudely stirred out of a hangover. He had missed one of the buttons of his shirt. Reluctantly, he allowed himself to be persuaded that Walters was right: he needed to pause, wash and eat properly before doing anything else.

The bathtub at the top of the house was tiny for a man his size, but stepping into it still felt like a great luxury. The idea of relaxing in a bath of hot water gave him only fleeting pleasure, the warmth and comfort instantly replaced by guilt. From the moment he had discovered Florence and Henry gone that morning, more than three weeks ago, he had rushed to find them. Even when he was sitting at Crewe Station, waiting for his connection to Liverpool, or when he spent those long days and nights on board ship for Canada, or on those slow, rattling trains into the United States he had not let himself relax: he had paced the railway platform and the ship's deck or drummed his fingers like a man in a desperate hurry. He had maintained the urgency he had felt that first moment, when he had dashed out of

249

the front door of their house in Norham Gardens, calling out their names. He might have crossed an ocean and half the world, but he still felt the fierce urgency of a man who had just lost his family. And stopping, even for ten minutes in the bath, felt like a kind of betrayal. Worse, it frightened him, suggesting a time when he might get used to being without his wife and his son, a future in which he was fated to be as alone as he was now.

He looked down at his shoulder, the bone collapsed, the skin stretched. As the water in the bath began to cool, James remembered how his son, then a baby, had once used his little hand to touch that damaged patch of him, his infant face curious. Harry had never recoiled from the sight of the scar because he had never known anything else.

James realized that his eyes were stinging. Reflexively, to make it stop, he sank his face into the warm water.

Dressing as fast as he could, he made for the Owl Shop. He would pretend his purpose was merely to offer thanks to the bartender who had vouched for his presence there last night. But he was looking for someone else. And to his relief he was there: the young man he had met on his first visit, now polishing glasses.

After a short greeting and a little small-talk, James came to his question. He began elliptically. "So what's all this about secret societies, then?"

"You mean like Skull and Bones and all that jazz?"

"Maybe. Assume I know nothing."

"Oh, well I'm not a member or anything. Most of them are for juniors and seniors." When he saw James's puzzled expression, he smiled. "Oh, you really *do* know nothing. OK. Freshman, first year; sophomore, second year; junior, third year; senior, fourth year."

"So once you're in your last two years, you can join."

"No! It's not like that at all. Not just anyone can join. You have to be asked."

This all made sense so far. Oxford was no different: it too had its drinking societies, like the Assassins or Piers Gaveston or the Bullingdon Club. They were secretive, too, in that they didn't exactly publish the minutes of their meetings, but most undergraduates had a pretty good idea of who belonged to which. The Bullingdon even had its own costume, with navy blue tails and a garish, mustard-coloured waistcoat. Membership tended to be wealthy and aristocratic, young men rich enough to reduce the private room in a restaurant to rubble and pay the repair bill on the spot and in cash.

But the Yale societies — Wolf's Head, Skull and Bones, Scroll and Key — sounded different. For one thing, they had their own buildings in the heart of Yale. "Oh, they're extraordinary, you gotta see them," the bar boy said. "They look like ancient Greek temples. Doric columns and all that. They call them 'tombs'."

"So they're not secret at all, then."

"Oh, they are. Completely secret. No one knows what goes on inside. And only a handful of people are allowed to join. I think Wolf's Head only has fifteen or sixteen members at any one time. Mainly juniors."

"But however exclusive they are, whatever it is they do can't be that important if these groups are — with

all due respect — made up only of undergraduates."
James smiled.

"But they're not, not really. That's the whole point. After your year as a member, you become a *past* member. And you keep that for life. They say President Taft was a Skull and Bones man."

"And, what, they meet afterwards?"

"They help each other out. Like a secret network." That too was familiar. Oxford academics pretended to be above such things, but James knew of the Freemasons and their cat's cradle of connections, one man giving another a leg-up, the beneficiary then lending a hand to a third, who in turn would help the first — a perpetual motion machine of favours and patronage.

James had just pressed the bartender for a few specifics when the door opened and two men came in, instantly demanding martinis. James left a coin on the counter and hurried out.

Once outside, he reached for the notebook he had kept in the inside breast pocket of his jacket: he hadn't wanted to scribble notes while the bartender had been talking, fearing it would look odd or at least break the young man's flow. Instead he had relied on a mnemonic technique he had used a couple of times during his brief, abruptly-terminated career in intelligence in Spain. If discretion barred him from using a pen and paper, he would take in information — nodding along, absorbing what he heard — and then, in his mind's eye, visualize it in written form, the words appearing one by one on an imaginary page. Once the page was full, he would snap a mental photograph of it in his head and commit that to memory.

He now jotted down what he had just heard, rather than risk losing it: the locations of those three secret societies. As he walked he checked his notes against the Yale street map he had picked up from Walters earlier. Wolf's Head was not far at all; he would pass Skull and Bones en route.

The boy from the bar had not been wrong. If most of Yale looked like a transatlantic transplant from Oxford, the "tomb" of this secret society appeared to have been grafted on twentieth century America from ancient Greece or Rome. It consisted of identical twin buildings, each in reddish stone, smooth and windowless, save for two strips of dark, leaded glass framed by a flat, pillared portico: fake entrances. Buckling the two buildings together was a real entrance, similar in design to the other two — with pillars that were flat, rather than round — but with a genuine, solid door. There were no markings and no sign. It could have been a house of worship for an anonymous religion. And while James was tempted to mock the vanity of such a structure, as he probably would have done had this housed a student society back in Oxford, he could not deny the effect here. The closed austerity of this place exuded secrecy — and power.

He continued west on Chapel Street, then turned right almost immediately on York. At first, he couldn't see what he was meant to be looking at. There was none of the immediate grandeur of Skull and Bones, no imposing, temple-like entrance. Instead, there were just glimpses of amber stone behind the lush green foliage of a garden full of trees. He would have guessed this was the home of a wealthy recluse, newly-built, like the Sterling Library, from stones given an artificial patina of age.

He walked around to get a different view. Now he could see that, where Skull and Bones reached tall and high, the Wolf's Head "tomb" was spread lower and wider, its edges softened by gentle lawns all around. It could have been a chapel in the English countryside.

He followed the low wall around until he saw a path, shrouded by trees, leading up to a side door. He was sure that few outside the clandestine, gilded circle of Wolf's Head members dared to tread here and that he was breaking a dozen different secret society rules, but if he was to find Harry and Florence, Lund's promise — *I can help you* — was the closest he had got to a clue. The Assistant Dean's last act, embedding that pin into his cheek, had been to point here, to the Wolf's Head, so James had little choice but to find out why. This was the best lead he had, largely because it was the only lead he had.

At the door he found a simple push-button bell on the right. He pressed it but heard nothing. He pressed it again, assuming he had not pushed it hard enough. Still nothing. Perhaps it was broken. Or else the bell was sounding in some distant room, the doors thick, the floors lushly carpeted, from which no sound could travel. He leant in, pressing his ear against the wood. The place seemed utterly empty.

He walked a few paces back, his eye seeking out windows, drainpipes, ledges. Without planning to, he had begun sizing up the building for a break-in. He retreated further, to see if there was a path leading around the back, when he heard the sound of a twig breaking under foot. He swivelled to his left and saw nothing, then round the other way and there, standing right by him, much closer than he expected, was a woman — watching him with a calm, steady gaze.

She was tall, with hair that was neither blonde nor brown but somewhere in between, the colour of honey, tumbling loosely onto her shoulders. To add to his confusion, she was wearing trousers, wide at the bottom, wider than any he had seen worn by a man, but unmistakably trousers. She was young too, perhaps one of Yale's select population of female graduate students. In one hand she held a notebook, in the other a cigarette. She brought it to her lips, drew on it hard and then released a wreath of smoke. Then, unhurriedly, she discarded the cigarette, ground it out with a neatly-shod foot and extended a hand. "I'm Dorothy Lake of the *Yale Daily News*. How do you do, Dr Zennor?" The emphasis on the second syllable, Zenn-or.

James was about to answer reflexively, but caught himself. "How do you know my name?"

"Well, you just confirmed it. Thanks. But I'd worked it out. What other Englishman would be sniffing around outside Wolf's Head except the man Yale police were questioning this morning over the death of —"

"How do you know about that?"

"I'm a reporter. My job is to know what's going on in this city. Just like your job is to know what's going on in people's heads." She tapped an index finger at her temple. He noticed that her nails were painted blood red. "Besides, the editor has very good links with the Yale police department. Very good."

James tried to reply, but the words would not come. He was flummoxed, and not only because Dorothy Lake had wrong-footed him with that reference to his academic field. There was something about the way she stood which suggested a confidence, bordering on aggression. He was used to that in men; he saw it all the time. But he had never before encountered it in a woman.

Finally he spoke. "When the police mentioned my name, I hope they also told you I had been released. I had nothing to do with Lund's death, Miss Lake."

"Yeah, I heard that. But an innocent man would put the whole thing behind him, don't you think? Get on with his work, reading Sigmund Freud, analysing ladies' fantasies or whatever it is you psychologists do. But here you are."

"I'm here to find my wife and child."

"What here? At the Wolf's Head tomb?" She cocked her head at him in a way that was downright impudent.

James could think of no reply. Instead he turned and walked down the path and was almost back on the street when he felt her hand on his arm, lightly at first, then with greater force. "Stop," was all she said, but her eyes said more, a tiny concession. "I think we should talk."

256

"So that you can get a story for the student rag? I don't think so. Now if you'll excuse —"

"You don't need to worry about that, Dr Zennor. We don't publish during the vacation. I'm just gathering string for the first edition of the next semester: 'The strange death of Dr George Lund.' I might not mention you at all . . . if I don't feel like it."

"And what does that mean?"

"You help me, I'll keep your name out of it."

"I couldn't care less what you write. Put my name on the front page if you want. I'll be long gone from here by then." He wrenched his arm away, suppressing a wince as he did so.

He had walked no more than two paces when Dorothy Lake stepped in front of him, blocking his path. "What if I can help you find your family?"

He stared at her, hope rising. He forced it down: the woman was playing some sort of game. "You can help me by leaving me alone." He tried to walk past her. She moved to her right, blocking him again.

"What if I tell you what I know and you tell me what you know." She arched a single, elegantly pencilled eyebrow. "You know, you scratch my back and I'll scratch yours."

James tried to ignore the flush in her cheeks and the fullness of her lips. He had barely noticed any other woman since marrying Florence — since he had met Florence, truth be told — but there was no denying that this Dorothy Lake, as tall and lean as his wife, was very striking. Her features were not as refined as

Florence's, but nevertheless she was magnetic. She had what Harry Knox would have called a "bedroom face".

"You'll tell me what you know about what?"

She gave a small smile and nodded towards the building they had just left behind. "About this place."

"Wolf's Head?"

She nodded, then leaned in, close enough that he could pick up her scent — feminine, with a hint of musk — and whispered, "I've been inside."

James pulled back, so that he could face her but also to put greater distance between them. The moment had been unnerving in its proximity. He was about to speak when she looked up and over his shoulder. He turned, to see two students approaching. She signalled to wait, conversation suspended, until the men had passed; then she spoke again. "You know what, it makes no sense talking like this on the sidewalk. Why don't we get some lunch?"

Without enthusiasm, he agreed. She was persistent and canny, she had demonstrated that much already. Maybe she had picked up something useful. And he was not exactly inundated with offers of help. He needed to take what he could get.

They went to a place she described as a "diner" on Elm Street, where they were presented with hamburgers and chips, which she called French fries. In an attempt at small-talk, there was a brief exchange about the correct pronunciation of "tomato". "*Tom-arto*," she said mockingly, as if she were a house guest in an Evelyn Waugh novel. "It's *tom-may-to*: don't you Brits know anything?"

A few minutes later she pushed her unfinished plate aside and lit up another cigarette. "So why are you so interested in Wolf's Head?"

"I think you know the answer to that."

"I do, but I want to hear it from you." The confidence of this young woman was quite unsettling. She seemed to make no concession to the fact that James was older than she was, that he was a man or that they had only just met. He took another gulp of coffee. "Listen, Miss Lake. It was you who wanted this deal, not me. So why don't we let me decide the terms? You tell me what you know and then I will do the same. But you go first."

Dorothy took a long drag on the cigarette then ran her fingers through her hair, a gesture that instantly reminded him of Florence — though he was sure his wife would not make such a move in front of a stranger.

She rested her cigarette in the ashtray where it sent up a little curl of smoke as if in protest, then extended her hand across the table: "Deal." They shook hands, and she held on a fraction longer than she needed to. Her fingers were cool to the touch as they rested against his palm.

James withdrew his hand. "Let's start with the Wolf's Head. What can you tell me?"

"It's a secret society, set up around sixty years ago — the same way all these societies were set up."

"How's that?"

She retrieved the cigarette, took a drag. "By people who'd failed to get into the other secret societies."

"Like Skull and Bones and —"

"And Scroll and Key. You learn fast." She blew a ring of smoke, revealing a set of perfect white teeth. James was trying to work out her accent, which was different from the others he had heard here. The way she kept her lips tight together, the jaw slightly clenched, and clipped her words made him wonder if this was the American equivalent of posh. "Anyway, that's how it works. Scroll and Key was set up by Bones rejects, Wolf's Head by Scroll rejects."

"And who decides who gets in?"

"Who gets *tapped*, you mean. The existing members decide."

"And they're all third year students? Sorry, 'juniors'."

"Correct. But maybe not just by them."

"Who else?"

She stubbed out the remnant of her cigarette. "None of us know for sure. They're secret, remember? And women are not allowed anywhere near them."

"Except for you."

She ignored him and went on. "The members are top-drawer, chosen for all the usual reasons."

"Which are?"

"Brains, athletic ability. Pedigree."

"You mean their family backgrounds?"

"Sure. Grand-daddy was a Wolfie, Daddy was a Wolfie, you're a Wolfie."

"And what do they do, exactly, these 'Wolfies'?"

"The usual fraternity stuff: drinking, hazing, fooling —"

"What's hazing?"

"You don't have fraternities in England, huh? Hazing is an initiation ritual. New recruit has to be humiliated. You know, stand naked reciting the Declaration of Independence while getting towel-whipped." She mimed the snap of a towel.

"And once you're in?"

"That's when the fun starts."

"Like what?"

"More drinking, more larking around. But also," she lowered her voice, leaning in closer so that he could smell that musky scent once more, "parties."

"Fifteen male undergraduates drinking together doesn't sound like much of a party to me."

"Who said the guests were all men?" Her eyebrows twitched.

"Ah, so that's how you got inside. You were invited to a party there."

She nodded, her eyes briefly drifting faraway as if savouring a memory. "It was last year. When I was an undergraduate."

"I thought there were no lady undergraduates at Yale."

"I wasn't at Yale then. We were all from Vassar."

"All?"

"Yes, a group of girls from Vassar went to Wolf's Head for parties."

"I see."

"They brought us to Yale in a special bus. Took an age to get here."

"And what happened at these parties?"

She gave him a look. "Do you want me to draw you a map?"

"I'm just trying to work out what this bloody society is all about, Miss Lake. Just in case it's relevant. Please."

"You sound like you need a cigarette, Dr Zennor. Calm your nerves." Without asking if he wanted one, she took a cigarette from her case, put it to her mouth, lit it and then passed it to him. He hesitated before taking it, unsure whether he should collude in such an intimate exchange. But she was right; he did need to calm himself. He inhaled deep and long and then spoke again. "And you had a friend at Wolf's Head who invited you to these parties?"

"No, it didn't work like that. Vassar decided who went on the bus."

"Oh, so that was an exclusive club too."

"You bet. And discreet. Only those girls who were picked even knew about it."

"And I bet they were the smartest, prettiest girls in the college."

"Now you're asking me to be immodest, Dr Zennor." She smiled. "Put it this way, I'm sure Vassar was careful to choose girls the men of Wolf's Head would enjoy meeting."

"And inside? Did you see anything, anything that might be useful to me?"

"There's lots of wood panelling in there, I remember that. You know, honour boards listing past members, names painted in gold letters."

James leaned forward. "And do you remember any of them, any names?"

"I was a nineteen-year-old girl surrounded by some of the most eligible young men in America, Dr Zennor: I had my eye on other things."

"I need to see a list of past members."

"I might be able to help you with that."

James exhaled loudly. "That would be excellent, Miss Lake. Really."

"But now I think it's your turn to help me."

"Not yet, I'm afraid. I have a few more questions to ask first."

"Come on, this is not —"

"What, fair? Perhaps not. But there are probably a hundred people in this town who could tell me about the Wolf's Head Society. There's only one who can tell you about the death of George Lund. Remember, I was with the lead detective on the case a matter of hours ago. So, another question."

She raised her hands in defeat.

He cleared his throat, signalling as much to himself as to her, that he was getting to what mattered most. "I want to know what you know about the Oxford mothers and children."

"This is about your wife and child, right?"

"Right."

"Well, they arrived here on July twenty-fourth. They —"

"I've read your newspaper, Miss Lake. I want to know what *more* you know."

She crinkled her brow, as if she was struggling to think of anything interesting. "I didn't cover this story, so I don't really know much beyond —"

"Try."

"OK. I know they were invited by a few faculty members at Yale. It was their initiative. I know that it had to be arranged real quick, over a few weeks. I also heard that Cambridge said no."

"Cambridge? As in the university? Why would they say no?"

"I have no idea. I just heard that they did. People were asking, 'How come we're only doing this for Oxford? Is Yale Oxford's sister university? Will Harvard be hosting Cambridge children?' And the answer was no, Cambridge were offered but said no."

"How odd. And you don't remember where you heard that?"

"Just around." She lit another cigarette. "Oh, there is one other interesting thing."

"Yes."

"Both camps agreed on this plan."

"I don't follow."

"You know, pro- and anti-war. Those who think we should join the war backed the Oxford rescue, saying it's part of our historic ties to England and all that. And the anti-intervention people agreed, probably to show that just because they're against the war doesn't mean they don't care what happens to sweet little kids."

James resisted the desire to give her a brief lecture on why anyone who truly cared a jot about British children would be agitating to join the war this instant. Instead he asked, "Where did they go?"

"All over. They're staying with different families. People volunteered to open their doors. I heard there was one family who had their heart set on having a little girl and were shocked to receive four adolescent boys." She smiled at the thought of it.

"And you didn't hear anything about a mother with just one son, a two-year-old boy?"

"I'm sorry, but I didn't. I'm really sorry." What was odd about that last remark was that this otherwise unsentimental woman appeared to mean it.

Then she sat up straight. "Now it really is my turn."

"All right," James said, in a voice that suggested a reluctant concession. "But then we go back to past members of Wolf's Head, yes?" She nodded.

And so, as Dorothy Lake scribbled in her notebook, he ran through his meeting the previous day at the Dean's office, the second encounter at Pepe's restaurant, the rushed conversation over pizza and then the police visit this morning.

"He also appears to have taken something from the killer," James said coyly, building up what he planned to be his big revelation.

"You mean the pin in the cheek?"

"Oh. So you know about that?"

She rolled her eyes. "Of course. Why else would I have been sniffing around the Wolf's Head? Come on, Zennor. Tell me something I don't know."

He contemplated describing the photographs he had seen in Lund's bag. But he would not do it. Part of it was respect: why defame a dead man as a pervert, in the college newspaper of all places? But part of it was a more hard-headed calculation. He needed to hold something back, currency to be used later if needed.

"I'll tell you more if you tell me about these past members — and there's something I need you to do for me."

"I have a better idea," she said.

"What's that?"

"Why don't we cut the deal-making and the horse-trading and just agree to work on this together? You need to get to the bottom of this and so do I. I can't do it alone and nor can you. You help me, I help you. No more bartering. What do you say?"

"I say that's a much better idea."

"OK, then." She flicked through her notebook, finding an earlier page. "There's only one document I could find that makes any mention of past members. It's from an alternative college magazine that circulated a few years ago, before the Dean's office shut it down. It was called *Rebel Yale*. Luckily the Sterling keeps everything."

"And you've seen it?"

"I read it this morning. As soon as the editor got the tip-off about the link to Wolf's Head."

James leaned forward. "Go on."

"The formal group of Wolf's Head alumni is called the Phelps Association. Named, I think, for Edward John Phelps, who went on to become ambassador to London, as it happens."

James nodded. "OK, who else?"

"All kinds of big shots. Politicians in Washington, lawyers in New York, professors, doctors, business tycoons, you name it."

James sat back, trying to sift through what he was hearing. "And presumably Lund's killer was one of them?"

"No one else gets the pin."

James furrowed his brow again. "These former members, the Phelps Association. Do they stay involved in the university in any way?"

"There was something on this in the library too." She turned several pages of her notebook and began reading out loud. "'WHS' — that's Wolf's Head Society — 'alumni have been central to some of the most significant changes in the life of Yale. The recently-established residential college system was the inspiration of former WHS member, the late Edward S Harkness, while it was another one-time bearer of the Wolf's Head pin who in 1934 established the Yale Political Union'." She began speeding up, skim-reading as if looking for something else. "'Other innovations credited to WHS alums include the founding of the Elizabethan Club, as well as the composition of the unofficial Yale anthem —' "

"Hold on, go back."

"'. . . in 1934 established the Yale Political Union —' "

"No, the next bit."

"'. . . the founding of the Elizabethan Club, as well —' " "That's it. The Elizabethan Club. That's where I'm staying."

"I know."

"That's quite a coincidence, don't you think?"

"Well, not really. I mean, these WHS fellows also wrote the college song. They did a lot of things. It has no connection to Lund, does it?"

"No, I suppose not." He gestured at her notebook. "Go back to the rebel magazine. Does it list any names?"

"It does, but it seems to be purely speculative. Rumours and gossip."

"Can I look?"

"Sure," she passed the notebook across the table.

He saw a series of scribbled notations he could not decipher and then, continuing onto the next page, a list of names, apparently in alphabetical order: Harrison, Hayes, Hinton. He scanned ahead to McLellan, Merritt, Moore, Morton. Then to Simpson, Sutton, Symes, back up, his eye stopping briefly at the F's, where he saw a Ford and wondered if it might be the Ford of the motor car company, and then back down again. He was about to hand the list back when he saw an entry that halted him.

He turned the notebook around, his finger hovering over the name. "Well, that one certainly means something to me."

She peered at it, as if struggling to read her own handwriting. James's finger rested on the name of Theodore Lowell: the pastor James had heard within hours of arriving in New Haven, preaching so effectively from his pulpit at the Battell Chapel, urging his fellow Americans to stay out of Europe's war.

CHAPTER
TWENTY-FOUR

"All you have to do is provide a distraction," he said, after he had explained the plan for the first time.

"At the administration building?"

"Yes."

"In the Dean's private office?"

"No need to make it sound harder than it is. Not the Dean's *private* office, his outer office. I am fully confident in your abilities, Miss Lake." When he saw that she was still not convinced, he decided to take a risk. "I can't imagine any of the men on the *Yale Daily News* hesitating like this. Isn't this the kind of thing intrepid reporters do all the time?"

Lake signalled for the bill then said, "If you talked to her like that, I'm not surprised your wife left you."

James glared at her. "How dare you? My wife did not leave me. She evacuated our child to safety. That's all she was doing." He could hear a catch in his own voice, like a dry, repressed cough, but he could not stop himself. "Because what none of you people seem to realize is that our country is fighting a war. You'd never know it here, with all your milkshakes and pizza and three-egg omelettes. Might as well be on another planet. But England is in danger, do you see? We might lose. We might be bloody well invaded. That's what Florence was frightened of. She believed our child was in danger. She worried that he was not . . . safe. That was all. She came here to be safe. To be safe . . ."

He drew to a halt, avoiding her eyes. He hadn't blubbed: he'd caught himself just in time and hoped she had not noticed. But he knew what had just happened — and he was ashamed of himself.

And yet when he eventually caught her eye, he was surprised by what he saw. He had imagined a gaze that was chilly or, at best, pitying. But this was neither. Instead, her eyes had welled up in sympathy. Then, "How old is Harry?" she said, in a voice she had not used until then. "You never told me."

Soon James was back where he had been twenty-four hours earlier, though this time he had a woman, rather than a newspaper, to hide behind. The administrative building was a matter of yards away. He thought he saw Dorothy Lake chewing her lower lip in anxiety.

"Now remember," he was saying. "There are two entrances to that corridor. You have to do whatever you're going to do at the far end, on the other side of the office. Are we clear?"

"We're clear."

"All right then. Best of luck."

She straightened her blouse and was taking her first stride towards the front entrance when he spoke again. "Oh and Miss Lake —"

She turned around, a movement that briefly — in its suggestion of long, taut limbs beneath the clothing —

reminded him of Florence; Florence how she used to be, when they had first met, before the weight of war and her shattered husband had borne down on her. "Thank you," he said. And she was gone.

He waited for about thirty seconds, as they had agreed. Then he approached the entrance, making sure to stay far enough away that the doorman would not see him. He counted ten more seconds and then, true to their script, he heard a yelp of pain coming from inside the building: Dorothy, far down the corridor, crying out in apparent agony.

The commissionaire did what they had expected him to do: he left his post and rushed to help. Now was James's moment to slip inside.

From the hallway he craned his head round just long enough to see Dorothy sitting on the floor, clutching her leg. She had done as she was told, staging her fall at the far end of the corridor, well past the Dean's office. James had a clear run from here to there. But it was still not safe to move.

Judging the moment perfectly, Dorothy ripped the air with another howl of pain. James stole another glimpse into the corridor, and saw her struggling to stand up. At last, people started emerging from their offices, among them, James was relieved to see, the secretary to the Dean.

He could hear voices now, Dorothy's loudest. The echo made the words indistinct, but he got the gist. She was asking for someone to help her get to the bathroom, so that she could clean herself up.

Now. James began his walk down the corridor, affecting the gait of a man who was not visiting, but worked here. He took the five or six strides to reach the Dean's office, then turned left.

The plan had worked: they had timed Dorothy's little accident just right, the two secretaries' desks were both empty. Instantly, James moved around them to the bank of filing cabinets behind. There were cards placed on the front of each drawer, starting at the top left: "Admissions — Disciplinary Code".

His eye moved to the drawers below, picking out the subject headings, arranged alphabetically: Dwight Chapel, Endowment, Geography Faculty. He found a drawer labelled "Memorial — Saybrook College". He tugged at it, surprised to see that it extended well over a yard. It must have contained several hundred files, each identified by a tab.

He went past the M's — Memorial, Monroe, Montana — and overshot, landing in the P's — Political Science, Posture Study, Professional Training — before tracking back to the O's. His heart leapt when he saw a divider labelled "Oxford", which preceded perhaps a dozen more files: "Oxford, Chancellor", "Oxford, History faculty" and "Oxford, Rhodes scholarships". Not what he was looking for.

He went back, slower this time, and his heart jumped. Just after the "Chancellor" file was a tab he had missed: "Oxford, children". He pulled it out, only to discover that the tab was attached not to a file but a single sheet of card. On it was stuck a typed label: "See

Yale Faculty Committee for Receiving Oxford and Cambridge University Children".

James looked up. There was a sound outside: two voices. Instinctively, he straightened his back and took a pace back. He held still as, out of the corner of his eye, he saw two men deep in conversation pass the door. Neither of them looked his way. He wondered what bathroom theatrics Dorothy was engaging in to keep the Dean's secretary busy: whatever she was doing, she would have to keep doing it a bit longer.

He now looked towards the floor, finding the drawer that would contain files labelled with a "Y". There it was.

There must have been a thousand files crammed together: "Yale, Alumni Association"; "Yale, Divinity School"; "Yale, Faculty Committee". He burrowed deep into the last category and found that too was subdivided into a score of files, one for the Faculty Committee on pay, another for the Faculty Committee on ethics, until finally he found what he was looking for: "Yale Faculty Committee for Receiving Oxford and Cambridge University Children".

He pulled it out and rushed to the first sheet. A letter from the Dean, Preston McAndrew, to his opposite number at Oxford, inviting him to send Oxford's children to Yale for the duration of the war. Behind it, the same letter, though this time addressed to Cambridge; letters of grateful reply from Oxford, then a response from Cambridge. James skimmed over it just long enough to see that Dorothy had been right: here was Sir Montague Butler, Master of Pembroke College,

Cambridge declining Yale's offer, explaining that no particular arrangements should be made for university children, "since this might be interpreted as privilege for a special class". Then more letters, back and forth, to Oxford about dates, visas, shipping routes . . .

Then, at last, he had it: a list of participants, his eye motoring through them, rushing as it always did to the end of the page. There: *Walsingham, Harry, two y.o. (accompanied by mother, Florence)*.

He turned to the next entry, a sheaf of papers held together by a bulldog clip. The first sheet was dedicated to three children by the name of Anderson, including their dates of birth and home address in Oxford, as well as details of their parents, alongside what James assumed was the address of the family who had taken them in — in this case the Mansfields of Prospect Street, New Haven. He turned to the next sheet: the Arnolds, brother and sister, children of a Fellow of Jesus College, a medieval historian, now relocated to Swarthmore, Pennsylvania. Why so far away, James wondered for the briefest of moments, but there was no time to think. These papers were arranged in alphabetical order which meant Harry and Florence — and their new address — would be at the back.

He went to the last sheet: Zander, a boy, evacuated to St Ronan Street, New Haven. He turned to the penultimate sheet: Wilson. The one before: Walton. His hands trembling now, he struggled to separate the next two pages that clung together, refusing to come apart. At last, they separated. This sheet, surely, would bring him back together with his family.

Hands shaking, he read the name: *Victor, Ann*.

There must be some mistake. His thumb and forefinger rubbed frantically at this sheet, praying for it to yield another page, the one that would tell him where he might find his wife and child. But it refused to separate.

He ran through them again: Victor, Walton, Wilson, Zander. No Walsingham. No Zennor.

It must have been filed wrongly. He started back through the whole sheaf, turning the pages as fast as his fingers could do it: Anderson, Arnold, Boston, Champion and on through the Falks, Macbeths and Somersets. No misplaced Walsingham, no randomly filed Zennor.

There was a clicking sound on the corridor, footsteps coming nearer. It must be someone else: Dorothy had promised she would keep the secretary busy in the ladies' lavatory long enough to give James a clear five minutes among the filing cabinets, staging another fall or weeping about her good-for-nothing boyfriend if that's what it took.

James went back to the first sheet he had found, the list of Oxford arrivals. He ran his finger down the names: Anderson, Arnold, Boston and on and on, ending with Walsingham and then Zander. This document mapped onto the bulldog-clipped set of papers perfectly, the same families listed in the same, alphabetical order. Except for Harry and Florence, who appeared on the first register but were missing from the next, the one that revealed where the Oxford children were now living.

He was about to go through the rest of the file when he sensed the change of light in the doorway. He hurriedly shoved the document back in the drawer, but it was too late. When he looked up he saw not one person watching him but two. He recognized the first figure as the secretary, Barbara, but he instantly worked out the identity of the other. He knew without being told that he had come face to face with Preston McAndrew, Dean of Yale University.

CHAPTER
TWENTY-FIVE

London

Taylor had shuddered with boredom when he first heard of the job his father had arranged for him. It sounded so technical, as if he were going to be a grease-monkey, wearing overalls and thumping away at machines all day. He had been educated expensively enough to expect — no, to deserve — better than that.

And his colleagues were, as he feared, dull as a weekend in Ohio. They barely talked about anything, let alone anything interesting. One spent the lunch hour reading the baseball scores from the *Paris Herald Tribune*, which might have been tolerable had he not insisted on reading them aloud. Thankfully, since the fall of Paris, the paper only reached London sporadically, if it was published at all.

The consolation came, surprisingly enough, from the work itself. He would tell Anna that he worked in the embassy's "nerve centre" and, though at first that had been mere self-aggrandizement on his part, he had come to believe it. He had become convinced that there was not a significant document that did not pass through this office, whether coming in or going out.

He used to prefer the incoming traffic, enjoying the thrill of knowing what the rest of London did not, feeling as if he were eavesdropping on the conversations of the most powerful men in the world. Outgoing was often a chore: either it was humdrum stuff about consignments of this and container loads of that or it was rehashing what he had already read in that morning's London *Times*. Even the cables which purported to offer the skinny on what was really happening in Whitehall or Westminster rarely offered anything juicy — and nothing to rival what he was picking up around Murray's dinner tables (or from Anna's pillow talk, for that matter).

But he was good at his job, faster than the others. He had the advantage of youth, that was what the secretaries said: "It's always the young men who master the new gadgets." The machinery did not faze him: he could operate it without thinking about it. And so, before long, he was given the most urgent material, which often meant the most important.

Some of his colleagues didn't even bother to read the paperwork in front of them. Of course they read each word before rendering it. But they were not really reading it, not taking in its meaning. Taylor Hastings, however, found he could do both, effortlessly. And as he did so, he grew aware that he was becoming supremely well-informed about both the progress of the war — as reported by British officials to the US Embassy, and then passed on by US diplomats to the State Department in Washington — and the shifting moods and sympathies in the American capital.

278

Of course he knew he was getting only half the picture, and even that half was jaundiced. Most of the Brits were putting the best possible gloss on their efforts for the benefit of their American contacts: telling them that they had detected chinks in the German armour, that it would not take much to bring down the Nazi ogre, that victory was possible. But that message was tempered by the advice given by Ambassador Kennedy, whose thrust, however subtly disguised, usually amounted to the same thing: Britain was doomed and there was no point America coming to its aid, not economically and certainly not militarily. The replies Kennedy received, and which passed through Taylor's hands each morning, told him which way Washington was leaning that day — towards isolation or intervention — and where the various competing US officials, in State or in the White House, were positioning themselves.

Reading this material first hand, reading it indeed before the principals themselves had laid eyes on it, fed Taylor Hastings's feeling that he had somehow landed close to the summit of world affairs. Had destiny placed him there? Was this the work of the God his mother worshipped so faithfully? He wasn't sure. But the sense that he had been granted an opportunity he should not waste, that he was being called to act, was growing within him.

A fresh pile of papers awaited: incoming traffic from Washington that had arrived during the night. His job, here in the cipher room of the London embassy, was to decode the messages, turning each cable of gibberish back into English, to be read by those far above him in the hierarchy, those who would never meet him or know his name. They would read these documents soon enough — but only after Taylor Hastings had read them first.

CHAPTER
TWENTY-SIX

"Barbara, would you get Dr Zennor a cup of coffee?" The Dean turned to him, attempting a smile. "I'm afraid we don't run to tea here."

"I don't want a cup of bloody tea or coffee. I want some answers."

"Why don't you sit down, Dr Zennor?"

"I will sit down when someone tells me what the hell is going on here."

"Barbara," the Dean said, his voice still even, his smile still in place, "why don't I take Dr Zennor into my office where he and I can talk in private. And perhaps you could bring us that coffee." He gave his secretary a look which suggested he did not want her wandering too far away, just in case.

James allowed himself to be ushered through the inner door. Wisely, Preston McAndrew did not try to put a hand on his shoulder as he guided him, otherwise the Dean would have been on the receiving end of an English fist.

"I must tell you, something very strange is afoot in your university, Dr McAndrew. Something very strange indeed."

"Please, sit down." The Dean pulled his chair out from behind his desk so that he might sit closer to James, as if they were two men in a club drawing room rather than an office. He gestured towards the seat for James, but his gesture was ignored.

"I have twice been barred from enquiring after my wife and child by staff at this office. On my second visit, the Assistant Dean promises he can help me — only to end up dead that same evening. And now I see that my wife and child's records are missing from your files. What on earth is going on here?"

"I can see you're very exercised —"

"Don't talk to me as if I'm some kind of lunatic! I'm quite —"

"I am not accusing you of being a lunatic, Dr Zennor. But you must appreciate this situation is highly irregular. I find an intruder rifling through my files and he starts putting *me* in the dock. I think most men in my position would have called the police by now. And from what I hear, I suspect they would be most interested to learn what you've been up to."

That pulled James up short. He suddenly became aware of himself, standing here, shouting in the office of a man he had never met. He thought of what Bernard Grey had said about him: *not suitable for sensitive work*. Slowly he sat down.

"Good man," said the Dean, who let out a barely audible exhalation of relief. When the secretary knocked on the door with two cups of coffee, he leapt up, apparently grateful for a break in the tension.

Only now did James take a good look at him. He was not at all what he had expected. The title of Dean had planted a picture in his mind of an American version of Grey, white-haired and ancient. But this man looked to be in his mid-forties, no more. He was as tall as James and handsome too, with a full head of dark hair lightly flecked with grey, the touches of silver suggesting distinction rather than old age.

"Look, the truth is, I blame myself for this situation, I really do," he was saying, as he stirred cream into his coffee, a habit that would, James reflected, have seemed like reckless indulgence back home in the land of the ration book. "Oxford notified me that you were coming on a fellowship and I really should have made arrangements to meet you. Forgive me for that mistake."

James said nothing, wondering if this was a deliberate attempt to wrong-foot him. The Dean had not summoned the police; he had not even raised his voice. Disarming an opponent with courtesy was just the sort of trick Grey would pull.

"Barbara has already filled me in on the history here, as we medics say." The hint of a smile was realized, revealing a set of straight, white teeth. "And I need to apologize for that too. As you say, you came here to make a perfectly reasonable request for information on your wife and child. Florence and Harry, is that right?"

"That's right. The point, Dr McAndrew is —"

"Preston, please." The Dean looked directly into James's eyes. "I'm afraid Barbara and Joan are very good at what they do, but they're used to guarding the information they have here as if it were the Ark of the Covenant! So, let's see what we can do."

"I hope you agree it is odd. That file contains a complete list of locations for every Oxford mother or child, but there is no record for my family."

McAndrew held up his hand. "I completely agree with you. Something doesn't add up." He rose to retrieve a piece of paper from his desk.

Perhaps, James thought, he had rushed to judgment on this man. McAndrew exuded competence and a degree of sympathy too. And there was surely no one more capable of reuniting him with Florence and Harry. He needed an ally, especially one so well placed.

"I ought to apologize for resorting to . . ." James hesitated. "Unorthodox means." As he said the words, he thought of his accomplice. He guessed that by now Dorothy had hobbled out of the ladies' lavatory, leaning on the secretary, only to see the Dean returning to his office — and had then tiptoed away, lest anyone suspect a link between her and James. That would have been the canny thing to do and that girl was nothing if not canny.

"No need to apologize at all," the Dean said, distractedly. He was reading the sheet in front of him, briefly looking up to add, "I don't have kids myself, but if I did I'm sure I'd have done exactly the same thing." He suddenly stood up. "So let's go and look at these files, shall we?"

James followed him into the outer office where the secretary, Barbara, was hammering away at a typewriter. She glanced up only briefly, returning her gaze to the machine hurriedly and, to James's mind, guiltily.

"So," McAndrew said loudly, "why don't you show me where you'd got to?"

"Well, this is slightly embarrassing."

"On the contrary, the embarrassment is all ours." The Dean shot a reproving look in Barbara's direction. "Go ahead."

James walked over to the cabinet containing the "Y" files, pulled open the drawer and, tentatively now, in deference to the fact that he was in another man's office, thumbed his way through a few of them until he found the one marked "Yale Faculty Committee for Receiving Oxford and Cambridge University Children". He pulled it out and handed it to the Dean who opened it immediately.

"Well, of course I'm familiar with this document." Smiling, he pulled out the letter of invitation he had signed less than two months earlier. "As Dean I was charged with issuing our offer on behalf of the university."

"I saw that. The relevant papers come later. The list of names."

Both men stood by the wall of filing cabinets as McAndrew flicked through the pages, eventually stopping where James had asked.

"The name you're looking for is Walsingham." Noting McAndrew's quizzical expression, James added, in a quieter voice, "my wife's maiden name."

A momentary pause and then: "There they are!" The Dean was delighted. "Look," he handed James the document in triumph.

"Yes, I've seen that Dr McAndrew —"

"Preston."

"But this is my point." He could hear the nerves jangling once again in his voice. He wanted to be calm and suave, one accomplished scholar talking to another. He knew that would be more effective. But he could not do it. He desperately wanted to see his family again and desperation is one of the few things impossible to hide. "She is on that list — but nowhere else."

"So," said the Dean, his lips pursed in concentration. "This document confirms that Florence and Harry made the crossing successfully from England and that they reached New Haven."

"Yes. But when everyone else on that list has an extra sheet, detailing their host family, address —"

"Yes, yes. Quite so."

The Dean was holding the bulldog-clipped sheaf, making the same search James had done, furtively, a few minutes earlier. Back and forth he went, drawing the same result. "Hmmm," he said eventually. Then he turned to his secretary. "Barbara, this is most odd," he said, explaining the problem and asking her to search all the files thoroughly. "If it's there, Barbara will find it," he said, turning back to James. "There's none better!" He gave her a warm smile and she immediately set to work, crouching down by the "Y" drawer and working her way through it. "Why don't we go back into my office, while we wait to see what miracle

Barbara produces? There's something else I'd like to discuss."

James hesitated. He wanted to stand over the secretary, watch her go through those papers, get down on his knees and sort through the files himself if necessary, rather than talking, talking, talking. The muscles in his back were tense. For over three weeks now he had had that same taut feeling in his body: that every minute not spent searching was a minute wasted. But he forced himself to be polite — and patient.

McAndrew closed his door and took off his jacket, draping it over the back of his chair. Whether that was in recognition of the heat, mitigated in this room by the whirr of the ceiling fan, or a cue that they were now having a less formal conversation, James was uncertain. Though when he saw McAndrew head towards a drinks tray in the corner of the room and pour two glasses of Scotch, he concluded it was the latter. And he knew precisely what topic the Dean was about to raise.

"This is turning into an afternoon of apologies," he began, handing James a heavy tumbler of whisky, "but I wanted to say how much I regret that you were drawn into this very unfortunate business with the Assistant Dean."

"Yes." James paused. "Very tragic."

"Tragic is the right word. The Yale Police Department are zealous — as they should be, of course — and they pounced on you, I'm afraid. When anyone could have told them, as I now have told them, that this was hardly unexpected news."

"Oh?"

The Dean looked into his glass. "I'm afraid so, yes. A very troubled man, Dr Lund." McAndrew hesitated, as if unsure how much he should let on. "You're too young to have served in the last war, but I saw it there too."

"Saw what?"

"Men in the grip of demons, Dr Zennor. Demons. I believe they had been tormenting poor George for some time. Why he latched onto you, I don't know. Who can know what fantasies rage through such a troubled mind? But I guess he told himself that you had some role in his nightmares."

James drunk from his glass, tasting what he knew instantly was a malt of the highest quality. He decided to take a risk. "And what about Wolf's Head? The badge in the mouth and all that."

McAndrew did not react; confirmation that this had not come as news to him. He swirled the liquid in his glass for a moment or two, then smiled. "Such a lot of nonsense is spoken about these clubs, you wouldn't believe."

"Perhaps Lund didn't think it was nonsense. He went to some lengths to connect Wolf's Head with his death."

"Is that what the police said?"

"That's what I assumed. That his killer had been wearing the pin and Lund managed to tear it from him in the struggle. Shoved it in his mouth, so that the police would find it. You're not convinced."

"Well, I suppose it could be that. If this were the movies, Dr Zennor, the killer would have left the pin

288

there deliberately, as his 'calling card'." The Dean gave an indulgent smile, the crows' feet crinkling in the corner of his eyes. "But I suspect the truth is much more humdrum than that. More humdrum and infinitely more sad."

"And what is the truth?"

"Lund had a first-class mind, you know. Really one of the best in his class at the Medical School. But it began to unravel. I suppose his past membership of Wolf's Head went into the stew, along with everything else, including his meeting with you."

"So the police told you he was a member?"

The Dean gave another smile, the wistful expression of an older man speaking about a wayward son. "The police didn't need to tell me, Dr Zennor. I already knew."

"I thought these clubs were all terribly secret."

"Oh, they are. But the members tend to know who's who."

James sat back in his chair. "So you too, then?"

"I'm afraid so. It was me who brought George in."

James took another sip of the whisky, enjoying the warmth of it in his throat. "And your view is that Lund took his own life?"

"I'm certain of it. More than that: I had feared it. For some time now."

There was a light knock, followed by the appearance of Barbara's head around the door. "Dean McAndrew, I'm afraid I've looked. There's nothing there."

"You've checked thoroughly?"

"And checked again, yes, sir."

Briefly soothed by the alcohol, James had, for a minute or two, allowed himself to forget about the files and the missing information on Florence and Harry. But that made the disappointment now all the heavier. He had been sure the Dean, backed by the full bureaucratic muscle of his office, was about to solve his problem; he had half-expected the secretary to come in waving a piece of paper, telling him she had tracked down the errant Mrs Zennor and that she was living twenty minutes away.

The Dean stood up, placing a consoling arm around James's shoulder. "I know what a letdown this is for you. I also find it very frustrating. But I promise to get to the bottom of this. Would you please let Barbara know how we can be in touch with you? One way or another, we will reunite you with your family — I give you my word."

CHAPTER
TWENTY-SEVEN

James left the administrative building, stepping into the summer evening. His son Harry had once called this "the orangey time of day", when the sun begins to dip, turning the sky pink, crimson and every shade in between. It felt like midnight, such was his exhaustion — from the heat, from the whisky, but above all from the disappointment. Sitting in the office of Preston McAndrew, he had allowed himself to believe that his journey was all but over. Each moment in the Dean's office had pumped him ever fuller with hope. And now that hope had been punctured.

He always thought of himself as a rational man, a man of science. Faced with any conundrum, he always favoured the explanation that was both simple and supported by evidence. He had no patience for theory, for hypotheticals or speculation. And so, no matter how curious Lund's behaviour had been, no matter how bizarre his death or connection to the mysterious Wolf's Head society, James had believed that the true explanation for Harry and Florence's disappearance would turn out to be straightforward and mundane: a mislaid file, a document that had been filled in incorrectly. There would be apologies, perhaps even laughter at the rotten luck of it all and the whole ordeal would be over. At bottom, that was what James had believed throughout — and wanted to believe still.

But it was becoming harder to hold onto. Lund was dead and all the rational, empirical evidence pointed to murder rather than suicide. Florence and Harry were proving impossible to trace. Again it was now logical, not hysterical or paranoid, to conclude that something had happened to them, even that they could be in serious danger. Lund had been agitated when he made his offer of help, hardly the behaviour of a man aware of a mere administrative mix-up that, once resolved, would reveal Florence's whereabouts. He had acted as if he were privy to information that was itself dangerous.

James suddenly became aware that he was walking very fast, adrenalin pushing him into a rush he could hardly control. What was more, though it took him another moment to realize it, he had no idea where he was going.

It was as he headed into College Street that he sensed someone behind him. He didn't turn at first, his training telling him to wait. His brain automatically offered up the options: McAndrew catching up with him, to tell him they had found Florence's address after all; the men who had killed Lund, now come to kill him; Florence herself. That last thought — however unlikely — made him turn and what he saw made him wonder why he had not considered this possibility first.

"Hold up, Dr Zennor. Some of us are wearing heels."

"Christ, you gave me a start." He realized he was panting. "How long have you been following me?"

"And there I was, expecting a nice 'Thank you, Miss Lake'."

James stopped, looked down, then said, "I'm sorry. And thank you for doing what you did. But it was no good. They have details for every Oxford family but mine."

"No! That *is* disappointing." Something in her eyes, clear and blue, suggested a sympathy that was more than merely polite. "Where are you going?"

"I don't know, Miss Lake." He let out a bitter laugh. "I really don't know."

"You don't know or you don't want to tell me?"

A thought that had been incubating in James's mind since he had sat in McAndrew's office now came to life. It was laden with risk, something he would not consider in normal circumstances. But these were not normal circumstances. "Actually, I do know where I would like to go. But I will need your help."

He had often thought badly of himself in recent years, especially when regarding his damaged body. His opinion of his own worth had sunk low. But he had never felt what he felt now. He had never despised himself.

Standing here, on the doorstep of a small, colonial house on Church Street, his hand hovering by the brass knocker, he felt contempt for what he was about to do. For this was the home of Margaret Lund, a woman who had become a widow that morning. To intrude on such a person was appalling in itself; to do so with a reporter in tow was vile. And yet here he was.

When he had mentioned the idea to Dorothy Lake, he had half-hoped she would talk him out of it, tell him it was wrong and that he should leave Mrs Lund in peace. But who was he fooling? She was a journalist and an ambitious one at that. He had barely got the words out before she had found a telephone booth, with a directory hanging on a metal cord, and discovered the home address for Lund, Dr G.E. If he had known it would be that simple, James would have done it himself.

"Don't be too tough on yourself," Dorothy had said as they turned onto Church Street, the harder edges on her voice softer now, as if they had been planed away. The change made him wonder which of the two voices he had heard from her over the course of this day was real and which the fake. "You're paying a condolence visit."

"I'd hardly call it that."

"She may find it comforting to talk to someone who saw her husband at the end."

"For God's sake, he wasn't ill, was he? It's not as if I visited him on his deathbed. We met and he stormed out. Besides, that's not my motive, is it, to express my condolences? I'm there for my sake, not hers."

"And what about me?"

"That just makes it worse."

"Oh thanks."

"Because you're a reporter." He had shaken his head as he walked, his pace quickening in time with his nerves. "I can hardly believe I'm doing this."

"We'll say I'm your friend and that I'm helping you find your wife and child."

James gave her a sideways glance. She was about the same age Florence had been when they had first met, in Barcelona. Florence's poise had stunned him then; he had fallen in love with it. But it was nothing next to the brazen confidence of Dorothy Lake.

"What, and lie to a grieving woman?" He had stared straight ahead. "We'll try to keep it vague."

He now took a deep breath, lifted the knocker and let it fall once, then twice. He could hear voices on the other side of the door: the low hubbub of a house of mourning. He wished he could turn and sprint away. But it was too late for that: a woman answered the door, much older than he expected, her hair silver-white at the temples.

"Mrs Lund?" James said tentatively, his voice gentle.

The woman shook her head. James saw that she was clutching a handkerchief, balled up in her fist. "Mrs Lund is my daughter. Were you a colleague of George's?"

James considered saying yes; it would be so much easier. But he could not do it. "No, I only met him yesterday. I was hoping to —"

"Who is it, Mother?"

The voice came from the other end of the hallway, from a woman with similar features to the first, though she was taller and fuller-figured. When she emerged into the light, James could see she was cradling a baby in her arms.

He had thought about this moment in advance. He had prayed to the God he didn't believe in that the police had already told her that the Englishman had a cast-iron alibi for the murder of her husband, that he was no longer a suspect. But what if they hadn't?

"My name is James Zennor. I was with your husband last night."

She was close now, shooing her mother out of the way so that she filled the doorframe. The baby was tiny and new. Margaret Lund's belly was still rounded, as Florence's had been in the weeks after Harry's birth. Her eyes were raw. They looked into James's for a long moment, as if trying to see into him, to see what material he was made of. Then they diverted to his side. "And who is this?"

"This is Dorothy Lake, she's helping me while I'm here at Yale." Perhaps he had spoken too gently, because Mrs Lund leaned forward. "I'm sorry, I missed the name."

"Dorothy Lake." She extended a hand, which Margaret Lund ignored, her brow furrowed. Lund's widow reminded James of the men he had seen during the university battle in Madrid, stumbling around, dazed, after they had seen their friends drop to the ground. "Lake, you say?"

"Yes." It was James who answered. "I wonder if we could come inside. Just for a moment or two."

Mrs Lund turned around and walked back down the hallway. James chose to interpret that as an invitation to follow. Conscious of being watched by the older woman, he kept his eyes focused ahead, fighting the urge to look around, to guess where the dead man's corpse had been found.

They were led into the kitchen, where Mrs Lund had already taken a seat. (Perhaps the living room was out of bounds; perhaps it had happened there.) She was looking down at her baby, stroking his bald head.

Without being asked, James found a chair. He did not know how or where to begin, so he just started talking. "Your husband performed a great act of kindness to me yesterday. He offered to help find my wife and child. They came here to New Haven from Oxford, you see, but there is no trace or record of them. Your husband said he could help. We met yesterday evening. He became agitated; I'm afraid we argued — and I didn't see him again. But I believe he was trying to help a man in distress. A fellow father in distress." James could feel his eyes turning salty. He had not expected to become emotional. Maybe it was the sight of the baby. He rushed towards a conclusion. "And so I wanted to pay my respects."

Through this, Margaret Lund kept her gaze on the infant, soothing him as he slept. She did not raise her eyes to James when he finished talking. He now saw the futility of this visit; it had been a mistake to come. What had he really expected her to say? "Oh yes, George mentioned you to me. He told me your wife is staying at number seventy-eight . . ." What possible light could she shed on his problem, especially now, in this state?

He got up to leave, rising from his chair slowly, as if too sudden a movement would be disrespectful. He wanted to ask about Wolf's Head, about the pin in the mouth, why George Lund had seemed so nervous and, if she had spoken at all, if she had given him even the slightest cue, he would have found a way to do so. But asking cold, like this, was impossible. He was not a detective; he could not start bombarding a widow on her very first day of mourning with questions. She was clearly catatonic with grief.

It was Dorothy who spoke next. "Mrs Lund? Might I use your bathroom?"

Now the widow looked up, an oddly serene expression on her face. "Upstairs, first door on your right."

James wondered what Dorothy was up to. He hoped to God she wasn't planning on snooping around up there; he would not have put it past her. He got to his feet. "Once again, Mrs Lund, I am so sorry for —"

"Close the door."

"I'm sorry, I —"

"Close the door."

James did as he was told.

"Listen to me. Don't tell anyone else what I'm about to tell you, do you understand?"

"Of course."

"No one. Not for my sake. For yours."

"I don't —"

"My husband did not kill himself, Dr Zennor. Whatever else anyone tells you, don't believe it. He

298

would never have done such a thing." She glanced down at the baby. "He did not kill himself."

"I thought not."

"There are some very powerful people around here, Dr Zennor. I think George had found out something he shouldn't have. In the last few days, he had become very anxious." The eyes, rimmed with red, were afire.

"Did he tell you what it was?"

"No. But he wanted to tell someone. Maybe he was going to tell you."

James gazed at her, his mouth dry. "Yes."

"It had something to do with his work."

"You're certain of that?"

She nodded tightly, impatient to get on. She cocked an ear as a voice became audible on the other side of the door. "With you in a minute, Mother!" she called out, to ward off any interruption. In an urgent whisper, she resumed: "Every night George brought home a briefcase full of papers. Every night. He worked so hard." Her voice sounded like a broken reed. "But when I found him . . . this morning." Her eyes were brimming now, the words cracked. "When I found him, his case was empty. Nothing there but a few pencils. No documents. Not a single sheet of paper." Her gaze pinned him: he could not look away.

"Whoever killed him took those papers, Dr Zennor. That's why they killed my husband. To keep their secret safe."

CHAPTER
TWENTY-EIGHT

"We ought to stop and get something to eat," Dorothy said. When he hesitated, she added, "As a purely practical necessity."

He was indeed exhausted and hungry too. Though sitting down for a meal seemed an indulgent act with Florence and Harry missing, he nodded his acceptance. "Good. I know a little place just a few blocks from here."

She took him to a restaurant off Wall Street, where she gestured at a table outdoors. He had not eaten outside since Madrid three years earlier; he recoiled from the idea of doing so now, with someone other than Florence, particularly a young and, it had to be admitted, pretty woman. So he moved inside, where he instantly saw a set of newspapers spread out on a table, each one attached to a wooden pole, like those kept in a public library. He jostled aside a couple waiting to be seated and all but fell on the papers, scanning them for word from home.

They were from across the United States, almost all yesterday's rather than today's. He started with the *Chicago Tribune* and its headline: "Leading Congressman brands Roosevelt a 'warmonger'." He read the first few paragraphs, which were plainly slanted in favour of the congressman and against the President. Was this what people here were thinking, that to come to Britain's defence against the bloody Nazi menace amounted to "warmongery"? He could feel the bile rising in his throat. He shoved the paper aside, searching for some word on the war itself. He flicked through the *Boston Globe*, eventually finding, on page four, a story headlined "Stoic Britons gird themselves for invasion". It was accompanied by a photograph of the "Home Guard", the renamed Local Defence Volunteers that James had seen parading in the college quad, under the command of Bernard Grey. He wanted to weep for his country: weeks, if not days, away from Nazi conquest, with only a few feeble geriatrics to protect her. And America, her young, strong child, standing aside, refusing to help.

Dorothy ordered a bottle of wine and James didn't bother to object. He drank more than he ate, listlessly turning over the steak that had been laid before him. As the sky outside turned a deep red, then indigo and finally fell into darkness, she tried to get him to discuss what they had learned, to speculate and theorize about George Lund and the secret fraternity of the Wolf's Head Society, but he was sick at heart and could barely respond.

She tried a different tack. "So how long have you been married?"

"It will be four years this winter."

"She as smart as you?"

"Smarter."

Dorothy whistled. "And what is she smart about?"

"Her subject is biology."

"I bet it is."

"What's that supposed to mean?"

"Scratch that. You fall in love right away or she play hard to get?" She lit a cigarette. "Or maybe *you* played hard to get? I could see you doing that. You're the type."

Without meaning to, James found himself telling the story — of the People's Olympiad in Barcelona, of the outdoor swimming practice, of his confusion over Florence's departure for Berlin. Dorothy nodded in the right places, asked the right questions. Not that he needed prompting. Once he started he found it hard to stop. He could hear his own voice, calmer and quieter as he talked about his wife and their life together. He found it comforting, as if the next best thing to speaking to Florence were speaking about her.

"And you left Spain in thirty-nine, right?"

"No, we left in thirty-seven."

"Why's that? You lose faith?"

"No. Not at all."

"Why then?"

"I'd rather not talk about it."

"Oh, you never say that to a reporter, Dr Zennor." She lightly smacked his hand, the touch of her skin sending a current through him. "That just makes us more interested. Or in my case, *intrigued*."

"What intrigues you exactly, Miss Lake?"

"You, exactly, Dr Zennor."

Feeling uncomfortable, he shifted the subject back to Florence, like a man returning to the warm part of the bed. He found himself describing her — her height, the muscles of her back, her posture. He was speaking about her athletic accomplishments, how she had trained for the Olympics, but the effect on him was more direct than that. Not for the first time, the physical memory of his wife recalled his desire for her. He had a memory of her stepping out of the shower, her skin glistening, the shape of her visible under the towel and how, when she spotted him gazing at her, she let the towel fall to the floor . . .

"So what went wrong, Dr Zee?" Dorothy Lake lit another cigarette, dipping her head to meet the lighter, so that James caught the scent of her hair. That too sent a charge through him, one that somehow combined with the yearning he felt for his wife, the longing for her touch, to produce an effect that confused him. He pushed away the sensation by trying to address her question.

"You'd have to ask Florence."

"What would she say if I did?"

"That I became unbearable. And that she feared for our child."

"Why?"

"Because of the war." James, now smoking too, inhaled deeply. "And because of me."

"You? You didn't hurt the baby, did you?" For once the alarm was genuine, a look that made James wonder if this was Dorothy Lake's real face, if the rest of the time she was posing.

"Never deliberately." He saw Dorothy's reaction. "I never hit him, for Christ's sake! There was an accident with a boiling kettle. A near-miss. Nothing happened. But it could have."

"And you blame yourself?"

"I deserve the blame."

"You're very hard on yourself, do you know that? I've noticed that about you. It's very unusual in a man."

James looked up at her, with a faint smile. "How old are you, Miss Lake?"

"I'm twenty-one."

"And yet you know all about men."

"I know plenty."

"Yes? And why's that?"

"Same way a birdwatcher knows about birds. I pay attention." She held his gaze after she spoke, lifting the cigarette to her lips, letting her eyes close for a fleeting moment as she sucked on it and inhaled, then looking at him again. In the end, it was he who broke the contact.

"So what's your story going to say then?"

"I don't think I have enough to go on yet. We need to find out more. The wife didn't give us much, did she?"

"No." He decided not to mention the widow's impassioned, urgent final message.

"Other than that she doesn't believe Lund committed suicide."

James sat back. "How do you know that?" He pictured Lake on the other side of the closed door, her ear pressed to the wood, hearing Margaret Lund's warning.

Not for my sake. For yours.

Dorothy took a sip of wine, licking her lower lip afterwards like a cat. "Oh, sometimes you just know, don't you? Call it woman's intuition." She briefly touched his hand as she said that, her fingers as cool as they had been when they had shaken on their deal all those hours ago.

"It's a lovely evening," she said as they headed outside. "I'm going to walk a bit. Care to join me?"

James looked at her — this young woman who knew how to get a man to talk and how to listen, whose hair was a perfect, lustrous honey-blonde, who through the cloud of cigarette smoke still managed to smell so alluring — and settled on his answer. "I'm tired, Miss Lake. I enjoyed our dinner very much, but I'm going to turn in."

"Of course," she said. "I'll walk you back to the Club."

The stroll was short, but seemed to take an age. His chest seemed to be crackling with a kind of static energy; he was breathing unevenly. Neither of them said a word.

At last they were at number four hundred and fifty-nine. He was about to knock on the door when he felt her hand on his arm. She guided him round so that they faced each other.

"Good night, my handsome Englishman," she said, and she moved her face close to his. He could have moved at that moment, but he did not and, an instant later, he felt her lips touch his. Lightly, the slightest brush of her mouth, but the taste — of the wine, of her lips — was strong. Combined with the smell of her perfume, the freshness of her skin, it was intoxicating. One second became another and another, until he felt the first tiny touch of her tongue.

Suddenly, and without conscious volition, he sprung away from her, appalled. Reaching in his pocket for the key Walters had given him, he pivoted and opened the door of the Elizabethan Club, mumbling, "I really am dreadfully sorry. Good night." He stepped inside, shutting the door loudly behind him.

He pressed his head hard against the wall. What had he just done? *What the hell had he just done?* Florence's last message to him, delivered twice, had been a declaration of love — and how had he rewarded her? By embracing an American girl, a perfect stranger. Kissing her . . .

But he had broken away, he told himself. He had resisted. But not straight away. He had held that kiss for at least a second or two; he had not rejected it immediately. No wonder Florence had left him. He was a loathsome rat, unworthy of her love. He lifted his head and let it fall against the wall and then did it again, harder this time. How could he have done such a thing?

"I'm sorry to disturb you, sir."

Immersed in guilt and self-disgust, James had not heard the butler approach.

"It's just I thought you'd want to know."

"Know what, Walters?" James tried to compose himself.

"That a lady came here looking for you today. An English lady — with a little boy."

CHAPTER
TWENTY-NINE

The butler might as well have slapped him in the face. The effect of Walters's words was instant, as if he had been abruptly woken up. James stared at him for a while before speaking, then peppered him with questions.

"When were they here?"

"About four o'clock this afternoon, Dr Zennor."

"And how old was the child?" He locked the butler with a gaze that did not waver.

"I'm not good at these things. I'd guess he was —"

"How tall was he? Show me how high he stood. Here? Or higher? And tell me again, what she said. Her exact words, please."

"I opened the door to her and she said she had heard an Englishman was staying here, a Dr James Zennor and she wondered if she could speak to him."

"And what did you say?"

"Please Dr Zennor, you're making me a little uncomfortable staring at me like this. Please. Let me tell you what happened my own way."

James exhaled. He had to get a grip on himself, not to descend any further, not now. Florence and Henry here, in this very spot a matter of hours earlier: the very thought of it made him feel light-headed. He took a deep breath and followed Walters as he shuffled out of the hallway and into the first sitting room. Too agitated to sit, James grasped hold of the top of one of the high-backed leather chairs.

"All right," Walters began. "There was a knock on the door just after four or so. A quiet one, kind of uncertain. I opened it and there was this lady there, holding her son's hand. She looked kind of nervous. She didn't even come in at first, just asked if you were here and if she could speak to you. I told her I was expecting you back later. I asked her in, but she said no. Just could I tell you she'd called. The little boy seemed shy: he kept staring at me from behind his mother. I don't think he ever saw a black man before. Round eyes, he had. Very quiet."

"Very quiet." *Yes*, thought James. *That sounds like Harry*. "And can you describe what she looked like, Walters?"

"A tall lady, sir."

"Very beautiful, very straight-backed and upright? With smiling eyes?"

"She looked very kind, sir."

"Kind, yes . . ."

"Though she looked worried too."

"Did she tell you how she knew I was here?"

"Yes, sir. She did. She said she had seen you. In town."

James felt himself unsteady again, as if his legs were about to give way. The thoughts were rushing into his brain so fast, they were falling on top of each other. If

308

Florence had seen him, why hadn't she rushed over to him immediately? Where exactly had she seen him? And when? Surely not today, when he was with Dorothy Lake? Had Florence seen the two of them just now . . . His stomach twisted. What if he had come all this way, if he had crossed the Atlantic, only to be rejected as a faithless husband now, here in America? He cursed himself and his weakness all over again.

It took a moment to compose himself. At last he said quietly, "And did she leave anything for me, a card or a letter?"

"She just had me write down her details, so that you could get in touch with her. I'll go get them."

James watched the butler shuffle off to the backroom that seemed to serve as both his office and his home: there was certainly no other bedroom in evidence, and yet he seemed to be at the club day and night. James waited a while, pacing and clenching his fists. But even the thirty-second delay was too much. He walked out of the sitting room, meeting a returning Walters in the hallway.

"Here it is, sir." The old man passed him a small square of paper.

It was as if a slab of stone had landed on James's chest.

Elizabeth Goodwin, staying with Mr and Mrs Swanson, New Haven. Telephone number . . .

The words were swimming on the page, the disappointment clouding his vision. His head began to throb, the pain from banging it against the wall suddenly asserting itself.

The butler must have seen his desperation because he began muttering some kind of reassurance, the words lost and muffled in James's ears.

What an idiot he had been, once again succumbing to foolish optimism. The warning sign was there in how Walters had described the appearance of the woman at the door: *kind*, he had said. Florence certainly could be kind and generous. But kind was not the first word any man used to describe her. If it had been Florence at the door, Walters would not have hesitated to have agreed that she was stunningly, heart-breakingly beautiful.

So this was one of the other Oxford mothers, who had somehow tracked him down to the Elizabethan Club. Where had she seen him? And would she be the one who would, at last, tell him where he could find his wife and child?

From up here, he had a clear view over the treetops towards New Haven harbour. For the first time he realized what a beautiful place this was, no doubt lush and green in the springtime, scenic even in the arid summer. And yet he was barely two miles away from Yale.

He had called Mrs Goodwin first thing this morning, just after seven — the moment he felt it socially acceptable to make a telephone call. Her American host, Mrs Swanson, had sounded wary, but Mrs Goodwin herself had been perfectly polite. She explained that her son was attending summer school during the daytime hours and that she would not have a chance to meet till 4.30pm at the earliest.

310

"Why don't I meet you at the school?" James had suggested. To his surprise she had agreed, and so he had hired a taxi to take him up the winding, tree-lined road to Hopkins Grammar School for Boys. En route he had looked on in envy at the large family houses, with their lawns, an occasional tyre swinging from a tree or basketball hoop on a post. Such space compared with the cramped, ration-book England he had left behind. But it was not America's prosperity he envied, typified by the sleek, curved black motor car now purring along behind the cab — a moving sculpture in metal, topped off by natty white rims painted on the tyres — no, it was not America's wealth that made James pity his own country. It was the peace. The peace of that woman there, checking her roses, or of that old fellow in the house next door, oiling the garden gate. No Yale colleges were given over to organizing munitions or fish and potato stocks. No men here had to learn how to polish their boots like mirrors or clean a rifle. No mother in America had to fear her two-year-old son would die under a falling bomb or be crushed by a Nazi jackboot, as Florence had feared for Harry. How serene this summer morning seemed. And yet, under the same sky, even at this very moment, he knew there was a continent at war with Britain — and that shabby, grey Britain was fighting for its life.

Now, as the cab got closer, he could read the sign that announced Hopkins Grammar, dedicated to "The Breeding up of Hopeful Youths".

They had arranged to meet at the school office, so he walked through the arched entrance, past the portrait of Hopkins's seventeenth century founder, musing that this might have been any boarding school in the English countryside. He ran into a secretary who told him he needed to go to the playing fields and promptly offered to walk him over there.

She chatted away, explaining that the school had only moved from the centre of New Haven fifteen years earlier. "I'm afraid the city is not quite what it used to be. So crowded there now."

"Cramped?" asked James, making conversation.

"Well, we've had so many immigrants in recent years. It's not the country your ancestors left behind any more."

The words were neutral enough, but James detected a note of distaste and snobbery that he did not like. "I see."

"Not that we're complaining about being here, gosh no. It's wonderful here. So good for the boys to be outside in the countryside, away from all the dirt and grime of the city."

She led him down a slope, and now a large lawn came into view. On it were perhaps three dozen early teenage boys, in white shorts and plimsolls but no shirts, engaged in physical jerks. As James approached, they were doing press-ups, in unison. Watching on the sidelines were five or six mothers kitted out in their own uniform of floral dress and sunhat.

"Mrs Goodwin!" the secretary called in a sing-song voice and the tallest of them turned around. In her early forties, she was just as Walters had described: not pretty, her hair mousy, but kindly.

They shook hands while the secretary politely excused herself. The lady gave a gentle smile. "Well, I'm glad my eyes didn't deceive me."

Just hearing the rhythm of those precise, enunciated words filled James with a rush of emotions. Until that moment he had not particularly registered that he had not heard an English accent in more than three weeks. Hearing it now evoked home, as if he had been transported with just those few cadences back to Oxford, to its stones, its bicycles, its scones, its afternoons. He realized in that instant just how far away he was. Above all, it made him want to be with Florence, to hold her and to feel her holding him.

He said none of this of course. He simply shook her hand and said, "And so am I, Mrs Goodwin, so am I. Where on earth did you see me?"

"In church, Dr Zennor: the Battell Chapel. I was there with Thomas." She tilted her head in the direction of the boys, who were now extending their arms and legs in a series of rhythmic star jumps.

"On Sunday? During that debate about joining the war?"

"Quite so."

So that explained that fleeting sensation he had had, the nagging feeling that somewhere in that congregation he had glimpsed a familiar face. He had thought it was a trick of the light, or exhaustion after his journey, but it had been real. Not that he had any idea where or when in Oxford he had seen Mrs Goodwin. Was she another friend of Florence's he had all but ignored?

"I must say, I found the event rather sobering," she went on. "It seems our little island is to fight this war all alone, wouldn't you say?"

"Joining the war hardly seems popular in America, if that's what you mean." He cleared his throat. "Mrs Goodwin, I've come here to Yale to find my wife. Do you have any idea where she is?"

"You mean, you don't know?"

"I'm afraid, I don't."

She looked away, embarrassed. "It's odd, but I had an inkling that that was the case. When I saw what I thought was you in church, I dismissed it at first. I assumed I had just glimpsed someone who looked like you. Such things do happen, you know. But then I was buying some cigarettes at the Owl Shop and the young man there mentioned an Englishman on his own, looking for his wife, and I began to wonder. I called in at the Elizabethan Club really on the off-chance —"

"Mrs Goodwin, do you know where she is?"

"I *did* know. She was with the rest of us at the Divinity School when we arrived."

"The Divinity School?"

"Yes, that was where we were first received. Before they allocated us to our respective host families."

"And where was Florence allocated?"

"Well, that's just it, you see. I don't know. She was still there when I was picked up by the Swansons last Friday. They've been terribly nice. And settling in took a few days, inevitably, and before I knew it everyone had been scattered to the four winds. A few ladies are in Pennsylvania."

"Do you not know where any of the others are?"

"I do know where *some* are staying. A few of us have made contact with each other. Plenty of our hosts know each other of course. Especially those of us who have been housed here in New Haven. But there's not many in that position, you see. Others are with professors who live away from here, or else have summer houses in the country."

"I understand."

"But surely the university must have records, Dr Zennor? What about that committee that arranged everything for us, have you spoken to them?"

"Not exactly. But I have . . ." James hesitated. "I have consulted their records, as it were. And Florence and Harry are the only ones about whom there is no information."

"What about the Dean, Preston something, I forget his name —"

"Dr McAndrew?"

"That's it. He's been perfectly wonderful. He was the driving force behind the whole scheme, I hear. He's in charge, he must know."

"He's drawn a blank too."

The woman bit her lip. "That really is most odd."

"Can I ask, Mrs Goodwin, when is the last time you saw Florence?"

"As I say, at the Divinity School. We were there together for the first day or so."

"And can you remember anything that happened there, anything my wife might have said, that could perhaps explain where she is?"

315

Just for a second, the woman looked at her feet, a fleeting aversion of the eyes that suggested — what? — guilt, embarrassment, James was not sure. "Anything at all, Mrs Goodwin."

"Well, it's rather awkward but —"

At that moment she gave a slight jump, shaken by a sudden bellowed roar from the exercise ground as the boys shouted a slogan: "Straight backs and good posture are essential to good health!" The instructor cupped his ear, a pantomime gesture suggesting they had shouted too quietly. They tried it again, this time at the tops of their just-broken voices.

"They're very serious about all matters physical here, I've noticed," Mrs Goodwin said with a smile. "If they're not hiking, they're wrestling or playing basketball. Thomas always enjoyed playing cricket, but this is —"

"You were about to tell me something, Mrs Goodwin. About Florence at the Divinity School." He paused. "You said it was awkward."

"Yes, I did." She looked towards the boys, about to embark on a run around the perimeter. "It's a question, really. Tell me, Dr Zennor, have you ever written to your wife?"

"What? Yes, of course. Every day, as soon as I knew she had come to Yale. I sent several letters from Liverpool, then perhaps a dozen from Canada. I'd stored them up on the ship. I've sent some from here too, not that I've got an address. I've just been sending them 'care of Yale University'."

"Oh I see." Her brow furrowed. "That confuses me rather."

"I don't understand. Why?"

"I don't like to be rude, Dr Zennor. And this really is none of my business."

"What? Tell me."

"Well, my husband's been doing the same. Addressing his letters 'care of Yale'. And they've all arrived, every one of them. There were several items of post waiting for me and the children at the Divinity School. But I'm afraid . . ."

"Yes?"

"Florence had nothing from you. Not even a card. She was quite distressed about it. We all sympathized as best we could. Now that I see you here, having travelled all this way, I realize we must have got the wrong end of the stick. But I'm afraid at the time we did think it a rather poor show."

CHAPTER
THIRTY

He sprinted back to the school office, asking the secretary to order him a taxi as soon as she could. His head was pounding.

He was not paranoid, he was not deluded: something dark and dangerous and awful was going on here and, God knows why or how, Florence and Harry were at the centre of it. An image of his son, cowering and terrified, entered, unbidden, into his mind. Little, beautiful Harry. Oh God, what on earth had they done to his boy? And what did they want with the woman he loved?

There was no writing this off as a coincidence. At first, maybe, it could have been just that. A missing document in the files, a mislaid sheet of paper: it could happen to anybody. But this: concrete proof that his letters to Florence had been intercepted. Who would want to do such a thing? And why?

As he paced by the school entrance, round and round that sign — "The Breeding up of Hopeful Youths" — he could feel again the clamminess of Lund's hand as the man, sweating frantically, had clutched his own. *You have no idea what you've walked into here, do you? You've stumbled into something much bigger than you realize. Bigger and more dangerous.*

The poor bastard wasn't deluded. He was damn right. This was something dangerous enough to have cost Lund's own life — and perhaps, who knows, it posed an equally grave threat to James's wife and child. Unless it was already too late . . .

He shook his head, as if the action would shake away such an insupportable thought. He had been such a fool and the worst kind, a clever fool; foolish, indeed, *because* clever. The signs had been there from the beginning: that rattle of the letterbox the morning after Florence had disappeared. They had been tampering with his post even then, getting to the card from his wife before he could, deliberately depriving him of the few hours in which he might have got to her in time. He should have suspected a plot then — a careful, meticulous plot. But did he? No. He was too bloody rational for that, too *reasonable*. There had to be another explanation, that was what he had kept telling himself. Another, more sensible, rational explanation for why his wife was missing from those files, why Lund had latched onto him, why Lund had ended up dead. James had been a prisoner of his own damned rationality. But he had been wrong. If only he had been stupider, thought with his gut rather than his head, he would have got to the truth so much faster.

At last the cab was here and they were bumping back down Forest Road towards and into New Haven. He would go to see McAndrew right now. He would storm in there if necessary and demand to know the truth. If the Dean could provide no answers, then James would refuse to leave his office until McAndrew had ordered an internal investigation, preferably calling the head of the Yale University postal service into the room, right there and then.

James stared out of the cab's passenger window, breaking his stare only once, to glance in the rear-view mirror — and he did not notice it at first. His mind was too full to register it.

But then some other zone of his cerebral cortex processed the information for him. He checked the tyres of the vehicle behind, to see if they had the telltale white rims on the wheels. They did. There was no mistaking it: the same car that he had seen on the way up to Hopkins Grammar was now behind him. It had tailed him then and it was tailing him now. He would not try to make rational excuses for it, not this time. He was being followed.

"Driver, can you take the next left turning, please."

"But we don't want to go —"

"Just turn left!"

The driver did as he was told and, sure enough, the car behind — stately and solid — followed suit. Right, thought James: he would add that to the list of questions he would hurl at McAndrew the second he saw him. *Why the hell am I being followed?*

Through side streets and residential avenues, the cab eventually arrived outside the administrative building that housed the Dean. The black car parked up just a few yards away, brazen in its refusal to conceal its purpose. James marched towards the entrance, past the

320

commissionaire and barged straight into the office where he had been less than twenty-four hours earlier. He only realized what a determined, even crazed, expression must have been etched on his face when he saw the way Barbara the secretary looked up at him as he strode in. She was aghast — and petrified.

Without speaking to her, James made straight for the inner office occupied by the Dean. He grabbed the doorknob as if these rooms were his own, making no concession to good manners. As the door flung open to reveal an empty room he heard Barbara's plaintive cry behind him: "The Dean's not here! He's on leave."

"On leave?" James bellowed, wheeling around to face the secretary, on her feet and quite pale. "On LEAVE? Where the hell has he gone?"

"I can't tell you that, Dr —"

James took a step forward, prompting the woman to leap backward in a panicked, animal gesture of retreat, clearly afraid that he was about to hit her. The sight of that terror halted him. He could now hear his own breath; he was, he realized, panting.

A moment longer and he would, he knew, be escorted out of the building and into the arms once again of the Yale Police Department. He gathered his strength and, walking backwards — so that he was able to see the lines of anxiety on Barbara's face gradually smooth out as the threat receded — he left.

James rushed out through the lobby and into the street. He looked to his right: the black car, which he now identified as a Buick, was still there. Right. That was it.

He stormed across the street, plunging into the middle of it with barely a glance at the traffic that now dodged around him, and marched right up to the car, slapping his hand on the bonnet.

"Get out!" he said in a loud, clear voice. "Come on, out with you." He rapped on the window, hard. "Don't be a coward. Show your face, come on."

He banged on the glass again. "I want to see you, you bloody coward!" He was shouting now; people were staring at him. Dropping into a squat so that he could see inside the car, he realized that he had been banging on the wrong side; he was looking at the passenger seat. But there was no one in the car anyway. It was locked and dark.

He let out a long sigh of exasperation. He was chasing shadows. Chilling though it was to know he was being followed, and infuriating though it was to let his pursuers go unpunished, he knew this was a diversion. It was not them he had to find, it was Florence and Harry.

The immediate task was to make a call. He looked around and spotted a telephone booth on this side of the street, no more than thirty yards away. He sprinted over to it.

Maddeningly, he didn't know what to do, having to read the laborious instructions on the printed card above the telephone. Eventually he heard the voice of an operator.

"*Yale Daily News*, please."

He knew he was playing with fire, making this telephone call. The sensible thing would be never to see or speak to her again. And yet who else could he turn to for the information he needed this very instant?

There was a click and then a voice on the end of the line, announcing the name of the newspaper.

"May I speak with a Miss Dorothy Lake, please?"

"Is she a typist?"

"She's a reporter, I believe."

"Hold the line."

He heard a hand placed incompletely over the receiver and then a muffled voice calling out for Dorothy. There was a rustle and then her breath and then her voice.

"Miss Lake, it's James. James Zennor."

"Well, how are you, my disappearing Englishman? I was beginning to get worried about you." He could tell that she was smiling. He could picture her lips, full and slightly parted in that same knowing, playful expression he had seen over dinner last night.

"I'm well, Miss Lake," he replied, his voice overly stern and businesslike. "I'm afraid I need your help. I need to go and see the Dean right away." He checked his watch. It was quarter to eleven. "I need his home address."

"Well, that's easy."

"Really?"

"The Dean has an official residence. It's on St Ronan Street. Number two hundred and forty-one."

CHAPTER
THIRTY-ONE

The map was trembling in James's fingers as he searched for St Ronan Street. His eye went west: York, Park, Howe, Dwight Streets. No sign of St Ronan. He checked east: High, College, Temple, Church. Now he looked north: Wall Street, Grove, Trumbull. Where the hell was St Ronan Street?

He looked outside the centre of New Haven, his finger running along what appeared to be one of the main arteries northward, Prospect Street. Nothing here. He looked across to the east, tracing the long Whitney Avenue. Nothing here either —

There it was, between the two main roads. It was a long way, but not complicated. He would not walk there: he would run.

As he pounded down Wall Street, ignoring the stares of the mid-morning strollers, he wondered how it had come to this: running through strange streets in a strange country, searching for his family. That he was now confronting an enemy — faceless and unknown — he did not doubt. But he could not deceive himself that that was why he was in this situation. Whatever evil his unseen adversary had wrought, this was still his fault. Florence would never have so much as considered leaving Norham Gardens, let alone England, if he had been the strong husband, the good father, she thought she had married. Instead, within months, he had become a stranger to his wife — a seething geyser of rage and resentment, a man who had turned inward, away from the two people in the world who most loved and needed him. His wife was young, vibrant and beautiful; yet what happiness had she known in recent years? They did occasionally go to the theatre or a concert, but only after she had cajoled and persuaded him. As for parties, she had learned not even to suggest such a thing. If she wanted a good, long walk in the countryside, she had had to turn to Rosemary Hyde and her Brownie pack rather than to her own husband who, when he did venture into the outdoors and the fresh air, did it alone and at dawn, when there was no danger of meeting another soul. His wife was a woman who flourished in the sunlight and he had kept her in the dark. It was not a shock that she had left him when the fear of invasion became too much. It was a surprise that she had not done it earlier.

He needed to tell her all this, to tell her he understood. But he could do nothing if he could not find her. Which was why he had to talk to McAndrew right now, face to face. He would start by demanding to know where Florence and Harry were and then get to the bottom of exactly why they were missing from that file. He would not be brushed off with vague promises this time: he wanted answers.

By now he had left behind the cluster of science laboratories that flanked the earliest stretch of Prospect

Street and was running uphill through botanical gardens, hot and sticky in the morning sun. The gradient was steep; his shoulder was throbbing with pain. He looked down at his map; not far to go now.

This was clearly the expensive part of town, the timber-clad houses large, the street wide and leafy. Perhaps this was where he and Florence would be living if fate had made them a pair of young American academics at Yale, rather than Oxford. They would be together now, enjoying a calm, peaceful life, no fear of war scaring her half way around the world. He might never have gone to Spain; not many Americans did. He would never have been shot, his shoulder would still be intact, but he would never have met Florence, they would never have had Harry . . .

James was gasping now, his lungs craving oxygen. He let his head fall, his palms resting on his thighs. He was sweating hard, even with his jacket bundled half a mile ago into his satchel.

Now he resumed at walking speed, turning right onto Canner Street. It would not do to turn up a panting wreck at the Dean's home. James gripped his shoulder, trying to squeeze the pain away. One more turn, left, and he would be on St Ronan Street.

The house numbers were in the eighties; he was nearly there. The houses were even wider and grander now than on Prospect Street, with their smooth lawns and their five-step staircases up to the front porch. How safe it seemed here, thousands and thousands of miles away from the blacked-out towns and cities of England where, right now, they were girding themselves for another night. Soon they would be huddling in their Anderson shelters. The damp smell of soil, waiting for the siren to come, the exhausted desire to go back to bed . . .

There. Number two hundred and forty-one, a house as substantial as the others. The style, James decided, was colonial; the door was painted a solid, respectable black. He walked up the path and rang the bell, mentally preparing his lines in case Mrs McAndrew answered the door. *I met the Dean yesterday and he said I should contact him any time if I needed any help.* He wiped his forehead to remove any remaining traces of sweat.

There was no response. James rang again, this time leaning close to listen for any sign of movement on the other side. Nothing.

He moved onto the porch, so that he could peer through the window. Pressing his face against the glass, he saw that the living room at least looked empty. There seemed to be no lights on anywhere.

James turned to see if anyone was around, if he was likely to be seen. No one. With all the confidence he could muster, trying not to look like a burglar, he strode over to the side of the house and began walking down the path. There was a bicycle propped up against the wall, but then the path dead-ended in a wooden gate.

Another look over his shoulder and James placed his foot on the bottom timber. One more pull and he was halfway up, sufficiently high that he could look over the top of the gate and at the garden. His shoulder was screaming again.

James scoped left to right, confirming in an instant that the house was entirely empty. There was a table and two chairs on the paved area, a large, well-kept lawn with a single, stand-alone child's swing in the middle, a couple of fruit trees towards the back, and lots of well-kept bushes and shrubs all around.

James was just wondering if there would be any value in vaulting over the gate altogether, perhaps even trying to get into the house from the back garden, when he felt the grip around his right and then his left ankle.

He turned awkwardly, trying to look down, which only sharpened the agony in his shoulder. He let out a howl of pain, which prompted the grip around his ankles to grow tighter.

He heard a voice, instantly familiar. "Do not resist, Dr Zennor," it said. "You've reached the end of the road."

CHAPTER
THIRTY-TWO

He looked down at his feet to see that they were in the firm grip of Detective Riley of the Yale Police Department. From above he could see the same white, fleshy features, slightly flushed this time, probably on account of the slight incline of the front lawn the police officer had just climbed to reach him.

"I'm going to need you to come down, sir."

"Oh for God's sake! Please, this is not what you think —"

"Just come down, sir."

James gestured towards his feet, indicating that he couldn't jump until Riley let go.

Once down, he started again. "Detective Riley, please. I was not burgling this house. I came here to speak to the Dean. I need to speak to him urgently, I've —"

"Wrists."

In the moment James hesitated, Riley produced a pair of handcuffs. Now James understood. He felt a surge of fury and then, like a wave that breaks only to trickle back into the sea, he felt it recede. He was too exhausted for rage. Curiously, too, he felt no anger towards Riley. Instead he blamed himself and his own stupidity.

He had not been seen, he was sure of that. The side path of McAndrew's house was not overlooked by any neighbours; he had checked left and right, up and down, before he had ventured down here. Yes, he might have been spotted by a vigilant neighbour across the street. They might have suspected a break-in. But he didn't care how technologically advanced these Americans were, there was no way they could have telephoned the police and brought a police car here that quickly. He had arrived at the house no more than two or three minutes ago and would have struck even the most nervous neighbour as acting suspiciously only in the last minute. Until then, he was just a man ringing on a doorbell.

"Detective Riley, can I ask a question?" James said, as Riley and his partner frogmarched him down past the sloping lawn towards their vehicle.

"You can ask what you like. Don't mean I'm gonna answer."

"Are we still technically under the jurisdiction of the Yale Police Department?"

"On this property, we sure are. This is the Dean's residence, part of Yale University territory."

"Of course. But this *area*. This would fall under the New Haven Police Department, surely?"

"Yeah, but you ain't in this *area*. You're on this *property*. And you're trespassing too."

"I understand. But if someone was to call the police for help, someone who lived in this street, they wouldn't get you, would they? Their call would be answered by the New Haven police force, am I right?"

Riley fell silent, pushing James's head down as he folded him into the backseat of the car. That settled it. He had not been spotted by a neighbour or passer-by out walking their dog. He had been betrayed. Only one person knew he was coming here — and she had betrayed him.

The journey into town was brief; only minutes later they were back in the police station where his day had started yesterday morning, though it felt like weeks ago. He didn't say anything in the car, just stared out of the window wrestling with a question that spun around him like a whirlpool, trapping him ever deeper and lower: why?

All he wanted was to regain his family. That was all. He did not want to know the truth of the death of George Lund. He did not want to know how Preston McAndrew was caught up in this, nor even why Dorothy Lake had kissed him last night and betrayed him today (though he did wonder, fleetingly, if the two events were connected, whether she had tipped off the police in revenge for his rejection of her). He did not even particularly care why he had been followed earlier. He did not want to know any of that. All he wanted to know was where he could find Florence and Harry. He wanted to find them and hold them, to stroke their hair and smell their skin. That was all he wanted.

Soon they were back, he and Riley, across that blank table in that blank interview room. Wearily, James asked, "Do you do everything for your police force, Detective?"

"What are you getting at?"

"Well, one minute you're investigating a murder, the next you just happen to be on call for what must have looked like, at worst, a minor break-in."

"Let's say I like coming out on special occasions."

"And why exactly was this a special occasion?"

"You're an important man, Dr Zennor."

"Ah, so you knew I was involved, did you?"

"I know now."

"I see. So when Dorothy Lake told you to dash over to the Dean's house on St Ronan Street, you dropped everything and ran."

Riley's failure to react, his lack of surprise or puzzlement at the mention of Miss Lake confirmed it: she had made the call. "I see you're not denying it."

"It's not me who's under arrest for criminal trespass, Dr Zennor. So why don't we say that I ask the questions and you answer them, OK?"

"Fine with me, Detective."

Riley plodded his way through the interrogation, James responding with a simple, straight, if not complete, account of the truth. He had discovered that his post — sorry, his *mail* — had been intercepted and wanted to take this matter up urgently with the Dean. That was it.

"Talk to him, eh? Do you break into the houses of all the people you wanna talk to?"

"I wasn't breaking in! I was looking into his garden. Just in case he was there."

They went round and round, Riley trying to make two and two equal five, trying to get James to stumble on an inconsistency, James stubbornly offering a straight bat. Finally the detective, who seemed as weary as James, sighed heavily and said. "I'm going to arrest you, which means you have the right to make a telephone call. Most people call their lawyer."

He led James out of the interview room and into a tiny cubicle which contained nothing but a plain chair and a telephone on a small shelf. "I'll be right here."

James picked up the receiver and heard his own breath. After no more than a second's thought, he responded to the operator's enquiry by asking to be put through to the office of the *Yale Daily News*. James checked his watch. It was mid-afternoon, it was summer. There was every chance there would be no one there. But the call was answered.

"The editor, please."

Another delay, then a second voice. "Can I help?"

"Yes, I hope you can. My name is Dr James Zennor and I've been dealing with one of your reporters, a Miss Dorothy Lake."

"Yes, I know. Is there a problem?"

"No problem at all. She's been extremely diligent. She is keen to have my co-operation on the story she's working on and I just wanted to check her *bona fides*, if you will. Do you mind if I ask how she came to you?"

"She was an undergraduate at Vassar and on the paper there, I think. She comes very highly recommended."

"I'm glad to hear that. By whom?"

"Excuse me?"

"You said she comes very highly recommended. Recommended by whom?"

"Well, I'm not sure I should say. I don't want people to think nepotism plays a part in these decisions."

"No, no, of course not. This is strictly for my own reassurance. It will stay between us." James looked over his shoulder to see Riley pointing at his wristwatch. He could cut off this call at any moment.

"In that case, I'm glad to reassure you that Miss Lake came with the highest possible recommendation."

"Oh yes?"

"Yes. She was recommended by the Dean, Dr Preston McAndrew. And here I would appreciate your discretion, Dr Zennor. But Dr McAndrew is Miss Lake's uncle."

He lay on the hard, narrow bed in the cell. Part of him welcomed the chance to lie down and rest. He was exhausted and needed to think. But the other part was desperate to act, to get back out into the daylight and onto the streets, to see if this new knowledge might somehow lead him to Florence. First, though, he had to think.

He went over and over again the events of the last twenty-four hours, since Dorothy Lake had found him outside the Wolf's Head tomb, reviewing them in light of the discovery of her family connection to the Dean. Theoretically, it might make no difference: yes, she had got her start with the *Yale Daily News* through him, but now she was an ambitious young journalist whose sole desire was to get a good story.

But the other possibility was just as likely, that she was, in fact, working for her uncle — doing what he had asked her to do. Perhaps that amounted to no more than a request that she keep an eye on James, letting the Dean know what he was up to. But he had to consider that her duties went far beyond just that.

He thought of the list of names of Wolf's Head alumni in Miss Lake's notebook, how it had included everyone except one of the society's most eminent past members: the current Dean of Yale University himself. He should have become suspicious of her the moment McAndrew had revealed his connection to the Wolf's Head. But he had not even thought of it.

In the same way, James had accepted that it was just rotten luck that he had been interrupted by the Dean himself as he went through the files in the outer office. But what if Dorothy had tipped her uncle off? She might have recovered from her fall earlier than agreed, then gone to find McAndrew or sent the secretary to get him. It would mean that her telephone call to Riley and the Yale Police Department just now would have been her second betrayal of James in as many days.

So for all his courtesy and promises to help, the Dean had been suspicious of James and had despatched someone, his own niece, to watch him, so that she could sound the alarm if he ever got too close for comfort. But too close to what? What exactly was the Dean hiding? Whatever secret it was, he clearly believed James was getting dangerously close. But why would he believe that? Because James had been in contact with Lund? Or simply because he had been making enquiries about the Oxford children?

James's head hurt. His shoulder was throbbing, as it always did after strenuous exercise. It would be so easy to fall asleep, to slip into a stolen hour of rest and dreams, where Florence and Harry might visit him. His eyelids were growing heavier. But then he heard the sound of metal scraping against metal. His jailers were unlocking the door.

Without speaking, a junior officer ushered him into the hallway. Preparing himself for release — to sign a form, have his belongings returned to him and be sent on his way — he was instead greeted by Riley, mug of coffee in hand, a curl of steam rising from it. The detective nodded towards the interview room. "Shall we?"

James followed him inside, tasting the sourness of his own mouth. The sweat from his earlier run had congealed on his skin, leaving a clammy film on his back; he hadn't eaten for hours. He wanted to be almost anywhere but this room. Surely the Yale Police Department had better things to do than prosecute an English academic for climbing a garden gate?

"Detective Riley —"

"Hold on, Dr Zennor. I need to check something with you."

"All right," he said, shaking his head at the exasperating endlessness of it all. "Fire away."

"It's not a question exactly. I need to look at you. Can you stand up a second?"

336

"Look at me? What the devil is this about?"

"It will only take a moment." The detective moved closer, so that he was just a few inches from James, then raised himself on tiptoes — and began looking at James's hair.

"What the hell is this?"

"I'm nearly done." Riley began touching James's hair, probing into the scalp. Instinctively James reached up to push the man off and away, but the detective was strong, grabbing James's right arm with one hand, using the other to touch James's hair, repeatedly rubbing a lock of it between finger and thumb.

"Get off me!"

"There we are, all done," the policeman said, stepping back and wiping his hands on his handkerchief. "Sorry about that."

"You better have a bloody good explanation, Riley, or I shall be lodging a complaint. I've never —"

"Calm down, Zennor. I'll decide who's in trouble here. I caught you engaged in an act of criminal trespass, remember? Take a seat." James remained standing, his eyes burning. "Now."

Slowly, James sat down, reining in his temper, bringing the dog to heel.

"Good. Forgive my little impromptu exam, but this job ain't always pleasant. Now, I just had a very interesting visitor here."

James, still struggling to keep the lid on his anger, said nothing.

"The lady who lives next door to the Lund residence, as a matter of fact. Says she heard some noise late Monday night. Went to her window to check and — guess what — she saw a man leaving the house."

"We've been through this. You know I was fast asleep at the Elizabethan —"

"Will you shut the hell up and listen for a moment? Turns out there's a street lamp right by the Lund house. Lady says the man was tall, roundabout your height. She didn't see his face, but the lamp did pick out his hair. Very distinct, she said it was. What they call salt-and-pepper. Little bit black, little bit silver."

There was a pause as James said nothing and sought to ensure his face did the same.

Riley went on. "Hence my little poke around up top just now. Wanted to see if you'd dyed your hair, you know, to cover it up."

"But I haven't," said James, quietly.

"No, you haven't."

"Which means someone else killed George Lund."

Riley leaned back in his chair. "I think you're jumping to conclusions again, Dr Zennor. This could still be what it looked like. Suicide."

"Except you said his wife said he was planning for his future. A baby upstairs."

"I know what I said."

"And how many suicides die with a metal badge in their mouths? Tell me, Detective, there was no sign of a break-in at the house, was there?"

"No. And that usually means no one else was involved."

"Either that," said James, "or someone who Lund knew well enough to let into his home late at night."

338

"Don't try to do my job, Dr Zennor."

"OK, I won't." James could feel the blood pumping around his brain; he pictured it, different zones lighting up like the pinball machine he had seen at the drugstore on College Street. "But could I ask you a favour?"

"Depends what it is now, doesn't it?"

"I'm presuming you're going to release me. When you do, it would be a great help if you told no one that you have — especially not the editor of the *Yale Daily News*."

"You're making a lot of presumptions there, Mister. I mean —"

"Not even your superiors here, if you can help it. I can't explain why, but if you trust that I'm an honest man — and I suspect you do — then I'd like you to believe me when I say it may help. Not just me, but you too."

"Maybe it's normal to talk to police officers this way in England, but I got to tell you, this is not —"

"Now, where do I sign?" James asked with a smile. "I have somewhere I need to get to as quickly as possible."

CHAPTER
THIRTY-THREE

What they call salt-and-pepper. Little bit black, little bit silver.

Distinct, Riley had called it and it certainly was. His hair was one of the first things James had noticed about Preston McAndrew. The man the neighbour had seen was the right height too.

If he had heard it described to him, he would have dismissed it as fantastical, the kind of tale feasted upon by the Sunday newspapers back home: the dean of a university involved in a murder. But in the light of the evidence, surely it was rational to conclude that Preston McAndrew had murdered George Lund, that despite his veneer of charm and scholarly sophistication, the holder of one of the most prestigious posts in the American academy had strangled his immediate subordinate, then strung up the body to make it look like a suicide. For James, one implication stripped ahead of all the others: it meant that McAndrew's warm reassurances about his endeavours to find Florence and Harry were worthless. This man was not to be trusted, but feared.

James was striding quickly now, right on Wall Street, left on Church Street, navigating entirely from memory, glad for the simplicity of New Haven's layout and for his own memory. His shoulder was sore, urging him to rest, but adrenalin was beginning to kick in and it was an effective anaesthetic.

James could see it now, the same walk-up, two-step entrance to the modest, pretty Lund house. How idiotic he had been to bring Lake with him, McAndrew's niece. No wonder the woman had clammed up. And then he and Dorothy had gone from here to eat dinner together. He had talked about Florence and he had dropped his guard, allowing himself to believe that Dorothy liked him. When of course she was nothing more than a woman doing a job.

James was furious with himself. He was nearly thirty, too old to be guilty of such naïveté. He should have seen through the sudden appearance of a beautiful, intriguing young woman at the Wolf's Head, ready to help and be at his side. But he was also — what was it? — not angry, exactly, but disappointed in Dorothy. Despite all their negotiations and gamesmanship, he thought he had detected a connection between them. And then there was the concern, almost maternal, he had seen in her eyes when he spoke about Harry . . . He could not accept that that was entirely fake.

It was late afternoon but the sun was still bright. As he stood on the doorstep he could not see inside the windows; too much glare.

He knocked on the door. Silence. He knocked again, this time pressing his ear to the door to listen. None of the voices and hubbub he had heard yesterday. He stepped away from the entrance, towards the bay window of the main room. Shielding his eyes with his hand, he peered in. All was dark.

"You looking for the family?"

The voice came from the porch of the house next door. An elderly man in a blue blazer was sitting on a wicker chair, a newspaper on his lap. He spoke again, as if unsure he had been heard the first time. "You a mourner?"

James offered a concerned smile. "I'm here to see Mrs Lund, yes. Do you happen to know —"

"They left this morning."

"They *left*?"

"That's right. All of them, her parents, the baby. Early too."

"Really?"

"I can't sleep later than four, four-thirty these days. It'll happen to you someday, believe me."

"And, what —"

"I came down and I saw them packing up. In a hurry too. Just shoving those suitcases in the trunk of the automobile and off they went. She waved at me, the younger one."

"Margaret?"

"That's right. She was holding the baby. And then they were off."

"At dawn."

"You bet. Break of dawn. Yes, sir."

"Did they say where they were going?"

"No. They didn't stop to talk."

James thanked the man and headed back down the street, trying to digest what he had just been told.

342

There are some very powerful people around here. That was what Margaret Lund had said yesterday. She believed they had killed her husband *to keep their secret safe.* Those were her words. She must have concluded that they would be ready to kill her too, that she was in sufficient peril to warrant leaving her home in a dawn panic. Perhaps Lund had told his wife what he suspected. No wonder she had not wanted to pass it on, especially with the woman she knew to be the Dean's niece present. It would expose her — and whomever she told — to great danger. He thought of the intensity of her stare, so incongruous as she held her baby. *Not for my sake. For yours.*

The idea was both dizzying and dangerous. He had to make sense of this too, even this. He had no alternative, not if he was to find his way back to Florence and Harry.

Very well, he told himself. If he could not learn directly what George Lund had told his wife, he would have to work with what he had: the last communication Lund had made, even in death. He would have to discover the truth about the Wolf's Head.

For an hour he paced up and down, or sat at the bench across the street, all the time watching the entrance to the Wolf's Head tomb. He kept an especially vigilant eye out for a black Buick with white-trimmed wheels, but saw nothing. Good man, that Riley: apparently he had done as James had asked and let no one know that the English gentleman arrested for criminal trespass had been released from custody. On the belt-and-braces principle, James had stopped by the J Press shop on York Street to pick up a new jacket. Inspired by the Lunds' elderly neighbour, he had opted for a blue blazer as well as a Panama hat, which he now wore low, covering his eyes. If someone was tailing him, the least James could do was put him off the scent.

Still nothing. The building deserved its name; it was locked, empty and silent as a tomb.

James glanced at the copy of *Time* magazine he had picked up from a news-stand on his way over here. He had been drawn by the image on the cover of Lord Beaverbrook, first occupant of the newly-created Ministry of Aircraft Production. The magazine was full of praise for the man Churchill had brought in: "Even if Britain goes down this fall, it will not be Lord Beaverbrook's fault. If she holds out, it will be his triumph. This war is a war of machines. It will be won on the assembly line."

The magazine was clearly impressed and the overall assessment was upbeat, but the opening line made James's heart sink. *Even if Britain goes down this fall* . . . Florence had not been hysterical to fear a Nazi invasion. It was a possibility, maybe even a probability.

Looking up, he saw a white-haired man approaching. At that moment, James recognized his face: it was Theodore Lowell, the university chaplain and pastor he had seen preach at the Battell Chapel on Sunday. He froze, but Lowell did not even glance at him, just looked left and right to check traffic before crossing the

344

road. Without altering his pace, he slipped in among the lawns and bushes leading to the Wolf's Head's building.

That was not in itself a surprise: Lowell's was the only name James had recognized on the alumni list in Lake's notebook. As a former member of the society, he had every right to pay a visit; as chaplain, he might even have been there on pastoral duty. (James imagined him counselling a wayward young man to drink a little less and pray a little more.)

But there was something about the way he walked, an urgency, that struck James. No, it was more than urgency — it was furtiveness. Lowell didn't want to be seen. He looked quickly behind him and disappeared into the side door.

James had just resumed his position on the bench when there was another rustle of movement and someone emerged from the tomb, from the same concealed entrance. This figure was taller and, James guessed, younger; his hair was darker. Just in time, James raised his magazine so that he would not be seen.

This second man now reached the pavement and started walking north towards Elm Street. James waited five, six, seven seconds and then began to follow.

The voice of Jorge, the Spanish republican who had coached both him and Harry Knox in the art of shadowing suspected members of Franco's Fifth Column in Madrid three years earlier, remained in his head throughout. *Remember, you walk at the same speed as the subject. Slower, and you will lose him. Faster, and you reveal yourself at once.*

The pursuit was challenging, James having to part a large group that emerged from Davenport College when he had barely got into his stride — muttering apologies and "excuse me's" — having to shield his eyes from the afternoon sunshine, all the while keeping his gaze fixed on the man twenty yards ahead of him. He was walking with purpose this man, whoever he was, at a pace that suggested his destination was not far off.

The hardest part of any pursuit is the turning of a corner, when the risk of losing the subject is at its greatest. The temptation is to accelerate, but that too carries a risk: the subject, if vigilant, will notice that someone previously distant has come much closer. And once a pursuer has been noticed, he is useless.

James maintained his speed, but as he turned the corner, he looked to where he expected the subject to be — and saw nothing.

Damn. Hurriedly, James scanned the other side of the street. Not there. He examined his own side of the road, and again saw nothing. He stared into the distance, to see if the man he had followed had cottoned on and broken into a sprint, but there was no sign of him.

There. He had been searching for a moving target, and so his eye had passed over the static figure. His prey was just one building ahead, standing by the front door of what looked like a large Georgian house. His demeanour suggested he had no idea he had been followed.

346

James sucked in his breath, a predator trying to shrink into invisibility and avoid detection. Now, at last, he could get a decent look at the man. He was tall, impressively built, but much younger than James would have guessed, perhaps even an undergraduate. Was this a "junior", and therefore a current member of Wolf's Head? His right leg was vibrating slightly under his trousers, a sign, James decided, of impatience. The man knocked on the door a second time. A moment later the door opened.

Instinctively James stepped back, trying to recede into the street scene, as he watched the young man hand over a large white envelope. There was a brief exchange and then he appeared to be invited inside. The door clicked shut behind him.

James walked past the building, as naturally as he could manage. He glanced rightward once, noticing that mesh curtains blocked any view inside the windows. A brief flash of sunlight dazzled him: a reflection bouncing off the name-plate by the front door.

The least risky option would be to move fast, right now. Wait, and the young man he had followed might re-emerge. Wait, and he would eventually be noticed. James marched to the front door, his stride purposeful, as if he too were making a delivery. He pretended to ring the doorbell, instead taking a quick look at the brass plate just beside it. Then he looked again to make sure he had read the words properly.

What he saw there surprised and baffled him, but there was no mistaking what it said in clear, engraved letters.

AMERICAN EUGENICS SOCIETY,
NEW HAVEN OFFICE

CHAPTER
THIRTY-FOUR

London

He remembered this feeling sharply. The same hot blend of nerves and pleasure, of fear and excitement. The last time he had experienced it had been in his junior year at St Albans. A few of the seniors had got hold of some "erotic" pictures, a set of photographs rumoured to be utterly depraved. Everyone in his class was desperate to see them and it fell to young Taylor Hastings to get his hands on them.

He had done it through a series of negotiations, trades and promises — but he had done it. As he left the seniors' dorm that night, his satchel containing the all-important "documentation" slung over his shoulder, he had felt his face grow hot. He was aroused in anticipation of seeing those pictures, most certainly — indeed, he made a stop at the squash court bathrooms in order to have his own, personal private viewing — but he was also engorged with the thrill of the forbidden. His bag contained a set of photographs of women in a variety of poses, some acrobatic, others shocking — including one of a bare backside greeted by the smack of a cane — but all in violation of at least a half-dozen school rules and perhaps a couple of state obscenity laws into the bargain. What's more, he had, through a rather smart sleight of hand, taken more pictures than the seniors had agreed to. The result was the pleasure of a deception, the kick of committing a small, but elegant crime — and that, he understood at that moment, was a sexual pleasure too.

He felt it now as he walked across Grosvenor Square, his bag once again weighty with illicit cargo. He had staged this heist with much greater sophistication than his little trick at the expense of the St Albans senior year. He had had to use his hands — switching papers from one pile to another with the panache of a magician producing the ace of spades from a handkerchief — but also his wits.

He had created a distraction, summoning his colleagues to huddle over an intriguing cipher that had just come in, asking them to pool their collective knowledge to work out what it could possibly mean. And, while they were puzzling over it, Cellucci scratching his ear with the eraser-end of his pencil, Taylor had salted away carbon copies of the key papers right there and then, inches away from their very eyes.

That, he complimented himself now, was the genius of it. At the moment he had chosen to strike, he had not ushered the dullards of the cipher room out and *away*. No, no, no. Nor had he done anything so cheap or pedestrian as wait for them to leave. On the contrary, he had beckoned his fellow decoders over to *his very desk*. As they gathered in a knot around the bait he had laid for them, he had taken one pace back before calmly and quietly taking exactly what he wanted. He had turned potential witnesses to his crime into alibis for his innocence.

As he walked back through Hyde Park on this bright summer evening, he felt the blood rush to his loins. He was hardening at the thought of what he had done. He pictured himself with Anna, looking at the papers together, tonight, in bed. He would read them out loud, impersonating the authors' voices. He imagined her praising him, calling him "her clever little boy", rewarding him with her tongue, starting at his chest and working steadily downward . . .

Or perhaps he would forego that particular delight, exquisite though he knew it would be. Perhaps he would show restraint and wait for the greater prize. It would mean going straight home now, stashing these documents where they would never be found — until he was ready to show them to the man who would understand their true power. The man, indeed, who had already entrusted him with his own great secrets, held together between the covers of the magnificent Red Book. Imagine what Rawls Murray could do with these papers. He would be overawed the instant he saw who had written them — but once he had digested their substance, well, he would fall to his knees.

Taylor Hastings would become an instant hero to Reginald Rawls Murray, that much was obvious. He would, of course, be a hero to the Right Club. But the young American dared dream of a greater accolade still. By his actions he, Taylor Hastings, would become nothing less than a hero to history.

CHAPTER
THIRTY-FIVE

Eugenics? James squinted at the sign to make sure he had read it properly. Eugenics? How on earth did the science of human breeding — improving the quality of the human race and all that that implied — fit into everything that had happened these last few days and weeks? Unless, of course, it didn't. Unless he had simply followed a random member of the Wolf's Head Society with a scholarly interest in eugenic ideas and no connection at all to Lund, the Dean and his niece or, crucially, Florence and Harry . . .

Reason told him to walk away and to think again. And yet he had learned since that early morning in Oxford that reason did not always deserve the last word, that there was more to him than the power to add up logical propositions, one following another. He was made of flesh and blood, with instincts and intuitions — as well as rages and sorrows — that he had tried to deny for too long. And so he listened to his gut as it told him to ring the doorbell and attempt to get inside the New Haven branch of the American Eugenics Society.

He did not have to wait long. A bespectacled man, his glasses misting up in the heat of this last day of July, answered the door. Judging from his expression, and the sound of voices coming from within, he had been letting people in for a while: it seemed a meeting was underway.

Once again, instinct intervened. Instead of offering his name, James simply nodded and stepped forward.

"Are you on our list?" asked the man with the foggy glasses.

"I should be," James said, in what he hoped was a tone that was part supreme confidence, part lightness and affability. The man on the door pointed James towards a table where two women were taking names. James thanked him and headed in that direction, only to drift away the instant the bell rang, summoning the sweating man on the door back to his duties.

The interior was cool and bright, like a London townhouse. He was standing in the hall on a floor made of stone tiles of black and white, like a diamond-shaped chessboard. Off it he could see a meeting room, the door open, the chairs already set out in rows in a fashion that recalled similar sessions at Oxford. This, he guessed, was that peculiar creature, the early-evening seminar: glass of wine, a show-off presentation, more show-off discussion.

He milled around, noting a crowd that looked utterly familiar: men, most of them middle-aged, in the crumpled linens and tortoiseshell spectacles of the academic. He avoided eye contact, fearing to be drawn into a conversation that might require him to explain himself. Instead, he chose to linger by one of the display tables covered with material relating to tonight's talk. The title was "Eugenics, the next steps" and the speaker was a Dr William Curtis of Yale Medical School. Was he another of McAndrew's protégés?

Also on the table was a neatly-stacked pile of copies of a thin red volume which James took to be a kind of manifesto for the society, apparently offered free of charge. All true believers did this, James had noticed: communists giving away Marxist texts, evangelicals handing out bibles to passers-by. He wondered if this would be a scholarly seminar or an exercise in evangelism.

He picked up the book and saw that it was, in fact, a primer on the topic: What is Eugenics? by Major Leonard Darwin. The book did not mention what James already knew: that this Darwin was the son of Charles.

Not that he knew much more than that. He had long been *aware* of eugenics; it would be impossible to be an educated man in the 1930s and not be aware of it. There had been a Eugenics Society at Oxford, though whether it was still in business he would be hard pressed to say. There was the occasional lecture on the topic as well as frequent letters and articles in the periodicals. And yet James had let it pass him by. The language of the subject did not appeal to him and its leading advocates he found especially grating: so often well-born, busybody types all too ready to condescend to a scholarship boy from the provinces.

Now James ran his eye over the contents page of the junior Darwin's book, picking out the chapter headings. Domestic Animals; Hereditary Qualities; The Men we Want;

354

Inferior Stocks; Birth Control; Sterilization; Feeble-Mindedness; The Deterioration of our Breed, Eugenics in the Future; Selection in Marriage.

He glanced up to see that the room was filling up and for a while he eavesdropped on the greetings and handshakes taking place around him, with their talk of delayed trains from Boston and long drives from New York. This was, James understood, a meeting of scholars from beyond Yale, one that appeared to bring together colleagues from several Ivy League universities: Harvard, Princeton, Columbia and the like. When James sensed that someone was looking in his direction, he quickly ducked back to the book, reading the first line of the first page:

When the time comes for the old dog to die and when with sorrow we shall have to replace him, will not the breed of our new companion be our first thought?

He jumped ahead.

Owners of cattle have always known that care in the selection of stock for breeding purposes will pay them well in the long run ... And if men, however savage or however cultivated, have always given so much time to the study of the breed of the animals they own, why have they not paid equal or more attention to their own breed? Before a marriage is contracted many questions may be asked as to the amount of money likely to be inherited by the bride, while no consideration is usually given to the qualities of mind or body which she is likely to pass on to her children — to her breed, in fact. The aim of eugenics is to prove that the breed of our own citizens is a matter of vital importance ...

James wondered again if he was wasting his time. Could there be any connection between Harry, Florence and all of this? All he could think of was that his wife's field was academic biology and eugenics was, he supposed, not too far away from that. Was it possible that she had been drafted here to Yale as a scholar on a research project, one that had to be kept secret, even from him? The thought made him shudder: it would have meant everything he had been told about her fear of invasion, her desperate desire to protect Harry, would have been a lie. He could not believe it; he would not believe it. If she had had work to do that entailed travelling to the United States, even highly confidential work, she would have told him about it, of course she would. And what kind of work on eugenics would demand secrecy? It was not exactly a matter of war or peace.

He felt an unspoken shift around him. People were no longer chatting or greeting friends, but slowly shuffling their way into the meeting room. The seminar was about to begin. He took a seat at the back, next to a man who had already produced a notebook, running his pen in a clean vertical line down the page to create a margin.

The speaker appeared. He was no older than James: sandy-haired, with an easy, smiling manner, dressed in a summer suit that hung lightly on him. To James's untutored eye, he looked as if he came from old money.

The man cleared his throat. "I'd like to begin by thanking you all for coming on this warm summer evening. Some of you, I know, have come from far and wide." There it was, the same accent as Dorothy Lake. Reflexively, James looked around the room, just in case she was here.

"As you know, this is an invitation-only gathering. Our usual discretion applies, but it is especially pertinent tonight. Some of the items on our agenda would be open to . . ." He paused, ". . . *misinterpretation*, were they to be disclosed more widely than I intend. I hope I have your co-operation."

There was a murmur of assent.

"Good. Some of you will have seen the copies of the Darwin book in the foyer. Of course, I don't mean to insult anyone here in making such a well-known text my starting point this evening. But I thought it might be useful to return to first principles.

"Let me begin with this important statement from *What is Eugenics?*". Curtis lifted the book to his eye-level as if he were an actor declaiming from a script, and read aloud: "'In order to improve the breed of our race, we should now take such steps as would result in all who show any natural superiority producing a greater number of descendants than at present, whilst making all who are definitely inferior pass on their natural inferiority to as few as possible.'" He lowered the book. "From that single paragraph we derive what we know of as the two different strains of eugenic thought. So-called 'positive eugenics', encouraging procreation by the fittest and most intelligent —" here he made a sweeping gesture as if to encompass his audience, which elicited a warm chuckle of approval, "and also so-called 'negative eugenics', which seeks to stop the unfit from reproducing. Forgive me for teaching grandmother to suck eggs in this way, but I hope my purpose will become clear in due course.

"Put simply," Curtis went on, "the eugenic idea holds that if we have more of the strong and fewer of the weak, then the nation itself will end up stronger. It's true of a herd of prize cattle and it's true of us. Note Darwin's own language in his summary of eugenics' primary aim."

Curtis raised the little red book once more, in theatrical style: "'A lowering of the birth-rate of all the naturally inferior types and an increase in the birth-rate amongst the naturally superior.'"

With each word he heard, the more James remembered his aversion to the whole eugenics business. It came back to him not as a thought, but as a feeling, a creeping sensation across his flesh.

Curtis was reading again, from the Darwin chapter entitled "The Men we Want".

"'It has been suggested that, whilst getting rid of these extremely undesirable types, we should endeavour to create a group of supermen at the other end of the scale. If a few perfect individuals were to appear on earth, and if their perfection were to be acknowledged by all, this would be very good. These supermen would rule over us to our great contentment.'"

Curtis lowered the book. "It's quite a thought, is it not, ladies and gentlemen? Imagine it, a latter-day pantheon of the gods, human and yet blessed with the strength of deities."

The man at James's side was scribbling furiously. No one had so much as raised a hand in objection, apparently unfazed by the notion of this "group of supermen" ruling the world.

Curtis too was moving on. "The question arises, how exactly is society to get rid of these 'extremely undesirable types'? Here Darwin's chapter on eugenic methods is extremely helpful, though he eliminates what would of course be the easiest solution from the start."

Another knowing laugh rippled across the room.

Curtis raised the book once more. "'As to the inferior types, we cannot, as we have seen, reduce the number of their descendants by the simple expedient of murder. All that can be done is to lessen the size of their families.' He makes it sound so easy, doesn't he? Easy enough for Major Darwin, sitting there in his study in Kent or Staffordshire" — he pronounced it *Stafford-shy-er* — "or wherever it was. But not so easy for those of us who wish to translate these ideas into practical policy. So what should we be doing? What action should we be taking to, in Darwin's words, 'lessen the size' of those inferior families?

"We're all familiar with the obvious methods: birth control, sterilization and so on. These are all useful, and indeed I'm proud to say the United States has been a leader in sterilization. But we are rapidly being overtaken, thanks to laws permitting involuntary sterilization or its variants right across Europe: Denmark, Sweden, Norway, Finland, even little Estonia. And of course the true lead is now set by

Germany, where forced sterilization has become a matter of state policy, the preferred methods being vasectomy for men, ligation — or tying — of the ovarian tubes for women and, in a few cases, the use of x-rays. Hundreds of thousands of Germany's feeble-minded or otherwise abnormal population have been prevented from reproducing under this programme. I hope it is clear that the old debate — on whether this range of available, medically-established methods should be used simply to *persuade* rather than to *compel* the naturally inferior to refrain from parent-hood — is becoming rather out of date."

James was watching the faces in the room, not one of which had so much as demurred. They were listening to this without a word of dissent, many nodding as Curtis moved onto definitions, quoting Leonard Darwin on what groups constituted the inferior: "'These include the criminal, the insane, the imbecile, the feeble in mind, the diseased at birth, the deformed, the deaf, the blind, etc, etc.'"

The man on James's left had now filled two pages of his notebook and was beginning a third, listing those whom Major Darwin, quoted by Curtis, further defined as undesirable for reproduction: the unemployed, those on low wages, who had thereby proved their lack of value to the wider society, as well as those who had experienced consumption or epilepsy. The lecturer helpfully spelled out Darwin's exact words on the matter: "'No one who has had unmistakable epileptic fits should become a parent.'"

"What, though, of those who seem sound enough in mind and body, but who have what Darwin calls 'many defective relatives'?" asked Curtis, affecting to sound genuinely vexed by the conundrum. "The answer is not immediately obvious, which is why such people, cursed by a family tree laden down with so much rotten fruit, should consult a doctor." Apparently Darwin was clear what the wise physician would propose in such a situation: "'a marriage which should result in no more than one or two children.'"

Suddenly James knew, to the depths of his stomach, why he had declined the Oxford invitations to hear Miss Marie Stopes speak on the merits of contraception — yet another leaflet about that had landed in his pigeon-hole the day after Florence disappeared — why he had turned the page at the first sight of an editorial in praise of the eugenic approach to population control, why the idea had repelled him.

What right did these people have to say how many children he, or anyone else, was allowed to have? To them it was no more than arithmetic, a matter of simple utilitarian calculus, working out what set of arrangements would result in the greatest happiness for the greatest number. On that measure alone, it made perfect sense to reduce the number of criminals, lunatics and imbeciles along with the deaf, dumb and blind. But couldn't they see that "utility" could never be the only measure, that every one of those "defectives" was a unique person, a person with a life and needs and desires and loves?

He thought of his parents, how they never referred to numbers of people but rather to "souls": *we had a good twenty souls at the meeting this morning*. It was a habit of mind, a reminder that people were not mere building blocks in the creation of some theoretical utopia, but that each one of them was individual and precious. He used to mock such talk in his youth, but now he had a good mind to start hurling the phrase "sanctity of life" from his back row seat, heckling the speaker and challenging this complacent audience of nodding heads by reminding them that human beings were not cattle to be bred but that each one was unfathomable and mysterious and full of wonder — that people were never a means to an end, but an end in themselves.

But there was something else, too. He thought of his shattered shoulder. He recalled the repeated rejections from even non-military wartime service, explained to him by Bernard Grey down the telephone at Liverpool docks: *not suitable for sensitive work*. He remembered the verdict the Medical Examination Board had passed on him and which they might as well have branded onto his forehead: *D1*. He thought of all that and he realized his loathing for eugenics was grounded not only in principle but also in bitter, personal anger. He hated it because he knew that the likes of this William Curtis and his precious Leonard Darwin and probably everyone else in this bright, civilized seminar room would regard him, James Zennor — with his broken body, his blackouts, his rages and his torment — as "extremely undesirable", as "inferior", as *defective*." And that, if Curtis and Darwin had their way, James too would doubtless have been told gently, and then compelled, to "refrain from parenthood".

And it wasn't just him, it was all the people these eugenicists were ready to throw aside like so much refuse. He thought of the young men born in the slums of Manchester, Birmingham or Glasgow who were now the defenders of Britain, risking their lives to save the country. Eugenics would have branded these soldiers sub-standard, not good enough to last another generation. He remembered a friend in the International Brigade, Len, who one night admitted that he was the child of a prostitute, that he had never known his father. Eugenics would have preferred he had never been born, yet he was one of the finest, bravest men James had ever known. He thought of his own parents, his father the son of a Cornish tin miner whose lungs had given out when he was barely forty years old. What would Darwin and Curtis have made of him, eh? He would hardly have made the cut, would he? They'd have snuffed him out, along with his son and his son — all of them expendable, so much human rubbish.

Christ, the blood was boiling in his veins. His body seemed to be quaking with rage. He needed to get a hold of himself. In an act of will, his right hand gripped his left wrist and squeezed tight. He had to assert control. He needed to know what this group, the American Eugenics Society, was all about; what connection, if any, they had with the Wolf's Head and how they might lead him back to Florence and Harry.

So he calmed himself and, as if fiddling with the dial on the wireless, tuned in again to the speaker. Curtis seemed now to have turned to the specific task that confronted eugenicists in America. Quite baldly, as if it were entirely uncontroversial, the speaker explained that one fifth of the current population of the United States should never have been born — and that it was their duty, as the leaders of the coming generation, to ensure that such people were not born in the future.

"Happily," Curtis went on, "you find yourselves in the right place. While other cities in the United States of America still labour in confusion and uncertainty, we are privileged to gather at a university where eugenics has taken firm root. Take these words, for example." He raised his hand again to signal a quotation. This time he was holding not Darwin's little red book, but a sheaf of notes: " 'We could make a new human race in a hundred years if only people in positions of power and influence would wake up to the paramount importance of what eugenics means . . . we could save the bloodstream of our race from a needless amount of contamination.' Those," said Curtis with a beam of institutional pride, "were the words of the founder and first president of the American Eugenics Society, Irving Fisher, who, I'm glad to note, was a professor in the economics faculty right here at Yale. I don't need, I'm sure, to mention Ellsworth Huntington, who only stepped down as president of our society's board of directors a couple of years ago. He, as you all know, was Professor of Geography here at Yale. Or what about these words? 'Granting that society can decide just which individuals it wishes to eliminate as genetically inferior . . . how shall it proceed to eliminate them?' That was Edmund W Sinott, a botanist, here at Yale. Those of you who are not yet subscribers to the *Journal of the American Eugenics Society*, I suggest you become so immediately: there are gems like that in every edition!" he said to polite laughter.

"And lest you think we have no allies at the very top, let me reassure you by citing the name of James Angell." There were nods of recognition. "Angell was President of Yale University until three years ago. Well, let me — and I promise this will be the last one — let me quote him to you: 'Modern medicine, unless combined with some kind of practicable eugenic program, may result in an excess of feeble and incompetent stock. Certainly the preservation and increase of life for individuals unable to make reasonably happy and effective adjustments to the conditions of living is a highly dubious blessing.' So you see. We have support at the highest possible level."

A worm of suspicion was forming in James's mind, slowly and steadily turning through everything that had happened these last few weeks. He wanted to follow it, to watch it. But he needed to pay attention to what he was hearing in this room. Eugenics had crossed the Atlantic and seemed to have docked and found safe harbour here at Yale. Nor could it be dismissed as the marginal preoccupation of a few cranks: these people counted the former university president among their number.

The speaker was coming to his main point. "I tell you all this," said Curtis, "for two reasons. First, I believe we have wasted too much time on rather sterile — if you'll forgive the pun! — debates over persuasion versus compulsion, and that those debates arise only because there is still some uncertainty over definitions. We still lack clear-cut, unambiguous understanding of what, or rather who, counts as superior and what, or who, counts as inferior. The next step forward for our discipline is to arrive at some commonly-accepted definitions. The project I wish to propose to you tonight aims to settle this matter once and for all.

"Before I detail the specifics, I want you to be assured that I am not asking you or your institutions to take on anything that we here at Yale are not prepared to take on ourselves. Indeed, what we have *already* undertaken — with support, as I hope I have demonstrated, at the highest level."

James could feel the tension in the room, which was now hushed. Everyone was rapt.

"Two researchers," Curtis began, "one from Harvard, the other from Columbia, are pioneers in a field they describe as 'Physique Studies'. They argue that a person's body, properly measured, studied and analyzed, will reveal much about the intelligence, temperament, moral worth and even the future accomplishments of that person. But only if the study is extensive and meticulous."

He paused to let his words sink in. "They believe they can gather the evidence that will not only confirm that there *is* a connection between physical prowess and intellectual ability, but will also demonstrate how this connection operates. First, though, they need to establish a set of different bodily configurations. Once defined, and set alongside long-term data on performance — marital, professional and in all other spheres — it will, these men submit, be a simple task to correlate each body type and physiognomy with later life history. They believe that the correlation will be strong, that these bodily traits will be shown to be unswerving determinants of character. They believe, in other words — and forgive the crudity of my summary of their complex thesis — that physique equals destiny."

James could hear nothing but the sound of pen scratching on paper from his neighbour.

"But none of this will be possible without a comprehensive collection of photographs of young American adults, that might, taken together, form an Atlas of Men and an Atlas of Women. The subjects in such a study will, of course, have to be photographed without clothing, in order that the bodily configuration be correctly classified. Discretion may demand that this work be done in combination, as it were, with another more conventional activity. But a full range of subjects is essential, so any study must include those likely to be at the higher end of the scale of intellectual achievement and moral worth.

"Which is why today I call on you, my dear colleagues in our fellow Ivy League institutions, to give your best endeavours in assisting this vital project — one on which, I am glad to say, we here at Yale have already made a start."

Suddenly James felt a shiver run through him. He was back at Frank Pepe's pizza restaurant, George Lund's briefcase open in his hands. Inside it were those photographs of men, naked as they stood before the camera, posing as if at a medical examination. And all of them were young, just as Curtis had suggested. Was this part of what George Lund had discovered? What he had been carrying in his bag — and what had been deliberately removed — was not a collection of pornographic pictures to titillate Lund, the secret homosexual. They were proof that Yale was engaged in the first stage of a study to show that the intellectual elite were defined by certain physical traits, that "physique equals destiny". That was no crime; Yale could research whatever it liked. But what had Curtis just said? *Discretion may demand that this work be done in combination, as it were, with another more conventional activity.* Translated, that surely meant that the participants had not been told what they were posing for, that they had believed they were being photographed for some other reason. In other words, Yale had engaged in an act of deception, tricking its youngest members into posing naked for a camera. Was this the truth poor George Lund had stumbled across? Was this why he was killed?

James halted his train of thought before it ran away with itself. If Yale had been involved in such an act of academic chicanery it would certainly be embarrassing. The Dean would have to apologize, to be sure. But James knew what these university politicians were like: McAndrew would be able to say there had been a misunderstanding, that he had been misled, that he had thought this was a bona fide research exercise. He would do what all senior college staff did in such situations: he would blame someone else. James had seen that manoeuvre a hundred times before. And how shaming a scandal would it really be? Not that shaming, surely, if Curtis felt able to allude to this research exercise in a meeting of colleagues, albeit one that was invitation-only.

Besides, Lund had seemed convinced that Harry and Florence were caught up in whatever it was he had discovered. But how could they possibly have any connection with illicitly-taken undergraduate photographs? Both Lund and his widow had also suggested that much more was at stake than an academic scandal. *You've stumbled into something much bigger than you realize. Bigger and more dangerous.*

Curtis was still speaking, enumerating the challenges eugenicists like them faced in the coming years, identifying the potential sources of opposition, making the obligatory call for more funding for research. James was only half-listening, his mind furiously trying to assemble and re-assemble the pieces of the puzzle, desperate to construct a picture that might include his wife and child and that might reveal where he could find them.

The speaker was moving to his conclusion. "This, I know we agree, is an idea whose time has come. It is an idea that needs to be tested and taken to its logical conclusion, so that the world may be persuaded at long last of its truth and its urgency. Here I must defer to a man I know would like to have been here tonight — who indeed sends his apologies — a man who is a great friend to our cause. His latest thinking represents a new and exciting advance, one that understands the changing times in which we find ourselves, especially with regard to the unfolding events in Europe. I'm referring of course to the Dean of Yale University, Preston McAndrew."

James did not wait for the end of the meeting, taking advantage of his seat at the back to slip out while Curtis was still basking in applause. He walked briskly onto York Street, the stones of Trumbull College almost amber in the evening sunshine. He checked his watch. If he was fast, he should get there in time. Unbidden, his mind calculated the time difference and worked out that it was past midnight in England. German pilots were probably in the skies right now, at this very instant, dropping their deadly cargo on cities, factories, homes, bedrooms . . .

He quickened his pace. He was getting closer, he was sure of it. Lund had discovered what McAndrew was up to. The photographs were part of it, but not the whole, they couldn't be. There was something else. And Curtis had just confirmed it. *His latest thinking represents a new and exciting advance . . .*

What was McAndrew's latest thinking? What was he doing or saying or planning that had got Lund so agitated and so frightened? It had been sufficiently serious that he had been killed to keep it secret. And somehow it involved Florence and Harry.

It was only once he had walked through the grand entrance of the Sterling Library, and was standing in the echoing stone lobby, that James realized he did not know exactly which department he was looking for. Was eugenics to be found in Natural Sciences or in Philosophy? Was it classified as biology or politics? Given the grandiosity of eugenics' ambition, its desire to be taken seriously as objective, unarguable fact, he headed for the Natural Sciences reading room.

Approaching the librarian, a younger man who looked irritated to be taken away from his own reading, James attempted a smile. "I wonder if you can help me. I'm looking for the latest writings of Dr Preston McAndrew. He's the head of the Medical —"

"I know who Preston McAndrew is," the librarian replied. "Books or journals?"

"Is it possible to look for both?"

The librarian looked up at the clock. "I could do that. Come back tomorrow morning, say, any time after eleven o'clock and I'll —"

"No, I'm sorry. It really is terribly urgent."

"Well, you need to be more specific, sir. Otherwise I can't help you."

James said the first thing that came into his head. "*The Journal of the American Eugenics Society*. The latest edition. Let's try that." That was what Curtis had mentioned, after all. And if McAndrew was going to air his "latest thinking" on eugenics anywhere, it would surely be there.

The librarian looked at him sceptically, but eventually he turned to face the wall of drawers comprising the card index while James paced and paced, checking his watch, looking at the clock, replaying Curtis's words in his mind, in case he had missed something important.

After much checking and cross-checking, pulling drawers open and closed with exasperated sighs, the librarian returned to the counter. "I'm sorry, sir, but that title you requested is currently with another reader."

Damn. "I don't suppose you could tell me his name, could you? So that perhaps I could see if he's finished with it?"

The young man glowered, apparently weighing which would be more effort, acceding to this request or denying it and then having to argue over his decision with this troublesome-looking Englishman. He lingered for a moment longer, then went back to the card index and finally to a large ledger. Eventually he returned wearing an expression James had seen many times before. It said, *I shouldn't really be doing this, but . . .*

"I have the name, but this is rather —"

"Of course. I'll be extremely polite."

"All right. The book you requested is currently on loan to a reader whose desk number is four hundred and seventy-three. He's a member of the faculty. His name is Dr George Lund."

CHAPTER
THIRTY-SIX

As a young man, James had never had much of a poker face. His parents and their Quaker friends were straightforward, honest people and so he had never learned to dissemble. Only at Oxford did he start to understand that the face of the sophisticated man was opaque, but even then he was not much good at it. It was only after Spain that he became adept at hiding his feelings. Which is what he did now, as he showed what he hoped was no response at all to the words he had just heard from the librarian. Instead, he turned around and walked unhurriedly over to the section of the room where the desks were numbered four hundred and above.

So Lund had been down this exact same path just before his death, investigating the Dean and his "latest thinking". James counted the numbers of the desks as he passed them: four hundred and sixty-five, four hundred and sixty-six . . .

There it was, four hundred and seventy-three. James hesitated before sitting down, feeling a shudder of the dead man's presence. On the desk were two books, as if their reader had simply stepped away for a cup of coffee. As James sat down, he felt certain: it was something Lund had found in these books that had made him half-crazed with fear — and set him on the path to his death.

James picked up the first volume, which appeared to be an anthology, a series of short papers on eugenics. He flicked through it, turning the pages fast, desperate to find something he might latch onto. Maddeningly, there was neither a contents page nor list of contributors, nor any kind of printing history. Perhaps this was not a published book at all, but rather a collection of monographs that some institution — maybe Yale itself — had bound together.

There was, however, no shortage of familiar names. Indeed, to James's surprise, most of the authors seemed to be drawn from socialist circles back home. He had heard half of them lecture in person; the other half he had read. Here was George Bernard Shaw, arguing that if democracy were to be saved it would be by a Democracy of Supermen: The only fundamental and possible socialism is the socialization of the selective breeding of man. James skipped over the next bit, picking out only the sentence in which Shaw argued that the overthrow of the aristocrat has created the necessity for the Superman.

There was an editorial from the *New Statesman* of 1931. The magazine reckoned that the only people who could possibly oppose the eugenic vision were traditionalists and reactionaries, too selfish to see that their desire to have children should take second place to society's need for an improved breed. Or as the *New Statesman* put it: The legitimate claims of eugenics are not inherently incompatible with the outlook of the collectivist movement. On the contrary, they would be expected to find their most intransigent opponents amongst those who cling to the individualistic views of parenthood and family economics.

Here was that economist chap, Keynes, whom everyone so admired, putting the case for widespread use of birth control, because the working class was too "drunken and ignorant" to be trusted to keep its own numbers down. And look at this, Grey's big pal, William Beveridge, Master of University College, arguing that those with "general defects" should be denied not only the vote, but "civil freedom and fatherhood".

Next James came to a short essay by Harold Laski, who had once sat between James and Florence at high table: The time is surely coming in our history when society will look upon the production of a weakling as a crime against itself. And on the very next page, JBS Haldane. Harry Knox was always quoting Haldane, James remembered, chiefly because the eminent scientist and socialist supported the Republic in Spain. Here he was sounding the alarm: Civilization stands in real danger from over-production of "undermen".

James was tearing through the pages now, trying to find a reference to McAndrew or something else that might have caught Lund's eye. It was as if the dead man were right in front of him, James shaking his corpse, trying to get him to spit out what he had meant to say.

Next there was a paper on the sterilization of those deemed unfit to reproduce, with a long passage on the Brock report on the subject, commissioned by Britain's health minister in 1934. Apparently the eugenics crowd were delighted that Brock recommended exactly what they had been calling for: a campaign to encourage voluntary sterilization. There was an editorial of warm support from the *Manchester Guardian*, praising Brock for backing the sterilization "the eugenists soundly urge". On the next sheet was a table of recent statistics, showing which countries were already leading the way. Curtis had been right: Germany apart, the United States was ahead of the pack, having sterilized thirty thousand of the mentally ill and criminally insane by 1939, mostly against their will.

Come on, come on, James thought.

He flicked through a few more pages, coming across Bertrand Russell, star philosopher and another one of the Greys' high table chums. It seemed the great man had dreamed up a rather elaborate wheeze to improve the quality of the nation's stock. He wanted the state to issue colour-coded 'procreation tickets': anyone who dared breed with holders of a different-coloured ticket would face a heavy fine. That way people of high-calibre could be sure their blood was mixed only with those of similar pedigree. Why risk contamination by those whose blood might be dangerously proletarian, foreign or weak? Just check their ticket!

James was shaking his head at the arrogance of it all when he came across an essay suggesting that the problem was not that the poor were having too many children, but that they were having the *wrong kind* of children. The solution was a programme of artificial insemination, aimed at impregnating working-class women with the sperm of men blessed with high IQs. There was a quotation from that queen of the Fabian Society, Beatrice Webb, explaining why her sort were worth reproducing in the greatest possible numbers, describing herself as "the cleverest member of one of the cleverest families in the cleverest class of the cleverest nation of the world". Sounds just like Virginia Grey, James thought.

By the time he came to the end he was trembling with fury and loathing for these people and their contempt for anyone they deemed a lesser mortal than themselves. He pictured them all, sitting together in an Oxford college no doubt, deciding who was fit and who was unfit, who worthy and who unworthy, who shall live and who shall die. He hated them and their eugenic creed with the very core of his being.

He forced himself to focus. What had he discovered, except that Britain's greatest progressive bigwigs were as steeped in eugenics as the luminaries of Yale? Surely this could not have been what had so agitated Lund? What *had* the man been trying to tell him?

James had one more flick through the collection of papers. He was looking for pencil marks, some sign, however faint, that would reveal what had caught Lund's attention.

The funny thing was he saw it so fast he thought he had imagined it. He had to turn back through the pages slowly to pick it up again. He almost smiled to himself at the joke of it. What he was looking for was not in the text at all. It was in the footnotes — and one of James's greatest vices as a scholar was his aversion to reading footnotes. But there it was, with the faintest pencil mark alongside it.

I am indebted to the enthusiasm and support of two scholars, whose shared interest in this subject is not only a model for further eugenic study but for future academic collaboration across the Atlantic: Prof Bernard Grey of Oxford University and Dr Preston McAndrew of Yale University.

James fell back in his seat as if he had been shoved into it. He let out no sound, but his mouth had fallen open. And then he cursed himself — for not seeing it sooner, for failing to grasp what had been in front of his nose all this time.

He was thinking of Harry. Not the little boy he knew, but the child these people, the authors of these papers, would imagine. They would see him as the offspring of two Oxford fellows, blessed with a genetic inheritance that would doubtless have placed him in the top fraction of the top one per cent in the country. He thought of Curtis and his researchers in the new field of "physique studies". What would they make of Harry's mother, with her tall, lean, flawless body that had, not long ago, made her the fastest female swimmer in the world? If physique equalled destiny then any child of Florence Walsingham was surely destined for greatness. Too bad Harry's father had had to ruin his chances. Except that was not how these eugenicists would see it, would they? When Harry had been conceived, James had been just like Florence, an accomplished scholar-athlete, sound — better than sound — in mind and body. To the likes of McAndrew and Grey, Harry was the product of two perfect specimens of mankind.

No wonder Grey and McAndrew were collaborators. Of course they were. That was why it had been so easy for Grey to set James up at Yale, why Grey was the natural point of contact when Yale had offered to take in the Oxford children. That was surely why it had been Yale — rather than Harvard or Princeton or anywhere else in the United States — that had opened its doors to those young Britons in the first place.

James now remembered what Mrs Goodwin had said about the Dean, that he had not only been in charge of running things for the Oxford families once they had got to New Haven, he had been *the driving force behind the whole scheme*. James didn't doubt that the families who had taken in little English boys and girls and their mothers had done so out of the goodness of their hearts. But now he could see that McAndrew's motives — and Grey's — were very different.

James digested everything he had heard at the American Eugenics Society and what he had read just now and watched the picture as it took shape in his head. What had once been a faint pencil outline was now being filled in, in blocks of solid black. Of course, of course, of course.

What were the Oxford children if not the cleverest members from the cleverest families in the cleverest class of the cleverest nation of the world? All self-respecting believers in eugenics would see it as their duty to protect such children, Harry included. If Britain was going to be bombed, if its people were soon either to be killed or to become slaves to a foreign occupier, who should be saved first? The answer was obvious, at least to all those elitist academics he had just been reading.

And not just to them. To all those people in Oxford he had brushed past or ignored, whose last names he had forgotten. Magnus Hook, wittering on about "superior" social categories and "those we might classify as defective" — he doubtless would have seen the matter the same way too. As would Rosemary Hyde, with her improving walks in the fresh air and the countryside, her zeal for rambling as a way of improving public health and increasing the quality of the national stock. Leonard Musgrove and those other blasted Fabians would have had the same view.

No doubt they had all conspired together in this plan to spirit the children out of Oxford, holding their secret meetings, keeping that unreliable chap Zennor in the dark, even stealing a postcard from his letterbox to ensure he didn't find out too soon where Florence and Harry had gone and have time to stop them. They were all in on it together, with Bernard Grey in charge of the operation, colluding with his fellow eugenicist across the Atlantic, Preston McAndrew. They all believed that those one hundred and twenty-five Oxford boys and girls were the best and the brightest and had to be saved. They would be returned to England after the war, little saplings to be replanted in the soil. Even if everything — and everyone — they had left behind had turned to rubble, these saplings would take root and grow tall, blossoming into the next generation of the elite: they were the cleverest of the cleverest of the cleverest, to be preserved at all costs.

A page appeared in James's head, popping up as if on a spring. It was the letter he had seen when he rifled through those files in McAndrew's outer office, the letter from Cambridge declining Yale's offer, "since this might be interpreted as privilege for a special class". Cambridge had understood what James had not. Except this was not a question of mere interpretation. Given who was behind this scheme, privilege for a special class was precisely its purpose.

He wanted to run out of the library, find the nearest post office and send an urgent telegram to Grey: *I know what you've done STOP I know how and why you did it STOP*

But even if this was the true motivation for the Oxford evacuation, it still did not answer the question that had been devouring James for nearly a month. Where on God's earth was his wife? Where was his child?

There was still one more book on the table. He picked it up. It was the latest edition of the American Eugenics Society journal, the volume he had requested. He only had to read the contents to see that it included a lecture by Dr Preston McAndrew of Yale University. His fingers rushed to the page, fumbling in their haste. Finally, he read the introductory paragraph, explaining that the talk had been delivered at a colloquium — not at Yale, but at some far more obscure institution — on

Charles Darwin, held the previous November to mark the eightieth anniversary of the publication of *On the Origin of Species*. It was entitled *Cleansing Fire*. James read every line, carefully and slowly.

The greatest human frailty, common to those of both strong and weak intellect, is sentiment. Perhaps it is this trait, more than any other, that sets us apart from the animals. Watch any collection of beasts and you will soon see displayed a cold calculation of collective self-interest which eludes us humans. A cat with a litter of kittens will immediately identify the weak one and discard it. Not because she is especially cruel, but because she has calculated what is best overall for her litter. Any animal confronted by a runt will be similarly ruthless; the runt has to go for the good of the whole. We like to call ourselves rational, but in this regard it is the animal kingdom which is the domain of reason. It is human beings — who tend to be moved by the sight of a struggling runt or feeble kitten — who are irrational, so clouded by sentiment that they are unable to make the basic calculations of utility.

If we were not so impaired, we would be able to see quite clearly, even automatically, where our best interests lay. It would be obvious to us that the species as a whole would benefit if we were no longer burdened by those who take much and offer little. If the human litter, as it were, were free of its runts, society would no longer have to provide for the weak and dependent, for such people would not exist. It would, instead, consist solely of those able to make their contribution, to carry the load rather than to be carried. What place would there be for poverty in such a society? Why, none at all. For every man would be a driver, with not a passenger to be seen.

It sounds fantastical to imagine such a society, utopian even. And yet in every generation an opportunity to create that very utopia presents itself. The trouble is that, just as regularly, the human race — soft-headed and sentimental as we are — misses that opportunity. Worse than misses; we actively reject it.

What is this opportunity I speak of? I shall answer that with reference to the man whose work we honour tonight. I know the purists among you dislike the phrase "survival of the fittest" as an inexact summary of Charles Darwin's work, but it serves as a useful shorthand for my current purpose and I hope you will indulge me.

Since the dawn of time, different animal species have come and gone. Natural selection has proved remarkably effective — ruthless, but effective — in eliminating those who, by definition, were too weak to survive. When cosmic disaster struck the earth, the dinosaurs were eliminated. It was as simple and brutal as that.

Human beings should be no different. When disaster strikes, the weakest should be eliminated, leaving only the strongest to survive. But we humans have made ourselves the exception. We feel compelled to intervene, to get in Nature's way, to protect those who would otherwise be discarded. Just as we weep at the sight of that rejected kitten, so we become overwhelmed by irrational pity — and prevent Nature from taking its course.

And what is the disaster I have in mind? It is the same as the opportunity I spoke of a moment ago. I am referring, ladies and gentlemen, to war.

War is the human equivalent of that great meteor striking the earth, separating weak from strong. Or rather it should be. But every time it comes we meddle and get in the way, trying to hold up a shield to stave off disaster.

But what if, just once, we stood aside and let war run its course? What if we let it act as Nature intended, as a cleansing fire that might burn through the entire forest, destroying the deadwood, leaving only those plants and flowers that were beautiful and strong enough to survive? Imagine the human stock that would be left: only the very best.

It sounds fanciful, but I believe it is no such thing. Just such an experiment could soon be played out before us, with a single, island race as its subject. The only task — the only duty — for us as American scientists and as American citizens is to make sure that we don't get in the way. War is coming to our mother country — Great Britain — like a cleansing fire. But it will cleanse nothing if the United States puts out the flames.

CHAPTER
THIRTY-SEVEN

He left the book unclosed, sprinted to the nearest exit and galloped down the stairs two at a time. Heading back onto York Street, his mind was running faster than his body, processing and analyzing what he had just read. He could not say he had absorbed its meaning: it was too big, too important.

He turned left and crossed Elm Street, dodging the yellow beams of car headlights switched on in the summer twilight. As he walked down York Street he knew he was taking an absurd gamble, one that was almost certainly doomed. And yet he had no idea where else he could turn.

She had mentioned this location only once, in an aside during their dinner, but it had lodged in his memory. And there it was, just next to the School of Architecture, confirmed by a small sign in the window: the offices of the *Yale Daily News*.

Dorothy Lake had also said that even in summer, when there was no daily newspaper to produce, there were usually people around — ambitious, would-be editors preparing for the new term. And indeed, when he pushed at the door, it opened.

He seemed to have entered some kind of basement, exposed brick arches rising around him as if he were under a railway bridge. In front were tables covered with newspapers, battered typewriters, rulers and scalpels. The floor was littered with old ink ribbons, photographs, discarded flashbulbs and piles and piles of paper. All around the walls were recent front pages of the newspaper.

James picked his way through this paraphernalia to reach a staircase on the other side, its first few steps similarly covered with debris. To his relief, he could hear voices. He had not even reached the top when he saw Dorothy.

She had her back to him, turning only when a young man — who, from his posture, James took to be the editor — gestured in his direction. Her face, a picture of shock, told him what he already knew. A moment later, she recovered her poise and gave him a bright smile. "Dr Zennor!"

James said nothing. He held her gaze for a long moment and felt some small gratification when she blushed. So she was capable of feeling shame. "Could we speak? In private?" he said at last.

Dorothy looked away. She said something he couldn't quite catch to the editor then walked briskly across the room, her heels clicking on the stone floor. As she passed James on the staircase, he caught the scent of her, as potent as it had been last night, and for a moment felt a renegade stab of desire. Then he turned and followed her.

She tried to seize the initiative, speaking even before they had reached the bottom. "James, it's so good to see you. I'd wondered where you'd —"

"No need for any of that, Dorothy."

"I don't know what you mean." She bit her lip, a gesture of feigned innocence, but he hardened his heart.

"Yes, you do. The Dean is your uncle and you've been telling him — and the police — what I'm up to."

For a moment he wondered if she was going to brazen it out, but then she looked down at her feet, which was all the confession James needed.

"What kind of woman does that? Getting a man to trust you, to spill his guts out, telling you everything that matters to him, then betraying him — for what? Did your uncle pay you for this information? Did he tell you to kiss me, Miss Lake? Was that his idea? Was that part of the job, too, eh? Because I know what kind of woman behaves like that and they're not called reporters."

She slapped him hard, across the face. It stung.

"OK, fine," he said. "But we're not even yet. I need to know where your uncle is. Where has he gone?"

"My uncle?"

He found himself looking at her, his gaze taking her all in. She was tall, her body curved and shapely, her hair styled just so. She had the patina of a charming, sophisticated woman polished to a shine. And yet he was sure he had glimpsed something else, *someone* else, a moment ago, beneath that hard veneer, just as he had for a fleeting moment when they had had dinner together, the moment he had talked about his son, Harry. His voice softened.

"Dorothy, you do this so well. Playing the sharp, beautiful cynic. The woman of the world. I bet they love it here." He gestured at the wall of yellowing front pages. "But you weren't always like this. And you won't always be like this."

She gave him a curious look, almost a smirk, as if he were being a sap.

He carried on, undeterred. "One day you'll be a mother. And you'll be a good one too." He watched her eyes narrow, puzzled, assessing. "You'll love your child so much and that child will love you. And the only thing you won't be strong enough to bear will be being apart from that little boy or little girl." The smirk began to fade. "If someone took your child from you, you'd fight like a tiger to get them back, I know you would. And you know it too. So I'm asking you, Dorothy, as a father addressing the good mother you will one day be, and as a husband speaking to the loyal, loving wife I know you will one day be — please, help me. Tell me where Preston McAndrew has gone."

For a moment she looked bewildered, a lost child herself. Then she took two or three faltering steps, gripping the shoulder of a chair piled high with old notebooks to keep herself steady. She kept her eyes down as she spoke, her voice so small he could barely hear her. "I don't understand how Florence and Harry are caught up in this."

"Leave that to me. Just tell me where the Dean has gone."

She touched her eye with just the side of her index finger, using the knuckle rather than the tip so as not to smudge her make-up, a minute, feminine gesture that made him instantly long for Florence. For long seconds she said nothing and James fought the urge to shake the information out of her.

At last it seemed she had reached a decision. She looked up, her blue eyes suddenly candid. "He left in a hurry. Very excited. More excited than I've ever seen him."

It required enormous willpower for James not to reply immediately, not to demand more information, not to speak too loudly and break the moment. But he forced himself to remain silent and to wait.

He was rewarded when she spoke again. "He said he was off to have an important meeting. 'The most important meeting of my entire life' is what he actually said. He said that he had to go right away, that what he was about to do would be the greatest act of service he could ever perform for his fellow man."

James reeled. It was confirmation of what he feared most, that the deadly idea McAndrew had articulated in that Cleansing Fire lecture was not some abstract hypothesis for rarefied academic discussion. It was a plan, one he aimed to implement in the real world — and soon. Of course he would describe it that way, not as an abominable act of wickedness but *as the greatest act of service he could ever perform for his fellow man*. He surely could not have been referring to anything else.

James could wait no more, repeating his question for the fourth time. "Where has he gone?"

Was he imagining it, or were those blue eyes wet with tears? Dorothy stepped closer, so that they were standing just inches apart. She gripped the lapels of his jacket and pulled him towards her. "I hope that one day I meet a man as good as you, James Zennor. And that he loves me the way you love your wife." She hugged him tight, then moved her mouth next to his ear and whispered, "Washington. He's gone to Washington, DC."

CHAPTER
THIRTY-EIGHT

London

He straightened the cloth across the small dining table one more time, cocking his head to check that it was right. Of course it was and of course it did not matter if it wasn't. Yet Taylor Hastings could not help himself. He was as nervous about this meeting as any in his entire life.

And yet the nervousness was three parts excitement to one part anxiety. He believed this would be, to quote that bombastic blusterer who was now Britain's prime minister, his "finest hour". He had done what all great men do: seized his opportunity and bent history to his will. His act of heroism would be secret now, but one day it would be recorded in the annals of human events. There, etched in brightest gold, would be his own name: Taylor Hastings, saviour of the European race.

He went back into the bedroom. The suitcase in the closet was still sealed firmly shut, as he had known it would be. But even so, he was filled with doubt once more: what if the envelope was not inside? He had checked it before, twice if not three times, but what if he had moved it absent-mindedly and failed to replace it? He knew consciously that no such thing had happened, but once the question had been raised he could not ignore it. So he unlocked the closet once more, turned the key in the suitcase, opened it and reached under the two carefully-placed blankets until he felt the reassuring roughness of the manila envelope. Then he put the blankets back as they were, closed and locked the case, closed and locked the closet, and reassured himself it was safe — until the doubts returned and the whole cycle started again.

He moved towards the window. Not too close: he didn't want to be seen. Or rather he didn't want to be seen *looking*. What faster way to attract surveillance than to look as if he feared surveillance? From this spot in the middle of the room he could see the other side of the street. The trees were bare. There were few cars; Sunday afternoon traffic was barely a trickle around here. As for passers-by, he could see governesses out with children, those Norland nannies in their oatmeal coats, felt hats and white gloves; the odd courting couple — but no men on their own, no one looking upward to this second floor apartment, no one he suspected of spying on him. He wondered, yet again, if they should have met in the park or in a café. But the idea of carrying that envelope, those papers, out into broad daylight . . .

He wished, for the tenth time that day, they had made this appointment for nine o'clock this morning rather than for afternoon tea. But Reginald Rawls Murray had insisted that he and Anna were "in the country" this weekend and could not get to London before four. "Any earlier and it will look distinctly fishy, old boy. Let's not give Churchill's squealers anything to go on, no break in the routine and all that."

Taylor had deferred to the older man's wisdom, unaware then of how slowly the Sunday hours would pass.

He was about to have another peek out of the window when at long last there was the knock on the door: three quick taps followed by a pause and then a single tap, as agreed. Taylor Hastings breathed in deeply and, with pride as well as apprehension, ushered into his modest digs the man who was simultaneously a Conservative MP, animating spirit of the Right Club and one of England's leading advocates of a peaceful settlement with Nazi Germany.

Murray kept the pleasantries short. He eyed the table, set for tea, and with a purse of his lips and barely perceptible shake of his head signalled that there would be no such time-wasting today. Instead, his coat still on, he said, "Let's get on with it."

Taylor tried to hide his disappointment. He was young and Murray was a busy man, he knew that. But he was about to hand over the Rosetta Stone and Holy Grail rolled into one; surely he deserved a bit of respect, if not outright praise and deference? Instead, he was being treated as if he were no more than the boy at a left luggage counter, his duty to hand over a stored parcel. He slipped into the bedroom with his head down.

There he performed the same drill he had already repeated four times that day, returning with the manila envelope he had removed from the cipher room of the United States Embassy just a few days earlier. As he walked back into the living room, he found Murray standing there tapping his foot, gazing at the ceiling, and he decided in that instant to assert his own power. After all, it was he, Taylor Hastings, who held the cards. The moment would not last long, but for now he would enjoy it.

"Take a seat," he said, gesturing towards one of the armchairs.

For a moment, Murray hesitated, displeasure drawing down the corners of his mouth. Then he removed his coat and did as he was told.

"What we have here, sir," Taylor began, still holding tight to the envelope, "is a series of top secret cables between —" He lowered his voice to a whisper, "President Franklin Delano Roosevelt and a 'Former Naval Person'."

Murray's brow creased, just as Taylor had known it would. He was milking the moment, but what the hell. "'Former Naval Person' is the secret codename of —" He paused, letting the MP hang on his words, then dropped the volume another notch. "Winston Spencer Churchill."

"Good God," said Murray, his hand covering his mouth in an involuntary gesture of genuine shock.

There was something else in that movement too, though it took Taylor Hastings a second or two to work it out. It was indignation. Reginald Rawls Murray, for all his anti-war, anti-Churchill rantings, was indignant that a foreigner, a Yank, should have stolen the private papers of a British prime minister. It offended his patriotic sense of propriety. But, the younger man noted, that reaction did not last long. Murray reached out to take the envelope.

Taylor pulled his hand back, ensuring the documents were out of reach. "Good God is right. God has been very good to us, Mr Murray. It turns out that these two men, who for ease we'll call R and C, have been corresponding for some time, long before C reached the top, as it were. The papers I have in my hand would cause great discomfort for R if they were to become public, especially now, with the election looming."

"Yes, of course."

"But there is one letter that I think will prove decisive. I'll let you read them for yourself." He removed the documents, representing six exchanges of messages between the two leaders, from the envelope, and gave them to the MP who took them with a hand that was, Hastings was delighted to see, trembling. At this angle, he could read along with Murray, though he all but knew the texts by heart.

London
May 15th 1940, 6pm

Most Secret and Personal.
President Roosevelt from Former Naval Person

Although I have changed my office, I am sure you would not wish me to discontinue our intimate,

*private correspondence. As you are no doubt
aware, the scene has darkened swiftly . . .*

Hastings watched as Murray's eyes scanned along the
page, his thumb indicating where he stopped next:

*If necessary, we shall continue the war alone and
we are not afraid of that. But I trust you realize,
Mr President, that the voice and force of the
United States may count for nothing if they are
withheld too long . . .*

That got Murray excited. As expected, the Englishman
turned the page, looking for Roosevelt's reply to this
direct appeal for US intervention. If the President
bowed to Churchill's plea, if he had secretly promised
to deploy "the force of the United States", then
Roosevelt would be finished, his re-election in
November doomed. He had repeatedly sworn before
the American people that no such decision had been
taken, that the US was still officially neutral. But if it
could be proven that Roosevelt had, in fact,
clandestinely committed the US to Britain's defence,
he would be exposed as a warmonger and, worse, a liar
— ready to trick his own nation into a global and
potentially disastrous conflict.

Murray was skimming the President's reply, all of it
exasperatingly non-committal. Taylor knew what the
older man was looking for; he had been looking for just
the same thing himself when he had first held these
papers in his own grasp, his hands clammy with

excitement. He wondered if he should put the Englishman out of his misery, but decided against it. He had worked hard for this moment; he had every right to savour it.

He let his guest turn over another sheet, so that Murray was now reading Churchill's cable to Roosevelt of May 20, 1940, despatched at one pm, his eyes darting across the page at double speed. Taylor particularly liked this one:

Excuse me, Mr President, putting this nightmare bluntly. Evidently I could not answer for my successors who in utter despair and helplessness might well have to accommodate themselves to the German will . . .

Taylor hoped the meaning of that passage had sunk in. Here was the British prime minister warning that, if no American military help was forthcoming, then his own administration would collapse and a pro-German regime would take its place. Wasn't that proof, from the horse's mouth, that he, Taylor Hastings, was about to make all the Right Club's dreams come true? Once Roosevelt was discredited and ejected from office, the US would stay out of the war and Britain would either be defeated or make its peace with Germany: Churchill himself was saying it! Hitler would be master of all Europe, with only the Atlantic — no longer defended by Churchill's precious Royal Navy — standing between the Third Reich and America. A new world was about to be born and he, young as he was, would be remembered as one of its fathers . . .

He could see a line of worry etched into Murray's forehead. That did not surprise, still less concern, Hastings. He understood. The Englishman had only read Churchill's increasingly urgent pleas; from Roosevelt, he had only seen a series of fence-sitting replies. The MP was fretting that these documents did not, after all, contain the lethal words that would unseat an American president and prepare the way for a new order in Europe and beyond.

He decided to employ a technique learned from Anna, Murray's wife and his lover. She always knew when a striptease had gone on long enough. It was time to remove the last veil and show the man what he was aching to see.

"June 13," he said steadily. "Turn to R's letter from June 13, 1940. One pm."

Murray's fingers were shaking in their haste to turn over one sheet and then another.

As at last he began reading, Taylor's eye accompanied him over each word, the pleasure of it now even greater than the first time he had read it.

Your message of June 10 has moved me very deeply . . . this Government is doing everything in its power to make available to the Allied Governments the material they so urgently require, and our efforts to do still more are being redoubled. This is because of our faith in and our

398

support of the ideals for which the Allies are fighting.

It began at the corners of his mouth, spreading slowly as if this were a delight not to be rushed. Reginald Rawls Murray read the words again, then sat back in his chair, at first relieved, then steadily — as the meaning sank in — elated. Colour was spreading across his face, brightening by the second.

"It's not one hundred per cent definitive," Taylor said, "but —"

"But it's as close as makes no difference," Murray said. "If even one sentence of this were to become known on Capitol Hill. I mean, 'our faith in and our support of the Allies'. What's that, if not a commitment?"

"That's not exactly what he said, Mr Murray. The full quote is actually —"

"Oh, don't you worry about that, young man. This is politics, not diplomacy. He's talked about 'faith and support', that's what matters. No one cares about the small print. And look at this." The MP, his cheeks now filled with a ruddy flush that extended to his ears, rapped the paper in front of him. "'Our efforts to do still more are being redoubled'. Well, what the hell does that mean except war? He admits he's doing everything else already, supplying materials and what have you. 'To do still more.' It can only mean one thing. No, I'm afraid your Mr *Rosenfeld* has hanged himself with his own rope here."

"Not my Mr Rosenfeld, Mr Murray. I never voted for him."

"Of course not. Not yours and not America's, if the truth be told. He works for the Jews, like they all do."

The MP got to his feet and reached for his lightweight summer coat, which he had left on the couch — the same couch, Hastings reflected, where he had been thrusting like a locomotive piston into Mrs Rawls Murray not a week earlier. The older man extended his hand. "You may never get any recognition for what you have done, Mr Hastings. Your name may never be known. But people of good blood will always owe you a debt. On their behalf, I thank you."

Taylor accepted the handshake and nodded gravely, the star pupil on prize day. He knew he should have left it like that, saying nothing more than bidding farewell. But between curiosity and decorum, curiosity was the stronger. "What will you do with it?" he asked.

"I shall put it into the hands of those who will make best use of it. And I shall do it tonight."

CHAPTER
THIRTY-NINE

It was dark and deserted on the platform at Union Station and, thanks to the cloudless sky, cold too. James had grabbed only what he could pack in thirty seconds from his room at the Elizabethan Club, received a warm shake of the hand and a "Good luck" from Walters the butler, then run almost the entire length of College Street — past the couples sharing milkshakes in the drugstore and the medics drinking beer at the Owl Shop — until the neighbourhood got decidedly seamier. Once he had reached the railway tracks, he took a sharp left, sprinting until he could see the lights and hear the shunting and braking of the railway yard. Perhaps a cab would have been quicker, but he was too impatient to wait for one to appear. What was more, running meant there was no one he had to trust but himself.

It was nearly nine o'clock; the chances, he knew, of a train leaving for Washington just when he needed it were almost non-existent. And so it had proved. The next useful train was the Federal, the overnight service that would — if it were anything like the milk trains he knew from England — trundle through the small hours at horse-and-cart speeds, stopping and starting at every tiny little hamlet en route.

And yet it would be better than standing still. More to the point, there was little else he could do until morning and that, surely, was equally true of Preston McAndrew. As long as he reached Washington, DC, early tomorrow, and was able to get started right away, he would not be too late. That, at least, was what he told himself.

But as he paced the platform, his shirt sticky with sweat and clinging to his back, he could not escape the fear that the reverse might be true. Dorothy's words had been clear. *He said he was off to have "the most important meeting of my entire life". He said that he had to go right away* . . .

What if that meeting were tonight, even at midnight? What if McAndrew were travelling to the capital by motor car; would that mean he would get there later or earlier than by train? James cursed himself. If only he had understood earlier, he would have got to the Dean while he was still in New Haven. If only he had had the wit to put Lund at his ease. Florence would have known what to do: she'd have had Lund spilling his guts, the Assistant Dean explaining that the naked photos had merely acted as the signpost, pointing him to McAndrew's larger, grander scheme, the one Lund had only truly grasped when he read the Dean's lecture, *Cleansing Fire*. Somehow Lund had made the mistake of letting on to McAndrew what he knew, or at least what he suspected. That, surely, is why the Dean had decided his assistant had to die, so that no one else should have the same inkling.

James now understood the Dean's aim well enough: the lecture had made that clear. He was determined to keep the United States out of the war, so that a great eugenic experiment might unfold. Let Britain suffer a catastrophic defeat and then watch the consequences, observing as the weak and the inferior were wiped out in their tens of millions while only the strongest would survive. Britain was to be a giant laboratory, its population mere lab rats, while McAndrew's hypothesis was put to the ultimate test. And once it was done, once this cleansing fire had burnt through every corner of England, devouring the "runts" from the British litter that were too feeble to save themselves, those still standing, stronger and better than the rest, would be reinforced by the return of one hundred and twenty-five of the fittest, cleverest children, safely incubated in New Haven.

It was a monstrous scheme. However much he loathed Bernard Grey and the rest of the Oxford circle that had connived in Florence and Harry's departure — and he did loathe them — James refused to believe they could have collaborated in the entirety of such a diabolical plan. What they had colluded in was a plan to spare a special, privileged class of children, so that, in the event of catastrophic defeat, this elite might be sprinkled like top-quality seed into the soil of a devastated Britain. They doubtless believed they were saving the lives of a hundred and twenty-five innocent children who were, yes, more deserving than others because of their value to the English national "stock". That was morally reprehensible enough. But there was a world of difference between planning for the *contingency* of a British defeat by the Nazis and positively *willing* that outcome. Whatever nonsense Grey and the other socialists, Fabians and do-gooding social reformers believed, they were still British patriots, firm in their support of the war effort and in their opposition to Hitler. They did not long to see German bombs flatten British cities and a jackbooted Gestapo gauleiter in every English parish hall. McAndrew must, surely, have hidden from them his ultimate purpose — that what they saw as a doomsday to be planned for, he saw as a dream to be desired. For the Dean actively yearned for calamity and slaughter, for the sake of his warped, repulsive notion of "science".

But if that was the end the Dean was pursuing, James still had no inkling of his chosen means. Which meant he had no idea what he would do once he got to Washington, how on earth he would find McAndrew who would, after all, be one man in a capital city, a man who could be anywhere. If only he had understood all this yesterday or even earlier today, when there was still time. If only he could ask Lund, who might have known the answers, who might have uncovered the details of the Dean's plan, thereby signing his own death warrant. If only, if only, if only. James kicked the gravel, the toe of his shoe sending up little clouds of dust.

Through the gloom he now saw a light, some distance away. It was getting larger and now came the first rumble of noise. He looked at his watch for the fifth time in twenty minutes. The overnight train was not due to pull in here for another quarter of an hour. Only as it got nearer did he realize that this was a train coming into the other platform from the opposite direction.

There was a sudden commotion and a flurry of colour on his own side of the tracks. James wheeled around to see a woman gesticulating at a station guard. All he could see clearly, picked out by the sodium lamps of the station waiting room — no blackout here — was a bright bulb of honey-blonde hair. And then he heard the voice and knew instantly that it was Dorothy Lake.

She saw him at the same moment and broke into an athlete's sprint, running towards him with no restraint. She began shouting long before she had reached him. "You must get on that train! Quick! Get on that train!" She pointed across the tracks at the small locomotive, drawing no more than three carriages, now slowing to a halt, hissing with steam.

James could hardly hear her. "What? That's going the wrong way."

"No," she panted, catching up with him at last. "No, that's the right way. That's where you need to go. Take that train to Greenwich. Get off there and ask for Hope Farm. Harry and Florence are there."

James felt his heart stop. For a second, he and everything around him froze. He stared at Dorothy Lake and knew in an instant — from the earnest, pleading urgency of her face — that she was telling the truth.

"I don't und —" he started, but she cut him off.

"Don't say anything!" she said, the glow of her cheeks visible even in the half-light. "Just get on that train. I can't tell you how I know, but I know. Your wife is waiting for you. Your *son* is waiting for you. Go!"

"I . . . I can't."

"Yes, you can. The train's right here."

"I have to get to Washington. There's something I have to do before it's —"

On the opposite platform the guard was marching through clouds of steam, inspecting both ends for any passengers still getting on or off. He had a flag in his hand.

Dorothy turned back to him, her eyes afire. "You must go now. I don't know how much longer they'll be there. Now's your chance!"

"Dorothy —"

"You said that all you wanted was to see them again." Her eyes were both pleading and baffled. On the other platform, the guard was raising his whistle to his lips. "Or were you just lying?"

"I want to see them more than anything in the world. But there's more at stake here than me and my family."

The guard bellowed, "Last call! All aboard!"

Dorothy's eyes were now two wells of tears. "I wanted to help you."

He gripped her by her shoulders. "I know you did. And I will never forget what you've done." A piercing sound cut through the air: the guard's whistle. "I love my wife and I love my child. Very much. But I also love my country."

They were suddenly engulfed in a fresh cloud of white steam, their voices swallowed up in a loud hiss as the pistons of the locomotive cranked back into motion.

"There's still time," Dorothy cried as the train inched slowly forwards. "You could jump on. Florence and Harry are less than an hour away."

James did not answer. Instead he watched the train gather speed and move away, its tail-lamps becoming smaller and smaller until they were a mere pinprick of light, no bigger than a distant star. He did not know what to say to this young woman but at last, when the train had disappeared from view, he turned to her.

"Dorothy, I know what this looks like. And I know what you're thinking: that men like me, maybe all men, are snakes and that we can't be trusted. But it's not true. There are some bad ones, I can't deny it. But the rest of us try to do our best, we really do. Even when it doesn't look like it, we try to do what's decent and what's right." He wasn't making any sense.

Now she looked at him. "What is it my uncle is doing in Washington that would make you sacrifice your own family?"

"I don't know yet and I don't want to say until I'm certain." He gazed at her damp, flushed face, her distraught expression. "And it's nothing you're responsible for."

"I could telephone him and tell him you're coming after him."

"You could, Dorothy. But I'm taking the chance that you won't. Because you're a good person and you have your whole life ahead of you. And look what you were prepared to do to save just one family."

"I don't understand," she said.

"No, nor do I. Not completely. But we will. And you will have done the right thing." They stood in silence for a moment until he spoke again. "Besides. You don't know where in Washington he is."

"How do you know that?"

"Because if you did you would have told me."

The stationmaster was back, checking his pocket watch. He called over to them, the only passengers on the platform. "The Federal to Washington, DC, this track. Federal to Washington, arriving this track."

James looked at Dorothy Lake, and as he did so her face crumpled, the sophisticated veneer completely gone now. Impulsively, he hugged her for just a moment. "Thank you, for what you've done." He pulled away from her to give her an exhausted smile. "Wish me luck."

CHAPTER
FORTY

James spent the first minutes of the train journey staring into the dark, thinking of Harry and Florence. He could see nothing outside as the train headed into what he imagined to be vast acres of American farmland, empty and endless. Instead he saw Harry's face, his wide eyes looking into his father's, asking him where he had been, and why he had not come for him when he had the chance.

Alone in that rattling carriage, James tried to formulate an answer. He imagined himself perching his son on his knee, explaining how there were moments in life when you had to do things you did not want to do. How sometimes your own needs, your own desperate hunger to see the two people you love most in the world, had to come second because of an even greater need. He heard himself saying these words to his son; and then he heard his son's husky voice answer him back with a single word, repeated over and over again: why?

James closed his eyes and pictured Hope Farm. As the train clattered over the tracks at a pedestrian nocturnal speed, he saw it in bright summer sunlight, a place of white fences and orchards teeming with shiny apples, of yellows and ambers and the golden colours of American plenty. And the next moment in sharp contrast he imagined Harry and Florence huddled together on two bare wooden chairs in a tiny freezing kitchen, the whole scene bathed in blue-grey light. He knew it made no sense; that if they were just an hour away, as Dorothy had said, then their weather was no different from his. But he pictured it that way all the same.

What was Hope Farm? Why were they there? Dorothy had insisted she would not tell him how she knew — but he had not even asked, pressing her for no details. He had not wanted to hear anything specific, anything too real, because he knew that would make it harder to resist. His choice was hard enough already.

At intervals, as the night-time minutes turned to hours, he would be gripped by panic, becoming convinced he had made a grotesque mistake. What, after all, did he have to go on? The text of a lecture and a few casual remarks by McAndrew to his impressionable young niece. It was quite possible that the Dean had been thinking aloud in that Darwin anniversary lecture; that he was heading to Washington merely to boost his career. *The most important meeting of my entire life*. Perhaps the President had summoned him to serve in his cabinet, the way British politicians were always wooing Bernard Grey.

But James's gut said otherwise. He knew what he had read; McAndrew could not have made his intentions much clearer. And surely only Lund's discovery of a plan this ambitious could explain the poor man's agitation — and indeed his murder by the Dean.

He thought back to those final moments at the station with Dorothy. The train had taken time to leave, as they shunted on new rolling stock. The delay had been awkward; neither knowing what to say to the other. To fill the silence, James had asked a question that had popped unannounced into his head. It came in the voice of William Curtis, the lecturer at the American Eugenics Society. *The subjects in such a study will, of course, have to be photographed without clothing . . .*

"This will sound strange and rude, but tell me something. Have you ever heard anything about students at Yale being photographed without —" He hesitated. How to put this delicately?

"Without what, James?"

"Without their clothes."

"Oh, you mean the posture photos?" She said it matter-of-factly, as if it were something perfectly normal.

"The what?"

"The posture photos. We had them done in our first week."

"'Posture photos'? Why 'posture'?"

"Because they were taken to help us with posture. You stripped off, they put steel pins on your back and then *snap*. Took your picture."

"Pins?"

"Yes, about four inches long."

Suddenly James was seeing those pictures stashed in Lund's bag. "They put pins in your back?"

"No! Not *into* our backs. They taped them on. Afterwards they looked at the shape of the curve made by the pins. Any of the girls, or boys I suppose, whose 'postural curve' was not good enough were sent to posture improvement classes."

As the train now rattled through the darkness, James heard the voice of Curtis echoing in his head. *Discretion may demand that this work be done in combination, as it were, with another more conventional activity.* Now it was confirmed: this was what Lund had first discovered. That Yale was taking nude photographs of its new students under the spurious cover of a posture-improvement drive.

James's memory instantly threw up a sight he had not registered at the time but which he had stored all the same. He was in the Dean's outer office, rifling through the filing cabinets. He had gone past the M's — Memorial, Monroe, Montana — and landed in the P's — Political Science, Posture Study, Professional Training. His eye had glided past, as if it were just another, regular field of university activity: *posture study*.

Now he knew better. This was a secret research programme aimed at proving the link between physical strength, intellectual prowess and "moral worth". The men behind it were trying to answer the question Leonard Darwin had asked in that damned book of his: *If our object is to try to improve the breed of man, should we not first decide on the kind of man most to be desired?* Those photographs, which doubtless included not only Dorothy, the boy behind the counter at the Owl Shop and every other young person entrusted to Yale's care, were the attempt to provide an answer. It must have been Lund's discovery of the bogus posture study that first alerted him to the Dean's unflinching brand of eugenics, that led him ultimately to realize the "bigger and more dangerous" scheme his superior was embarked upon. Had he kept those photos in his briefcase as his only hard evidence?

James was disturbed by a sound so muffled, he first wondered if it was inside his own head. He looked up and over his shoulder; the carriage was still empty. It must have been a loose bit of gravel, thrown against the window. He went back to looking into the void outside, searching for the glimmer of even a solitary farmhouse. But he could see nothing.

A minute passed and there was another sound, louder and more metallic. James looked up again. All was quiet behind him and, apparently, at the far end of the carriage. There was a click.

He looked closer now, rising from his seat. Unlikely to be an inspector on this ghost train, doubtless loaded with sacks of mail and churns of milk rather than paying passengers, but not impossible. There was definitely movement on the other side of that door.

"Who's there?" James called out, without thinking.

Now he saw the handle of the far connecting door, linking this carriage and the next, begin to twist.

The train hit some kind of rut and jumped, sending James stumbling towards the windows on the other side, his left shoulder slamming into the wooden seat post. He let out a cry of pain. At the same instant, the carriage door flung open.

All he could see was height, a tall man made taller by a hat that appeared to rise to a sharp peak, covering his face in shadow. He was walking this way, in brisk, deliberate steps. Only when he was about two yards away did he speak.

"Hands in the air, Dr Zennor."

Reflex sent James's hands towards the ceiling, even before he had noticed the small, dull metal ring hovering in the air, parallel with the man's waist. It took another second for him to understand what he was looking at: a revolver, its barrel covered by a silencer.

Time seemed to slow down; he felt detached from the scene, as if he were an observer rather than a participant. Something similar had happened during gun battles in Spain. It meant that, at this very moment, instead of fear or alarm, he felt irritation at his own foolishness. He had shouted "Who's there?" in his telltale English accent. He had betrayed himself.

"Walk backwards. And keep your hands in the air." The voice was rougher than any he had heard in New Haven. Instantly James decided that this man knew nothing about him, that killing him was a job.

James did as he was told, reversing down the aisle between the benches, counting two, three, four paces. He stopped when he felt the blast of wind coming through the gap between the carriages. He was now in the standing area at the end of the car, a door on each side. The cold air seemed to slap him back to reality.

414

Now his heart surged, a flood of adrenalin as he desperately tried to think of what he might do to save his life.

"OK, that's good," the man said. In the light, James could see he was thick-necked and square-faced, maybe a former boxer. His mouth carried the suggestion of a smile, like a man who enjoys his work. The gun was still hovering; his finger was on the trigger. *What's he waiting for?*

The second-long delay provided the answer. In that instant in which he had not squeezed the trigger, James understood how this man wanted him to die. It was like Lund: *he wants it to look like a suicide.* He was going to try to shove James from the train, so that the police would conclude he had jumped.

The gunman stepped forward, confident that James would step back in terrified retreat, leaving him just inches from the door. James did as he was expected, trying to win himself another second or two in which he could think. He could not take his eye off the revolver. He could be shot right here before he had drawn his next breath, his body then kicked off the train, where it might not be discovered for days, unless the animals got to it first . . .

As the man took another step, instinct took over. Instead of walking backwards, James leapt forward, deliberately colliding with his attacker, his right hand reaching first for the gun, pushing it away.

The advantage of surprise paid off; the gunman fell back, slamming against the far door. Still gripping the man's gun-holding hand, James rammed it into the doorframe, hoping to shake the weapon loose. But now the attacker had recovered his strength and his fingers refused to let go.

The train swerved around a bend and, in time with the movement, the gunman pushed back at James, sending him careering into the opposite door. To his horror, James felt it open — the rush of cold air against him, the carriage filling with noise. Only his fingertips, clinging to the wooden surround above the door kept him inside.

He was filled with rage. He would not die like this, not here, not now — not without seeing Harry and Florence one more time. This bastard would not stop him. All the fury and agony he had endured over the last weeks — and years — now flowed through him. Still gripping the doorframe, feeling his jacket billowing in the wind, he swung forward, kicking out with both his legs so that his feet landed directly in the attacker's face.

The man stumbled backwards and James dived onto him, searching for the gun. The attacker reacted fast, firing a shot, but not fast enough: the bullet went straight into the ceiling. James gripped the man's wrist and the pair of them wrestled on the floor, the gunman supine, James on top of him and with the advantage. He forced the man's gun hand to the ground, where it would be useless. It was nearly there . . .

But the assassin refused to give up, his hand curled around the butt of the revolver ever tighter. And now James's left shoulder began screaming. The exertion of this struggle was becoming too much.

James shifted his weight, so that his knee landed firmly on the man's private parts. When he heard the yelp of pain, he did it again, shoving his attacker's prone body along the floor, his knee pushing upwards against the man's groin. One more shove and he had rammed the man's head into the door.

But the gun hand was twisting, the barrel turning to face James, like the head of a snake. No matter that James had moved his left hand onto the assailant's windpipe, where he hoped to strangle him, one squeeze of the trigger was all it would take . . .

He had only one option and he would have to rely on his left hand to do it for him. With his right still curbing the attacker's gun hand, he reached up with his left, found the train door handle, turned it and, with the last of his strength, propelled the man forward, sliding him head-first into the fast, night air.

James remained there, kneeling on the floor of the train, buffeted by the wind coming in from doors open on both sides. He was panting. And, as the adrenalin faded, he became aware of the acute pain in his wrists, his legs and especially his left shoulder. At last he staggered to his feet, closed both doors and slumped onto a seat. His head hurt and he reached up to touch his forehead. When his hand came away there was blood on it. Even in a year of combat in Spain, even when he had seen his friend Harry's brain shattered before him, he did not believe he had ever come so close to death.

He spent the rest of the journey pacing, like a captive animal that had been dangerously provoked. McAndrew had sent this man, there was no doubt in James's mind. How had he known where to find him? He considered the possibility that Dorothy had betrayed him yet again, considered it and dismissed it. Her help for him, her feelings for him, had been genuine, he was certain of it. No, McAndrew had relied on more direct means. James remembered the Buick with the white-rimmed tyres. He might have shaken off his watchers for a few hours after Riley released him from jail, but they had clearly caught up with him. The gunman must have been at the station, watching from the shadows, seeing what train James took, then quietly climbing aboard.

And even though he felt no pity for the dead man, even though James believed he had every justification — in law and in morality — for what he had done, he could not shake the image of the man sliding off the train to a painful death. Back in Spain, James had shot at the enemy many times. Statistical probability alone meant he had surely killed at least one man, if not several. And yet he had never done it like this: he had never seen the face of a man he had killed. James thought of his parents and their lifelong vow of nonviolence. What prayer would they utter after committing such an act?

To dispel the thought, he checked his watch. It would be hours before he reached Washington. He still had no clear plan how he was going to find McAndrew once he got there. He desperately needed help.

Twenty minutes passed and at last he saw lights in the distance, not just a few but whole constellations of them. The train was approaching New York.

Slowly, the suburbs gave way to busier, city streets. Billboards began to appear: for Dairy Queen ice cream, for *Time* magazine, for Peter Pan Peanut Butter. James watched them go by, clasping his aching shoulder.

Suddenly an image floated before James's eyes: *Time* magazine, the edition he had read while watching and waiting outside the Wolf's Head tomb, the page opposite the article on Lord Beaverbrook. He had scarcely registered it at the time, but now the whole double-page spread appeared to him — including the name, middle initial and all, waiting to be found. The only man James knew in Washington; probably the only man he knew in the whole of America.

He jumped onto the platform while the train was still moving, not wanting to waste a second. The station was deserted except for two men with brooms and an older man with a nest of a beard, peering into the dustbins looking for food. Remembering their location from his first visit here, he sprinted over to the phone booths, entering the first and nearest one.

He lifted the handset and was glad to hear the dial tone. He waited for the voice of the operator, nasal and metallic, yet still female: "Local or long distance?"

"Long distance, please."

"What city?"

"Washington, DC."

"What name?"

"The name is Edward P Harrison."

There was a long delay. James pictured a woman, middle-aged and bespectacled, leafing through a fat directory of thin pages, listing name after name. H for Hammond, Hanson, Harris . . .

"There are two Harrisons, Edward P in the DC area, sir. I have a Dr Edward P Harrison?"

James wanted to smile. "No, the man I'm looking for is not a doctor."

"Connecting you now, sir."

He heard a series of clicks, then a long ringing tone and then another. Damn it all, he wasn't there. Damn, damn, da —

"Hello?" A woman's voice, sleepy.

"Hello. I'm sorry to call so late. I need to speak —"

A man's voice now, taking the phone. "Who the hell is this? What's the idea, calling after midnight?"

"Ed, is that you? It's James, James Zennor. From Barcelona. I mean, we were in Spain together, remember, when you were covering the People's Olympiad?"

There was a pause, into which James spoke again. "You took a letter for me, do you remember? When you went back home, through London?"

"OK, now I remember. Zennor. You were writing your girl who'd left you for Hitler, wasn't that it?"

"She'd gone to Berlin, that's right. You've got a good memory."

"Jeez, you sound terrible. You OK?"

"Just ran into a spot of . . . bother, that's all." He could feel the ache in his jaw, where he had slammed into the train door.

"The thing is, I don't know what time it is where you are, James, but it's real late here. So if —"

"My train's just made a stop in New York, Ed. And I need your help."

"Call me in the morning and I'll arrange for Western Union —"

"I don't need your money!" The words came out faster and angrier than James intended. He cursed himself. He had only a minute or two before he had to get back on the train. "I mean, that is very kind of you, but I'm not asking for that sort of help." He was getting this all wrong. He thought of Dorothy Lake and the ambitious young staff of the *Yale Daily News* and hoped the same urges drove seasoned reporters as motivated new ones. He took a different tack: "I may have a very important story for you."

An instant change in tone, sharper and more alert. "What kind of story?"

James had to think quickly. "One that could affect whether or not America enters the war."

"I'm listening."

"It involves the Dean of Yale University. He's in Washington. I have reason to believe he is involved in a secret campaign to keep the United States out of the war. He told his niece that he was about to have the most important meeting of his life." James heard himself. He sounded like a lunatic. In a moment, Edward Harrison, *Time* journalist and James's only hope in Washington, would surely hang up, explaining to his wife that it had been "some British guy" he knew back in Spain who had clearly lost his marbles during the war.

But Harrison said something else. "A meeting? I've been hearing rumblings about this. I thought it was all happening in Chicago. They're calling it the America First movement. Or America First Committee. Committee, I think. So what's the secret plan?"

James heard a whistle, coming from his platform. "There's more I can tell you. I'm on the slow train to Washington, it gets in at seven fifteen. Meet me at the station."

"But —"

"Please, Ed. I promise you, it'll be worth it."

Ed Harrison acknowledged James not with a wave, but by holding up a brown paper bag, as he greeted the train that had just pulled under the shelter of the vast, arced roof of Union Station. The bag was soon revealed to contain two doughnuts, both for James.

"I figured you'd be hungry," he said, looking hardly a day older than when the pair had met amid the sunshine, high hopes and infinite bottles of Sangre de Toro in Barcelona in 1936. Even unshaven, ten years older than James and with a head of unruly hair, he was still craggily handsome.

"I wasn't sure you'd be here," James said between mouthfuls.

"What, and have you call again first thing in the morning? No thanks."

"I'm sorry about that. Will you apologize to your wife for me, for ringing so late?"

"Who said anything about a wife?"

422

James saw the familiar wicked sparkle in Ed's eye and remembered how women had flocked around Harrison the famous reporter, playing in the jazz band, drinking the men under the table and still staying sober. That type didn't tend to get married.

"So," Harrison said. "It's been a long time. Four years, almost to the day, I'd say. What you been up to, James?"

The words that comprised the question were inoffensive enough, but in between them James detected a comment on the state he was in. He had tried to clean up after the battle on the train, but his jacket was ripped, his trousers stained and his face bruised, with dried blood along his jaw and in his scalp. Even before, his face had become thin and drawn, his shattered shoulder distorting the shape beneath his shirt. To Harrison, who had last seen James fit, tanned and youthful in the heady summer of thirty-six, he must have looked a wreck — a premonition of James's future, aged self.

"It's not been an easy time, to be truthful. I stayed on in Spain; fought with the International Brigade."

"I remember."

"And I was wounded."

Harrison nodded.

"Shot in the shoulder. Took a long time to recover."

"And your buddy, what was he called? Fine man."

"Harry. Harry Knox. Killed, I'm afraid."

"Sorry to hear that."

"Same incident." James tapped his shoulder in a gesture that cursed the sheer dumb luck of it.

"I'm real sorry. I went back, you know. To Spain. To cover the war. Several times, even at the end."

"I was back in England by then. Oxford."

"I thought I was doing my bit for the cause by reporting the war, 'telling the world' and all that. But you guys, taking up arms — you're all heroes, you know that."

"I didn't feel much like a hero."

"You were taking a stand against fascism, that's the point. Not many ready to do that. Especially not here."

"So I've gathered."

"My magazine's on the right side: the boss would have Roosevelt declare war tonight if he could. But you know public opinion, it's . . . Well, put it this way, not many Americans have seen what I've seen."

"In Spain, you mean?"

"Spain, Germany, Poland. I've been covering this story as best as I can, telling it like it is, but —"

"People don't want to know."

"People don't like war, James."

"That's where you're wrong, Ed. Some people like war very much. In fact, some people want to see this war run its course, unimpeded, till Britain is reduced to ashes."

"You talking about the Yale guy?"

"Yes, I am."

"Before we get to that, what about the girl?" the American asked, as they walked out of Union Station, the dome of the US Capitol visible and bright in the early morning sunshine. James had seen it in paintings;

424

maybe the odd news photograph. It was like a pristine version of St Paul's.

"What girl?" For a brief, guilty moment James thought he meant Dorothy Lake.

"The girl I had to get the letter to? The one in England?"

A shot of pain went through James, as he thought of Florence and Harry at Hope Farm, wherever that might be. Were they still there? Or had they already left? The thought that they might have been spirited away once their location had been discovered, that James had forfeited his one chance to see them again, did not go through his brain, but his flesh, like an electric current of sadness.

"I'm proud to say Florence Walsingham is now my wife. And the mother of my child."

Harrison slapped him on the back. "Well done, old man. Well done! You couldn't have married a more beautiful girl. They back home in England?"

James took that as his cue to fill Ed Harrison in — as briefly as he could — on what he knew and how he had come to know it. He did not linger on the disappearance of Florence or Harry, instead focusing narrowly on the Dean's "Cleansing Fire" lecture and the mysterious death of a subordinate who had apparently stumbled across his plans.

"You mean to say that one of the country's most senior scholars actually *wants* the British to lose the war, just so he can see what happens? Like, for an experiment?"

"Yes, but also as an end in itself. He's simply taking eugenic theory to its logical conclusion: we want more of the strong and less of the weak, so why not let war do what it does best?"

"And eliminate those too weak to survive." Harrison shook his head. "You've had quite a month, haven't you, my friend? No wonder you look like duck crap."

"Thanks."

"No offence. But, Jesus. And you think this is why he's come here?"

"Based on what he told his niece, yes."

"Well, you may be right. Look what's on page sixteen." Ed handed him a newspaper. "That's what I love about the *Washington Post*: you never know where you're gonna find a front-page story."

James read the headline. "Demanding 'No foreign entanglements,' anti-war campaigners plan next move." He skimmed the details: business leaders and politicians coming together . . . promise to build mass opposition to intervention in the war in Europe . . . no shortage of funding, several millionaires . . . political backing in both Senate and the House . . . strongest support in Chicago and Illinois . . . lead spokesman the illustrious aviator, Charles H Lindbergh . . . socialist allies in the Keep America out of War Committee . . . prime mover Yale Law School student, P Alexander Tudor, who hopes to launch a formal anti-interventionist movement in September, likely to be called the America First Committee . . .

One word stopped him: *Yale*. As if reading his mind, Harrison leaned over, pen in hand, and circled the

426

same word. He then said, "I've asked around. Turns out they're meeting today, trying to secure some big names on the Hill in time for launch in September."

James felt a tremor of anticipation run through him. "Where?"

"Willard Hotel. Right by the White House. Sending a message to FDR, nice and direct."

"Can we go there now?"

"I'm ahead of you, Dr Zee." As he spoke, Harrison gestured for them to turn right down Constitution Avenue, as wide and grand as a boulevard in Paris. James shot a glance over his shoulder, to check that no one was following. Soon, if not by now, McAndrew would learn that the killer he had hired had failed to complete his mission — and he would surely send another in his place.

"The meeting's closed to the public, of course," said Ed.

"Damn."

"Worry not, Jimbo. When I say closed to the public, I mean closed to the *public*. Not the press."

"So you'll be allowed in?"

"As will you." And, with a flourish, Harrison reached into his bag, a deep satchel slung over his shoulder that James remembered from Spain, and produced a camera. Bigger than an encyclopaedia and twice as heavy, with a flashbulb post doubling as a grip for the right hand, it was the object James had seen in a hundred newsreels, but never up close. "Congratulations, Jim Zennor, newest addition to *Time*'s legendary team of photographers."

They passed a series of imposing, governmental buildings rendered with imperial grandeur in grey-white stone. This must have been how London looked a century ago, James thought: a capital city with the power to rule the world. How that had changed, the great British Empire now reduced to praying that the young Americans would ride to their rescue. Without their help, his country was doomed. All that muscle, but so useless if America refused to flex it.

He was just beginning to feel the heat — a damp, humid, almost tropical heat — when Ed signalled that they had arrived. The hotel was tall and wedge-shaped; it too would not have looked out of place on a European street corner. Through the windows on one side, he could see waiters in white aprons fussing over guests, lifting chrome plate covers to reveal steaming hot breakfasts. Even from the pavement, James could see a custard-yellow cloud of scrambled eggs placed before a moustached man, distractedly reading his morning newspaper. Even in his agitated state, James worked out that there must have been three weeks' egg ration on that plate.

They walked into the lobby, as tall as a cathedral and as opulent as a palace, the floor shiny, the pillars dizzyingly high in amber marble, the ceiling decorated in gold. It could have been Versailles. "Remember," muttered Harrison through gritted ventriloquist's teeth, "you're the snapper. Hang back."

James dipped his head to hide his face and whispered back, "But you don't know what McAndrew looks like."

"Sure I do. Joy of working for a news magazine, Jimbo: we have a photo archive. I checked."

While Harrison strode over to the reception desk, James loitered in the lobby, his eyes scoping the room for a familiar face. No sign of the Dean. No sign of any groups at all, in fact; just individual businessmen coming down for breakfast. It was not yet eight o'clock. Once again James tormented himself with the probability that he had got here too late. McAndrew had had a head start of several hours; he had probably had his meeting last night . . .

James could hear Ed Harrison demanding to speak to the manager, wanting to see the full list of associations holding meetings in the Willard Hotel. Just from the tone of the exchange, James could tell the reporter was being rebuffed. Perhaps McAndrew had left specific instructions to keep out the press. James strolled, as nonchalantly as he could, to the concierge desk. As he did, he called up before his mind's eye page sixteen of that morning's *Washington Post*. In that image, he found what he was looking for.

"Excuse me," he said to a young man standing by a lectern-high desk, wearing a bell captain's uniform at least two sizes too big for him. "I'm here for a meeting booked in the name of P Alexander Tudor. Could you tell me where I need to go?"

"Oh, that would be a question for reception, I'm afraid, sir."

"I know," James said with a smile. "But they seem a little tied up." The sound of raised voices, Harrison's the loudest, reached their side of the lobby.

They exchanged a brief smile of shared understanding. "Of course, sir," said the concierge, reaching for a pile of papers. After he had run his finger down one and then another column, he looked up. "You need the Buchanan Room, sir. On our lower level."

James nodded his thanks and hissed in Harrison's direction, eventually succeeding in breaking him away from his altercation with the front desk. He led the way down the carpeted stairs, following the signs until they came to two closed wooden doors bearing the name Buchanan.

James paused, not sure whether they were about to barge into a room where a dozen people would be having a quiet — and private — discussion around a single table or where four hundred people would be arrayed like a theatre audience, listening to speeches from a platform. Against the first possibility, and the chance that he would see and be seen by McAndrew instantly, he held tightly onto the camera, ready to lift it to his face.

Harrison pushed at the door confidently, notebook in hand. Everything about his demeanour, down to the tilt of his hat, announced him as a newspaperman. What a weapon it was, James reflected now: both a licence to pry and a protective shield.

The instant the door was open, James recognized the scene. They had walked into an event that had not yet started, clusters of men standing together engaged in pre-meeting conversation. There were perhaps forty of them, hovering and shaking hands; behind them, a long boardroom table laden with untouched notepads and pin-sharp pencils. A portrait of George Washington in a cheap wooden frame appeared to have been hastily attached to the wall.

James raised his camera and began to look through the viewfinder, hoping no one would realize what he had just realized: that although he had once been quite a keen photographer — an interest discarded, like so much else, after his injury — he had no idea how to use this machine. He let his finger feel for a shutter while surveying through the room. To his right he could sense Harrison advancing, plunging into the middle of the room as if he were the guest of honour apologizing for his late arrival.

In the small glass window, James saw a series of faces, none familiar. That they were well-heeled, he could guess — from the silvery smoothness of their hair, from the effortless cut of their suits. But no sign of the salt-and-pepper of the Dean. He let the lens glide slowly across the room. More captains of industry, a dishevelled overweight figure James took to be another pressman.

And then the camera froze in his hands.

It was the dog collar he saw first, only later raising the lens to confirm the man wearing it: the Reverend Theodore Lowell, pacifist, chaplain of Yale University and alumnus of Wolf's Head. Quite a crowd from Yale then, gathering here in this Washington hotel just yards away from the White House to stop the march to war. Perhaps he and McAndrew had travelled here together; maybe Tudor had acted as their chauffeur, driving his two most distinguished allies down here. James concentrated his lens on Lowell's lapel and then focused on the same area of the man to whom the chaplain was speaking.

Both wore the same Wolf's Head pin.

He could hear Harrison's voice above the others now, buttering up the politicians and plutocrats in the room, no doubt the first step to extracting information — not that different, James supposed, to the way the reporter approached girls.

And suddenly he was struck by a crucial realization. Though James knew what Lowell looked like, Lowell had no idea who James was.

Emboldened, he strode over to the cleric, the camera still covering at least half his face. "OK, a group picture, gentlemen," he said. He gestured for Lowell to gather closely with his colleagues, guessing that one of them was young Tudor. And then, as naturally as he could make it, he said from behind the camera, "And let's have Dr McAndrew in this one, shall we?"

"Oh, darn, you've just missed him," said the younger man, gesturing at an exit James had not spotted, at the other end of the room. "He had to dash out for a breakfast meeting, must have been half a minute ago, tops."

James clicked and turned away, winded as surely as if he had been punched hard in the gut. After travelling all night, to miss him by just seconds . . .

He swivelled back towards the door, catching Harrison's eye. James glared at him with such intensity that the American understood immediately, broke off whatever conversation he was having and followed.

432

They took the stairs outside two steps at a time.

"He must have gone while we went downstairs or we'd have seen him," Harrison panted.

"Not necessarily. He could have found another exit out of the hotel. Especially if he thinks he's being followed."

"And does he?" Harrison said, as they burst back into the lobby.

James thought of the corpse lying by the railway tracks, the confirming phone call the gunman was doubtless meant to have made to McAndrew but hadn't, the Dean's knowledge that James was therefore still alive. "Probably."

Dashing across the marble floor, they emerged into the Washington morning. The warm, damp air hit James's face in an instant, smothering blast. He looked left and right then right again, focussing on the other side of the street.

He couldn't see the man's face. Nor was it the hair he recognized, though once he was in pursuit he caught sight of the familiar salt-and-pepper. It was, instead, the purpose that caught his eye. Unlike everyone else strolling down Pennsylvania Avenue, Preston McAndrew was walking with unrelenting intent.

So that he could move faster, James thrust the camera back towards Harrison, who took it and shoved it in his bag.

James crossed the street with barely a glance at the traffic.

The eyes are your most lethal weapon. Never let your gaze waver, not even for a second. If you stay watching him without a blink, then you will never lose him — and he will be yours.

Jorge's voice was his own now as James let his pace quicken and then slow, quicken and slow, synchronized with his prey. When McAndrew moved to cross Constitution Avenue, James did the same, reflexively making a three-quarter turn of his body, so that — had the Dean thought to look over his shoulder — he would have seen nothing to catch his eye.

The buildings had given way now to green lawns on both sides. Up ahead, poking into the sky, was the pale golden obelisk of the Washington Monument. McAndrew was marching towards it.

Suddenly James felt dangerously exposed. Buildings are a kind of shield for tailing a man; the pursuer always has the possibility of darting into an entrance or down a side alley. Jorge had warned him a dozen times. *Once you are on open ground, you are in danger. Your subject will think, why is that man here, except to follow me? And he will be right . . .*

James slowed to a stop and Harrison was at his side within moments. The American was breathing hard. "What do we do now?" he gasped.

"We watch." James's gaze followed McAndrew up the slope towards the needle. "And we walk slowly. That way." He indicated a curved path towards the monument, leaving McAndrew to take the straight route.

The Dean was slowing down, just as James had hoped. He had guessed the rendezvous was here and it seemed he was right. He checked his watch.

Twenty-five minutes past eight. *Meet at the Washington Monument at eight thirty*. He could almost hear McAndrew saying it.

He watched him take a seat on a bench among the forty-eight flags of the forty-eight states, and felt the fury bubbling and boiling inside him. This man who had so nearly had him killed, this man who had kept him from his wife and child, this man who through lies and deceit was determined to pass a collective death sentence on the people of Britain.

It would be so easy to have his revenge, James thought. The sprint across this patch of grass would take what, twenty seconds? McAndrew would run but he would not be as fast as James; few men were, despite his wound. He could tackle him at his knees, bring him tumbling to the ground and then it would require the smallest exertion of the fingers to choke the life out of him, to press his fingers to his throat and squeeze. And squeeze . . .

It would be justified too. Not just as self-defence, but as vengeance — vengeance in advance for the crime of plotting the agony of England, and vengeance for the torments he had already inflicted on James. All he had to do was run a few yards and he could have this man in his hands.

And yet he knew he had to resist that urge. It would not be enough simply to lash out and kill McAndrew. The Dean was here in Washington because he clearly had a plan, an operation involving others, and it was that plan that had to be stopped. Watching the Dean die now would be satisfying, but it would almost certainly leave the threat to England intact.

James turned to Harrison. "In a minute or two, someone is going to join him. I need you to tell me who he is."

"I'll have to get closer."

"You can get as close as you like. He has no idea who you are."

Ed Harrison walked ahead, gingerly and, to James's mind, obviously. He had the studiedly casual gait of the amateur; so ostentatiously nonchalant it was immediately suspicious. It didn't help that he was identifiable as a reporter from a distance of two hundred yards.

But Harrison was no fool. He had the wit to hang back, so that he was not in McAndrew's immediate field of vision. Besides, James, his focus still on the Dean, could see that the subject was too preoccupied with his appointment to notice much else. McAndrew checked his watch three times in as many minutes.

At last, another man came into view. He approached the Dean's bench, slowed, looked down and then appeared to hesitate. McAndrew said something and the man sat down. They then shook hands in a way that struck James as odd, looking straight ahead rather than at each other. But they were certainly talking.

James stared at them, wanting to miss nothing. He certainly did not recognize the second man and, he concluded from McAndrew's posture and that initial hesitation, neither did the Dean. They were strangers who had nevertheless arranged a meeting.

So fixed was his gaze that only now did James notice that Ed Harrison had rejoined him. He heard him before he saw him, the same fast exhalation. Except this time it was not exertion that made the American breathless, but excitement. "You won't believe who that is," he said. He looked back towards the two men conversing on the bench, surrounded by blue sky and fluttering flags. "Your Dean is locked in discussion with Hans Stoiber, the most senior diplomat at the Washington Embassy of the Third Reich."

CHAPTER
FORTY-ONE

James couldn't help himself. He turned to Harrison, his eyes wide and his mouth open, utterly aghast, before remembering his task and turning back. That man in front of him, just a matter of yards away from him, was a Nazi. Elegantly tailored, well-shod, a man you would pass without objection on one of these Washington streets — and yet a servant of a cruel regime bent on crushing and mastering all of Europe, if not the world. It was one thing to glimpse their planes in the skies, to witness the havoc their bombers could wreak, as James had first hand in Spain, or to see their leaders, Hitler, Goebbels and the others, in black-and-white on a newsreel. But to behold the enemy in the flesh and in colour, so near . . .

And there was Preston McAndrew, happy to shake this man's hand, happy to engage in polite chat with him, happy — more to the point — to do business with him. Was there no end to this man's wickedness? Even the sight of it turned James's stomach. He could feel his loathing turning into a physical thing, a viscous fluid flowing through his veins and vital organs.

Of course James knew the Dean had come to Washington with evil intent: to prolong Britain's agony.

But he had assumed that his method would be . . . what? Perhaps some discreet lobbying, a quiet word in the ear of an official or two in the State Department? The scene James had witnessed in the Buchanan Room at the Willard Hotel, those lapel pins on Lowell and the other man, had reinforced that thought. He had expected McAndrew to be engaged in looking up his fellow alumni of the Wolf's Head Society, doubtless spread throughout the higher reaches of the US government, using that network of old members to advance his cause, patiently putting the case for non-intervention. *You're too young to have served in the last war*, he would say to those officials in the administration, as he began to detail the horrors of conflict . . .

But he had never bargained for this, McAndrew supping with the devil himself. Sitting with the enemy — not America's enemy, perhaps, not while the US remained so devoutly neutral. But James's enemy: the enemy of his country.

And then he was struck by a kind of premonition. His parents might have called it a divine visitation. Or perhaps it was just a lucky instinct. Without looking at Harrison, he whispered, "Give me the camera."

Then, in a walk that was stealthy, noiseless and fast, James got closer — though not so close that his camera would be heard. He put the device to his eyes and watched. He snapped once, moved the winder on, then snapped again. As he was moving the winder on again, it happened and just in time for him to capture it on film. In a movement so swift that it was barely noticeable, the German reached into his briefcase and produced a white, foolscap envelope. Just as James pressed on the shutter, the diplomat handed it to Preston McAndrew, who in a similarly unfussy movement slotted it into a slim leather portfolio case which he then fastened and lodged under his arm. They shook hands — which James photographed too — and rose to their feet.

At once, James pivoted around so that should McAndrew happen to look into the middle distance to his right, he would see only the back of a man walking away from him.

James caught up with Harrison. "Can you see him? Which way is he going?"

"West. Towards Lincoln."

"Lincoln?"

"The Memorial."

James counted to three, then turned and walked in the same direction, wincing to hear the sandy gravel of the path crunch beneath his feet. He could see McAndrew clearly, perhaps thirty yards ahead of them, that same purpose in his stride.

"Please tell me you got a picture of that," Harrison said eventually.

"I hope so. I pressed the button, it made the right sound. I only hope you put film in the camera," he said, handing the machine back to the American.

"You sure you didn't become a reporter in England and you're just not telling me?"

James's eyes were locked on the Dean, now about to cross 17th Street. Always the riskiest moment in any pursuit, the crossing of a main road. So many chances to lose the subject: he could turn left or right; he could get in a car; he could cross in a break in the traffic, leaving you stranded on the other side.

"I mean when you said I'd get a story, I didn't —"

"We don't have anything until we see what he does next," said James, his voice as firm and unwavering as his gaze.

Now they were by a long, ornamental stretch of water with grass on either side. James estimated the length at less than half a mile, perhaps a third. The sunlight was reflecting off the water, making it hard to see. He used his left hand to shield his eyes, aggravating his shoulder, and forced himself to ignore the pain. All he had to do, he told himself, was keep McAndrew in view.

They were no more than two hundred yards from the end when he heard a voice that made him shudder.

"Stop right there."

It was from behind him. James pictured a gun, silencer attached, as it had been on the train, aimed at his back. Or perhaps it was the police: they had found the corpse by the railway, had realized that no one else had been riding the overnight train. He turned around slowly.

"Eddie Harrison as I live and breathe! Well, I'll be."

Standing, arms outstretched, was a round-faced man in a white suit, his face glistening with sweat in the clammy Washington heat. "Congressman, always good to see you," Harrison said. James let out a gale of air in relief.

"Now, Ed, I've been wanting to talk to you about this metal embargo for Japan. You sure you can't get Luce to run something —"

James looked over his shoulder to see that McAndrew was still striding ahead. This delay had cost him valuable seconds and therefore yards. He wanted to sprint, to catch up, but feared that could trigger another bellow from this blasted congressman: "Hey, where you off to, son?" It would be disastrous to make any kind of scene. Raised voices and McAndrew would turn around.

Eventually desperation propelled him. He muttered an excuse, swivelled round and carried on walking. He could hear protests from the Congressman, the reporter apologizing on his behalf, as James quickened his pace. He looked ahead but could see McAndrew nowhere.

James's heart began to thud. In front of him was a crowd of women, advancing in that slow amble characteristic of out-of-towners. They were blocking his view. Had the Dean realized he had been tailed and deliberately shielded himself behind this group of sightseers? *Damn.*

James broke into a jog, always a calamity during surveillance. At intervals he leapt, endeavouring to see over the heads of the women. No sign of McAndrew. He looked to his left and right: had the Dean taken a different route or, realizing he had been discovered, aborted his plan altogether?

James had come to the end of the Reflecting Pool now. Before him was a vast edifice in white stone, a Greek Doric temple of columns, fronted by a wide,

442

steep staircase. So this was the memorial to their President Lincoln. How ingenious of the Dean to choose this place for whatever move he planned to make, rather than skulking about in some back alley. Jorge would have been impressed: *hide in plain sight*.

But McAndrew had vanished.

Suddenly the pain in his shoulder violently asserted itself. James put his hand to the wound as he squinted up to look at the staircase. There were too many people, all in motion. If you checked one side you risked missing someone on the other. Scan one section and the section above or below had already changed. In this shifting throng, McAndrew had concealed himself. James's shoulder was screaming. He had been outwitted.

Now Harrison was at his side. "Where is he?" he asked unhelpfully. James nodded toward the steps, then added "Come on!" He took the first two in a single leap.

Maybe the Dean had ascended to the memorial itself, entering the temple at the summit, but even as they climbed the steps James forced down the fear that they might have lost their subject for good.

Behind him, he could hear the reporter breathing heavily. James guessed they were both thinking the same thing. That Preston McAndrew had received Nazi documents with a direct bearing on the war effort and, thanks to their failed attempt at surveillance, was about to get away with it.

"Keep walking," Harrison said suddenly, his tone urgent. "Ahead, two o'clock."

James's heart raced in anticipation at seeing his prey again. He could see a man — brown suit, felt hat even in this heat — walking with an intent that set him apart from the tourists, but it was not McAndrew.

"What?"

"Brown suit."

"I see him, but —"

"Just a hunch. Keep an eye on him."

"Who is he?"

"Karl Moran, *Chicago Tribune*. Biggest anti-war paper in the country."

"I don't —"

"Just watch."

They slowed their pace, letting Moran reach the top first.

"Give me the camera," James said. "I'll go right, you go left. Remember, McAndrew won't recognize you. If Moran sees you, it's a coincidence."

James dipped his head and climbed those last two steps. A moment later he was aware of a change in temperature, the close, muggy heat replaced by the cool of marble. His eyes took a second to adjust to the shade.

He stole only the briefest glance upward, to see the largest statue he had ever seen: a seated, stone Lincoln the size of a mythic god. He and the others in here looked like ants at the president's feet. And there, on the other side of this shaded space, next to the engraved words of the Gettysburg Address, stood Karl Moran, talking to a man whose hat was pulled low over his face

444

— a man who, James knew at once, was Preston McAndrew.

James raised the camera, just in time to see the men shake hands and part. He did not catch the moment of exchange, but in Moran's hand there now rested a white, foolscap envelope. The journalist turned sharply and headed for the staircase.

Now, James told himself. *Now*. It would be so easy to walk those few paces, grab McAndrew, bring him to the ground if necessary, watch him gasp for air. The desire for revenge bubbled up inside him once more, hot and red. He would make that man pay for whatever wicked trick he had just performed, for depriving him of his wife and child, for murdering George Lund . . .

He took a step forward, ready to do it, even here, with all these people. He could feel himself throbbing, the blood thumping through him. But reason, the same rationality he had come to curse, held him back. He repeated to himself what he had to remember: that the threat to his country now was not McAndrew, but those documents. It was the envelope, and whatever dastardly information it contained, not the Dean, that had to be stopped. McAndrew had given those papers to Moran because he wanted them to be published so the goal now — the only goal that mattered — was preventing that from happening. To reveal himself at this moment, by apprehending, even killing McAndrew would not stop that. Rage could not help him now.

And so, biting down hard, he smothered the urge seething through him, watching instead through the viewfinder of this heavy, newsman's camera as Preston McAndrew adjusted his hat, touched the cuff of his jacket and, with the tiniest smile of satisfaction on his lips, walked just a few yards away from him out of the shade, back down the steps and into the sunlight. How James longed to wipe the smirk off that face, to shatter it with the same force with which he had despatched that goon on the train. He swallowed the rising bile of frustration that rose in his throat.

Looking down, he could see Ed Harrison heading down the steps too. James caught up with him. "Where are you going?"

"I think we need to have a word with my esteemed colleague, Mr Moran."

"What are you going to say? How on earth are you going to persuade him to —"

The slower-footed Moran was within sight and within reach now. Harrison smiled. "Oh, I'm not going to *say* anything. It's just I know one thing about the man from the *Trib* that your Professor McAndrew does not." He glanced at James. "That for Karl Moran, it's never too early for a martini. I hope you can hold your drink, Zennor."

This, James concluded with admiration, was the secret of Edward P Harrison's success. He had noticed it even in Spain, when Harrison was thumping away at the double bass in that impromptu

446

Olympians' jazz band, knocking back the Sangre de Toro with the rest of them — yet somehow remaining standing when everyone else was keeling over, upright enough to woo one of Florence's swimming team-mates once he had regretfully concluded that Florence herself was immune to his rugged adventurer charms.

Now James could only look on in awe as Ed filled and refilled the glass of the *Chicago Tribune*'s correspondent in Washington. He had made a brilliant show of running into Moran on the walk back down Constitution Avenue, calculating that it would be too much of a coincidence for them both to be at the Lincoln Memorial at the same time.

"Moran! Hold up," he had cried, slapping him on the back. "I need a man to celebrate with me and you're just the fellow. What do you say to a pick-me-up at the Old Ebbitt Grill? Oh, and I'm buying."

Moran — his hair ginger, his skin florid and his nostrils permanently flared — had glanced guiltily at the white envelope in his hand. "I really ought to get back to the office, Edward."

"Please, it's Ed. And I shall have you back at your typewriter within the hour. That's what, Karl, eight hours before deadline? That should be enough, even for you. And remember, today's the first day of August. And what do we always say?"

"Nothing happens in August," the two men chorused.

"Now, meet my friend Jim, photographer for the *Picture Post*." James raised a silent hand, not sure if he was meant to risk the revelation of his accent. "And let's get ourselves some refreshment."

Ed kept chatting away, clearly keen to get to the bar before Moran had a chance to change his mind. Then, as they turned onto 15th Street, the three of them walking three abreast heading north past the White House, Ed looked over at James. "Oh, you needed to pick up some supplies, didn't you, Jim?"

"That's right," James answered, entirely baffled. "Some new film."

"And you were going to get some stationery for me, weren't you?" At that Harrison had given the merest glance in the direction of Moran's hands and James understood.

So now he watched as Moran downed what, by James's count, was his fourth martini. At long last, the reporter who had been expounding on the scandal he was sure was brewing in Henry Morgenthau's Treasury Department, how he reckoned Harold Ickes must hold some "stinking dirt" on the president to have stayed in the Cabinet so long and why he couldn't stand his father-in-law, finally rose to his feet and, swaying, moved towards the men's room. To the horror of both Harrison and James, he took the white envelope with him.

"That's it," Harrison said, so sober he might as well have been drinking tea. "We're just going to have to prise the damn documents from his hand. I'm going to pay a visit to Mr Moran in the men's room."

"You'll do no such thing," James said immediately. "You do that and, two minutes later, Moran will be telling McAndrew we're onto him. He'll have time to rethink."

"Damn."

"He mustn't know we know."

"Damn, damn, damn."

"Here," James said, handing him the white envelope he had bought nearly an hour ago. "Let's stick to the original plan."

Harrison quickly opened his briefcase and pulled out a series of papers, which he scanned and assessed, then deposited inside the envelope. "At least these should keep him busy," he muttered.

"What are they?"

"Just a story I've been working on."

"A real one?"

"Real enough to confuse Moran, even when he straightens up. Sprat to catch a mackerel."

Moran was back. James had known only one or two dipsomaniacs in his time, one a friend of his parents, but they all had the same telltale trait: the smell of alcohol oozed from their pores. Moran was no different. But he was still sufficiently alert that, as he sat down, his hand remained on the precious envelope.

Harrison resumed the offensive, more talk, more laughter, more drink. But none of it was working. James, who had mainly kept quiet, murmuring his assent, adding the odd chuckle but no more, now took the floor.

"You know," he began. "I was in Spain during the war."

"*Covering* it, for the *Picture Post*," Harrison added quickly.

"Of course. Which is how I met this reprobate." James pointed affectionately in Ed's direction. "And I got talking to some of the men, the volunteers. You know, you were deemed unfit for service if you couldn't stand up straight, touch your toes, stand up straight, touch your toes — five times in ten seconds. They all had to do it. Hemingway, all of them. Not as easy it sounds."

"Don't be ridiculous," said Moran. "Anyone can do that."

"Harder than you think," said James.

Moran drained his glass and rose, with surprising grace, to his feet. There were others in the bar now, the early lunch crowd, a few of whom turned around to watch. In a gesture that was almost balletic he sent his arms soaring towards the sky, then flung them down in the direction of his toes, then pulled himself back upright. There was a small smattering of applause from the other end of the room.

"You didn't touch," said Harrison.

"What?" Moran slurred.

"Your toes. You didn't touch your toes."

"Come on."

Moran had another go, his nostrils flaring wide as he went down as if to draw in more oxygen. This time he lingered as his fingertips drew level with his calves, seeking to find the extra flexibility that might carry

450

them to his feet. Keeping his eyes on the *Tribune* reporter, James picked up Moran's envelope and replaced it on the table with the one he and Harrison had just compiled.

Moran was back up again now, his face red from the exertion.

"Three more," James said, pretending to time the *Tribune* man's efforts on his watch.

Down he went, giving James a second to slip the original envelope — the one that had passed from Stoiber to McAndrew to Moran — into Harrison's briefcase. Then he sat back, heart beating. At last it was done.

"See, I did it," said Moran, exultant as he returned to his regular altitude.

"As good a man as Hemingway," said Ed, admiringly.

"And now I'll be on my way." Moran picked up his envelope and walked towards the exit, where the sun was streaming in to drown these noontime drinkers in reproving light. He took a peek inside the envelope and then turned back towards the table, a furious look on his face.

James's heart skipped a beat.

"You didn't let me pay for my shout," he said to Harrison, in mock admonition.

"My treat," said Ed, raising his hand. "Like I said, I felt like celebrating."

Ed insisted they wait a good five minutes before repairing to the private snug known only to the bartender's favourite guests, just in case Moran came back for more.

James could not help but stare at the briefcase, inside which lay McAndrew's secret. "Patience, Jimbo," Ed said, more than once. "We gotta play this one real cool."

To make the minutes pass, James asked the American what papers Moran would now be looking at in the office of the *Chicago Tribune*. What sprat had he served up in place of the mackerel they were waiting to examine?

"Not a bad story, as it happens, though it will confuse poor Karl Moran and confuse his bureau chief even more. It's evidence there's a German agent working on the staff of a United States congressman."

"No."

"Yes. And very active he is too. Writing full-page advertisements for the national newspapers, timed to appear during the Republican convention — all bought and paid for by the government of Germany, no less."

"And you gave that to Moran?"

"Yes. I've been working on it for days. Mind you, I don't think he'll use a word of it."

"Why not?"

"Because the *Tribune* is the Defend America First paper: they're not going to crap on their own doorstep, if you'll pardon my French."

"So he'll know it's fake straight away?"

"It's *not* fake. The papers are real. But he won't understand why McAndrew will have leaked them. If I were him, I'd guess there was some kind of tension among the America Firsters, and that I was being used by one faction to damage another. He may think McAndrew has a beef with my senior congressman. And if he knows the Dean's little parcel comes from the Embassy —"

"He'll think the Germans are trying to discredit the politician."

"Maybe my congressman has outlived his usefulness. The point is, it will take time for Moran to decode. Which is what we need. So long as McAndrew didn't give any hint to Moran about what he was getting; if he did, Karl will be disappointed as well as confused. Nothing we can do about that. Come, that's our five minutes."

They walked through the wood-panelled booths, past a small staircase and then into a room no bigger than a first-class rail compartment. There was a fireplace, mercifully unlit in this moist summer weather. Doubtless, this town was full of rooms like this, where the business of power was played out.

Harrison placed his briefcase on the table, pulled out the white envelope and passed it to James. "Reporters' code of honour. You reeled this fish in, Jimbo; you get to slit it open."

James was surprised to see that his hands were trembling. He was nervous, he was excited; but above all he was exhausted. He had had next to nothing to drink, slipping most of his martinis into Moran's glass, but he was lightheaded. Taking a deep breath, he pulled out the wad of papers.

There were six separate documents, each consisting of two or three sheets paperclipped together. He read the first lines on the first page:

London
May 15th 1940, 6pm

Most Secret and Personal.
President Roosevelt from Former Naval Person

Although I have changed my office, I am sure you would not wish me to discontinue our intimate, private correspondence. As you are no doubt aware, the scene has darkened swiftly . . .

It took him another paragraph or two to realize what he held in his hands.

If necessary, we shall continue the war alone and we are not afraid of that. But I trust you realize, Mr President, that the voice and force of the United States may count for nothing if they are withheld too long . . .

"Good God up above," James said, covering his mouth. "Good God."

Harrison read each sheet after James had finished, alternately gasping and swearing, swearing and gasping. When they had both read Franklin D Roosevelt's secret message of June 13th, with its language of redoubled efforts to help because of "our faith in and our support of the ideals for which the Allies are fighting", Harrison shook his head silently.

James looked over at the grizzled, world-weary American and saw that his eyes were welling with tears. Harrison extended his hand and said simply, "Dr Zennor, I think you may have just saved your country."

CHAPTER
FORTY-TWO

The train was too bright and too full to sleep, but even if it had been dark and empty, like the one he had ridden in the opposite direction a matter of hours earlier, James would not have slept. His body might have been drained and yearning for rest, his mind utterly spent, but his heart would not be quieted. And it was aching for Florence and Harry.

It did not matter that Ed Harrison had continued to lavish him with praise. The journalist kept insisting that had the *Chicago Tribune* got hold of the Roosevelt-Churchill letters — cutting and editing them to support their own, fevered anti-war stance — then FDR's hopes for re-election would have been doomed. The paper would have used those letters to cast the President as a liar and a deceiver, a man prepared to vow to the American people that he had made no promises to fight for Britain when in fact he had done just that. Roosevelt's enemies would surely have seized on the correspondence to demand his impeachment, on the grounds of violating the United States's multiple Neutrality Acts. One way or another, the single American most committed to the defence of Great Britain — Franklin Delano Roosevelt — would have

456

been destroyed. The chances of the United States coming to Britain's aid would have been reduced to close to zero: Britain would be abandoned, its defeat guaranteed.

Harrison had rushed back to the office, his first stop the darkroom, where he handed over the film from his camera, announcing it as a "triple urgent" job to be done this instant. Next he conferred with his editors, skating over the precise subterfuge he had used to extract this story from the hands of the *Chicago Tribune*. They read the documents and held their breath just as he had.

The discussion was short but intense. The news editor believed the magazine could not possibly sit on a story this momentous. Yes, it was good that the cables would not be published and distorted by the *Tribune*. But surely they could not be complicit in the suppression of information — even if, as it happened, *Time* fully endorsed the sentiment expressed by Roosevelt in that June 13th letter and even if it was clear that publication would fatally undermine both the President and his pro-intervention stance. Harrison hit back that that might be true in the abstract, but not when these documents had come from the most tainted source possible, an official of the Third Reich. Hans Stoiber's masters had wanted those letters — doubtless carefully selected to cause maximum damage to Roosevelt — to appear in print in America. If *Time* published them they would be doing the bidding of Adolf Hitler himself. The editor had listened to the argument and sided with Ed. "Besides, who knows what else Roosevelt has said to Churchill? For every letter like this," he tapped the June 13th document, "he may have written one leaning the other way. We're not in business to help the Nazis play games with American politics."

Harrison relayed all this to James, as they shared a taxi to Union Station. "But d'you know what your best work was today? The photos came out a treat." He passed James the pictures taken at the Washington Monument: grainy but unmistakable, they showed McAndrew receiving the envelope from Hans Stoiber. "That's going to look very good in our magazine this weekend: 'The Ivy League Dean and the Nazi'."

Time had passed the photographs and the rest of their information to the White House. Within the hour, the Federal Bureau of Investigation had put out a warrant for the arrest of Dr Preston McAndrew on charges of trafficking in US state secrets obtained from a foreign power. Ed Harrison had been careful to extract a couple of concessions of his own from his best contact in the administration, including a promise that if ever the White House decided to release the full Roosevelt-Churchill correspondence it would give the exclusive to Edward P Harrison.

The two men said goodbye at the station, Harrison handing James another doughnut in another brown paper bag. James offered him his hand and Ed did what no Englishman had ever done before, hugging him warmly. "No one is ever going to know what you did, James. So you'll just have to take it from me. Britain

458

and every person in the world who believes in freedom owes you a very great debt."

James waved away the praise, giving a shrug at the American bombast of it all. And yet he could not deny what had just happened: the Dean had been at the centre of a plot that would have consigned Britain to a bloody and terrible fate, that would have left Hitler as the master of Europe and perhaps the world. And that plot had been averted. The thought was so large, so daunting and impossible, it seemed easier to express in the passive. He could not bring himself to say that he, James Zennor, had averted it.

And now the pain in his heart returned, as he made the journey back to New York and from there to Greenwich, Connecticut, just as Dorothy had urged him to do last night. She had told him then that he had to go that very minute, that it could be his only chance.

I don't know how much longer they'll be there.

And yet he had not gone to them. He had put his family second. Florence had been right all those months — or was it weeks — ago, when she had condemned him for being ready to sacrifice his own two-year-old child, exposing him to bombing and invasion, out of his own misguided sense of duty. *You made your sacrifice, James. You don't need to do any more.* And yet he had done it again.

If they were gone, he would not forgive himself. He would have condemned himself to a life of misery and loneliness. The glory of Harrison's little encomium to him would be all he had to keep him warm at night. And it would not be enough.

At long last, the train pulled into Greenwich station. It was late, Harry's "orangey time of day". James walked over to the two cabs waiting for passengers coming off the New York train. Now that he was here, he felt his stomach knot at the finality that was looming. Up until this moment, he could always look forward, to the future possibility that he would see Florence and Harry again. But soon there would be certainty, a definite answer to the question of whether or not they were there. The idea of it terrified him.

He approached the first cab, the driver resting a tanned arm on the wound-down window.

"Hope Farm, please."

The man looked bemused. "Where?"

"I'm looking for Hope Farm. I'm told it's just outside Greenwich."

"OK, I know it. Get in."

As James, settled into the back seat, the driver eyed him in his rear-view mirror. "You a professor too, then?"

"Sorry, I don't think I understand."

"You did say Hope Farm, didn't you? That's the place that belongs to the Yale guy, right — you know, the Dean?"

James felt his insides dissolve, a physical sensation akin to nausea but somehow deeper, as if in the very base of his guts.

Each second passed like an hour. Had Florence and Harry been McAndrew's prisoners, held on this farm since the day the Oxford mothers had been despatched from the Divinity School to their new foster homes? That, surely, was why their names had been expunged from the record, so that no one would know that the Dean had taken two of those Oxford refugees for himself.

Then suddenly, with horrible force, he remembered something. How could he have missed it? The garden at the Dean's residence in New Haven. In the middle of the lawn, there had been a single child's swing — on its own, surrounded by none of the other paraphernalia of childhood. Yet what had McAndrew said? *I don't have kids myself, but if I did . . .*

That lonely swing, freshly added to the garden, had been put there *for Harry*.

The truth is, he had suspected this somewhere. The worm of this thought had formed in the darkest places of his mind, but he had not dared drag it into daylight. Now a more sickening thought took its place. What if they were not his prisoners? What if Florence had *chosen* to live in that house on St Ronan Street, then chosen to come here? Perhaps she had only escaped to the countryside once she had learned that James was in New Haven looking for her. Was that it? Had his wife fallen for Preston McAndrew, for his suave intelligence, his maturity, his body still intact, unbroken by war?

His skin was crawling, as if he were covered with insects; his nervous system seemed to be waging war on itself. He felt the familiar lava welling up inside him, a seething river of molten rage rising higher and higher. It had no clear target, but was ready to burst, drowning both McAndrew and his faithless, adulterous wife —

she who after less than a month away had begun sleeping with another man, she who had been ready to give her body to the very man who was bent on destroying all she had once held dear . . .

He began pounding the side of the car door with his fist, only stopping when the driver braked suddenly and threatened to shove him out and make him walk.

That caught him. His right hand gripped his left wrist. He had to calm himself, he had to quell that fury. Reason, he told himself, reason. He did not know the truth; he needed to find out what had happened. The James Zennor Florence had left had been a slave to his rage; he could not be that man now. He could not be that man any more.

Finally, the car slowed. They were on a narrow lane, where a break in the hedge indicated a path leading to a house. James paid the driver and stared for a second, taking two long, deep breaths. He was bracing himself for a terror that surpassed anything war had thrown at him. What if the fear that had tortured him just now was about to be realized? What if there was something worse? What if they were not there?

He feared his legs might collapse beneath him as he took first one step and then another. In front of him was a beautiful farmhouse, the white clapboard glowing in the dipping evening sunshine. It was flanked on all sides by apple and pear trees, scenting the air with a sticky fragrance. It was, James understood, just the kind of place Florence loved.

Girding himself, he knocked on the door and waited. Silence at first and then the sound of footsteps on

462

wooden floorboards, a woman's. He knew instinctively it was not Florence: too heavy, too slow. The door opened to reveal a black woman wearing a maid's uniform.

James said his name, though all that emerged was a croak. At that moment, he wondered if he would ever have the strength to speak again.

And then he heard the sound of wheels turning on the wooden floor, toy wheels, small and rattling. He looked behind the maid and saw it inch into view, emerging from a side corridor, a wooden truck pushed along by an infant hand. And then a face — the round face of a little boy, the hair the colour of English chestnuts, the eyes wide and deep.

"Harry?"

The boy looked up, his brow furrowed for a second in confusion.

"Harry, it's Daddy!"

The two moved towards each other at such speed they nearly collided. James took his son in his arms, lifting him and enfolding him in a single motion, closing his eyes as he felt Harry's hair tickling his skin, savouring the smell of him, the warmth of his solid little body. And when he felt a dampness on his cheeks, he held the boy apart from him so that he could stop the child's tears. Only then did he realize that it was he, not his son, who was crying.

He kept his eyes closed, his head bent over Harry's. How long he stood like this, he did not know. Then, as if in a dream, he heard someone say his name.

Just one word, but it flooded through him. Raising his head, he opened his eyes to see her there, in the centre of the hallway, as tall and proud as he had remembered her. Her skin was browner, her eyes older, but it was her.

Florence.

She looked as if a bomb had gone off, her face stunned and frozen. James moved towards her, with Harry in his arms. "Florence," he said. "I'm here."

CHAPTER
FORTY-THREE

Florence did not come to him, but hesitated. She moved slowly, as if she were approaching a dangerous animal. James wondered if it was the way he looked, if the beating on the train, along with the pain of the last month, had turned him into an object of terror to his wife. She glanced to her side, "You can go home now, Ethel," she told the maid.

The woman collected her things, passed him, mumbling a goodbye — and still Florence stood there, watching him warily.

With Harry in the crook of his arm, James stepped forward and slid his free arm around her. Her body was stiff, uncertain. Still, he drank in long draughts of the smell of her, the scent taking him back in an instant to Norham Gardens, to the college gardens, to Madrid, to Barcelona, to every moment they had ever known together. He could feel them both, Harry and Florence, alive and in his arms.

And then, what seemed an eternity later, he felt her tremble, her body quaking quietly and gently. Her head buried in his chest, she was sobbing. Florence, who never cried. He moved to stroke her hair — but she sprung back from him.

"When I heard the motor car outside, I thought it was him. I thought he had come back. I thought you were him." Her eyes were bright with fear. "But then you knocked. And why would he knock on the door of his own house?"

"Florence. It's all right." Suddenly he noticed a suitcase in the hall, the same one his wife had taken three weeks ago.

She saw him looking at it. "We were about to get away. Ethel was going to help me."

"You wanted to escape?"

"Yes."

"So you weren't here because —" James put Harry down. "You weren't here because you were . . . with him?"

She recoiled. "No, of course not. James, I could never —"

"Because it's taken me so long to find you, Florence. It's been so hard to find you."

"But you never wrote to me. Not one letter. All the other mothers —"

"He had my letters blocked. I wrote to you every day, sometimes three times a day. I wrote to you on the ship coming over here. He blocked them, Florence."

Now she took Harry from him. "I thought you had decided to forget us, that you didn't forgive me for leaving you like that. What else was I to think?"

James stepped forward, getting closer to his wife. "Why are you in this house, Florence? Why are you in his house?"

466

She blinked, a gesture of disbelief that her husband was actually there in front of her, that they were in the same room, hearing each other's voices, no longer thousands of miles apart. "The day they allocated us to foster families, they said we would be rooming with the Dean's elderly mother, at the official residence."

"On St Ronan Street?"

"How do you . . ." She regarded him curiously, then shook her head, dismissing the question, for now, at least. "But the mother never appeared."

"So you lived there with him?"

"It wasn't like that. The residence is enormous. There were staff living there. We had our own quarters; he respected our privacy. He bought a swing for Harry. As a temporary solution, I thought it would be all right."

"And when did you move here? Don't tell me: I bet it was Monday."

"Yes, as a matter of fact. It was. How do —?"

"Because that's when I turned up at McAndrew's office looking for you. Surely you suspected something, Florence?"

"It was nearly August. Yale was almost deserted. It didn't seem odd that the Dean would want to move to his summer-house. And I thought it would be good for Harry to be in the countryside."

"And were you together, the three of you? Like a little family?"

Florence looked at James, then lowered the child. "Harry, why don't you show Snowy his favourite cherry tree?" The boy turned to give his father a smile, then skipped off towards the garden.

She spoke quietly. "Preston started . . . taking an interest. Asking me about my research, having Ethel prepare dinner for us after Harry was in bed."

"Dinner? What, just the two of you?"

"Yes. When he heard that I'd had no letters from you —"

"'Heard'! I like that. He bloody *arranged* —"

"I didn't know that then. He came over so sympathetic. He started telling me that if he had a wife as 'intelligent' and 'radiant' as me, he would never let her out of his grasp."

"The bastard . . ."

"Just listen. He told me he had never married because he had never found the right mate. That was the word he kept using. *Mate*."

James knew where this was heading. His hatred of this man was growing harder and colder.

Florence went on. "Then something strange happened. He asked if I ever drank. I told him that I had the occasional glass of wine. He told me to stop. He said alcohol was disastrous, that it ruined the eggs of a woman and the sperm of a man."

James suddenly had an image of the Dean in his study, pouring those full glasses of warming, amber whisky. He had been happy enough to drink then . . . Except now James could see it: McAndrew regularly raising the glass to his lips, but never actually drinking from it. He was keeping himself in impeccable condition, just waiting for the right "mate".

468

Florence was still speaking. "Another evening, we were talking about science. He began speculating over what kind of children we — he and I — would have together. Hypothetically, of course. 'We're both so accomplished academically,' he kept saying. 'We're both in flawless physical health. I believe our offspring would be perfect.' "

The fury James felt on hearing those words was like a flood of lava he had to fight to keep dammed. But he knew he must. He needed Florence to see that he was in control of himself now, that he was his own master.

And yet precisely this had been his subterranean suspicion, the very thing James had imagined. That the Dean's belief in eugenics did not apply only to the human race in general, but to himself in particular. He wanted to create a world of supermen, most certainly, but he also yearned to breed a family of physical and intellectual giants in his own image, a latter-day pantheon of the gods: mythical men and women who would be blessed with perfection of body and mind. And he, Preston McAndrew, along with Florence — the Oxford scholar gifted enough to have been an Olympic champion — would be their founding father and mother.

"And what did you say?"

"I was frightened, James. Really frightened."

"Did he touch you?"

"He tried, once. But I never let him anywhere near me. Nowhere near."

James closed his eyes briefly as he digested what he had just heard. It made sense to him that McAndrew would not force himself on a woman who was reluctant. His goal was not immediate pleasure. He had clearly waited so long for a "mate" he deemed worthy of his seed, he would be nothing if not patient. Of course, once he had found as rare a genetic specimen as Florence, he would have wanted her to produce several children for him. And that, he would have known, required consent. McAndrew was playing the long game, waiting for the beautiful Englishwoman to accept at long last that her useless, crippled husband was dead or at least that he was never coming back.

He caught Florence looking at him in a way he had not seen before. "What is it?"

She stepped closer. "When I planned this moment, seeing you again — which I did, a hundred times — I didn't know how I would tell you all this. I worried that it would, that you would —"

"Fly into a rage?"

"Yes. That you would be so hurt and so angry that you would lash out, that you would do something . . . terrible."

"A month ago, I'm sure I would have done. But I left that man behind in England, Florence. Just as you did."

She let her eyes look into his, the two of them joined in a single gaze. Before his injury, they could do this for minutes on end, content to dive deep into each other. She spoke quietly. "I left because I didn't know how to protect Harry any more. Not because I stopped loving you. I never stopped loving you, James."

"I understand why you did what you did. You wanted our child to be safe and I wouldn't listen. I couldn't

470

listen to anything or anyone except myself, Florence. I see that now."

"But I shouldn't have done it. It wasn't fair. You're Harry's father. I shouldn't have done it." He watched as she fought the tears. "But everyone around me said I had to, it was my responsibility. Virginia, Rosemary, Bernard, they were all so certain, I —"

"Shhh," he said, stroking her hair. "You're a good mother. You were doing what you thought was right."

"I won't ever leave you again," she said. "Never." She turned her face up to him and their lips touched in a kiss that was tender, full of the melancholy and ache of the long, last month.

The moment was broken by the sound of Harry crying. Instinctively James went towards the back garden, but Florence realized the sound was coming from the front. She rushed towards the front-door and opened it, letting out a dry scream that made James's blood freeze.

There at the door, holding a tearful Harry in an awkward grip, was Preston McAndrew.

"What a nice surprise," the Dean said. "Here we all are, playing happy families."

"Put my child down," James said in a voice that was pure steel. "Now."

Harry was writhing, weeping as he tried to wriggle free. But McAndrew would not let go. "Don't give me orders in my own house, Zennor." He was, James noticed now, dishevelled, the usual smoothness gone. He looked what he was, a man on the run.

471

"Put Harry down," James said again. "If you want to hurt someone, hurt me, not my child."

"All right," McAndrew said, that smirk returning to his lips. "As you wish." He discarded the boy the way a man might cast aside a used cigarette, throwing him casually to the floor. Florence caught him and comforted him, but over Harry's bowed head her eyes were huge as they focused on what the Dean held in his other hand. A revolver.

"Now, how about I get comfortable in my own house?" McAndrew stepped inside, the gun trained now on James.

"The police will be here soon, you must know that," James said. He looked over to Florence. "He's on the run. He's wanted for talking to the Nazis and taking stolen American secrets."

"Of course," said McAndrew, his upper lip clammy with sweat. "I knew it was you. It couldn't be anyone else."

"Yes, I'm afraid your friend on the train failed to do his job — and kill me."

Florence looked aghast and confused.

"It's quite true, Florence, dear," the Dean said. "For once your deranged husband is speaking the truth." He stared at James. "When are you going to realize you're not wanted, Zennor? You don't *fit*. I have plans for Florence and me and there's no room in them for you."

Florence, still holding Harry, was burning, her eyes wild. "I wouldn't touch you if my life depended on it."

"Hush, Florence dear, this doesn't concern you. Now, James. I'm going to be generous. Leave us now and I will let you go in peace, no need for me to use this." He waved the gun.

"Listen to me, McAndrew. The police will find you eventually. And when they do you will go to jail for what you've done. But if you kill me, you won't go to jail. You'll go to the electric chair."

"Oh and what difference would that make to you? Don't tell me you care whether I live or die."

"Personally, it would give me great pleasure to see you die right now, McAndrew. But you need to go on trial first and not only for the murder of George Lund. America also needs to hear what you were planning, who you were prepared to help to get what you wanted."

"What, so that they will be shocked into fighting for your washed-up old country? Forget it. Now, Zennor, I won't repeat myself. I'm giving you the chance to save your life. Just agree to say no more about Lund and leave now. Leave me here with Florence and Harry."

"Never." He glanced to his right.

"All right, then take the child. I don't want him anyway. He's not perfect: he's a weakling like his father. Leave me and Florence to make some perfect babies."

James bit down on the anger that rose at these words, for he could not allow himself to be diverted. He needed to act calmly and decisively — and now was the moment. In a single, swift motion he ducked and grabbed up Florence's suitcase, then charged at McAndrew's midriff. But he wasn't fast enough. The Dean squeezed the trigger and the gun went off with a noise like thunder.

Florence screamed, while Harry — who had been crying steadily — stopped, frozen.

Where was the bullet? James felt no pain. No time to think about that. He slammed into McAndrew and felled him, then drew back his free arm — the damaged, weaker left arm he had despised for so long — and used it to deliver a smart left hook to the Dean's jaw, knocking him out cold.

He looked down at himself, fearing that he would, for the second time in his life, see a stain of red blood, spreading and expanding like a deathly inkblot. But there was no blood.

His eyes darted to Florence and Harry. Thank God, they too were safe and unmarked. He looked around the room, and saw eventually that the bullet had plunged harmlessly downward and was lodged now in the hard wood floor.

James stood up, exhausted. He reached for Harry, pulling him up so that they were looking at each other eye to eye and said the only words he could think to say. "Daddy's here, son. Daddy's here."

CHAPTER
FORTY-FOUR

One week later

The crew made an absurd fuss of them. Not because they knew what James had done — though that was the only reason they were allowed on the ship at all — but because they were the only civilians on board, possibly the only civilians heading this way on the entire North Atlantic. They gave Harry a seaman's beret that was too big for his little head and insisted on calling him captain.

James had Ed Harrison to thank. Or rather Ed's contact in the White House. Once he learned that it had been an Englishman who had thwarted a plan to leak the stolen Roosevelt-Churchill correspondence — a plan involving a group of British fascists, German intelligence, their allies in the US and a mole inside the American Embassy in London — they were ready to grant his every wish. They offered all kinds of rewards; there was even talk of a presidential medal. James said no to it all. He just wanted to get home.

So they hitched a ride on board a small cargo ship, part of a large convoy taking war material from America to Britain. It had been Florence who insisted on sailing back immediately, whatever the risks.

"If I could do my bit for Spain, then I can certainly do my bit for my own country. Our place is back home in England, on the right side in this bloody war."

"It may not be the winning side, Florence," James had said.

"I know," she said. "But it is right. And it's where we belong." She paused. "We can pick up where we left off, can't we?"

"No, Florence. I don't think that's a good idea."

"Why?" she asked, biting her lip in that familiar gesture of anguish.

"I think we need to make a fresh start, you and me. No going back to old habits. Or rather, *I* need to make a fresh start."

"James, you —"

"No, I mean it, Florence. I had become a bitter, angry old man. I wasn't a good husband to you. I wasn't a good father to Harry. My own son was frightened of me. Imagine that, my own son . . ." His voice gave way and his wife put her hand on his shoulder. He pressed on. "I changed, Florence. I was no longer the man you married."

"You were shot, James. You saw your best friend killed. I've studied cases like yours. You'd suffered a great trauma."

"Yes, but I can't keep blaming that. I *won't* keep blaming that. Not any more. I was so busy with my bloody shoulder, I didn't see there was a whole world out there — and my family right in front of me. I promise you, Florence, I changed once. For the worse,

476

admittedly." She laughed. "And I can change again; for the better this time. I want to be a better man."

"We'll both do things differently."

"We will. I can't promise it will be perfect, but I will try. I promise."

"But that's just it, James, don't you see? I don't want it to be perfect. I don't want to live in a perfect world of machines and robots and straight lines, where no one feels a thing. That's McAndrew's world. I don't want that. I want to live in the world of real people — with all their flaws and vices and stupid ways, with their crooked noses and funny voices and, yes, James, wonky shoulders. It's the cracks that make us human, James, you must see that. That's the world I want to live in. And I want to live in it with you."

AUTHOR'S NOTE

Pantheon is a novel and James, Florence and Harry are fictional creations. And yet their story is rooted in the most extraordinary facts.

A ship packed with one hundred and twenty-five Oxford children and twenty-five of their mothers did indeed leave Liverpool for Yale University in the second week of July 1940. The organizers in Oxford did spend the previous weeks in hurried preparation, a process the historian AJP Taylor would later describe as "an unseemly scramble". Once they had reached their temporary home, the local paper did indeed run the headline, "Refugees Find New Haven in Land Holding Promise of Peace".

As for the larger mystery eventually uncovered by James Zennor, there is little direct evidence of any such plot. Those who sailed across the Atlantic on the liner *Antonia*, now in their seventies or older, take the same view James did: that the Yale families who opened their homes to strangers' children, hosting them for nearly five years, did so out of altruism and kindness, nothing more. This much is lovingly recounted in two very touching books, *Havens Across the Sea* by Ann Spokes

Symonds, herself one of the Oxford children, and *See You After the Duration* by Michael Henderson.

And yet, some of those who were rescued have long wondered about the motives, not of their hosts, but of the effort's organizers: why were they singled out, was it perhaps their status as the offspring of the academic elite that made their plight particularly pressing? Tellingly, Dr John Fulton of Yale Medical School, a prime mover behind the effort, said that the Yale Faculty Committee for Receiving Oxford and Cambridge University Children hoped to save "at least some of the children of intellectuals before the storm breaks". It is also the case, as James discovers in the novel, that Cambridge rejected Yale's offer, fearing that, in the words of Sir Montague Butler, "this might be interpreted as privilege for a special class".

If there is a hint of eugenics about all this, then it should not be too great a surprise. For the belief that society should encourage the strongest, fittest and brightest to have more children, while pushing, or even forcing, those deemed inferior or weak to produce fewer children or none at all, held great sway over the elites of pre-war Britain and America. In some, it fed dreams of a new breed of supermen, a pantheon of almost godlike people destined to rule over an ever-stronger human race. In others, it meant dangerous — and lethal — schemes to weed out those branded unfit for life.

The historical surprise is that the advocates of eugenics were not, as one might expect, right-wing cranks and racists. Enthusiasts included some of

Britain's greatest intellectuals, many of them on the left, all revered to this day. The quotations and arguments James comes across in the Sterling Library — from the great writer George Bernard Shaw, philosopher Bertrand Russell, the father of the welfare state William Beveridge, the lauded economist John Maynard Keynes and many others — are real and accurate. The pioneer of birth control, Marie Stopes, was so dedicated a eugenicist that she disinherited her son on the grounds that he had married a woman who wore glasses — thereby risking that his children would be short-sighted — preferring to leave much of her fortune to the Eugenics Society.

Across the Atlantic, the idea had an equally strong hold on the most privileged circles. Eugenics was particularly in vogue at Yale, as the genuine quotations cited by the fictional Dr Curtis in his evening seminar attest, including the one attributed to the former president of the university, James Angell, described by historians as "a fanatic eugenicist". All the italicized passages and chapter headings from Leonard Darwin are quoted faithfully from his book *What is Eugenics?*

Evidence of the extent to which eugenic theory ran deep in the American academy is to be found in the bizarre saga of the naked "posture photographs". Two scholars did indeed dream of compiling an Atlas of Men and an Atlas of Women and, to that end, persuaded several Ivy League colleges to trick their undergraduates into posing nude, with pins taped to their back. The full story was revealed in "The Great Ivy League Nude Posture Photo Scandal" by Ron

Rosenbaum, published in the *New York Times* magazine in January 1995: the phrase "physique equals destiny", uttered by Dr Curtis, should properly be credited to Rosenbaum. He discovered that among those snapped without clothes in this effort to establish a link between physical prowess and intellectual ability were the younger selves of the first President Bush, Hillary Clinton and Meryl Streep, along with the journalists Bob Woodward and Diane Sawyer.

The two authors of the initiative, one from Harvard, the other from Columbia, were apparently inspired by Francis Galton, a half-cousin of Charles Darwin's, who was fascinated by questions of intelligence and inheritance, and who had earlier proposed a comprehensive photographic archive of the British population. His US heirs aimed to realize that dream in their own country, appropriating the already-existent practice of freshmen posture photographs as cover for the project.

Related was the apparently harmless practice of bussing girls from women's colleges to Harvard, Princeton or Yale to meet boys, the experience recounted in the novel by Dorothy Lake. Again, this did actually happen and is widely thought to have had a eugenic motive, encouraging the young men and women of the educated elites to meet and to mate in what one account of the period calls "a kind of eugenic dating service". The Wolf's Head Society does exist and does have a "tomb" of the kind James sees, but there is no record of it having any association with eugenics. The same is true of the Elizabethan Club.

As for the rest of the story, much of that too is borne out by the historical record. The Right Club is no figment of the imagination; it did meet at the Russian Tea Room in London, with the participation of the organizations and individuals named. My Reginald Rawls Murray is fictional, but some will detect a resemblance to Archibald Maule Ramsay, the Conservative MP and anti-Jewish agitator who did indeed pen the ditty "Land of Dope and Jewry", its lyrics reproduced here exactly as he wrote them. After 1940, Ramsay spent the rest of the war behind bars, interned under Defence Regulation 18B, partly because of his involvement with a suspected spy at the US Embassy.

That man was Tyler Kent, a truly remarkable character who has much in common with the Taylor Hastings of this novel. A cipher clerk at his country's embassy in London, he became involved with the Right Club and was eventually entrusted with its membership list, kept in a leather-bound, lockable red book — which can now be read in full in *The Red Book: The Membership List of The Right Club* edited by Robin Saikia.

The young American removed from the embassy multiple secret documents, including the clandestine correspondence between Franklin D Roosevelt and Winston Churchill. He passed those papers onto Ramsay, apparently in the hope that they would reach isolationist US politicians bent on thwarting FDR's march to war. Scholars agree that had those letters to Churchill become public, Roosevelt may well have been wounded beyond recovery. In the event, they fell into the hands of German intelligence. The extracts appear here exactly as they were written. The full exchanges can be read in *Churchill & Roosevelt: The Complete Correspondence, Volume 1, Alliance Emerging, October 1933–November 1942*, edited with commentary by Warren F Kimball.

Kent was eventually exposed. When the authorities raided his home, they found nearly two thousand stolen documents as well as the keys to the US Embassy cipher room. He was tried and sentenced and, like Ramsay, served out the rest of the war in prison. Later he resurfaced in the United States, as the publisher of a newspaper identified with the Ku Klux Klan. He is said to have died a pauper in a Texas trailer park in 1988.

The American milieu in which James Zennor finds himself in late July 1940 is, I hope, also faithful to the facts. At that time the United States in general, and the Yale campus in particular, were riven by debate over US involvement in the war. The university chaplain, the Reverend Sidney Lovett, was a pacifist; others were strongly in favour of coming to Britain's aid.

In Washington, there certainly were senior politicians aiming to discredit Roosevelt, both to sabotage his re-election in November 1940 and to thwart his advocacy of military action. Hans Thomsen, the then Chargé d'Affaires at the German Embassy, actively sought to influence US domestic politics, backing vocal isolationists and even covertly paying for newspaper advertisements making the case against war.

It is also well-documented that the *Chicago Tribune* was the leading mouthpiece of the America First movement, formally launched in September 1940, while *Time* magazine under its campaigning editor Henry Luce, was a loud advocate for US intervention.

The novel's earlier action is also grounded in fact. Barcelona did indeed host an alternative Olympic Games, the People's Olympiad, in 1936 on the eve of the Spanish Civil War. The battles I refer to during that conflict are anything but fictitious, with James Zennor's war experience tallying in part with that of the real-life Esmond Romilly, in whose story I was educated by the excellent *Rebel: The Short Life of Esmond Romilly* by Kevin Ingram.

Preston McAndrew is entirely fictitious and based on no one. And yet his notion of war as a cleansing fire is, I believe, no more than the idea of eugenics taken to its logical conclusion — an idea that was utterly mainstream in the pre-war period. Painful though it is to admit, a veritable pantheon of British and American intellectual heroes believed in a theory that today would make most of us shudder.

Three generations on, we take pride in the belief that the Second World War was fought out of moral revulsion at the ideas embodied by the Nazis. The awkward truth, however, is that intellectuals on both sides of the Atlantic were deeply in thrall to a set of principles we would now regard as horribly close to Nazism. This fact, one of the last great secrets of the Anglo-American elite, has lay buried for more than seventy years. It may be time to exhume it and give it proper examination.

ACKNOWLEDGEMENTS

First thanks must go to James Purnell, who in a chance remark mentioned the mother of a mutual friend who had been evacuated to Yale as a child during wartime. That child turned out to be Juliet Hopkins, who was kind enough to speak to me about her experiences more than seventy years ago. I should stress that the speculation as to the true motives behind the rescue effort offered in *Pantheon* is mine rather than hers.

Felicity Tholstrup proved a patient guide around Oxford, conjuring up how that city might have looked in wartime. Dr Michael Freeden, a former tutor of mine, was gracious enough to play teacher again, sharing his wisdom on the history of eugenics. I read his insightful paper *Eugenics and Progressive Thought: A Study in Ideological Affinity* nearly fifteen years ago and it surely helped plant the seed that grew into *Pantheon*.

In New Haven, Michael Morand spent many long hours showing me around Yale as well as introducing me — over tea at the Elizabethan Club — to the university archivist Judith Schiff and its pre-eminent historian, Professor Gaddis Smith. Both were extremely generous with their knowledge, but I am indebted especially to Professor Smith for sharing with me the chapter on eugenics at Yale from his upcoming history of the university. The hair-raising quotations cited by my fictional Dr Curtis were unearthed by the very real Gaddis Smith.

Two other scholars deserve my thanks. Dr Nigel Townson of the Complutense University of Madrid guided me expertly on the history, language and geography of Spain during the Civil War. Professor Tony Badger, Master of Clare College, Cambridge, became a virtual co-conspirator on the US political dimension of the novel, pointing me to both the Roosevelt-Churchill correspondence and the figure of Tyler Kent. Oxbridge academics do not get unalloyed praise in this novel, but I have only the warmest respect for Tony Badger.

The great American journalist Jacob Weisberg shared his expertise on the ideological dispositions of the US press in 1940, while Jo Rodgers was kind enough to cast an American's eye over the manuscript. Additional thanks to my former *Guardian* colleague, the irrepressible Tim Radford, for joining my search through the eugenics canon; Steve Coombe, for advising on matters of intelligence and surveillance; to Rebecca Lloyd-Evans for getting her hands on a key quotation; to Scott Barlow of the BT archives for guidance on 1940s telephone numbers; and to the staff of the British Library for directing me to the relevant parts of the Mass Observation Archive, which shed so much light on everyday life in the Britain of this period.

Thanking Jonathan Cummings is a pleasure that only becomes greater with repetition: once again, he proved a gifted plunderer of the archives and a constant comrade. Jonny Geller knows the word "agent" does not do justice to what he does: he is a regular source of inspiration and moral support as well as being the very best in his business. At HarperCollins, Jane Johnson, backed by the ever-dependable Sarah Hodgson and Emad Akhtar, lived through this novel with me, once again proving herself to be an exacting editor who somehow manages to combine rigour with encouragement. That I have not yet driven her mad is a tribute to her rather than me.

Finally, I want to thank my wife Sarah not only for her love, but also her wise counsel. She and our two boys, Jacob and Sam, had to put up with so much during the gestation of this book: I am more grateful than I can say. In the end, *Pantheon* is about a husband and father who realizes that it is family, above all, that makes life worth living. That's something I realized long ago.

Jonathan Freedland, October 2011

487